Gracie's Lending Library

Breathless

BY THE SAME AUTHOR

The Man From Marseille

Body and Soul

The Blue Hour

The Discovery of Light

J. P. SMITH

Breathless

VIKING

VIKING
Published by the Penguin Group
Penguin Books USA Inc., 375 Hudson Street,
New York, New York 10014, U.S.A.
Penguin Books Ltd, 27 Wrights Lane, London W8 5TZ, England
Penguin Books Australia Ltd, Ringwood, Victoria, Australia
Penguin Books Canada Ltd, 10 Alcorn Avenue,
Toronto, Ontario, Canada M4V 3B2
Penguin Books (N.Z.) Ltd, 182-190 Wairau Road,
Auckland 10, New Zealand

Penguin Books Ltd, Registered Offices:
Harmondsworth, Middlesex, England

First published in 1995 by Viking Penguin,
a division of Penguin Books USA Inc.

1 3 5 7 9 10 8 6 4 2

PUBLISHER'S NOTE
This is a work of fiction. Names, characters, places, and incidents either are the
product of the author's imagination or are used fictitiously, and any resemblance to
actual persons, living or dead, events, or locales is entirely coincidental.

LIBRARY OF CONGRESS CATALOGING IN PUBLICATION DATA
Smith, J. P., [date]
Breathless / J. P. Smith.
p. cm.
ISBN 0-670-86046-8
I. Title.
PS3569.M53744B74   1995
813´.54—dc20   94-31270

This book is printed on acid-free paper.

∞

Printed in the United States of America
Set in Adobe Garamond #3
Designed by Kathryn Parise

FOR SOPHIE

We have left undone those things which we ought to have done;
And we have done those things which we ought not to have done;
And there is no health in us.

—The Book of Common Prayer

Breathless

CHAPTER *1*

This was the land of wait and see.

She had been there since six, sitting, pacing, standing in a vast hall painted in shades of brown, furnished in beige, where the sound of shoe against floor rang out like gunshot. At the time there were few others there, a woman in a state of controlled agitation, smoking cigarette upon cigarette and knitting a scarf; an old man so vaguely aware of the life around him that he seemed as undefined as a photograph. A mother and her child filled a small corner with bags of diapers, playthings, a stroller, and when the child coughed it was like the harshness of metal, brazen and menacing. The others in the room sat apart from one another, staring at the angles in the corners, held tight in the imminence of bad news. The air bore the scent of chemistry and decay, the odor of death and failure. Soon a contingent from some sporting event arrived, people with bloody lips and torn eyelids, with matted hair and ripped shirts, grown men in tears mutilated beyond words by fists and pucks.

She hadn't thought to bring anything to read. In fact in her rush to get there she had left her bag at the university and had actually found herself behind an ambulance just as it was turning into the hospital, and imagining Peter was inside she watched helplessly through the window as in the brilliant sterile space of light and chaos two attendants held masks to his mouth, took his blood pressure, inserted a drip into his vein. On her car radio someone spoke with calm indignation of atrocities in the Balkans and affliction in Africa, and then came a musical interlude, a reflective six measures in a minor key.

In her bag had been her purse with its credit cards and means of identity, eighty-seven dollars in cash, a photo of her daughter, spare tampons in a blue plastic case.

Still she heard nothing. Four times she had begged the receptionist for information, and four times she was told that there was no news, and when she attempted to invade the actual corridors of the hospital, the same corridors that had swallowed up her husband, a guard in uniform stepped away from his post and glared at her.

"If you won't let me find out what's happening with my husband I'll call my lawyer," she shouted to the receptionist, because she could think of nothing else to say, and a white-haired woman in a nightgown, her elbow bleeding into a thick pad of gauze, said, "Yes, that's right, God love her."

"I'm only a volunteer," said the receptionist.

"I've been here for hours."

"I understand this."

"It's past midnight."

"I know that."

"Now it's morning."

"I'm sorry."

"And I still know nothing."

"No," said the receptionist, taking a hard look at the woman. In that look she must have been able to decipher the bend and ache of grief, the knotty muscles of anxiety, the veins and arteries that were taut. "Let me try to get hold of the doctor for you." The woman remained standing by the curved desk. "I'll call you back if I have any luck," said the receptionist.

The woman took a few steps away, idly picking up a leaflet that spoke of sexual disease and things made of rubber, the slow death that was inevitable.

"One more thing," the receptionist said, beckoning her. "Is your husband an organ donor?"

"What?"

"Did he sign a release to donate his innards? Just in case."

"I don't know," she said, her mind tumbling in wonderment.

She began to walk. She followed the signs to the gift shop and cafeteria and in her ears was the sound of doctors being paged, the names remaining especially vivid to her after they blared from the ceiling: Wardell, Roussel, Hirsch. She stopped to gaze into the window of the gift shop. Even though a sign said that the shop had closed at ten she tried to open it, she turned the knob and pushed it back and forth. In the window were shelves of cheap dolls and stuffed animals, trolls with mad hair and bad boy smiles, sad-eyed puppies in toy hospital beds, efficient little doctor ducks, stethoscopes at the ready. Beyond were magazine racks, and she carefully read the titles: *Time, Newsweek, Sports Illustrated.* A tabloid claimed in a headline that NASA scientists could now prove that Elvis's face had been carved into the Martian surface some twenty million years ago. Along one wall were the get-well cards and a row of condolence messages, black-and-white doggerel laced with crucifixes and saints, lilies erect in the morning light, veined hands joined in prayer and meditation. The flower shop was also shut, its blooms in deep freeze.

When she walked into the cafeteria two or three customers sat up as if suddenly awakened. She wondered what she looked like, if the ordeal of the past few hours had taken its toll on her, if her hair was in disarray, her face grown puffy. The woman behind the counter, dressed in apron and hairnet, said "Coffee?" and she nodded. Her eyes passed over the parched samples of Danish pastry, a selection of boxed cereals, a placard speaking of baked beans and bagels, English muffins, two eggs, bacon extra. She wasn't hungry: the events of the evening had destroyed the urging for food, and she wondered if this would be permanent, if she would simply starve herself, perhaps to death, until her husband could walk out of the hospital with his health.

"I haven't any money," she said, suddenly remembering. "I left my bag at my office. It's my husband."

The woman behind the counter looked at her, her eyes vaguely suspecting crime and falsehood.

"I'll pay you back. I promise I will."

She took her cup to a table and began to leaf through a newspaper someone had left. Because it was a daily tabloid there were more photographs than text. The pages in the center, some fifteen of them, contained simple word games, comic strips, advertisements for films and nightclubs. She glanced at the horoscopes, something she usually never did. Hers spoke of a blossoming romance; his of a brilliant business deal clinched by midnight. An advice columnist suggested that Surprised in Topeka should mind her own business when it came to her mother-in-law's peculiar habits. Her coffee was bitter, as though it had sat stewing for five hours, and she winced as she took the cup from her lips. An ill-shaven man at another table looked at her and attempted to smile, his merry eyes narrowing, and she stood and left the room.

She looked at her watch, and then up at the large clock on the corridor wall. It was morning, but not yet light, and when she glanced out the window she saw a darkened city, and beyond it a flashing beacon somewhere near the airport, and she realized that for the past five or six minutes not one of her thoughts had turned to Peter.

When she came back to the waiting room a uniformed policeman and a man in a suit were standing by the desk. They spoke quietly to the receptionist, and at that moment her eyes met those of the distraught woman. The two men turned to look at her and were joined by a policewoman, who must have been asked to park the car or fetch coffee, for she carried a small brown paper bag.

Things grew vivid; colors took on luster and outline, sounds began to absorb the fragments of silence that lay about. Suddenly it was as though pieces of a huge puzzle had lain around her like the ruins of an archeological treasure-house; and in the odd way that children have just by looking at the fragments she was able to make the preliminary connections in her mind. Silence; receptionist; police: the geometry of grief.

Layers of civilization began to fall away: what before had been a complicated network of details and superficialities, a life held together by a system of customs and manners, the way she intended to wear her hair, clean the sink, let the cat out, put on the yellow sweater, have the muffler checked, had become nothing more than the life of her husband, and the sudden absence of breath that would bring it to an end.

The world had grown thick and crowded with effect, though cause was nowhere to be found. Once again she went over it. Peter had made reservations earlier that week for dinner at a restaurant, Marta's, down by the harbor. Long before it was awarded four stars by the newspaper's restaurant critic it bore a reputation as a superb eating place featuring delicate entrées and spectacular desserts, where lawyers who published their memoirs and senators with pasts dined variously with their wives and lovers. It was where he had made reservations for seven o'clock. She could then drive him to the airport for his flight at 9:25. They would eat at their leisure, speaking easily of this and that, the conference he was scheduled to address, the seminars in which he had been asked to participate, the things they would do when he returned. She would broach the subject of an impending vacation; they would debate the merits of driving up the coast or flying out of the country. Beyond that the details of the last twelve or fourteen hours were as nothing to her, they had become like water, fluent, turning mucky, slowly evaporating.

"Mrs. Freytag?"

She looked at them for a moment.

"Mrs. Freytag?"

"I, . . ." and she didn't know what to say, because for all of her life, from birth until this moment, she had been known as Jill Bowman.

The man in the suit made a gesture in the air and the four of them, man in a suit, policeman, policewoman and Mrs. Freytag, walked down a brightly lit corridor where a young bearded physician in white was waiting for them at the end. His expression was utterly neutral. On his lapel were two red droplets. He held his hands before him: "We did everything we could."

And then someone gently touched her shoulder and they walked inside a small room.

"He died before we could operate."

Jill opened her mouth and said nothing because the taste in her mouth was bitter, as though, as she once had as a child, she had attempted to drink the elusive beauty of mercury. She turned to the others. The policewoman pressed close to her, took her hand. The man in the suit quietly described how Peter had been found in a hotel four blocks away from the restaurant. This man who lived in a realm of fact and statistic seemed about to add something, then stopped, as though he had been stepping away from her and had lost all ability to communicate. She remembered he said something like: he died from a knife wound. She wondered how a man who had innocently been on his way to dine with his wife could have met with such an accident. "I don't understand," she said, her hands churning the air before her.

"Do you want coffee?" the policewoman said.

"No. Yes. Just some water."

"Have a seat."

Outside in the corridor voices were raised in merriment, and the doctor, in a sudden rage, leapt to the door and told the people there, members of the custodial staff armed with mops and buckets, to keep it down.

"We found your husband's passport in his pocket," the man in the suit, a detective, said. "He was born in Switzerland," and he looked at her, expecting clarification.

Jill looked at the policeman. She couldn't quite understand what was taking place. Peter had shown no signs of sickness. The policewoman brought her water in a paper cup. "How did he die?" Jill asked.

"But he has an American passport."

"He was born in Zurich," Jill said. "He became an American citizen five years ago. How did he die?"

"He was about to go on a trip. There was a ticket."

"That's why we were going to have dinner in town. Because I was going to take him to the airport. He liked it when I saw him off."

"What kind of business was he in?"

"Where is he?" She pictured him in a darkened hospital room, trying to lift himself from the bed, gesturing helplessly, begging for her.

The policewoman squeezed her hand.

"Where is my husband?" She turned and looked this way and that, her eyes wide.

"He's not here," the policewoman said, and there were tears in her eyes.

"He's gone," said the detective.

"He's not," said Jill, and the detective said: "He's no longer alive."

"Your husband died an hour ago," the doctor said.

They had planned to meet at Marta's. A reservation for two had been phoned in by Peter. And having reiterated these points the detective looked at her. "And then what happened?" he said.

"I stayed late at my office. Then the hospital called." She

looked at the detective. "Nobody said anything else. Nobody told me what had happened."

She stared at them. Even though she had drunk the cup of water her mouth went suddenly dry. Her mind turned to her walk to the cafeteria, the things she had seen in the gift shop window, the newspaper she had leafed through, Peter's horoscope—all the things she had been doing when the breath escaped him and left his room. "Why wasn't I told?"

"You mean an hour ago?" the doctor said.

"Because of the nature of the case," the detective in the suit said. "What had been attempted murder is now homicide."

"But we had reservations."

"He never got to the restaurant, Mrs. Freytag. Did your husband have any enemies?"

"I don't know."

"How long was he going to be traveling for?" the policewoman asked.

"Ten days. I have to call them."

"His office?"

"The people he's supposed to be seeing in London. His hotel. He has appointments."

"There's plenty of time for that."

"But they'll be waiting for him."

"There'll be time."

The phone rang and the doctor picked it up. He smiled and said, "Oh great," and then he remembered what was happening and he stopped smiling and said goodbye.

And the detective looked at Jill Bowman.

"I'm bleeding," she said, feeling as though her body had begun to melt from the inside out. The policewoman instinctively reached for her arm and led her to the ladies' room. She put a coin into a dispenser and handed the tampon to Jill, and then waited outside the stall for her. "I've seen this happen before," she said, her two sturdy legs visible to Jill in the space beneath the door. "A shock sometimes brings it on. Were you due?"

"Not for another week."

"Just like me. Always regular."

Jill sat for a moment, then crushed her panties into a ball, adjusted her skirt and opened the door and, almost as an afterthought, threw her bloodstained underwear into the white wastebasket. She felt nothing; she was living in a world of words: husband, death, knife. None of it yet possessed the heart to move her.

CHAPTER 2

Because they said there was nothing more she could do, she was allowed to go home. For the first time that morning the detective smiled at her, offered his hand. "My name is Resnick. I'm a detective sergeant. I'll give you my card. If you need to get in touch with me call this number night or day. I'll get back to you even if I'm not in the office. I'll have you driven home. We'll need to talk later today. Would it be possible for you to come down here?"

Peter was dead, things would have to be done, and what moments earlier had seemed something solid and unbreachable had become like the sea, vast and fluid, a place of depths and shadows. She would have to call Peter's mother in Zurich, who was eighty-three and had never liked her daughter-in-law. There would have to be a funeral. A coffin would be chosen, and a vision of brass handles passed through her mind, a memory of when her father had died and she'd had to choose what the funeral director suavely called the hardware.

People would have to be called. She began to mouth the words to herself: *Something terrible happened.* She thought of the scene in the hotel room, of her husband walking, talking, washing his hands, looking out the window, lighting a cigarette while someone waited for him, stalked him, leapt to his back, plunged the knife. There was something pathetic about the scene, for no matter how someone died one became at that moment a child once again, startled and sad and in pain, and the thought of it brought tears to her eyes.

"I have a car," she said. "I'd prefer to drive myself."

She turned and walked back down the corridor, the police-woman following close behind. She could hear the doctor on the phone ordering a pizza, speaking of pepperoni and olives, a Diet Coke. She tapped on his door. When he opened it he stared at her as though his memory had abandoned him and she said, "Did he suffer? Did Peter die easily?"

The doctor continued to look at her. He hung up the phone. "It's difficult to say. Victims of such crimes are often numbed by the shock before they die. Let's hope it happened this way, for your husband's sake." He spoke in tentative phrases, the language of an uncertain world.

When she got out to the street a breeze rose and carried a swirl of dust down the avenue towards the river. On the horizon a crack in the overcast had appeared, and in the distance she could hear the trolleys gathering speed in the thin air of this Saturday morning. Few people were outside at that time, and those few passed her by without a glance, as if oblivious to the slow pain of Jill Bowman.

There was no traffic that morning, especially leaving the city. She stopped at the university to pick up her bag. She thought of what she had planned to do that weekend, two loads of laundry, call her sister in Montreal, visit the stable, and she saw that none of it made any sense, not anymore, and that nothing would ever be the same. She drove and listened to the silence, and watched the sky grow blue and cloudless.

When she reached her street she began to feel an ache in her body, the kind she had felt that second time she'd miscarried. It was a deceptive pain, the pain of impending birth, the pain too of rupture and sorrow. She slowed down by the driveway, then drove on at speed, turning the corner and approaching the street from a different direction. A neighbor was out with his children, walking, and all three waved at her, and for some reason she smiled and waved back as if nothing unusual had happened, as if the previous evening had been as all previous evenings. This time she stayed in the car in front of her house and looked up at the windows that together she and Peter had looked out of, never seeing this future moment, the blossoming of widowhood. They were windows she had sometimes gazed out of when they made love, when she turned her face slightly to the left, and in an odd way their forthright angles provided a contrast to this pleasure so full of ripple and curve and thus made it all the more sweet. Now it dawned on her: they had made love the night before his death, and the memory simultaneously thrilled and pained her.

And yet at that very moment, the moment this occurred to her, she realized that there was something different about their lovemaking that last evening, or at least about his, and whatever it was, whatever indefinable aspect there was to it, it came to her mind now that it felt not like an enigma of the past but as an omen of the future. Past and future: as though death were a great hand holding in its palm the brief roundness of his life.

She switched off the ignition and got out of the car. A bill for an oil delivery was stuck in her mailbox, for routine had not taken a moment to stop and pause for her, as if she were waiting on a railway platform and one train after another was passing her by, leaving her stranded late into the night. When she unlocked the door she counted to four before pushing it open, and then she counted to four again, then looked at her watch. It was when she shut the door behind her that she saw how everything had changed. On this morning Peter Freytag would never see, in the time before the evening and night and all the succeeding days through which he would never pass, Jill Bowman stood and looked up at the stairway and felt the emptiness like a sudden drop in temperature. And there was something familiar about it.

The living room with its walls of bookshelves, the stacks of volumes on the tables, the stereo, the lamps, the curtains; the hallway leading to the dining room with its mahogany table and six chairs: all seemed on the verge of something, as if this silence were about to give way to something wrenching, some appalling roar, the invasion of something monstrous and malign that would tear the heart from her body.

On the floor was yesterday's mail, letters, bills from Peter's dentist, from the vet, a reminder that a subscription was about to lapse. There were catalogues and magazines, little cards fluttering out of them, and as she stood in the kitchen going through them as if it were just another day she looked out the window into the woods, at the leafless trees of early December, and watched as the sky beyond them grew coppery. Time moved and she was standing still. Time pushed on and she had been left behind. Grief was a wall that stood between her and the ticking seconds of the future: thick, solid, windowless. This would be a moment she would never forget, that would always remain a touchstone in her memory, a meridian against which time would now begin anew. There would be the time before Peter and the time after Peter, and his death would reduce the calendar of her life in some significant way not yet obvious to her, as if all future Saturdays would be denied her, and life thus diminished just that much more.

She walked up to her bedroom and sensed a sour unpleasant odor, realizing after a moment that it was she who carried the smell, the reek of a woman who had sustained great injury, or struggled and lost. She stood by her bed and began to undress. She unhooked her skirt and was alarmed to see that she wore no underwear, and then remembered what had happened. The thought that she had driven home from the hospital in such a state made her feel as though she were a teenager again, and had for once stepped beyond the limits of childhood. She unbuttoned her blouse as she went into the bathroom. Her tampon was thick and blackly red. She made the water in the shower as hot as she could bear it. She wanted only to feel the heat and moisture, to hear the rushing sound of the water, to sense the pain.

When she was drying herself the phone began to ring, and wrapping the towel around her she went into the bedroom and answered it. It was Resnick.

"I hope I didn't wake you, Mrs. Freytag."

"I was in the shower." She opened the towel and began to dry herself with one hand: the pale cleft between her breasts, the hollows behind her knees. Her breasts, her thighs, her knees: things Peter loved to caress.

Resnick apologized. "I'm sorry I'm calling you so early, Mrs. Freytag. It's just that there's a question of time here."

"I understand."

"I'm sure you'd like to get some sleep."

"It's all right."

"But I need to ask you a few questions. More than a few. I'd like you to come into the city if it's at all possible. This afternoon would be all right with me. Otherwise," and she said it was fine, she'd be happy to drive back in. She looked at the clock on her bedside table and realized she'd been in the shower for nearly an hour. Her hair dripped water onto her shoulders and streams of it soaked into the duvet on the bed. When Resnick said goodbye she didn't bother to hang up. She pressed the button and called her sister, who taught linguistics at McGill University in Montreal. When she answered Jill said, "Peter's dead," and she dreaded the silence she knew would follow.

She heard Sally's husband saying, What, what is it, what's happened? He had seen her eyes, the sudden change in them.

"There was some sort of accident," Jill said. "He was murdered. Someone stabbed him in a hotel."

Sally began to laugh. "What?"

"We were supposed to meet for dinner."

"You're joking."

"He was supposed to join me at a restaurant and then a doctor called me and said Peter was on his way in an ambulance."

"My God."

"I haven't seen him since. He's gone from me."

"Where are you?"

"I'm at home. I have to go down and talk to the police again."

"Oh God."

Jill's mouth began to chitter and contort and as the towel fell away from her shoulders to the floor, as the world in her eyes began to melt, her body folded and she slipped onto her knees, and when she was finished and Sally's voice, small and distant, had stopped calling for her, she looked at herself in the mirror and then covered her eyes, for to see herself alive while Peter was dead was a kind of sin, as if the universe had become twisted and deceptive, its natural laws overturned.

CHAPTER *3*

What was usually a forty-minute drive to get into the city took her nearly an hour: it had nothing to do with the traffic, especially as it was early on a Saturday afternoon, nor had there been an accident, no scenes of torn metal and speeding ambulances, but rather she found herself unhurried, driving just over the speed limit, completely calm, in fact at peace with herself, taking in every detail of the trip, the bridges and edges of the river, the gas tanks and motor hotels, church spires and fiberglass dinosaurs, as though the trip down were a long unwinding sentence, pregnant with subsidiary clauses and asides, coming to an end only when she pulled into an empty space behind the tower that served as the metropolitan police station.

When she approached the glass doors of the front entrance

Resnick, who must have been waiting for at least half an hour, stepped out and took her hand. "Mrs. Freytag."

"I'm known as Jill Bowman. I never assumed my husband's name." She wondered if at that moment and with those words she had become a suspect. He smiled and she watched his eyes linger here and there as they divided her into sectors—chest, abdomen, legs—before his gaze returned to hers. She was more than presentable, she was an attractive woman, to her husband very beautiful, quite irresistible. It would have been unlike her to drive down without having showered and changed. She was full of herself because she had not yet completely begun to miss Peter.

The main room of the police station was quiet. A duty officer sat at the desk, smoking a cigarette, going over paperwork. A man in handcuffs, turning once to take in Jill Bowman with a smile, was led to an opening in the partition. "My office is just upstairs," Resnick said. They stood by the elevators. "One of these has been out of service for a week now. They can't figure it out. Instead of stopping exactly at a floor it stops at a place midway between floors. The doors open and you're faced with a wall. Already people have begun writing graffiti on it. Phone numbers, pleas for mercy."

She thought this was appropriate for a house of detectives, and said so. Resnick smiled and the doors shut. In silence they rode up to his floor. He stared at the toes of her shoes. She looked at him: short, sandy-haired, a pleasant man, handsome in an interesting way; a little tanned, still, from summer, as if he had spent his time not on the beach but at the tennis courts or on the deck of a yacht. She thought of detectives rather as subterranean, sipping bitter coffee and shunning the sunlight as the city disintegrated above them.

His office was simple and bright: the light from the sky seeping through the venetian blinds sent patterns onto the walls, bars of shadow, odd angles. On his desk were two photographs in Plexiglas frames: children playing in the dry autumn leaves, a wife taking a lock of hair away from her eye. Her mouth, the way her smile creased the corners of her face, was her best feature. The color of her hair matched that of her husband. Jill said, "What a lovely family you have."

The comment made him uncomfortable, as if, because one-half of her family had been murdered, he had no right to such happiness. "I'm sorry," she said, and he said, "No, it's fine."

He indicated a chair before his desk, and together they sat. "Let me get some coffee. How do you take it?"

"Black."

He rose and stepped out of the room and a minute or two later returned with two styrofoam cups. "I'll need to ask you some questions," he said. He looked at a page on his desk, then up at her. For a moment he said nothing. "Are you all right?"

"I'll be fine."

"I understand this won't be pleasant for you. Let me begin by saying that it still isn't clear your husband was killed for any specific reason."

She stared at him.

"Do you understand what I'm saying? We still don't have a motive."

She said nothing. The air in the room became oppressive. What had been a reflection of order was becoming something shapeless and malign, it weighed upon her heart like a nightmare.

"We don't believe your husband was robbed. His passport, plane ticket, wallet, cash, traveler's checks, and credit cards were all in his pockets when he was found," and he unlocked the cabinet behind him, sliding a metal tray out, displaying these objects to her. She could not bear to touch them. She raised her eyes from them.

"So there was no reason for this to happen," she said.

"I didn't say that."

"What hotel was he in?"

"A place called the Hubbard. It's really nothing more than a transient's hotel. You can take a room there for as long or as short as you like."

"Even a few hours," she said.

He looked at her. "Yes."

"Was he alone?"

"I—"

"Was he alone?"

"When he was found he was, yes. There's no evidence he was with anyone else."

"You can tell me the truth. If he was with a woman I suppose I should be the first to know it."

"We have no indication he was with a woman."

"A man, then."

"Apparently he was alone."

She could not now imagine Peter, essentially a serious and responsible person, engaging in the furtive routine of infidelity. It reeked of giddiness and the bending of rules, of codes and shared glances, of unfamiliar scents and midday showers.

"Why was he in such a place?" she asked, and a momentary image of her husband ascending the dark stairs passed through her mind. She saw his hand on the banister, his feet scuffing in the dust and broken glass.

"I was just about to ask you the same question," Resnick said.

They looked at each other. "I know how hard this must be," he said.

"But you're not telling me everything."

"I'm telling you everything I'm allowed to say for now. The investigation is still in progress, Mrs. Freytag."

"Bowman. I told you, my name is Jill Bowman."

"How long had you been married?"

"Thirteen years. Does it matter?"

"I'm just asking. Would you say you were happily married?"

"Very much so."

"This was your first marriage?"

"Second. I was married for two years before I met Peter."

"Your husband was a psychiatrist."

"That's right."

"And he was on his way to a conference in London."

"At the Tavistock Clinic."

"But you're not in the same field."

She shook her head. "I teach at the university. I'm a historian. I teach two seminars and spend the rest of my time in research."

"History."

"I'm especially interested in how people view the past. How they so easily forget it. I'm working on a piece on how the coming of plague affected people's concept of time. The past and the future. Looking back on a time of pestilence reminds perfectly sane people that before the disease came they saw apparitions and visions in the air. Floating coffins. Hands with swords. With every new plague comes the end of the world, and after it's over it'll never come again."

"You're interested in disease, then."

"No, I'm interested in fear."

He looked at her and moved his face very slightly from left to right, as though trying to read her. "And afterwards?"

"What do you mean?"

"After his conference."

"He was going to visit friends of his. Of ours. In London."

"Psychiatrists."

She nodded. "One of them is."

"But friends nonetheless. So there was no rush for him to come home?"

She shook her head.

"You have no children?"

He watched with interest as her mood changed. Her face seemed to age in a matter of seconds. She mouthed the word "no" and shook her head.

"I need to fill you in on some of the details. Obviously I can't tell you everything."

"You're speaking of Peter's body?"

"The circumstances of his death. An anonymous caller phoned first the police and a few minutes later the city hospital. This person said that a man was in a room in the Hubbard and needed help. The fact that he phoned the police indicates that he knew then that your husband was the victim of a crime."

"You said he was stabbed."

And he hesitated.

"You said he was stabbed with a knife. You told me this, you said it."

"Your husband was seriously wounded by a bladed instrument," he said after a moment's reflection.

"I can't accept this. I won't accept this."

"I understand that, Ms. Bowman."

"My husband was not killed out of pure bad luck. Being in the wrong place at the wrong time."

"No. He wasn't there by accident, Ms. Bowman." Resnick looked her directly in the eye.

"You know that."

"We seem fairly certain of it. There were no signs of a struggle. And according to his appointment book he did intend to have dinner with you at Marta's at seven o'clock. But he also had the time 5:30 circled and we assume he left his office at a quarter past."

"Was there a memo penciled in for that time?"

Resnick shook his head.

"May I see the book, please?"

"I can't let you do that now, Mrs. Freytag."

"Bowman."

"It's being examined in another part of the building. We've also taken custody of a list of his patients and notes he had taken down at their sessions. Every innocent person has to be ruled out."

It didn't occur to her then, but it would later, that she had been speaking to Resnick as though Peter had been on vacation, or off for ten days at his conference in London: the great depth, the dark hollowness of his absence, the knowledge that his return was infinitely impossible, had not yet moved into her life. "But you feel he was lured into this hotel room."

Resnick opened his hands. "I don't believe he would have gone there otherwise. We've already interviewed a few people who knew him, other members of his profession, and by all accounts Peter Freytag was a smart man, a very brilliant man. A man who examined the logic of his thoughts and movements. Not a fool." And he looked at her.

"But something drew him to his hotel room."

"Something very tempting."

"You're insinuating there was a woman."

"Temptation does not always take that form, Ms. Bowman."

"But you feel it was something he couldn't resist."

"Or something he needed to see to, that required his presence before he left the country. Try to look at it from this point of view, Ms. Bowman. Try to work it out with me."

She looked at the edge of his desk, touching it lightly with her finger.

"Please help us find out what would draw your husband to a place like the Hubbard."

"Someone tempted him."

"You said your marriage was a happy one."

"Yes."

"All aspects of it?"

She looked at him. "All aspects."

He stared at her for a long moment, reading her expression, the way her mouth worked. His eyes shifted down to the photograph of his wife and then he looked again at Jill Bowman.

"You sensed, I don't know, no need on his part to," and she said "None at all."

"Have you lately noticed any changes in your husband's behavior?"

"Sexual behavior?"

"Any behavior. Coming home late when before he was always prompt. Or that he was often distracted." He looked at her.

"No."

"More thoughtful than usual?"

She smiled. "Peter is always thoughtful."

"Were you in serious debt?"

"No more than anyone else."

"You weren't in over your head, you mean."

She shook her head. "No."

"Was your husband a gambler?" He threw the question out as though it were a scrap of lint, something inconsiderable, and yet there was a weight to his words that alarmed her.

"I don't ever remember him placing a bet. Or even talking about it."

"But did you sense that there was something in him capable of doing so?"

She thought about it.

"We don't always know the people we live with, Ms. Bowman."

"I know Peter. I know my husband."

"Then had he spoken of any of his patients, of experiencing any difficulty with them?"

"He never discusses his patients with me."

"Of course we've been checking out all of your husband's patients. Few of them seem to be the type. But of course you never know. Had he been having trouble sleeping lately?"

"I didn't notice any change."

"Was he the type of man . . . Let me rephrase that: was he a secretive man?"

"Not with me he wasn't."

"Let's go back to the beginning, Ms. Bowman. When did your husband first make the arrangements for his trip to London?"

"About six months ago."

"For the conference."

She nodded.

"And the dinner appointment with you?"

"Three or four days ago."

"And he made the arrangements, he phoned to make the reservation."

"He decided on the time. I was going to drive him to the airport."

"But he chose the time."

She watched as Resnick rose from his chair. He stood by the window and adjusted the angle of the light by twisting a plastic rod attached to the blinds. She watched his face turn yellow, then grey, then his eyes met hers.

"Before your husband's body can be released for burial we need to establish his identity."

"But I thought you knew it was my husband."

"His passport and license and plane ticket and credit cards say so. We need someone to look at the body. We require a positive identification."

She felt her heart run away with her.

"My car's parked just outside the entrance," and he gestured to the window.

His car was equipped with telephone and two-way radio, and on the backseat was a child's jacket, a pink windbreaker. Resnick drove slowly through the streets, keeping to the speed limit, obeying the law. They said nothing, and because there was silence, because she had not slept the night before, she felt completely serene. For a time—she wasn't sure for how long—she closed her eyes and began to drowse. Voices came into her head, scenes presented themselves, none connected to what had been happening to her over the last twenty-four hours. They seemed to rise up from the sea of time, showing their faces, just as quickly evaporating into the present, and suddenly the car came to a smooth stop. Resnick's hand reached across her and pointed. "That's the Hubbard, Ms. Bowman."

She looked at it. Five steps leading to the door, a building covered in grime, painted with graffiti: Noel 59; Atsaboy 143; Mr. Gringo I Love Your Mother. She wondered if Peter had had time to take these in, these messages from other lives.

"He must have had a business meeting here," and she lifted her eyes to the dark windows on each of the four floors. Next to the building, in a boarded doorway to what had been a nightclub, a burlap bag covered in plastic shifted and moved, and a hand emerged from it.

"At the Hubbard, Ms. Bowman?"

She turned to the detective. "Which room was he in?"

He said nothing.

"Was it on this side?"

He leaned towards her and when he extended his arm to point it out his hand lightly skimmed her breast. "The top one on the right."

The window was shut and she could see two cheap white curtains hanging behind it. She felt tears flood her eyes and when she began to sob, when the breath rushed from her, because this too seemed pathetic, this place where her husband had lost his life, Resnick took her hand and gently squeezed it. She turned into him, pressing her head against his shoulder, trying to brush the tears from her cheeks. The cry emanated from her heart, her body went into brief spasms as though it had become separated from this educated and reasonable woman.

Resnick's other hand rested against her back and it moved very slightly up and down in sad little attempts at comfort. "I'm sorry," she said. "I'll be all right," and she pulled away from him.

He switched on the ignition and drove away and at once they had to stop at a red light. The district was busy on this Saturday afternoon. Bars and lounges, peep shows and darkened doorways vied for customers. A man standing in front of Whitey's Bar and Grill sucked on a toothpick and eyed Jill and when she noticed that his hand was slowly agitating the front of his trousers the light turned. She looked at the names passing her by, Mr. P's Billiards, Ladyland Vegas, The Tattooed Vampire, Fugitive Comforts, and quickly they were out of the neighborhood and passing through residential streets, churches and corner markets, funeral homes and liquor stores. She became aware that Resnick was following the large blue signs with the letter H on them.

Now they were at the hospital, and he switched the engine off. She said, "I can't do this."

"You're the only one."

"It would be terrible for me."

"You need to do this."

"But when I last saw him he was alive, he was well," and her memory turned to their last night together, she saw his skin in the pale moonlight, she felt him curving inside her, moving slowly against her hips while suddenly and very gently he reached down and pulled her hair away from her face. She wondered if in his last moments of life he remembered this also, and the thought brought tears to her eyes.

Resnick touched her arm. "Let's get it over with, Ms. Bowman."

They walked through the door into a carpeted windowless corridor. Signs on the wall forbade smoking, indicated where certain offices could be found. They rode the elevator to the bottom floor and walked through another series of corridors, tiled in linoleum, smelling medicinal and forbidding, as they turned one corner, then another, still one more.

The doors to the morgue were shut. Resnick pressed a button on the wall and a buzzer sounded from within. A balding man in a white tunic unlocked the door and mumbled something. Resnick called him Albert and asked how he was.

It was obvious to Jill that Albert was an employee, not the city coroner. She had seen it before: the face puffy from medication, the ambiguous unsteady gaze, the way he seemed to reach for and lose the words he needed, as though trying to catch butterflies. Had he been born without his disability he might have been a physician, a policeman, the mayor. Now he pushed the dead around, tied tags to their toes, washed floors and went home to watch comedy on television.

Another man came out of an office and smiled. He was short and grey-haired and resembled someone she had once known long ago, a teacher or a shoe salesman, someone who had passed briefly through her life and had left an imprint of his face on it. He took Jill's hand. He said, "I'm so terribly sorry, Mrs. Freytag. I know this is not going to be easy."

"No."

"It'll only take a second." He turned and led the way through another set of doors.

There was only one table in the discreetly lit room. In fact the light, though flat and undramatic, was barely noticeable, more moonglow than the harsh brilliance of midday. The body was covered by a sheet. There was an intense smell of a biology lab.

The pathologist held a clipboard out to Jill. He said, "If you could possibly take a moment to look this over. You'll need to sign it when we're done. You'll notice that we've provided a complete description of the subject, height, weight, identifying marks and so forth. You will help us put a name to these details."

She could barely make out the words. Her eye kept angling to the thing on the table, the airy curves and arches, bathed in white, that suggested the solidity of Peter Freytag.

"I need a pen," she said, and her hand shook.

"Not until you've made a positive identification." Resnick reached down and took a corner of the sheet, then, lifting it slightly, as they do in the movies, drew it back to reveal the face.

His hair had been combed back, away from his forehead. It was out of character for him to look this way, and this first thought that came to Jill Bowman seemed a trite thing, a vain thing, and she was about to reach down to fix his hair, to bring it forward and part it properly, when Resnick touched her elbow. "Please don't disturb him," he said, and at that moment she realized Peter was no longer hers.

She turned and faced him. She'd anticipated seeing a man badly damaged, cut through and smeared with blood, scarred and disfigured. Yet he seemed perfect, clean and untouched, almost pure in the stillness of his death. The last time she had seen Peter he was alive, he exuded warmth, he was buttoning his shirt and speaking a mile a minute about his trip to London, and when he'd left in the morning for his office he'd put a hand on her hip when she'd turned to kiss him on the lips. At seven, then, he had said.

She took the corner of the sheet from Resnick and slowly began to pull it down and was startled to see that Peter was wearing nothing. His ribs were hard and prominent against his pale skin. She looked for his birthmark, a small brown stain in the shape of a woman's profile a few inches below his left nipple, and she found it. The rest of him was oddly lifeless, his genitals soft and childish, useless and wrinkled in their bed of brown hair. There was an inertness to him, as though something essential in Peter had simply risen up and abandoned the body. This was nothing at all like sleep. It was the essence of absence: because his body remained behind, his disappearance was all the more heartbreaking. Then she noticed that something was wrong with his face. The bottom half of it, from his chin to his upper lip, seemed somehow different, as though it had been taken apart and afterwards reattached. She wanted to reach out and touch his jaw, to tilt his head back, to make him look like her husband again. "His mouth," she said.

"Is it your husband?"

"The mouth is different."

"We know that," said the pathologist.

"What's happened to him?"

"There had been an injury," and she noticed how his eyes met Resnick's.

"Is it Dr. Freytag?" the detective asked.

"It's Peter." She looked at the detective.

"You've seen enough, Ms. Bowman." And he took the sheet from her.

Every step forward, every walk into the future, every stroll down a city street is a promenade into the past. Each smell and sound and sight has its antecedent. And so Jill Bowman turned her gaze inward.

CHAPTER 4

Deeply buried in time, it came to her in a series of tableaux, brief static scenes vividly lit, intense in their color.

The shadow dividing door and wall.

The warmth of golden fabric.

Between silence and word there lay the beguiling landscape of memory.

She had been living with her parents and her sister in an apartment in the west side of another city, an affluent neighborhood. Most of those who lived in the building had been there for years. Most were professionals, as her father had been, as her mother certainly was. Living across the hall from the Bowmans was the Viennese woman Rose Keller, who had arrived by train at Auschwitz with her parents and sisters and brothers and left its gates alone in 1945, a sixty-two-pound teenager. She taught French uptown at a prestigious women's college. Mostly she kept to herself, as though fearful of rubbing up against others, wary of contagion. To her neighbors she was seen only departing and arriving, a woman whose life was filled with vacancy and enigma. Jill remembered her as a tall auburn-haired woman who seemed surrounded by silence and the smell of European passageways. Occasionally Jill would be in the hall when Rose Keller stepped out on a Saturday morning in her gloves and hat, and the woman would smile at Jill and move her hand gently through the air, as though tossing affection across the dusty lethargy of the corridor.

Through the keyhole of her front door she would watch her neighbor return from the college, and for a few valued seconds she would catch a glimpse of her apartment: a momentary swath of golden brown, a fleeting vision of an old world. Sometimes music could be heard coming from Rose Keller's apartment: a Beethoven quartet, a sonata by Schubert, an opera. And sometimes, on a Saturday evening, it would be a tango, slow and languorous, passing through the accumulated hisses and scratches of ten, twenty, thirty years of memory.

One afternoon Jill opened her door and held it open because she heard something unfamiliar, a brief wrenching sound, a balloon being twisted between someone's hands, as though someone had begun to laugh and then changed her mind. She stared at Rose Keller's door. She heard a footstep; she shut her door and bent to see. The man who left Rose Keller's apartment took care to close the door quietly, because Rose Keller must have fallen asleep. Jill watched as the man wiped his lips with a white handkerchief. The man was large and heavily jowled, his hair combed flat against his skull. For a moment, and it seemed to her to be much longer, three minutes, five minutes, an hour, the man stood and gazed at Jill Bowman's door, probing a space between his teeth with a wooden toothpick, rocking a little on his heels. Then he turned and summoned the elevator.

Thirty years later she recalled again the moment they took

Rose Keller from her apartment, men in white suits bearing a stretcher. Her death had not even been worth a cry for help, a scream of agony. It had come quietly and swiftly to this woman who had walked away from the clank and grind of annihilation all those years before. She remembered how a cleaning crew arrived a few hours later to wash the walls and remove the stains from the floors before the apartment could be let again. It was the first time death—the horizontal existence—had entered Jill Bowman's life. For four months Jill was unable to utter a word. As an adult she always wondered what had set off this sudden silence. It could not have been Rose Keller's death: Rose Keller had been a stranger to her. Only now, with Peter's death, could she begin to glimpse something of the truth. It was not so much the death of the person that was so shocking. It was what her imagination had made of it.

Jill's parents took her to her doctor, who referred them to a psychiatrist, a Dr. Angelico, who declared the girl had suffered a trauma. In time she would come out of her shell. For a while she went to see him one afternoon a week, she would listen while he talked, while he described to her what she had seen, what she was seeing, what she was feeling, what she must be wanting to say. For four months Jill Bowman lived within herself, in the confined world of her imagination. Without tongue her universe grew vivid; time, instead of moving unnoticed, as if it were woven into the small events of her life, became slow and visible. Things moved in tiny increments: flowers died, and their passing was perceived by her. The words uttered by others—her parents; her sister, Sally—seemed to linger, displaying themselves for what they were, and often mendacity hung in the air like the delicate trap of a spider's web.

She became aware of her own growth, she kept track of her physical changes, of the shape of her body, the aspects that would one day make her a woman. She continued to attend school, like an outcast relegated to the back of the room. Her teachers spoke to her as though her mind had grown old and useless, as if, be-

cause she had lost the ability to speak, she had somehow been de-
prived of the talent to comprehend. At night, while she was lying
in bed, a man shut a door, picked his teeth, fixed his eye upon
hers, sucked the words from her mouth.

One morning her mother said to her at breakfast, "They
caught him." Her mother looked at her, touched her cheek. The
photo in the newspaper showed a small ratlike man with tiny eyes
and manacled hands. He lived with his common-law wife and
two children in a flat in another part of the city. The caption described him as cold-blooded.

The first words Jill said were, "But I saw the man who killed
Rose Keller."

Years later, when visiting her mother at the house on the island, she would sometimes mention the incident, describing in
vivid detail the sounds she had heard, the way the man looked as
he stood gazing, stabbing the food from between his teeth. But
her mother denied it had ever taken place. "You must have imagined it, dreamed it, Jill darling," and she would walk out onto
the porch and put on her straw hat and stare at the sea.

Resnick held the door open for her and she stepped gladly into
the air outdoors, the sudden heavy curve of the gritty breeze that
carried the scent of the harbor. Gulls defined low circles overhead,
cars passed down the avenue. Peter remained inside, in a darkened room beneath a sheet, his mouth clamped tightly shut over
the secrets of his death.

She said: "Will you tell me?"

He looked at her. "About your husband?"

"Tell me how he died. Describe the room where it happened."

He opened the car door. "I can't do that yet."

"I need to know it."

"I understand that."

"I need to hear the details."

"But not now."

"But you will?"

They drove off, past the bridge, the fruit and vegetable market with its crowds and jocular vendors, the ground miry with the blood of overripe tomatoes and corrupt melons. They went through the deserted maze of the financial district, and Jill Bowman opened the window two inches, just to feel the air again, to clear her lungs of the death of her husband.

"What will you do now?" he said.

She said nothing.

"You'll have to make funeral arrangements," he said.

She said nothing.

"You'll have to bury him."

"I may go away."

"That's a good idea."

"My sister lives in Montreal. I have friends in London. We have a family house on the Vineyard." She looked at him. "I don't know. I suppose I'll have to request a leave of absence from the university."

"Will they grant it?"

"I'm in no shape to teach or do any research."

"And you'll be coming back?"

They pulled up to the police station, the tower with darkened windows that looked over the four compass points of the city. Resnick seemed about to say something: the look on his face reflected the weight and significance of the thought, as though he were contemplating leaping across the gap between two cliffs.

"Thank you," Jill Bowman said, and shook his hand.

She drove home and listened to the radio. For once she played with the dial, eschewing the classical music she usually favored for something less contemplative. On a talk show a caller complained about everything. He railed against taxes, politicians, the color of license plates, the taste of cold shrimp. "Not to speak of the crime rate, I mean, Jesus, people are getting their throats cut, Howie, do you know what I mean, are you hearing me right?" and she pressed the button and Schubert filled the space in the car. She began to be less tense. The music moved her, and she found her mind drifting. Peter never entered it. She thought of

Sally in Montreal, and her mother, who until her death two years earlier had lived on the Vineyard with her friend, a cranky woman who wrote mysteries under an assumed name and treated Jill as though she were a girl of twelve craving the attentions of her mother. Since then she and Sally and their husbands had taken turns opening the house and airing it out on Memorial Day weekend, securing the shutters and locking it up on Labor Day, the smell of dampness and vacancy already beginning to cling to the walls.

Now the music came to an end, and as the news began to be read she switched the channel once again. A woman's voice said, "If you care you will give," and she pressed the button. A man exhorted: "Find Jesus or burn in hell for all of eternity." Now she found some music, piano nocturnes by Fauré, and though these had been some of Peter's favorite pieces she left them on, she forced herself to hear them, as though they signaled the continuing existence of even a small part of her husband.

The traffic moved at a greater speed than usual: cars and vans and small trucks packed tightly together, linked in speed, snaking rapidly up the highway, past the restaurants and miniature golf courses, the pizza parlors and tuxedo rentals, the cellular phone stores and ice cream stands. In a few minutes she would be on the interstate with its multiple lanes that cut through woods and farms. She thought of the house that awaited her with its invisible memories and empty rooms. There would be hesitant phone calls and condolence cards with their idiotic verses and sticky sentiments, offered to her by those who found themselves without the words to say.

The traffic thinned out. Now there were few cars around her. In her rearview mirror she could see a coach, a truck, a horse trailer. As she always did, she turned to look at the building nestled in the distant hills, visible as a brown Gothic imposition. Carrie lived there, and she would live there for the rest of her life, silent, enfolded in silence. Jill thought of her in her little room, staring at the window with its indiscreet iron bars, betraying nothing of her thoughts. She remembered her from her last visit only a week earlier: the essence of zero as Jill fed her, spoonful after spoonful of puréed apricots, "Now open," she would say, afterwards kissing Carrie on the forehead, cradling her in her arms, singing quietly. She wondered if she would be able to see Carrie this week. She wondered if Carrie would miss her. And sometimes she tried to see the pictures in Carrie's memory: the swipes of light, the astonishing darkness.

She turned the mirror to an angle and looked at herself, touching the side of her face before returning her gaze to the road. She thought of Resnick, who had stepped into her life to elucidate a mystery and yet brought her only confusion. As though he were made of glass she could make nothing of him.

Her husband's mouth.

The pallor of him.

These were the things that now came to her. Instead of driving on to her exit she turned off early and began negotiating the familiar narrow roads cutting through the pastures and farms and little villages which over the past ten or twelve years had attracted wealthier families. You could see them outside the video shops and post offices, climbing out of their Volvos and Range Rovers, their windows crowded with decals from private schools and Ivy League colleges.

The stable was deserted when she arrived late that afternoon. The top halves of the stall doors had been left open and one by one the horses turned from their rest to look at her. Only Blackjack hadn't bothered. She wondered if he was sick, for normally he recognized the sound of her footsteps, the little noises she made to alert him, responding with his eyes, a twitch of his ears. She fetched a whip and a lunge line from their hooks in the tack room and by the time she arrived at his stall he was watching her approach. She ran her hand lightly along the side of his neck and he lifted his head, his huge glassy eye swiveling to take her in. He pressed his nose to her neck and she could hear his breath, she could feel the warmth of it on her skin, and for some reason it aroused her, as though in returning to this world she had discovered as a child, she could shed the conventions of the other.

Peter disliked horses, though he tolerated Blackjack because he belonged to Jill. When on rare occasions she entered a show, or more often rode to hounds, he would come to watch her in her tweed jacket and velvet hat, the breeches that clung to her slim thighs, the sleek black leather boots. He disliked horses because he feared them, their frightened faces, their splayed nostrils and lifting hooves, and on the few occasions she tried to get him to mount up and walk the animal around the paddock, he shook his head. Now that he was gone it occurred to her that Peter was not a man to take risks. Invited by friends to sail he would sit in his lifejacket, suffering headache, gripping the side of the vessel, eyeing the dark curve of land with its familiar landmarks.

She attached the hook to Blackjack's halter and led him to the center of the ring. She began to unravel the long line that joined her to the horse and she took a position some distance from him. Anticipating, he held his head low and turned to look at her. She clucked at him and waved the thin tail of the whip just behind the horse's quarters. "Walk on," she commanded. And he moved off. After a half-circle she moved the whip again and he broke into a easy trot. "Get up there, Jack."

She turned and followed him as his pace grew faster, and occasionally she would take notice of the world beyond his body, the blur composed of trees and fences and low buildings. She and her horse were moving in crisp detail, hand, line, mane and tail, while everything else was in flux. Now he rocked into a canter, and his mouth opened to suck in air. She could feel him pulling away from her, keeping taut the extent of the cord, trying to make the circle larger, attempting to turn an endless curve into an infinitely long straight line. She let him make ten more circles, slowed him to a trot, then a walk, then came to him and touched his shoulder, patted his neck. She had talked to him the entire time, encouraging him, telling him what gait she expected, and when she didn't talk she made little birdlike noises with her mouth, noises of comfort and control. She must have worked him far longer than she'd thought, for his chest was slightly damp with perspiration. He made an exasperated blubbering sound and she led him out of the ring to the grassy area behind the stable. A rider she knew, an Englishwoman who had moved to the area a few months earlier, passed her on a large grey and waved, cried hallo, moved off towards the stable yard.

Jill watched her horse tear grass from the ground with his teeth, and beyond him the Englishwoman dismounting, putting up her stirrup irons, unbuckling the girth. Obviously the woman knew nothing of what had happened to Peter. Yet it occurred to Jill that the newspapers must have picked it up, or would do so in the next day or two, that his name would be printed in a story of lure and murder in a cheap city hotel. She wondered if she would become an object of curiosity, if people would drive by her house and slow down to gaze at the windows. There would be phone calls, words of sympathy from total strangers and torrents of abuse from those who envied her the attention. She remembered the calls that began a few years earlier, almost always coinciding with Peter's conferences, whether domestic or foreign, the muffled male voice questioning her about the shape of her body in the middle of the night, begging for detailed answers, speaking of ropes and leather. Eventually the calls were traced to one of Peter's patients, an attorney specializing in divorce who had seen her photograph in his office, a Kodachrome woman looking over her shoulder, squinting a little in the autumn light, laughing into the lens.

Now it would begin again; she who had been a stranger in the world would become an item in the newspaper, a name, an age, a photograph of a woman in mourning. She clicked her tongue and Blackjack looked abruptly up at her. She began to walk him back to his stall. She patted him on the neck and returned to her car. When she got home she called the funeral parlor and prepared to put her husband to rest.

CHAPTER 5

As though it were a sense of dread, darkness seemed to arrive by degrees, extending shadows, going to grey. And suddenly you looked up and realized night had fallen.

Peter Freytag stood at his desk, tipped slightly forward, resting his weight on the two tents he formed with his fingertips. For a moment he shut his eyes and then he reached over and switched off the lamp. He turned to the window of his office that looked towards the harbor. A yellowish haze had drifted over the vessels: tugboats nodding in the swelling tide; a docked battleship, arrayed with pennants; a fishing boat puffing slowly in from sea. Beyond them, its masts strung with the webs and lines of its rigging, an antique ironclad discharged the last of the day's tourists. Amidst the buildings, the banks and brokerage houses, depart-

ment stores and restaurants, the trees of the city's small unex-
pected parks glowed with the reds and yellows of autumn.

He looked at his desk diary: the time 5:30 had been circled in
the blue pencil he habitually used, and an hour and a half later
the dinner appointment he would have with her before his flight.
He stood and bowed his head slightly, looked at the palm of his
hand, took his jacket from the back of his chair and left the office.

His secretary must have left before him, for he locked his door
on his way out. In the lobby of the building a thin Cambodian
woman washed the floor, pushing the huge mop northwards, then
turning east, then south, squaring the compass. He stepped out
to the sidewalk, looked at his watch, turned to the telephone
booth on the corner, looked up for a moment at the window of his
office. North, south, east and west.

Now he was in a taxi, his briefcase and suitcase beside him. He
held a handkerchief to his face as though he were weeping or had
been injured, and yet when he took it away he was smiling. The
driver said something and Peter tilted his head slightly, as
though the subject held more than a passing interest for him.

The midtown traffic was heavy, advancing a few feet at a time.
A school bus came up alongside the taxi and children pressed
their faces against the window, trying to get Peter's attention.
They seemed to be begging for help instead of laughing, and one
little girl was crying, scratching at the window and weeping, her
face contorted with fear. Someone, an adult, walked up and down
the aisle between the seats, gathering speed, swinging her arms
back and forth. In the distance, on the bridge, traffic was locked
in a halt. The driver pointed to it and Peter looked towards the
bay, the way the setting sun made it glitter and shine, like mercury in the palm of your hand.

A man and a woman stood outside the Hubbard Hotel. The
man was gesturing with his hand, pointing to his chest, while the
woman shook her head and snapped her fingers once. The taxi sat
idling by the curb while Peter took some money from his wallet
and paid the man. He looked at his watch; he checked his pocket,

because there was something in it, something important. He did not notice the haze of fear that lay over the scene. The driver switched on his radio and a voice said, The burial of Carrie Bowman will take place on Thursday.

Dust on the stairs, dust and broken glass and debris of yellow chalk that someone had stepped on. The smell of urine and rotting fish. Peter ascended the stairs, and although the stairs seemed endless, though he climbed at least twelve sets of staircases, he moved without altering his speed, grasping the banister, hefting his suitcase and briefcase towards the darkness. When he reached the door it was shut. He set down his cases and lifted his hand to knock and suddenly, slowly, the door opened. A smiling face appeared. Now Peter disappeared inside the room. In the room were two people and it was impossible to tell whether one was a man and the other a woman, or both men, but they seemed pleased to see Peter. One of them sucked on a toothpick, occasionally bringing his fingers up to rearrange it between his lips. Peter seemed to know these people, and his gestures were of an intimate kind, he touched their arms and described little circles in the air, as though defining things with his fingers. The air was filled with the weight of menace and yet he sensed nothing of it.

One of them helped him off with his jacket and then, saying something in Russian or possibly Dutch, caressed him on the cheek, touched his thigh; the other reached into his pocket and took something out and clamping Peter's mouth shut with one hand began to draw blood from his throat. Peter seemed unmoved by what was happening to him, in fact he remained standing, turning his head to look at different points in the room, and while he did so the blood in his body flowed down his chest and grey trousers onto the floor. The two people in the room stood back, holding their hands in the air so as to avoid being splashed or stained. They watched Peter as his nonchalance turned to something inhuman, the odd angular gestures of a machine breaking down, the way his body shuddered and his head lolled, the manner in which his mouth opened and closed, and the peculiar things he did with his tongue, as though words, like shards of bone, had become lodged in his throat.

Suddenly he stopped moving. His eyes grew wide and he turned to her and then she woke up, sweating, gasping for breath, blinking her eyes against the sunlight pouring from the window, feeling the ache in the chest that had more to do with actual pain than heartbreak.

This was how it was going to be from now on: unending speculation about the lost hour of Peter's last evening on earth.

For a few minutes she lay on the bed, finding her bearings, reconstructing what she had done since leaving for the stable, as though events in time could build a scaffolding against the edifice of the future. Because she had an appointment at five to meet with a Mr. Kelly at a local funeral home she had planned on taking a shower. After removing her clothes she had lain down for a few moments on the bed. She felt like she hadn't slept in two days, and she realized that she was afraid to fall asleep, that sleep was a form of forgetting, that in the moments of waking she might relive once again those first moments of agony that come with knowledge. Yet seeing Blackjack, working with him in the ring, had lifted the weight of things from her mind. She had lain on the bed and shut her eyes and thought of Peter that last night they had spent together, how different it now seemed to have been. She remembered him reaching down to take the hair away from her cheek. She remembered the feel of him, the weight of him on her, the smell of his neck, the sound of his breathing. She remembered putting the palms of her hands on his chest, as though in the midst of their ardor she were supporting him, establishing the reality of their passion, taking command of the weight of her husband. She wondered if he knew then that he was going to die in less than twenty-four hours, and if, in those thirty minutes they made love, he had been trying to impart something to her, something significant, some clue to what was going to happen, a message, anything. Something that might lodge within her and make itself known only later, when her thoughts had grown clear, and her memory less dark.

The sunlight was on her body now and she looked at herself, at the body she had come to forget over the past few days, the body Peter had so adored. She loved to watch him looking at her running his fingertips lightly along her thighs, bending to kiss her breasts, taking her in as if she were something new, someone who until then had fleetingly passed through the tropics of his fancy. Now he was no longer alive to do it, he was nothing at all, a thing on a table in a refrigerated room.

Now it occurred to her: everything had been arranged in advance.

CHAPTER 6

When she came out of the shower the phone was ringing, and it stopped when she reached to answer it. She dried her hair with the towel and chose a navy blue dress from her closet and then the phone rang again.

"Ms. Bowman?"

She didn't recognize the voice.

"It's Dave Resnick."

Still naked she sat on the edge of the bed opposite her reflection in the mirror. "What's happened?"

He seemed surprised by her reaction. "Nothing. Nothing's happened. We still have nothing more on your husband's case. But we hope to very soon. Possibly by the middle of next week."

"I'm going to set a date for his funeral."

"That's your choice," and his sentence, apparently unfinished, faded to silence.

"I don't understand."

"It's just."

"I have to bury my husband."

"We need to keep his body here until morning. That's what I was calling to say. There's one more test we need to complete."

"Test for what?" she asked, and she could hear the anger in her voice, the desire to break through walls, destroy barriers.

"I'm not at liberty to say."

"I had a dream about him. About Peter. There were two people in the room at the hotel. He went there willingly."

"Yes. We believe he did go there willingly. But we don't know how many people were in the room with him. We're trying to track down the person who first phoned the police and hospital. All calls to the station are recorded. We're also trying to locate anyone who was staying in the hotel the evening of your husband's death. We'll get there, Ms. Bowman, I promise you that."

"Didn't the hotel clerk see anyone come in?"

"This is the Hubbard, Ms. Bowman. Someone sits in a chair at the bottom of the stairs and takes cash. No one signs a register, no names are ever asked for or given."

It was odd: she felt no sense of revenge, no need to reset the scales. It was almost as if Peter's death had taken place with his own cooperation; as though, like the birth of a child, it had been planned before its time.

"Today is Saturday," Resnick said for no apparent reason. "Tomorrow is Sunday. The earliest you'll be able to bury your husband is Monday. Let me know when you've made the arrangements and I'd be happy to call the funeral home and deal with them myself."

"Deal with them."

"About transporting your husband." There was a pause. "Ms. Bowman?"

Again she looked at herself in the mirror. Breasts, thighs,

knees. The humid darkness between her legs. She pulled the towel away from her hair and laid it across her lap. "I still can't believe it," she said. "I mean."

"I understand."

"It hasn't registered."

"It will. Maybe at the funeral."

"I just want to get it over with," she said.

"Is there someone staying with you?"

She realized she hadn't told anyone but Sally, and though Sally offered to fly down and spend a few weeks with her, she refused. Another human being would have constituted an intrusion. There would be pointless conversations, words and sentences uttered merely to fill the uncomfortable silences. She could see Sally touching her on the shoulder, embracing her at odd moments, unaware that the most comforting thing she could do would be to fly back to Montreal.

"I'm alone," she said.

"I may need to speak with you again. In fact it's important that I do it fairly soon. Tomorrow, if possible."

"Speak to me about what?"

"Your husband. His practice, his patients. His habits. There's no need for you to drive in. I'll come to you."

"Tomorrow."

"Is that all right?"

She thought for a moment, she remembered Resnick's soft voice in her ear, his inconclusive little attempts to comfort her. He would be there at noon. *I'll come to you.*

And then she began to wonder. She remembered that Resnick was a detective. She sensed that anyone who had even remotely known Peter would be a suspect, as though your merely being alive were a risk to everyone you met, a form of contamination, something radioactive. She had said little to Resnick about her marriage; she had said little because she'd resented the implications of his questions, the way the little pauses and tiny emphases seemed to link together like a spider's web, creating a complexity of guilty entanglements. Now she found herself moving with a renewed speed. She put on a bathrobe and went down to the kitchen. She looked through her bag until she found the little rectangular card and her address book. She stood at the counter and looked at the card, then at the scene beyond the window, a spiral of colored leaves gathering in a wind, twisting like a wave, falling like snow to the ground below. In the yard next door her neighbor and his children were playing catch with a large rubber ball. She had seen him earlier when pulling into her driveway, and he had waved at her as if nothing at all had changed. That was what was bothering her. Between herself and the rider at the stable there had been a line of ignorance. No one knew anything. Peter was dead only to her and Sally and a detective. To the rest of the world he was still alive, landing in London, expecting to attend a conference and see friends.

She dialed the number and Resnick answered it after two rings.

"I forgot to ask you something."

He seemed pleased she'd called.

"When is the press going to pick this up?"

"They already have."

She was stunned by his words. "What?"

"There was a small item in both of the major city papers. But we requested that the name of your husband be withheld."

"But why?" She realized she would have preferred people learning of it from any source but herself.

"There are still details that have to be cleared up."

"And you think by not saying anything about Peter you might be able to find whoever did this thing?"

"That's the basic idea."

"My neighbors still know nothing."

"I suggest you keep it that way, Ms. Bowman. I can't order you to do it, but I strongly urge you to be discreet."

"My sister knows."

"That's only natural."

"Am I a suspect?"

"Please call me Dave, Ms. Bowman."

"Am I?"

And he said goodbye and hung up.

She pressed the button and tried the number in the city, then remembered Neil would be at home. After eight rings he answered with a breathless hello.

"It's Jill Bowman."

Formerly her mother's attorney, Neil was an old family friend. He had drawn up their wills, and she saw then that she should have called him Friday night.

"Peter's dead. He's been murdered."

"Jesus."

"I suppose I should have called earlier. I just didn't think."

"It's all right, Jill."

"The police have been questioning me."

She told him the story, she could hear him taking notes on the computer in the office in his home. "I'll call Resnick," he said. "I'll get back to you within the hour."

She hung up the phone and for an extra moment kept her hand on the receiver. Added to her grief and confusion was now the suffocating oppression of fear and wonderment. It was the sensation of being gagged and hooded while events took place around you, events in which your role was prominent. Events over which you had no control. She opened the window a few inches and felt the brisk December air slip in. It carried with it the scent of someone's wood fire, of dry leaves. Soon the season would fold in upon itself, and winter would cover her like a blanket.

Now she decided: Peter's funeral would be private. She alone would watch him descend into the black earth.

CHAPTER 7

She had been through this years before, this unchanging comedy of death, the ceremonial farce of goodbye.

The man named Kelly urged her to purchase a lead lining. And although Peter had always despised ostentation, the man named Kelly also insisted she buy a casket fitted out handsomely with sturdy brass handles that folded neatly down. So it had been at the time of her father's death. "At the very least he can be carried with ease from the church to the hearse," and he demonstrated how they worked: up and down.

"My husband was not a religious man."

"He will still need to be carried. Whether from your house to the hearse or from some other place, handles always make it easier. Imagine traveling with a suitcase without handles." And he smiled at her and made a notation on a page in his leather portfolio. His manner amused her. To him death was much like life: one had to be as charitable to a corpse as to a living person, and the small conveniences of life never seemed to come to an end.

"I'm having a private funeral for my husband."

"Whatever you wish. Have you made an arrangement with a church or synagogue?"

"My husband wasn't religious. I simply want a graveside ceremony."

"Then you've spoken to a clergyman?"

She hadn't considered it. It must seem absurd to the man known as Kelly that Peter would simply be driven to the cemetery and buried. She didn't even have a plot. Death had never entered into their plans.

"Oh dear," said this man. He tapped his pencil against his portfolio. "You could have him cremated, you know. It'll cost you a little more for the transportation, but you can then consider a less expensive coffin or, if you like, no coffin at all. If this is the route you're thinking about taking I can show you some receptacles for your husband's ashes. We, of course, don't do cremations here. You'll have to go out of town."

She followed him to his desk. "We've done a lot of work with this firm," and he handed her a card. "They're very good, very considerate, with nice clean facilities. The added attraction of cremation is that there is then no rush to dispose of the remains. You could do it whenever you wish, for the most part wherever you like. Simply check with the town's health authorities. If you wish you may even keep the ashes in your home."

He looked at her. Possibly she didn't seem to be comprehending him, or had somehow absented herself. He said, "Mrs. Bowman?"

She didn't bother correcting the way he addressed her. In the shadow of events it made little difference: words seemed to have lost their potency, the exquisite little nuances of social intercourse counted for nothing. She looked around at the coffins on display with their decorative pillows and comfortable bedding, brass fittings and shiny wood. She thought that by cremating Peter she might destroy some secret that would eventually come to light; the truth of his death that in some way would illuminate the truth of his life.

"Perhaps you'd like a few moments alone, Mrs. Bowman?"

She turned to him. "All right."

"Are you sure I can't interest you in a cup of coffee or tea? A glass of cider?"

She shook her head. He looked at her as though she were demented. When he shut the door it made a muffled sound, like leather slipping along carpet. She remained standing by the coffin she felt she would choose, sliding her hand along the edge of it, feeling the smooth finish, the cool handles made of brass. Soon it would be soiled and damp, and the tiny insects of the earth would be battering their jaws against it, drilling holes, desperate to pry into its secrets. Beside it was a display of pillows, many carrying a motif or design. Ducks flew off beyond the sunset; a horse grazed at close of day; there was a sailboat silhouetted in the twilight. They belonged to a world devoid of people, as though after one died one's adored objects or pets simply carried on without their owner. A pamphlet stated that designs could be custom-made, possibilities were limitless. One could have the insignia of a unit of the armed forces, a Masonic symbol, the profile of a favorite peak. A wide range of sporting scenes was available: cycling by an Episcopal church, jogging through a mountain pass, skating on a frozen country pond. For infants and children there were ducks and bunnies, Big Bird and Mickey. For the devout, Jesus, Mary and St. Francis of Assisi struck familiar attitudes.

Then they shut the box and placed it in the ground and no one was ever the wiser.

There were two doors to the room. She carefully opened the one through which the man named Kelly withdrew and walked into another room. A woman lay in a casket, dressed in a pink blouse, her hair tinged with blue, and Jill was startled to see her lying there, smiling, as though dreaming of a wish fulfilled, her fingers tangled in a rosary.

"May I help you?"

Jill turned to the man as he stood by the door. "I'm looking for the bathroom," she said to the undertaker. And suddenly finding purpose in her day she walked out and got into her car.

The drive south took no more than twenty-five minutes. She had done it so often that she found her attention drifting. There were distant hills, apple orchards, stables, mansions surrounded by gentle lawns, the cuticle edges of swimming pools, the cool geometry of tennis courts.

The sun was setting as she approached the exit, and as her car followed the curve of the ramp the clinic came briefly into view with its turrets and darkened windows. Located behind an iron gate, at the end of a long driveway that gently curved and dipped through a kind of meadow, it rose above the horizon as you crested the hill, like a ship breasting the curvature of the earth, and each time she saw it she remembered the first time she had seen it: as though it were something constructed from the bricks and mortar of a madman's fancy. Yet it was surrounded by gardens and pathways, a place devoid of sharp edges and disturbing imagery. When all those years ago she first arrived there she was startled to see some of the patients even walking about, as though they had every intention of going out for the evening. Yet after a few minutes she became aware that most of them were moving aimlessly in circles or elaborate patterns, lost in the labyrinth of thought. Watching over them, nurses both male and female often had to chase after them, lead them back to the building for medication and rest.

Before taking the road to the clinic she turned, came to a halt at a red light, made a left into the parking lot of a large discount store. The bright lights, shrill music and smell of stale popcorn made her wince as she entered and moved towards the aisle she knew all too well. Families were spending their evening there,

men in baseball caps, bearing the weight of too much beer, led
their wives and snarling children this way and that, for there
was nothing else to do, there never was. It was a store in which
the checkout women brightly greeted you, asked how you were,
and because you left complexity at the door you always told
them, no matter what had happened, that you were fine, thanks.
To say that your husband had been murdered, that you were
not quite yourself, that the edges of your life had grown blurred
and ambiguous, would have been out of place, considered an
indiscretion.

Jill examined the shelves of toys. She flipped through a *Beauty
and the Beast* coloring book, and the implications of it made her
replace it on the metal rack. Everything seemed suddenly inappropriate: the turtles in paramilitary costume, pictures of infants
in garbage pails, the plastic Uzis, the pregnant mommy dolls and
bright exploding cars.

She looked through the bins of stuffed animals and smiled
when the bright eyes of a blue kitten came into view. She felt the
soft artificial fur, the stubby little tail, the tag attached to its ear,
and the awkward, helpless expression on its face endeared itself to
her. She bought also a bottle of bubble solution that came with a
little plastic wand. The purchase was just another act in an old
routine that had always excluded Peter: an inviolable part of her
life that graced Jill Bowman's life with meaning.

A small unobtrusive gatehouse was located a hundred yards
before the main building, and just beyond it a barrier. She came
to a halt by it and a man in overalls slid open the window. "Good
evening, Ms. Bowman."

She smiled at him.

"You're late this week," he said and for a moment she felt
panic, for his words seemed to imply that something had occurred in her absence, an event that could have been forestalled
by her.

"I'll let them know you're here." The barrier lifted with a soft
hum and she drove into a space in the parking area off to the side.

When she stepped through the door Dr. Bradley walked up to her and smiled. "Everything's fine, Jill," she said. Jill had known Jean Bradley for years, at least as long as Carrie had been under her care. "There's been no change, of course."

"There never is," said Jill.

"But there's always hope."

"Yes," said Jill, not believing it.

"She's about to have her dinner." Usually most of the patients ate together in the dining room in the basement, supervised by members of the staff. On the occasions when visitors arrived, though, meals could be taken in the rooms.

"I'll feed her," Jill said.

"She'll like that. I'll let Frida know." She picked up the phone and said a few words into it and Jill stared at her.

"I need to talk to you," Jill said.

Dr. Bradley looked at her, saw the words behind the eyes, took her arm and led her to the office.

"My husband died yesterday."

"What?" The word came out of her like something physical, a jab with the hand, a punch to the face.

"Peter died yesterday."

"I'm so terribly sorry, Jill."

"He was murdered," and Jean Bradley was hurled into silence. "I'm not going to say anything to Carrie, at least not right away. There's still so much to be done. There's just—they still don't know exactly what happened. I'm not even supposed to be talking about it. It's so confusing. I haven't even," and she let her sentence trail off into a daze of silence.

After a moment Dr. Bradley said, "Are you all right? You could have called, there was no need for you to come down."

"I wanted to see her," Jill interrupted. "What happened to Peter doesn't make a difference here."

"Still."

"Nothing's changed as far as Carrie is concerned."

Jill took the main stairway up to the second floor, then an ele-

vator to the third. The property had been once owned by a prominent newspaper publisher whose periodicals were notorious for
their mixture of insensitive editorials and fiery endorsements
for Republican candidates for office, reveling in revenge, begging
for the death penalty, destroying reputations with a hazy photograph, a suggestive remark. The publisher had shot himself in the
head after a scandal in his life had come to light, and the property
had been bought by a consortium of psychiatrists from Virginia.
It cost Jill two thousand dollars a month to keep Carrie there.

When she turned into the familiar hallway she saw the woman
with a meal cart making her way along it. Although her name
was Frida, she was known to the patients as Betty; to Carrie she
was nothing more than an open door, a dark pair of hands, a
curved mouth, an orchestra of sounds. The woman smiled and
greeted her and waited for Jill to reach the door. "I've got her tray
ready to go, Ms. Bowman."

She stood by the door and waited for Betty to pass, then turned
the lever which operated the shutters and looked into the little
window. Carrie was sitting on her bed, staring out the window.
The lamp over her desk had been switched on, and the room lay
in an artificial twilight, soft and drowsy, the afterglow of day.
Had she seen Jill arrive, was she waiting for her?

Her hair had been secured back in a ponytail, and she was wearing the blue stirrup pants and yellow turtleneck Jill had brought
for her last time. She sat very still and looked out the window.
She sat without moving. Her breathing was imperceptible.

Jill was joined by Dr. Bradley, who unlocked the door for her.
"Carrie," she said. "You have a visitor."

And as always Carrie remained still and unmoving, as though
suspended forever between two words.

Now Jill was alone with her.

Even when her mother placed the bag down by the side of the
bed Carrie seemed not to notice. Jill sat next to her and took her
into her arms and she felt something in her heart move.
"Mommy's here." It was only a whisper. She looked at her daugh-

ter. It would take time, sometimes no more than five or ten minutes, sometimes it happened after an hour, but she knew it would
come eventually, the flicker of recognition, maybe even a sound,
the rubbing up of a cheek.

"What do you look at, my darling?" she said, and her eyes were
led to the window and the rapid darkness that was filling it. The
road that cut through the lawns, that twisted its way beyond the
heavy gates, appeared as a wending grey line, a letter cut into
the landscape. The space her daughter occupied was a place of
profound solitude, and at that moment she realized that she, too,
was alone in the world. Without Peter she was only one. Even
though Carrie had all the attention she could wish for she was
alone, separate, an island distant from the mainland. What went
through her mind, what pictures, what sounds, what darkness
had closed in on her? She lived in a parallel world, a place of re-
versement, as a negative is to its photographic image, and for a
moment, now that the horror had fallen around her, Jill could
suddenly grasp the answer and just as quickly lose sight of it.

She kissed Carrie's cheek. "I've brought you a few surprises,
my darling. Look," and she took the little kitten out and held it
in front of her daughter, and Carrie said nothing, she looked at
the window. The wall by her bed was lined with little soft creatures, bears and monkeys and dogs, a dolphin, an elephant, sou-
venirs of previous visits. She wishfully imagined Carrie lying in
bed at night, taking hold of them, squeezing them tightly, learning to love.

Although never sure that Carrie noticed it, Jill had taken the
trouble to decorate the walls, periodically removing some pictures and replacing them with new ones. There was a photograph
of Blackjack in the stable yard, his ears pricked, eyes alert, Carrie
standing beside him, a little tentative as she touches his neck.
More than once Jill had taken her daughter out for a day to see
the horse and to picnic on a nearby beach. They were days that
left Carrie overwhelmed and weary: so much sunlight, so many
noises, the brackish smells of stable and sea. On the way back

Carrie would gaze out the car window while Jill either played a
tape or sang to her. "Sing along with me," she would say. "Try it,
darling." And, if she was in the mood, Carrie would moan along
with the song, her eyes wide, her hands unstill, and for her
mother the world would reach the pinnacle of creation.

Jill rubbed the kitten's cheek against Carrie's and she saw Carrie suddenly press against it. She took her daughter into her arms
and held her against her heart and kissed her. Carrie looked at her
with a familiar look, her eyebrows arched, her mouth pursed, and
Jill laughed a little, standing and taking the girl's hand. "I'll go
with you," she said. "I'll help you, my darling."

She flicked the light on in the adjoining toilet and watched as
Carrie pushed down her pants and underwear. She waited as Carrie finished and then helped her clean up. Together they washed
their hands, Carrie's within hers, and together they looked at
themselves in the mirror; a mirror that made your face a little
milky, because it had been coated in plastic against the possibility of shattering.

Jill began to prepare her daughter for dinner, placing the napkin on her lap, picking up the spoon, setting the tray in front of
her on the desk by the window. Carrie pushed her hand away and
jerked her finger towards the bag. Jill took out the jar of bubbles
and unscrewed the lid. Carrie loved bubbles and often expected
them, yet the delight in her eyes, the dull light that for a moment
shone in the blue of them, turned Jill's heart. She dipped the
wand into the thick mixture and blew gently into the little circle.
A bubble caught the air, reflecting in its swirls of color the faces
of mother and daughter, and Carrie watched it float above them.
When it burst in the air she let out a single cry.

"Again?" Jill said, and she sent another bubble into the air,
and when it, too, burst, Carrie let out a shout and pouted.

"Let's eat, okay?"

She secured the little bib around Carrie's neck. She dipped her
spoon into the plastic bowl that had been filled with shredded
beef, mashed potatoes and diced vegetables, opening her mouth

as Carrie opened hers, wiping the girl's chin when she finished swallowing it. It took nearly half an hour for her to finish. Jill fed her dessert, lime Jell-O with whipped cream that Carrie ate far more eagerly, and her enthusiasm, visible on her face and clothes, made her mother smile. This was what a child was like, what her neighbors' kids were like; this must be what being completely alive is all about: the enduring delight in something sweet, the sugary thrill of the illicit. The thought began to swallow up her grief, and she caught it just before she forgot it. I've lost Peter, she was going to say, then thought better of it.

They were words beyond Carrie's understanding, words the child would doubtless puzzle over for months and years, turning sense into four separate sounds, and the sounds would eventually slide into enigma and silence. She stood and pulled the curtains shut. The pastel flowers and birds on them only made the little room look bleak and cheerless, as though all the air had been sucked from it. Yet when you looked at it you realized, without quite being able to define what it was, that something was missing. Not a particular object, perhaps, nothing specific, but you would grow slightly vertiginous when you looked around, as though something had come to disturb your sense of perspective. And then, as happened to Jill one night all those years ago, it would dawn on you: this was a world of blunt edges and rounded corners, a place from which the enticing angles of danger had been sheared off. And when you touched the walls your fingers sank into them.

And her mind turned yet again to a hotel room, a polished blade dipped in red, and the sight of her husband in the morgue, his mouth clamped shut, his chin pressed against his chest, a hollow thing without meaning.

She stood and looked at Carrie, a grown girl yet diminutive and helpless in her eyes, an infant bird, pink-skinned and chilled, that had fallen from its nest in a gust of wind, and she reached down and touched her shoulder, as if to hold on to her silent daughter's existence. Now her meal was finished. Carrie had picked up the little kitten and was pressing her cheek against it, not carrying it up to her face but rather bringing herself to it. Then she looked up at Jill, who at that moment, not for the first time, saw herself in her child. What darkness had closed in on her? What stroke of unreason had driven her into this terrible seclusion?

Now there would be no men in her baby's life: no father or stepfather, no husband or lover. She had nothing to lose; her mother had lost nearly everything.

Lucky Carrie: at least she was spared the need to find the words.

She sat beside Carrie and looked at her as she held her kitten to her cheek. No smile, no sparkle, no sound.

This was the world of silence and shadow.

CHAPTER 8

She heard him only as crisp rustling. It was the restless ashy
sound of ghosts, the dry autumnal laughter of phantoms, and
when she looked down from her bedroom window she saw
Resnick emerging from the woods behind her house, shuffling
through the unraked signs of fall.

She had not slept well the night before. In fact she feared that
sleep might not come at all, and then she began to see that she
was terrified of falling out of wakefulness. To sleep meant to pass
through a tunnel of memory. Never having taken advantage of
sleeping pills or late-night television, she had instead sat in the
kitchen listening to the radio, leafing through the unread newspapers of the previous days, drinking scotch until she could
barely see. She became ravenous and made toast and scrambled

eggs, and while she waited for the butter in the pan to melt she opened a bag of popcorn she had bought in the supermarket a week earlier and gorged herself on it, leaving kernels on the floor, bits in her hair. Continually she reminded herself that Peter would never be there again, would never speak, never touch her body. She said his name over and over again, Peter Peter Peter, until it became noise in her mouth, sounds devoid of sense. A peculiar mirth overcame her, as if she were a child in December, drunk on anticipation, climbing off to bed on Christmas Eve. The thought came to her as she stumbled up the stairs that possibly it indicated that she had in fact survived the loss of her husband, that perhaps this was what death was like: for all of your life it lay just over the horizon, a deep flooded pit, horribly dreaded, dark beyond black. And then you died, and discovered that it was like jumping into the deep end of the pool that first time: you rose to the surface and everything, everything, was blue sunlight.

She slept dreamlessly until four, waking suddenly when she thought she heard a noise, rising in a state of doleful sobriety. She took off her clothes and went into the bathroom. With a damp cloth she dabbed at her face and chest, and the cool water refreshed her as drops of it trickled down her breasts, her belly, the thicket of brown between her thighs.

Now she was awake. Not bothering to put on her bathrobe, crossing her arms over her breasts, she walked quietly downstairs and sought in the darkness the origin of the noise. As if in her cool nudity she could defend herself. She said, "Hello?" and when there was no response she laughed a little at herself, as though all along she had been prepared to carry on a dialogue with an intruder, a thief, Santa Claus.

Her steps on the floor echoed as they never had before when Peter was alive. She looked outside through the kitchen window and it was like midnight, black and overcast; it was impossible to believe dawn would ever come. The air outside was heavy with moisture, thick with possibilities.

She returned to her bedroom. She felt something within her

begin to weaken and bend, a reed in the marsh wind, a tree be-
sieged by storm, and her eyes brimmed with tears. The simple act
of missing her husband filled her heart with pain. She switched
on a small lamp in the bedroom and standing against the wall
surveyed the landscape of her solitude. On Peter's dresser was a
photograph of Jill from one of their vacations on the Vineyard.
She was standing on the porch, dressed only in one of his blue
chambray shirts, her tousled hair falling about her face. She remembered why he liked the photo so much: only minutes before
they had made love. She had been standing on the porch, leaning
on the railing, and he had come up behind her and without a
word had taken her, holding her apart with his strong fingers,
thrusting, pushing her up against the railing. But it was not like
making love, with implications of tenderness and small touches, a
prolonged awakening of the senses, where every move was a profession of devotion. This had been an assault, completely unex-
pected, taking place in public, in view of nearby houses, the
sound of her gasps carried off by the wind. She picked up the
photo in its frame and looked into her own eyes, as if there might
be reflected in them something of the living husband who was
now so absent from her life.

The photo contained all the events of that particular day: the
breakfast they had eaten, a phone call from New York, the way
the sun looked just before setting beyond Chilmark and Gay
Head. It was a day in which nothing important took place, and
yet Peter's act, this sudden unanticipated explosion, was like a
great wave, carrying with it the detritus and small treasures that
otherwise would have sunk to the bottom of her memory.

She set the photo down and opened the top drawer. His socks
lay rolled in neat ranks, his underwear folded just so. It was too
familiar to her, the drawers full of his clothes, the scent of them,
the sheer orderliness of his things. It was reflected in the way he
considered matters, with an integrity that had about it an almost
aesthetic quality, as if it were something apart from him, that had
been created by his hands, hewn from a block of marble. When he

spoke his words were carefully chosen, slightly heavy in his mouth, whether because of his accent or the manner in which he had chosen them. She would tease him about his Swiss sense of order, wondering aloud where his clockwork was located.

Yet now that he was gone his clothes seemed the belongings of a stranger, and she began to look through them, feeling her way under shirts and sweaters, expecting to find some small anomaly, something that might hint of a life lived apart from theirs, a photograph, a scribbled note, a hasty telephone number on a shred of lined yellow paper. She found nothing: his death had been etched in air and water.

She sat on the edge of her bed. She watched the night trickle into shadow.

Now it was the end of morning and she watched Detective Sergeant Resnick walking out of the woods, stopping to look at the house, scratching his ear, looking at the ground: the studied indifference of a man following a trail of blood.

He stepped to her door and it swung open. "I saw you walking up to the house," she said. And she looked at him, a calm face against a grey sky.

"I thought I'd take a look around, see what kind of a neighborhood it is." He turned this way and that, as if in illustration of his technique. He looked at her. He was speaking nonsense. "It's nice here," he added.

She made coffee while Resnick sat at the kitchen table. She offered him cookies from a box she had bought the day before Peter's murder, imported things from Belgium, and the sight of these dainty little cakes killed her appetite. The detective leafed through a pocket notebook, making notations now and again as she watched him. He wore a green windbreaker and khaki slacks and loafers.

"Is it your day off?"

He looked up at her. It was obvious he didn't know how to react. He held a cookie awkwardly between his fingers, as though he had never meant to take one, as if he had picked up an acorn or a pebble from the ground. He said, "If it were my day off I wouldn't be here, Ms. Bowman. I have a family. I have children."

"You have a wife."

"I have a wife."

"And what does she do?"

"She teaches third grade at a private school."

She said, "Have you found out who murdered my husband, Sergeant Resnick?" The anger in her voice seemed false, it spoke of feigned vengeance.

Resnick looked up at her and shook his head. "Not yet. But you can make your plans for the funeral."

"So you won't need him anymore."

"No," he said.

"How did he die, Sergeant?"

"It was a combination of shock and a loss of blood."

"Was there a lot of it?"

He seemed unwilling to answer. Then he said, "Yes. There was."

"So he must have been stabbed in the back. It was the only part of him I didn't see."

Resnick said nothing. She remembered the set of Peter's jaw, and she felt like a child in a room full of adults, the significance of things hovering above her head, just out of reach.

She placed the coffee pot on the table and sat across from him. Outside the air filled with the shouts of her neighbor's children, the sound of leaves being raked. "I spoke to your lawyer," Resnick said. "I explained all the facts of the case to him."

"And?"

"It's just a matter of keeping everyone informed."

"Does your wife know about this case?"

"I don't bring my work home, Ms. Bowman."

"You mean you never mention cases you're working on?"

"Sometimes I do. Sometimes if things get a little heavy I might mention it."

"A little heavy."

"If I become too involved."

"Is it possible to become too involved?"

"Sometimes it happens. Sometimes it's unavoidable."

"Sometimes you let it happen."

"Sometimes," he said.

"But it's not a good thing to do."

"No. It's not a good thing to do."

"It means you have a personal stake in the case."

"You have to back off," he said.

"How heavy is this one getting?"

He looked at her. "I'm doing everything in my power to find the person or persons who murdered your husband, Ms. Bowman. I'm sure you would like that to happen as quickly as possible."

"It won't bring my husband back."

"Nothing can do that. No one can make it happen."

She said, "I would do anything to bring him back, Sergeant Resnick."

"Tell me about your husband, Ms. Bowman. Tell me everything you forgot to mention the last time we spoke. I don't care how insignificant it seems. Something will give me the lead I'm looking for."

"He was a psychiatrist."

"I know that."

"He was successful."

"That was obvious."

"He was respected. He had a name. He'd published a lot of articles. He was a good writer, he had a wonderful sense of humor."

"Could it be," Resnick began, taking hold of another cookie, "is it possible that he had written a piece on one of his patients that might have been offensive?"

"My husband was a very careful man. He was European, he was Swiss, he was cautious. He would never have tried to exploit a patient."

"Still . . ."

"He would never have done it deliberately. He had to respect the relationship he had with his patients. It is the law, isn't it?"

Resnick made a note on a page in his pad. "By accident, then?"

She began to move her hand through the air, making motions of protest. "Peter was always very careful never to offend."

"He had women patients as well as men," Resnick said, and he waited for a response.

"Yes?"

"I'm simply stating a fact. He treated women and men." He hesitated a moment. "Sometimes it happens that women become, I don't know," and he moved his hands in the air, as though words, a whole array of them, were floating, waiting to be plucked, as if what he really wanted was for her to finish the sentence.

"You're suggesting that one of his female patients fell in love with him."

"Not necessarily in love."

"Peter would never have allowed this to happen."

"Not to your knowledge."

"But why would it have to be a woman?" she said.

"Come on, Ms. Bowman, you're a college professor, you understand what I mean."

"You're asking if a student has ever fallen for me? Of course it's happened. But there's a certain ethic to be obeyed in the classroom."

"And outside of it?"

She very clearly remembered the young man, the first-year graduate student with his beard and thick hair—a bright and thoughtful man—recalling the look in Greg's eyes, the way his attention drifted when he was in her office, the way he looked at her. For a time she was flattered, then confused, and she found herself tempted to the point where she began to conceive of what might happen were she to allow herself to be seduced by him. Yet there was something youthful about his face, the wide open eyes, his pale complexion, things that indicated that she would have to give him direction, whisper in his ear to tell him how to touch, how to move, where to press his lips. She would teach him when to be a little rough, and to use the words she liked to hear. She would try to shock him, to startle him into a kind of desperate passion, she would toy with time and desire, holding herself back, pushing him away, touching herself before his stunned eyes. She began to play a kind of game with her imagination, drawing lines in the earth, daring herself to cross them. She began to dress differently: silk blouses that clung to her breasts, shorter skirts that revealed her legs. Sometimes she took larger risks, coming to her meetings with him wearing skirts and sweaters but no underwear. She watched his hands and imagined them cupping her breasts, parting her body as though it were made of two halves and could be divided at will. She found herself sensing a fullness within, some great warm potential.

She began to weigh the consequences. She considered the circumstances. It was at a time when Peter was doing some consulting work at a hospital outside New York City and was traveling there a great deal, at least three days and nights a week. Her husband had become a voice on the telephone, tired, running out of words. He spoke idly of his patients, the exceptionally mad people of Westchester County who heard voices and saw angels and spoke to unseen demons who devoured souls and huddled in corners, and whose affluent children, fresh from the tennis court, country club or department store, seemed to have inherited their parents' inability to negotiate the simpler levels of reality.

She could invite Greg to her house and begin to discuss notions of history; she would serve coffee, and she saw herself pulling his face against her body, losing control, letting him take her as he pleased, taking him in turn, passionately, without restriction. She could do things with him she'd never done with Peter, and no one, because of the illicit solitude of the relationship, would ever know. This was the nature of the criminal pact: two people suspended above the law by mutual guilt.

And yet she didn't. She didn't because it would have marked the end of her life with Peter. It would have meant the sacrifice of something bigger than herself, this continent in which she resided, a place where nothing really changed, and time stood still. And then Peter was murdered; and she saw that her delusions were many, her eyes shut tight.

"And outside it," she said in response to Resnick's question.

He looked at a page or two in his notebook. "From everything you've told me, Ms. Bowman, it seems that Peter Freytag was a fairly reclusive man, a quiet man, a man who respected the privacy of others."

"That's exactly right."

"And he had a wonderful sense of humor."

"That's also true."

"But he was a man who was guarded most of the time."

"In public, maybe, but," and she remembered an afternoon on the Vineyard, the way the sun looked just before setting beyond Chilmark and Gay Head.

"That's the whole problem, you see, Ms. Bowman. Here's this very professional, very serious psychiatrist, a man who's attentive to his patients, loving to his wife, and yet who goes off to a flophouse and gets himself murdered. I'm sorry, I didn't mean to put it that way."

Yet she could see he had meant to put it that way, it was the whole thrust of the conversation, the ultimate goal of the sentences and words that were coming out of his mouth, that were extracting her own words from her lips, he was attempting to make her see Peter in a new way, an objective way, to locate for the police the mysterious nucleus that was erased one Friday night in a downtown hotel.

Now it dawned on her: Resnick was beginning to reveal the character of Peter to her, he was trying to show her that like the moon everyone possessed another face bathed in eternal shadow, where craters were formed without fanfare or spark, and the scars of time fractured the surface in great rifts and valleys. She tried to imagine Peter as anything but the man she had known so intimately, the man who lay beside her in the pink coolness of his nudity, who responded in such predictable ways when she touched him just so, or moved her tongue in tiny circles over the surface of his body. This was the man with a repertoire of gestures and verbal formulae, whose very formality of movement and speech were as familiar to her as her own.

What was Resnick saying, trying to show? That somewhere amidst the geometry of Peter Freytag was something dark and irresistible, some asymmetrical figure that hid between the lines, beyond the angles, that one day, probably very soon, would become visible to Detective Sergeant Resnick, and Peter's wife, Jill Bowman?

"Did your husband bring his work home?"

"Sometimes he did."

"But he never mentioned names."

"Sometimes he did."

"First names, last names, the same ones over and over again?"

She watched him pour more coffee, the casual movements of a man pretending to be relaxed, off his guard. "Only first names," she said. "Arthur and Hollis and Mia and Monty."

"Did things ever get too heavy for him?"

She didn't know what to say. His smile was more like a smirk. He said, "How are you feeling now?"

"What?"

He laughed a little, he said, "I mean, how are you taking care of yourself."

"You mean how am I feeling? I'm not sure," and she laughed as well. "I did something last night I've never done. Or rather I haven't done in years. I drank until I passed out."

"Then you usually don't drink."

"Of course I do. I usually have a drink before dinner. At least I always did with my husband."

"And wine with your meal," he said, and she wondered if he was mocking her.

"Sometimes," she said.

"Your husband drank, though."

"He wasn't an alcoholic."

"But he drank. How many did he have every evening? Two, three? Did he drink until he became sloppy?"

"He had one vodka on the rocks and a glass of wine." She could hear the fury in her voice, shrill and thin in the corners of the kitchen.

"I know how hard this must be for you, Ms. Bowman."

"No you don't. You don't know how hard it is."

He looked at her. "You're right. I don't know."

"I still don't know. I haven't felt it yet. I keep thinking that any moment he might walk through the door. Or that he's still here. Watching me."

He referred to a page in his notebook. "You were married for thirteen years." He looked up at her. "It's a long time. How did you meet Dr. Freytag?"

She smiled a little at the memory of a hotel lobby in London. She could still remember the man at the desk, a Mr. Longman, and she realized now that it was he the man at the morgue had recalled for her: Mr. Longman, who bade you good morning and good luck, who told you which bus to take to the Tate Gallery and where you could get a decent meal.

"Peter was at a conference at Cambridge. Before flying back to the States he stayed in London for a few days. I was attending a conference at London University. We were at the same hotel."

Resnick waited for further clarification. After the silence of a few moments he said, "Were you married at the time?"

She shook her head. "No."

"Your first was a brief marriage, though."

It was as though he were winding twine about her, creating interesting braids and designs, working meticulously at what was apparently a kind of trap, and she began frantically to try to unravel it all, these questions about her marriage, the way she had met Peter. "I," she said, and words disappeared.

"Was it a mutually agreeable separation?"

"Yes," she said.

"Is your first husband still alive?"

"Of course he is."

"Are you still in touch with him?"

"He lives with his wife in Seattle. Occasionally I write to him about," and her face turned a deep red as she fell silent.

"It's only right that he should know how his little girl is doing. Your daughter must be getting big. She's what—fourteen, fifteen?"

She looked at him and the feeling inside her was of electricity. "How did you find out about her?"

He smiled and opened his hands. He finished his coffee and folded the little paper napkin in half, leaving it beside his notebook. "The sun's coming out. Why don't we talk outside?"

She went to the closet and put on a suede jacket. Resnick touched her lightly on the back as she stepped out the door. The air was crisp and the smell on the breeze was of burning wood and decaying leaves. In her pocket was a pair of soft leather gloves, tan deerskin, almost yellow, with a warm lining. She pulled them on over her long fingers, pointing here and there as she fitted them to her hands. Resnick zipped up his jacket, and she found it an oddly boyish thing to do, a little touching, an innocent gesture that seemed to indicate a man utterly devoid of corruption.

"Did your first husband know Dr. Freytag?"

"He knew I was getting married again. How did you learn about Carrie?"

"But they never met."

"You think Dennis had something to do with what happened to Peter?"

Resnick looked at her and smiled. "Anything is possible, Ms. Bowman." And her mind turned it over.

He opened the door to the garden shed and looked inside. There was a mower, a spade, some snow shovels, clay pots, bamboo stakes, other tools. He took out two rakes and handed one to her. "Christmas will be here before we know it," he said.

Christmas, Easter, Thanksgiving, the holidays when people

came together, gorged themselves, reveled in the skittish peace of home and family: these would come and go and she would still be there, in the house, by herself. She could see it coming; she would learn too well to live alone: the monologues conducted with fork and knife, the facial expressions executed for no one, the responses that answered the unasked questions. Plans would have to be made. She could impose herself upon Sally, even though Sally lived in Canada with her Québecois husband and two children. She could invite them down, then, she would have them all there, Sally and Luc and the children, she would fill the house with the sound of their voices, and then she would hint on the phone at what Christmas might be like for her, the empty snowscape beyond the windows, the sandwiches and whisky consumed in front of Barbara Stanwyck movies on obscure cable stations, and she in turn would be invited to Montreal, to dine on goose and drink Beaujolais and open presents in the shadow of an artificial tree bedangled with hand-carved ornaments. In the new year she would travel, she would flee the country and let her mind fill with other images, vivid images, pictures and sounds that would force her to forget Peter. Yes: she would fly off on New Year's Eve, fly away from the revels and parties, the horrible garish merriment of the last night of the year.

She thought of a narrow street in Paris, its name forgotten, at a particular moment when she had found herself alone there late at night, the road glistening with fresh rain, the air thick with the richness of dark tobacco. When she looked up she saw at the end of the street a building whose single lighted window silhouetted a man on his balcony, looking down at her. And she felt then as she did now, as she held tightly to the tenuous thread of recollection, that something in life had eluded her, something unique and worthy and ultimately indefinable, a vein of gold she had overlooked for years and years. And she had let it go. She had let it go.

How long would this go on? Months, years, a decade?

She watched Resnick pulling leaves towards a pile he had begun, and she watched the colors gather, the fading reds and yellows, the browns, until they reached the height of his knees. He stopped and leaned on his rake. "Are you going to tell your daughter about this?"

"She wouldn't understand."

"You just prefer to keep her separate from things, then."

"She is separate from things."

"What was her relationship with your husband? With Dr. Freytag, I mean."

Her eyes moved here and there as she sought a response. "Distant. Or rather he was distant with her. She wasn't his daughter."

"And you never tried to have children, you and Dr. Freytag."

Now a hardness shone in her eyes. "We tried. Things didn't work out. I had two miscarriages."

"And so you have Carrie. I did a check on your husband through a computer database. Just as a matter of routine. Your name came up, of course. So did your daughter's." He looked at her. "Everybody's in the machine, Ms. Bowman."

"I find it hard to speak about Carrie," she said. She moved noisily through the leaves, halfheartedly gathering them together with the claws of her green plastic rake. She and Peter used to do the lawn together, on Sundays, piling the leaves high on a huge square of burlap, turning it into a exaggerated bundle, pulling it out towards the woods, leaving them to rot into a rich black mat.

"Why can't you care for her at home?"

"For a lot of reasons. Her rages, for one. Sometimes she'll just fly into one, begin destroying things, try to scratch people's faces. Sometimes she needs to be restrained. I can't do it."

"You mean you don't want to do it."

"I'm not able to do it. I'm not strong enough to help her."

"And did her father help?"

"Dennis? No. Carrie was born after he began having his affair."

The doctors said that her birth had been a difficult one. Because Carrie was born just as Jill and her first husband were about to separate, Jill had always felt responsible, blaming her child's injury on the chaos and raised voices of the nine months before Dennis had left her. She had discovered that her husband had been having an affair not by accident, not by someone's indiscretion or the seed of veracity always detectable in a rumor, but rather with her own two eyes, returning home from work, finding her husband wriggling in the limbs of another woman, a younger woman whose flesh had not yet begun to wrinkle, whose breasts remained firm, whose thighs were as smooth as the skin of an apple. Jill and Dennis had been trying to have a baby for more than a year. Now that she was pregnant he wanted nothing to do with her. She had failed him in every way. Even her body on which he had bestowed his past attentions, the flat pale tummy against which he would rub his cheek and on which he would sometimes ejaculate, leaving to cool on her the wan residue of his exertions, was becoming swollen and distended. The veins in her body, the thick blue rings in her huge and painful breasts and the knots that came up dark and alluring, disgusted him. He understood nothing of what she was experiencing, the strange beauty of it, the fruity erotic sense of abundance and seed. He never even bothered to visit Carrie, not even when Jill calmly phoned him to say what was wrong: Carrie was an unresponsive infant, the look in her eyes was without sheen or brightness, she reacted either slowly or not at all to sounds. "Your daughter is damaged," she told Dennis. She thought: you have done this to her. And in the background she could hear the woman mixing martinis, anticipating merriment, erasing his memory.

They had raked nearly all of the backyard. A line of perspiration showed on Resnick's forehead, and she could feel that she, too, had exerted herself, that the skin beneath her clothes, between her breasts, under her arms, was damp. They said very little. The raking had taken her mind off things, had compelled her to fall into routine, the very routine from which her husband's murder had so suddenly jerked her. Their conversation had touched upon less dramatic things: Blackjack and her riding, her work at the university, a novel Resnick had recently read.

"What will you do now?" he said.

"I don't know. I hadn't thought about it." She wondered why he would ask such a question. Surely she would have to stay where she was, be prepared to answer more questions, possibly participate in a trial. She imagined herself entwined in the death of her husband for years to come, suffocating in vines of implication and innuendo, in the small facts of his private life, of patients and people he had casually met, words jotted down on bits of paper, pieces of a life she had never suspected. She wondered if each person's death was part of some larger conspiracy, if we left behind us a host of suspicious people strolling along rural railway tracks, brooding in cheap motel rooms, falling out of windows and collapsing in elevators, people who at one time or another had crossed our paths, spoke two words, scarred our lives, and in turn were marked by us. She said, "Am I free?"

He smiled.

"I'm serious," and she smiled also.

"You're not a suspect," he said.

She leaned her rake against a tree. "Why not?"

He stopped smiling and looked at her. "You had nothing to gain from his death." He took the rake from her and returned both of them to the shed. She waited for him at the back door of the house. "We've had a chance to examine the contents of his office. We found letters you had written to him. Cards. There's no evidence he was involved with anyone else. It seems pretty clear that Peter Freytag was a serious man, a dedicated psychiatrist. Why he felt the urge to go to the Hubbard is something we're still trying to understand."

She tried to think of everything she had written to Peter over the years of their courtship and marriage. There were passionate letters sent to him when he was away, traveling in Europe, visiting his ancient mother, attending conferences, letters speaking of her solitude and her desires, of the dark intimacies that linked them, and there were the cards sent for his birthday or simply because she saw one that caught her eye, amused her. Her words had been seen by another, the fantasies scribbled in black ink had become a matter of public interest, and she pictured other policemen passing them around, sniggering as they pulled on their cigarettes and filled the air with innuendo and glee.

"Did you find anything else?" she asked.

"Anything else."

"Anything personal."

Resnick took out his notebook and leafed through two or three pages, looking intently at them. "No. There was nothing else." He looked up at her. "Were you thinking of anything specific?"

She'd thought of the photographs and now remembered that they had never been taken out of the house, that they remained in their envelope, unperused for years, in the rear of the drawer in which she kept her underwear. She wondered if she would ever be able to look at them again. She wondered if she should destroy them. The detective's eyes betrayed nothing more. He said, "I'll just ask you to let me know when the funeral's going to take place. With your permission I'd like to be there."

She said nothing. He touched the zipper of his jacket, looked at his watch, looked at Jill. "What will you do with yourself?" he asked.

"I may travel."

"And you'll return to teaching?"

"I suppose I'll call my chairman tomorrow. I'm sure there'll be no problem about taking a leave of absence. But I'll come back. I won't leave my students forever."

"How old are you?" he asked.

She looked at him and smiled. "I'm forty-two, Sergeant Resnick. Not really young enough to start over."

CHAPTER 9

On the night after Peter's funeral Jill Bowman consoled herself with the thought that at some point in the future she would look back on this dark moment and, because time conveniently alters the taste of our memories, view it as the beginning of sweetness.

The coffin waiting to descend, the people standing, solemn and watchful, the hazeless blue brilliance of the afternoon, formed a circle around the depth of her grief. It was a grief that could not be expressed in words, that broke within her like a sudden premature birth as she stepped out of the car and walked to where Peter was to be buried. The pain spread to her fingers, it twisted her face, it hobbled her steps. So this was it, this was the end of things; nothing stood between her and this moment, no sudden awakening from a dream, no chance to stop time, to turn away or turn back. The smell of raw earth filled her with a sense of dread, the memory of something distant and terrible.

The faces of those who came to mourn spoke of nothing but pity. Some expressions could be seen clearly as something else, as terror, fearing how Jill might react, of having to watch a woman of composure and learning become something primitive, a grimacing, howling creature, something not of our time. And there were those few who could be seen attempting to put the pieces of this story together, to place Jill within a narrative, to find her position within the ripples surrounding the murder of her husband. And yet they had come, they had flown from other cities and towns, for in the end she had put a notice in the newspaper, she had made calls, and Peter's colleagues and former students, their friends and neighbors, Sally and Luc from Montreal, others she didn't recognize, stood in their ties and good shoes and looked at her as Resnick stepped forth to help her out of the limousine provided by the funeral home.

The coffin, the box she had chosen from the man named Kelly with its shiny brass handles and lead lining, was covered with flowers in baskets, tasteful arrangements that would later be either given away, swiped by the man who operated the backhoe or left to fade on the fresh mound that covered her husband. In a year the mound would be a sunken rectangle, sparse with fescue, yellow with weeds. Beneath it Peter would lie, slowly decaying under the press of time. Distractedly she fingered the little note cards attached to the floral tributes, the words meant for Peter that would never be seen by him. She looked at the coffin and thought of her poor husband lying within, dressed in his blue suit, his hands folded on his stomach. She had stared at him for a long time at the funeral home and again had been tempted to touch his face, to understand what had so changed him. His waxy complexion seemed like a mask to her, something that could be peeled away to reveal a more telling face. The pity of death is a sorrowful thing. At the mercy of the living, twisted and torn like dolls, the dead were nothing in their expensive airless crates. Instead they rotted in our imaginations, their hair stood on end, their fingertips receded, jaws fell open, skin became leather. One day Carrie would die, perhaps sooner rather than later, and she thought of her baby losing her identity, her little glances and sounds, the way she loved her toy animals, the soft milky smell of her. She thought of Carrie being lowered into the ground beside Peter. Then there would only be the pain of being Jill Bowman who, having lost, could no longer suffer herself to live as one. The thing that might spare a person from it was not having ever been born. The thought weighed on her, bowed her head, broke her heart.

At the funeral home people hugged her to their breasts and took her by the arm, as though she needed support, as if she were on the point of collapse. She wondered at the nature of their speculation, she considered their thoughts racing along unimaginable paths, seeing their friend Peter engaged in extramarital relations, devious sexual liaisons, quaint deceptions of his wife Jill. She found herself engaging in levels of conversation, making small talk, forcing herself and her guests to fill the air with words and noise, anything but silence. "Peter was supposed to speak at the Tavistock, but of course that's out of the question now," she actually found herself saying. "I suppose I should try to get a refund from the airline. He booked in advance. He'd accumulated a lot of frequent flyer miles, you know," and the person she was speaking to, a psychiatrist like Peter, gazed at her in astonishment. "I'm thinking about traveling. Maybe I could trade in his ticket for another. Do you think that's possible?" she added, breaking into a smile.

That night she sat at her kitchen table and drank vodka and thought about Detective Sergeant Resnick, who like a dark thread had become woven into the cloth that was her life. She remembered catching his eye at the cemetery when she saw an unfamiliar figure in the distance, an Asian man carrying a camera, occasionally holding it up to his eye, and for an absurd moment she wondered if Japanese tourists intent on capturing yet another corner of Americana were about to invade the cemetery.

Yet the incident seemed somehow connected to something else she had noticed lately, a car parked at odd times across the street from her house, a blue Ford that a neighbor had noticed and brought to her attention.

In the living room Sally and Luc began cleaning up the plates and cups and saucers. Thirty people had returned to the house after the funeral and they had dined off the platters of roast beef and turkey and cheese a local delicatessen had made up and wrapped in colored cellophane, specially for the occasion. People congratulated her on the delicious food. She watched their mouths as they chewed the sliced meats and tore bits off the rolls. Beer and wine filled glasses, and bottles of scotch and bourbon and gin magically appeared, the contents evaporating as though into thin air. There were tortellini salad and crusty rolls, and bottles of flavored soda water for those who shunned inebriation. Jill had wanted none of it. She had been the object of everyone's attention, for that afternoon alone inhabiting the corner of a collective eye as she moved among them, slipping away, answering the phone, seeking invisibility. Only Resnick, fork and plate in hand, had watched her openly with the artless gaze of the detective. Widows of murdered men were treated differently from those whose husbands had died in their sleep or on the operating table. They stood somehow apart from the rest, their rank in the table of grief was high, their power to command beyond belief, and she moved among her guests as though through some ancient myth that was even then being recreated by the whispers and indirect looks of the mourners.

That night as she sat at the table with her vodka she said to an empty room: "I have to make a phone call," and Sally rushed in to look at her. "I need to make a phone call," she said again. "A private call."

Sally said, "Are you all right?"

"I'm all right. I just need to make a phone call. I don't want to be disturbed." When she saw that Sally wasn't about to move she went upstairs and shut herself in the bedroom. The ice in her glass shifted, clicked, took a turn. She dialed Resnick's number at work and left a message. He rang her back seven minutes later.

"A man was taking photographs at the funeral today. A car's been parked near the house with someone in it. You need to tell me what's going on." Her voice had the hollow sound that comes with too much drink.

"They're police officers."

"Why are they here? Why were they at the funeral?"

He said nothing. He allowed her to work it out.

"Do you think I'm in some sort of danger?"

"Personally, no. But I'm not going to be responsible for anything that happens to you. I'll do everything I can to protect you. I think you did the right thing by not having a private funeral."

"So you could invite your cops along to take snapshots."

"It's not only that."

She waited a moment.

"I just think it's an important thing to do," he said. "Otherwise you would have gone home to an empty house."

"I can't wait for my sister and her husband to leave so I can have my empty house to myself."

"They seem like nice people."

"As long as they're far away, yes."

"I want to assure you that we're all working very hard at this investigation. I know it doesn't matter to you. I know you're not interested in vengeance."

There was something in his voice, not an edge, but a sense of weight, of some inner meaning that was straining to come clear.

"We no longer believe that your husband was killed by one of his patients."

"What?"

Suddenly Peter's death had taken on an external dimension, his life was no longer the perfect circle she had always imagined it to be. She thought of the clothes in his drawer, the way his words formed sentences, the sheer predictability of Peter Freytag. That he had not been murdered by a patient meant that there was another level to his life: like a hidden room in a house, a place secured by locks, its windows boarded and blind.

"We don't know who did it," Resnick said. "But we're ninety percent sure it wasn't a patient."

"Why?" It was all she could say.

"We've been able to rule all of them out. Including former patients."

"But . . ."

"I must tell you, Ms. Bowman, that I'm not the only person on this case. I have a team of people working with me. Our first priority was to look at Dr. Freytag's list of patients. It was the obvious thing to do."

She looked at her shoes against the hardwood floor of her bedroom. If at that moment she had been asked what she was seeing, she would not have been able to describe it, so radically was her world now changed. "So," she said.

"We're looking into other avenues of investigation."

"What are you saying?"

"His outside friendships. He belonged to an athletic club, for instance. He played squash. He swam. We're trying to identify the people he normally associated with there."

"It was perfectly harmless," she said.

"It probably was. But it's our job to be sure of it. Your husband willingly went into the Hubbard. He must have known who was waiting for him. Or at least whoever it was he was supposed to meet."

She felt her mind turning it over, this new world of Peter's she had always known but had disregarded. Even though Peter had tried to encourage her to join, she had never gone to the club, she could not picture herself lifting weights or dancing aerobically to synthesized rhythms, or even quietly sweating out her dread of menopause with other women in an adjoining sauna. Instead she rode Blackjack as often as she was able: galloping across fields, jumping stone walls, afterwards washing him down, feeling the muscles under his coat: an exercise in solitude and mastery, the state of being alone and yet not alone, for your horse was a part of you, a creature under compulsion to become one with you, yet forever trying to slip away like an uneasy reflection in a rippling pool of water. She'd always thought that in truth it was this that frightened Peter, an edgy game of dominance and escape played out in a wooden circle or in the hills and open fields that lay on the horizon.

"It was a woman," she said to the detective. "That's what you're saying, isn't it."

"I never said that."

"You're implying it."

Resnick said: "It's possible. There's no proof."

"No letters?"

"Only yours."

"Are you telling me the truth?"

"Yes I am."

"Am I free to go now? May I leave my home, this town, may I travel?"

"Of course you may."

She hung up the phone. She remained sitting on the bed, her hands resting on her thighs. She was wearing a navy blue dress she had bought for events such as academic conferences and the bestowing of degrees, for three-course luncheons with venerable department heads and visiting scholars; when she ventured forth to bid farewell to the remains of her elderly colleagues. It had fashionable wide lapels and was sleek against her hips in a subtly provocative way. She wondered if it smelled now of Peter's grave, of loam and sod and the decay of years. She looked across at her reflection in the mirror and slowly began to unbutton it, and when she was done, when she was still sitting on the bed dressed only in bra and tights and slip and a strand of cultured pearls, she realized that not tonight, not tomorrow night or the night after

would she be touched by Peter. Many things in her life had come
to an end. Until this moment she had only missed his soul. Now
she missed his body.

This was the beginning not of wisdom but of age.

CHAPTER *10*

Now it came to her. This was inescapable. Like a great metropolis
built above a subterranean world of tunnels and damp caverns
and the monstrous couplings of unimaginable beasts, their marriage, this system of customs and routine, of endearments and
touches, had hidden from her something dark and unfathomable,
too terrifying to explore. All his little habits—his unwillingness
to secure the cap on a tube of toothpaste, the way he abandoned
his damp towel on the bathroom floor after a shower, the little
names he used for her, Puppchen and Dilly—seemed now nothing but veneer, the useless decorative trappings of something
deeper, darker, more profoundly labyrinthine than she could ever
imagine.

At first she had considered departing on New Year's Day, then decided to leave at once, as though fleeing from a pestilence, something dark and invisible encroaching upon the community, which only she could see. She spent each day of the week following the funeral in her office at the university, preparing for her leave of absence. Although her work could have been completed in one or two afternoons, she made it last for five. To leave in the morning and return exhausted in the evening erased the wordless hours of a solitary day. To get back to the city, to drive each morning over the congested bridge, to sit in traffic and watch the haze form over the harbor, seemed a return to a life never shared with Peter, the hours that had always belonged entirely to her alone.

The routine was unchanging. She would sit and look at the faces of other drivers as they stared out over the water towards the ocean, or spoke with animation and hope into their cellular phones. School buses would pass by, carrying children on field trips to museums and zoos, and sometimes there would be a different kind of bus with special windows, bearing prisoners en route to a work detail or another facility, and the eyes of these men, black isolation behind protective glass, would meet hers with an indecipherable stare.

Planes would take off, defining angles as they rose towards the clouds above the city, and as she watched them on that first day she returned to her office, a day when she no longer lived with Peter Freytag, she again wondered where she would go. As if travel, a constant restless movement, would somehow make her loss easier to bear. She found it difficult to focus her mind on this, and often caught her attention drifting as she became entangled in increasingly elaborate fantasies. This was the first time in thirteen years she'd actually been truly, hopelessly alone. Peter would not return early from a conference. The phone would not ring. And the idea of it filled her with an appalling depthless feeling as well as a sense of danger, as though his death had thrown a dare at her feet, had traced a line in the dirt, had sat back and waited for the next move. Perhaps she would meet a man, someone who would simply cross her path, a person of intelligence and culture who would step into her life as casually as Peter had, eclipsing the memory of her husband's death, filling the emptiness of her loss. Like something not quite human he would enclose her in his arms and turn her memory into a river, its waters flowing into a larger, quite distant sea.

She imagined it taking place in London and wondered if when she arrived there Mr. Longman would remember her, if this genial pink desk clerk would come to see himself as some portly cupid, a mythic figure in the sensual life of Jill Bowman.

This woman of intelligence and logic began to think in terms of luck and omens. She consulted her horoscope in her morning paper, in the monthly magazines on the racks in the pharmacy. They spoke of lunar tendencies and planetary trines, of fortunate days and potentially catastrophic ones. She was counseled against purchasing electrical equipment and driving after dark, trusting those near to her and dancing with strangers. Some astrological columns dealt only with romantic subjects, as if a woman's life were designed exclusively towards that end, the rapture of marriage, the security of brown wingtips in the closet. She even found herself purchasing a magazine devoted solely to this subject, whose cheap paper reeked acutely of ink and advertised soothsayers in West Virginia and New Mexico who for a fee would decipher the significance of your birth date or the nuances of your speech, who would lay out cards and pick your mind. There were telephone numbers that would put you in personal touch with fortune-tellers armed with the ancient wisdom of the tarot, and on the same page there were advertisements for telephone services that would provide you with the voice of an unseen person willing to coax you to orgasm for only $2.95 per minute.

Sitting in traffic on the bridge she looked up and saw a solitary seagull circling over the harbor. It seemed odd to her that it was traveling alone; she wondered if anyone else noticed it, and considered it a sign of change, something for her eyes only. It began to swell with significance, to fill with meaning and omen as its wings rode the ceaseless currents above the bay. It meant that the great empty cave of her life would grow full again. She watched the bird as it flew out towards the sea, circled twice and, taking with it the last wisps of hope, disappeared from view.

She did not deserve such misery: she felt as though she had been pushed to the floor, that her heart had been somehow crushed by Peter's death, as if he had intended by his death to hurt her. It was a pain beyond words, beyond tears, and she wondered when she would be allowed to stand up again, to laugh at herself.

Would anyone actually take the trouble ever to look at her again?

She began to examine herself in the mirror, in the evenings when she undressed, standing away from it, turning to the side. She remembered doing it as a teenager, presenting herself to the privacy and glare of her bedroom, pleased beyond words with her audacious curves. Slim as she was she saw herself going to fat, and she would take what she imagined as handfuls of flesh between her fingers, pulling them away from her body, as though her corporality were somehow a burden to her soul, something that must be carried through the decades of life, fed and pampered and manicured like some inconstant beast forever on the edge of rebellion.

Now all she could do was support her helpless breasts in her hands, feeling their soft weight in the joints of her fingers. Her face became a map of the years and events of her life, each line and furrow representing a trauma, a loss, a moment of happiness. She remembered her mother in her last days, grey and wrinkled, loose skin and dead nerves on useless bones, and it occurred to her then, as it must occur to all women, that the beauty to which she is expected to aspire, the beauty that is required for advancement and seduction, to catch the eye and tempt the soul, will fade and break the heart.

At night under the covers she would again think of someone who would enter the hours of her days and nights, whose arms would hold her, and the feeling within her was like an itch, low in her body, its center devious and elusive. It competed with memory, it jostled the lingering touch of her husband, in fact it became Peter in those first days just after she'd met him, and the scent of his body, the texture of his skin, the way he said her name, came back to her all at once with the freshness and shock of cold water. But it wasn't a man she craved as much as a place: a street in Paris that shone like a mirror, an alleyway that held the scents of the day, tobacco and spice, wine and the angles of one's body: a place into which someone might wander and become lost. But a place nonetheless. The birth of potential; the source of possibilities.

And she had finally gathered up the courage to look at the photographs. They had been taken eight years earlier, in a hotel room in another city. Jill had been asked to deliver a paper at a conference at a university and had been allotted a room at a better hotel, a tower that like a finger stuck up fifty stories into the yellow cloud that hung over the grid of streets and avenues. Peter had arranged to fly down and spend the weekend with her. The conference had been what those sorts of affairs usually were, an unending drone of delivered facts and opinions, theories and rebuttals, shriveled hors d'oeuvres and cheap whisky in plastic tumblers. Smile, Peter had said as she'd walked through the door, and she smiled because she hadn't expected him till the next morning. He'd brought the Polaroid, and the flash left her laughing at the spots dancing in the air between them, that disturbed their kisses like too much punctuation in a line of verse.

They'd found that the new surroundings lent something illicit to their time there. They phoned room service and ordered a meal. They raided the minibar. They pulled the shades and for an additional $7.50 on their hotel bill watched a film called *Doctor's Night Off*. During the first minutes an operation on a naked brunette was being performed in a white room. When she awoke she felt much better and thanked the doctor by resting her legs on his shoulders and pressing herself against his mouth. Afterwards lunch was ordered, bananas and cream. When night fell nurses with frosted hair removed their clothes and with their feet in the stirrups of the examining tables masturbated to monotonous disco music. When the doctor unexpectedly arrived to pick up some scalpels he took off his clothes to display his Olympian penis which, to the women who assisted him in open-heart surgery, at once became an object of engorged pink devotion. The nurses could barely keep their hands off of him, and often he was nearly hidden from view by the number of nurses that descended upon him, squatting and kneeling over his body as they moaned and sighed. When he discharged with stunning theatricality they rubbed his sperm into their breasts, they licked it off their fingers, and Jill and Peter laughed, because this was supposed to be just another evening off for the eminent Dr. O'Toole.

Peter and Jill became drunk and when they kissed, when their tongues played in the heat of each other's mouth, the saliva ran down their chins. The film had aroused them more than they cared to admit. She lay back on the pillow and opened her legs for Peter and a few moments later watched the picture emerge from the camera like a tongue, curled and impertinent. There was a photograph of her touching herself between her legs, her other arm covering her eyes as if shunning the lens, escaping identification. The images were flat and drained of passion. Her legs appeared pale and thin, and the warm light of the room had been turned into the glare of the operating table or a place of crime, a scene of dissection and autopsy, assault and mutilation. There were photographs of Peter alone, and of Jill and Peter together, and when she looked at them now she felt not pity or arousal but rather suspicion and embarrassment: this man, this Swiss psychiatrist who was so regular in his habits, possessed another side. When he had taken these photos, when he had made love to her, had he been one step removed from her, observer more than participant? Why could men find such pleasure in that point of view and not women? She looked at his slitted drunk eyes. Had she been the only one to see it?

Feel me there, touch me like this, fuck me, she would say to him, her voice low and sibilant as it hid beneath her breath.

Peter had gone to a filthy hotel and had been murdered in a frenzy of crimson joy. He had gone willingly, happily. Who was she, who was the woman who had lured him there, what had she that Jill so lacked? It came to her: men walked to their deaths; women were dragged.

A shout in the street, and a woman dies, her agony falling on deaf ears. That's what history was, someone once said in a novel as he gestured towards a window. A shout in the street.

She looked at the photographs of herself, a slimmer, smoother version, firm and full of poise and swagger, and she looked at herself in the mirror and she felt the tears come to her eyes, the familiar tears that each day seemed to rise to her face, as though she had been condemned to cliché, destined to drown in her misery, belittled and helpless in the light of his betrayal.

She tore the photographs in half and not content with leaving them in the rattan basket in the bedroom tore them into even smaller pieces and flushed them down the toilet.

At the university she felt refreshed. Her department chairman, a man in his early sixties who as a child had suffered from polio and walked now with a pronounced limp, his withered arm fishlike and useless as it occupied the space beside him, called her into his office, rang for coffee, held out his one good hand to her. His name was Julius Rosenzweig. He said, "To say I'm sorry would be trite. I'll do whatever I can to help you get through this."

"I appreciate your coming to the funeral."

He lifted his hand in a casual sweep through the air.

"It made it just so much easier." She felt as though she were

going to cry. It embarrassed her, these tears, as though their flowing might somehow be a stain on her nature, like a splash of
blood on a yard of freshly laundered linen.

Julius said, "I knew Peter only slightly. But I'm so sorry."

"Don't be sorry for me."

He smiled a little. "I don't know what to say."

She looked at him. "Neither do I." And she added, "I'm just so
confused," and she blushed, for it was the first time she had confessed her true feelings, the first time she had dropped the cool
demeanor. She finished her coffee. "I'm hoping to meet with all
my advisees this week. I'll make sure they're given work for the
next month."

"Where do you think you'll go?"

"London. Paris." She shrugged. "Away." And the word carried
with it the vivid image of a damp street, a man in a window,
someone waiting around the corner.

When she rose to go to her office Julius took her hand once
again, then came around to her and embraced her with his good
arm. She imagined his eyes shutting as he pressed his cheek
against hers.

Now she was walking down the hall, past her colleagues and
the students who had attended her lectures, and it seemed to her
that she was present at her own notoriety: people saw not Jill
Bowman but a notion, an idea, a woman whose husband had been
murdered. It was as if she had witnessed some catastrophe, the
bombing and destruction of a great city, the extermination of a
population, and in consequence had been invested with an aura of
majesty and wonder.

How long would it be before she became, once again, merely
Jill Bowman?

On the Monday after the funeral she posted a sheet of paper on
her door, asking her graduate students and advisees to sign up for
a private twenty minutes with her, to discuss their work in
progress and the work to come, to find their bearings with the
guidance of this woman who was no more certain than they were.

Before Peter's death they were just young women and men, eager for research, impatient to receive their degrees. Now they had become embarrassed participants in the grief of Professor Bowman, or curious onlookers eager to gaze upon the face of a woman who had lost her husband at the hand of another.

She shut the door of her office and looked at the list. Most had signed it; a few had shunned it, including a girl named Dora Castle, who was thin and olive-skinned and who spoke little. She smoked Pall Malls and wore black. She was writing her thesis on the treatment of refugees in the twentieth century. Her mother's aunt had been on the *St. Louis* in 1939 when, after being turned away by one country after another, after sailing the seas and cutting through the waves, it had been forced to drop off its Jewish passengers on the very continent from which they had fled. Dora called it one of history's sickest jokes. She held out the photograph to Jill Bowman, and when she looked at it she saw the face of her student staring at her, yellowed and frayed, lost in time.

Perhaps it was easier for Dora to face the tragedies of the past, or those that took place distantly, in countries she had never visited, where people in rags, begging for potatoes, tried to cross the frontier of their homeland.

She counted the names of the students who had made appointments. She looked at her watch and sat at her desk, and because she had not been there since Peter's death she reached over and looked at the framed photograph she kept at the corner by the box of paper clips. It had been taken by a friend on the Vineyard, just after lunch one afternoon. Peter and Jill were sitting at the table on the porch, leaning back in the wicker chairs that were always in need of repair. Four eyes spoke of contentment and certainty. Or at least two of them did. Peter was wearing dark glasses, and the expression he displayed, the way his mouth seemed straining for irony, was in a language she hadn't yet learned.

CHAPTER *11*

Her last appointment on her last day at the office was for eleven-thirty. Although she had hoped to fly to London the next day, the only seat available was for that evening. It meant driving to the university and then passing the hours in the city, waiting to board her plane. Or she could see her students, drive home, and then take the airport limousine two hours before her flight. On the other hand it would be easier and less tiring for her simply to remain in her office and drive out to the airport. Parking was ten dollars per day. She expected to be abroad for two weeks. Somehow it didn't matter how much it cost.

"Two weeks," Resnick had said the night before when he'd called.

"I actually have a month off. But I'll be away for the first half of it. Is there a problem with that?"

"Exactly two weeks?"

"Fourteen days. Is there some reason why I have to be so precise?"

"I just wanted to know when you were coming home."

The statement struck her peculiarly, as if it had emerged from his mouth at an odd angle, as if—and now she saw it—as if he had asked her something extraordinarily personal, such as what her breasts looked like, or if she was wet between her legs. "Do you need me to answer more questions?" she asked, and there was a pause.

"Possibly."

"I don't know how I can help you, Sergeant Resnick."

"You were the person closest to him. In all probability you know or have heard the name of the person who is responsible for this crime."

"But he might have kept part of his life a secret from me."

"A person can't hide everything. And if his wife has no reason to suspect her husband of something, she won't see it, even if the evidence is staring her in the face."

She thought of Peter returning home each night from his office, from his patients, the people who spent hours every day talking, pouring out their dreams and nightmares, the desires and secrets they kept deep within them, and in her memory she considered his face as he walked through the door, approached her, kissed her lips, an aura of cigarette smoke about him. The smells of the city, of his day: these were the things he brought home, the small accretions of his eight hours away from her. Until his death the map of Peter's life was vivid in her mind: where he worked, where he took his lunch, the athletic club to which he went every Thursday evening. Often he would call her from there, and the sounds of the place, the opening and shutting of doors, the noises people made when they called out to their friends or asked for a can of balls or a towel, confirmed his location. He played squash with another psychiatrist, a man named Frank she had never met, and sometimes he played with an architect named Harbison. She sat on the edge of her bed and looked at the floor, on which her suitcase sat open, half packed. Resnick said, "I hope the file on your husband's murder will be closed by the time you return."

She waved her hand through the air, as though to frighten a fly or cripple a mosquito. She wondered why Resnick kept updating her on something that wasn't advancing in any measurable way. Couldn't he understand that once her husband was buried she no longer wanted to think of that room at the Hubbard Hotel, a room she had come to construct in her imagination, every vivid detail of it, each clot of dust, every stain, the yellowing curtains, the cheap furniture and filthy spotted mattress, the brown door-knob, the murderer brimming with bravado and blades, the closet jangling with coat hangers?

"I have to finish packing," she said. The words emerged from her mouth as though made of ice.

"Have a good trip."

And she quietly replaced the phone. It was nearly ten o'clock.

Resnick had called just after her conversation with Sally, who had taken to phoning her every evening to ask if Jill was all right and if she needed anything, as if, had Jill said yes and asked for a pound of coffee and a bottle of vodka, her generous little sister might have actually driven through the night from Montreal, possibly in a blizzard, to deliver them to her. Sally spoke of the minutiae of her day, describing her children's teachers and what the new weatherman on television looked like, she talked about her husband Luc's passion for word games and the latest restaurant opening, and it was clear to Jill that all of these endless phrases were a substitute for the gloating silence of a contented, happily married woman. "And how are you doing?" Sally asked for the third time.

"I'm doing fine," said Jill. "I'm packing for my trip."

"It'll be fun."

"It'll be different."

"That's what I meant. Different but fun."

"I don't want fun, I want different."

She found herself arguing with Sally as if they were still children, Gimme, want, mine, mine, and she shook her head with exasperation. "I'm just going away," she said.

"You could have come up to Montreal. You know that Luc and I invited you."

"I just wanted to be on my own."

"The children wouldn't have been in your way."

"Your children are never in the way, Sally," she said, though Sally's children were creatures of nightmare, spoiled and spiteful, ever on the edge of tantrum and violence. Windows shattered at their approach.

"And you could have been nearer to Carrie, you know. Montreal is only a short plane trip."

Jill sensed a growing rage within her, as if Sally had spent the phone call prodding with a steel object at the nerves in her body. "Carrie will do fine without me for two weeks."

"Would you like me to fly down and spend some time with her?"

"Listen to me, Sally. You've been very helpful. I appreciate everything you've done. But I don't want Carrie to know I'm going away. If you visit her she'll know there's something wrong."

"She won't even notice," said Sally, and the little noise she made afterwards spoke of her embarrassment.

Jill remembered when she'd lost her voice after Rose Keller's death, and how her parents, in the enlightened early years of their middle age, when they socialized with Pete Seeger and voted for Stevenson and Kennedy, had never displayed any shame for their daughter. "She's had a shock," her mother would say to relatives. "She'll get her voice back when she's damn well ready." In the same way, because her daughter's heart and body and soul were as one to her, she always acknowledged her circumstances. Yet she also knew that Carrie could easily have done without her mother.

In fact Jill was certain that had anyone walked into her room bearing toys and a willingness to feed her, to wait patiently as she relieved herself, to sing and wrap her arms around her, Carrie would have shown just the same affection. Mothering Carrie was akin to nurturing an illusion. Its essence was nothing more than speculation and wishful thinking.

Sally said, "Are you going to see your friends in Europe?"

"I may."

Sally said nothing. The conversation was turning to dust. "Have a good time," she said. "Have a safe trip. Take care of yourself, Jill." In the background Luc cried out with excessive cheer, "Bon voyage!"

"Thanks."

"Send a postcard."

"Don't worry."

"Be careful."

Of what? Jill felt tempted to say, as though to prolong the conversation, to enter into another round of malicious repartee, would be a kind of delicious torture. Instead she said goodbye, again promised to send postcards, refusing, when Sally asked at the last minute, to divulge either her itinerary or the names of her hotels.

She would vanish, walk away from things, as though to become someone else, and the idea felt like the tingle of sexuality.

Once again she examined her suitcase, she counted her traveler's checks, zipped her passport into a compartment in her bag. Did she bring her aspirin, a shower cap, her favorite shampoo, an extra pair of reading glasses? These were the concerns an old woman might have, a widow in fact, someone who could no longer rely on another, who brought certainty into her world by reducing it to a universe of small details, little bits of the puzzle that had to be fitted neatly into a dull and endless twenty-four hours. Again she went to Peter's dresser and opened the drawers. His socks and underwear. His shirts. As if all of a sudden she might be able to read them, to make sense of the code of his disappearance.

She went back downstairs and checked the timers she'd attached to the lamps. They would come on at different times to give the appearance of life, of movement, eventually of repose. But no one would be there save the ghosts that had begun to wander through the rooms and up and down the stairs, and which she had begun to sense late at night, as she lay in bed waiting for sleep. But they didn't roam the house, they survived in her mind, Peter and the birth of Carrie, the hard push, the exquisite and appalling pain, the way she lay on Jill's breast, her eyes sucking in the light of the world. And there was Rose Keller, who had been there for decades, waving to Jill, forever dying behind a shut door while a man with a toothpick returned to the streets and the life he was perhaps even now still living.

She sat at the kitchen table and looked at the postcard she had picked up in her college mailbox that day. She had looked at it at least ten times already, as though it were a Pandora's box full of things forgotten or abandoned, vain hopes and secret desires spilling out into to the world, slithering before the eyes of many. The picture was a photograph taken by Robert Doisneau of a couple dancing in a deserted Paris street one Bastille Night nearly forty years earlier. She had seen the picture before: *La Dernière Valse*, it was called.

Dear Dr. Bowman, it began, and told of his life in Madison, where he taught history at the University of Wisconsin. He thanked her for having so well prepared him. He said that he thought of her often. He had signed it Fondly, Greg, and her fingers shook as she held it. He came into crisp definition in her memory, a face haloed by thick dark hair and a neatly trimmed beard. She thought of his hands. She remembered his smell. She considered what might have happened.

She washed her face and brushed her teeth and removed her clothes and got into bed. She turned on her right side, and pressing her hands together as though in prayer, held them between her thighs, as she had since she was a girl. She felt the weight of her breasts, the smooth heat from between her legs, the feathery ends of the hairs. She turned onto her back and touched herself with her finger, once, twice, in a circular motion. She thought of everything but Peter. She wondered if at the heart of pleasure lay the great gift of forgetting. She reached over and took the phone from her bedside table. The buttons glowed a pale green in the darkness. She pressed in the first set of numbers. She didn't even need to consult the magazine: she had committed everything to memory. A recorded voice asked her to punch in a credit card number, and she did so, following the instructions and entering her date of birth and all the other information required. The reward came by way of a computerized voice, female and dark and impersonal, that allowed her the anonymity and safety of silence. The voice spoke of work and romance, of small rewards and large pleasures, of Saturn and Venus and an occultation of the moon; and when it was done, when the empty words had come to silence, she returned to a dial tone and pressed in another set of digits. She could feel the palms of her hands grow damp, something flutter in the pit of her stomach. And when the voice answered, the man with the cool intonation, she asked for Greg and entered her MasterCard number and date of expiration.

"You've called before, haven't you."

"Yes," she whispered.

"Your name?"

"Sandra."

"Greg's just getting changed, Sandra."

"I understand." She swallowed, and something intangibly large rippled in her throat.

"He'll be with you in a moment."

A moment later the familiar voice greeted her by name. She had already spoken to him twice this week. He said, "Miss me, babes?"

"Yes."

"Sorry I took so long. I just needed to change. I'd had a shower and just wanted to towel off and put on a robe. When I heard you were waiting for me I decided not to put on anything else. God, I'm hot. They've got us in these little rooms in the basement. Just a bed and a television set. How's everything, Sandra?"

"Everything's fine."

"You in bed, too, Sandy?"

"Yes."

"Yes what?"

"Yes, Greg."

"What are you wearing?"

Her voice, almost a whisper, told him that she was wearing nothing. She rested her right hand on the inside of her thigh.

"Are you lonely?"

"Oh yes."

"Are you wet?"

"Yes," the word went unsounded, it was the wind shifting the autumn leaves.

"You know I'm right next to you, don't you. You're not alone, babes."

"I know."

"My hand is on you. I can feel you. I can feel your heat. And you can feel me, can't you. You can feel me pressing up against you."

"Yes, Greg."

"I can taste you, do you feel me?"

"Oh God," and squeezing her legs together she twisted slightly to one side. The ache was unbearable, and had she taken the time to reflect she would have seen the moment as one full of pain and horror and humiliation, utterly devoid of pleasure.

"What would you like tonight, Sandra?"

"Anything you want."

"Are you mine?"

"Yes," she said, and she felt tears in her eyes.

"Same as last time?"

She remembered it.

"Same thing, babes?"

"Yes. Okay."

"Do you love me?"

"Oh God."

"Do you love me?"

"Please God."

"Do you want me?"

"Just do it, Greg."

CHAPTER *12*

Because her flight had been delayed for more than six hours, because in the end there was no one there to meet her, no tilting
smiles showing their familiar creases in the crowd beyond passport control, she stepped out of the terminal in search of a taxi
and found herself in what was becoming a snowstorm.

The flakes, small and dry, drifted past the window of the cab as
it made its way eastward towards London. She had been due to
land at seven in the morning. Now it was nearly three, and the
light of a lingering London autumn was quickly fading, turning
slate grey as the snow gathered in baroque patterns on the road,
in twists and filigrees. Things had changed since she was last in
England. The taxi was an unfamiliar deep red unlike the ma-
tronly black vehicles she'd been used to. She remembered the last

time she'd been there; it was with Peter, and they were on vacation. One night they dined in a fish restaurant in Covent Garden and had returned to their hotel leaning against one another, laughing and speaking loudly, and when they made love they began with her standing up against the window, pressed to the glass with her legs spread wide while people walked home below them, and she could feel Peter pushing up against her as she pressed her hand to herself, feeling him hard inside her. Had she taken the time to think about it she would have realized how uncomfortable a position it was. Yet in the heat of desire of the moment it was something delicious, something unreachable, unimaginable, and she wanted only to break the glass and show herself to everyone, to shout out her pleasure and cry with joy, and as she thought about this as she rode alone in the taxi through what looked like a blizzard she remembered something she had completely forgotten from that night, something peculiar that at the time had meant nothing to her but now seemed to blossom before her eyes, emerging from her memory like ectoplasm, filling the air with white viscosity and the tumult of haunted voices. They had been in the restaurant for nearly twenty minutes. It was crowded, filled with affluent tourists and wealthy Londoners, and perhaps because it was late, because a night at the theatre or opera or ballet was behind them, over and done with, the clientele was loud and merry, roaring with laughter and raucous with exclamations, almost on the brink of something dangerous. She looked at Peter across the table as he sipped his drink. His eyes were moist and caught the light from the ceiling. He looked at his watch, he looked beyond her shoulder, he excused himself to go to the toilet.

When he returned ten minutes later he came in not from the corridor leading to the bathroom but rather, and she saw his reflection in the wall that was a mirror, from the front entrance.

He sat down, a little out of breath. He said, "It was just," and she told him what she had noticed, that he had gone outside.

"I thought I saw someone I knew."

"You're joking," and she laughed.

"Yes. Christopher Hansel."

The name meant nothing to her.

"I went to school with him in Zurich. I haven't seen him for, what, thirty years. Maybe more."

He was still out of breath. The skin on his face was glowing and his eyes sparkled as though on the brink of an explosion. At the time it meant nothing to her. She knew how important his friendships were to him, how he spoke on the phone for hours to people he hadn't seen for years, how he reminisced about his school days and bored her to death with tales of his lost Swiss youth. She thought of his mother filling her armchair, gazing upon her with a granite stare, and she thought of her sitting there for weeks, months, years, decades, from the time of Peter's birth to the moment of his demise, absorbing the life from her son, draining him of his resilience, wearing him down until he could only flee to his death.

At first she wasn't going to call and tell her of her son's death, and when she mentioned this to Sally her sister insisted she do it, that it was only right. "But she won't understand what I'm saying."

"Doesn't she speak English?" Sally said. "How did you speak to her before?"

"She understands it well enough. She just doesn't respond."

"Pick up the phone, dial the number, tell her what happened and hang up. You don't have to put yourself through anything more."

Jill considered it. In the terror and frenzy of the moments that filled the days that followed Peter's death she could no longer think in a logical manner. She wondered if it would make a tremendous difference if she just didn't bother telling Helga what had happened. There was also the possibility, a very distinct one, that if she told her, if she calmly described how Peter had been taken to the hospital and had bled to death, Helga would at once suspect Jill of murder and pursue her through various means. "All right," she told Sally, "I'll tell her."

"Do it now."

"Tomorrow."

"No. Now."

"The detective in charge of the case is supposed to be here any second."

"Just get it over with."

"I'll ask him to do it."

"Stop it, Jill."

Jill looked up the number in her directory and dialed the various codes that helped her reach a little cottage in suburban Zurich. She remembered the faded rugs on the floors and the crucifixes that decorated every room. The furnishings in the kitchen seemed coated with a thin layer of grease, the residue of a hundred years of overcooking. A family Bible, black and untouched, the edges of its thick pages gilded with dust, occupied a table in a corner of the living room. The old voice said Ja? and then Jill very slowly told her what happened. She began by saying This is your daughter-in-law, Peter's wife, I have some very bad news, and then she told her the news, that her son had died, that he had been attacked by some unknown person and murdered. For a moment there was silence, and then the woman began to shout and suck in air, and when she voiced her feelings at rare moments they came out in German and were thus meaningless to Jill. Jill hung up the phone. She imagined his mother sitting in her cottage at that moment, sinking into the ancient cushions of her chair, lost in a whirlwind of memory and regret, soaring through time towards death. Language between the two women had broken down, just as it sometimes had between Peter and Jill, when he looked at her blankly in response to a question or observation, and sometimes she wondered why he had married her, why he had not set his sights instead on some Swiss fräulein, succulent and blond, favorably disposed to mountains and chocolate. She could have asked the same of Dennis, who had yet always been able to understand her perfectly, and through this ease of communication, through the fluency of words and looks, had deceived her into believing in their marriage. Perhaps Peter had all along been trying to tell her of some difficulty in his life, of something potentially dangerous that was lingering on the margins of his emotions, and that this catastrophe, of which she was entirely capable of helping him avoid, had been her responsibility alone.

It came to her again and again: forty-three years of life had been erased in a matter of seconds. Forty-three years that had been shared between Helga Freytag and Jill Bowman, and as her taxi inched slowly over the dampening grit of Hammersmith and West Kensington, the thought came to her that more than once her husband had rehearsed for his death. That this man who devoted his life to the study of the mind and its many and various unpredictabilities, its laws both adhered to and scrupulously broken, had traveled a road of fatal inevitability. "We're here, missus," the driven said, and his eyes filled the rearview mirror.

She opened the door and stepped out. The driver smiled at her and handed back the change. She tipped him and took her bag and stood at the entrance of the hotel, a chunk of Victorian solidity in a quiet London square. She waited until the taxi pulled away from the curb and looked up, counting the floors. There was the window at which she had stood as Peter had made love to her, and the memory came to her as something tangible, something that possessed weight and dimension, taste and sound, and yet was as delicate and breakable as a baked wafer or a crystal glass.

Things weighed on her mind as she unpacked in a room utterly different from the one in which they had last stayed. The thought of his mother silently mourning her son, railing against this younger woman who had stolen and then lost him; the sight of Peter rushing out of the restaurant, claiming he had seen an old friend; the idea that she had come to London for no purpose whatsoever; they intersected at a single point, as though each was in some obscure way related to the others, and this knot bore down upon her like something oppressive. As a teacher, as a wife, even as the mother of Carrie, she had had reason to live, to move forward, to tread lightly on the present and leave the past behind. Now time seemed something that demanded to be created by her alone, the arduous and painstaking work of a craftsman, the elaborate engraving of her future.

Evening arrived quickly, as it did in London in December. Street lamps came suddenly on, and when she looked out of her hotel room she could see across the square into others' apartments, the fragile dramas of people crossing rooms, sipping tea, preparing a drink. The snow had dwindled to flurries, the roads had become wet and reflective. A fine mist danced upon the air, shimmering like glitter in the haloes around the lamplight. The patches of white that had earlier gathered had either melted or remained only on the dormant beds of the garden in the center of the square. The evening filled with noise: buses braking hard in the distance, cutlery being laid out for dinner, someone laughing. She felt a sudden and brief sense of guilt in her chest: she had buried Peter only a week earlier. A week before that he was tying his tie, preparing to go off to work, expecting to meet her at Marta's. The night before that they had lain together in bed, she had touched him, tasted him, pleased him. Now she was in London, and the word freedom passed through her mind. Could you be free when someone you had loved had died, been taken from you? It didn't matter so much that Peter had been murdered. It was his absence that was so substantial, a kind of pressure on her memory, an anchor holding her painfully to the ground, forbidding movement, crippling her. So that the death of someone was not a moment of liberation: it was the beginning of something far worse, an eternal moment of pain and regret. The words, the sentiments, the looks and caresses you had meant to bestow upon the beloved were now trapped within you, circling about in the mind, the memory.

Where was Peter now? By his own admission, nowhere. He and Jill had never been religious, had never adhered to a set of be-

liefs. He was utterly secular: to him life was limited only to what
the senses could make of it. Yet she found herself speculating in
an elementary fashion. Was he in heaven? Or was he writhing in
hell, forever bleeding from his wound, atoning for his sins in the
heat and flames of some wretched sea, surrounded by the mon-
sters of history? When plague arrived at a city, people who before
had lived happily within the web of faith and ritual ceased to be
concerned with such things. Death came quickly, like someone
on horseback, nimble in his boots and spurs, and the ceremonies
of life, the watches and wakes, the Latin and the calm hopeful
words by the space in the ground, now counted for nothing. Bodies were tossed from windows, wrapped in rugs. They were abandoned on the floor where they had collapsed. Covered in sores,
gangrenous and in constant torment, they were left to die and
then late at night by firelight and torch were flung by the hun-
dreds into common pits not half a mile from where she now
stood, directionless and exhausted in the last years of another
century.

She shut her eyes and pressed her forehead against the window
of her room. Her skin felt as though it had been coated with
something vile; she realized that she'd been wearing the same
clothes for over twenty-four hours, that she had sat in them on
the plane, slouching into a light sleep while others in the cabin
watched a comedy. Because she had fallen asleep with the head-
phones on, tuned to the classical program, she could not shake
from her mind now the music she had heard perhaps three or four
times, Vaughan Williams's *The Lark Ascending*, and the voice of
your host André Previn introducing it by asking you to hear the
bird in the notes of the violin and then speaking highly of the
music scene in London, to which you were now flying, the orches-
tras and chamber groups and opera companies, and she did as he
suggested, she could hear the creature lifting its wings, taking to
the air, sailing over the bay, beyond Carrie's room and Peter's
grave, moving towards the sun, tearing the clouds to shreds, van-
ishing in the brilliant yellow. Now through repetition the piece

seemed trite, the bird cloying, the cottony voice of André Previn that of a murderer who has insinuated himself with flattery and excessive kindness into your life.

She showered in a trickle of London water and the suds of a complimentary bar of lavender soap ornately stamped with the seal of the manufacturer. When she bent to soap herself her legs felt unsteady, a little tremulous. Although it was nearly five, and she was still on the cusp of noon, she felt an exhaustion that frightened her a little, perhaps because fatigue had always been something felt within. Now her body seemed to fight to remain upright, and the feeling reminded her in a strange way of her mother arduously making her way up the path to the house on the Vineyard, stick in hand, grappling against gravity to achieve her rest. Again it occurred to her that with Peter's passing something of herself had gone, something intensely personal, something physical, even. She leaned against the side of the shower stall and watched her thighs tremble, she felt her heart straining in its rhythm, and so alarmed was she that when she dried off she looked at herself in the big bathroom mirror, just to make sure she hadn't aged forty years.

Jill Bowman dressed and walked out into the city's rush hour. In the distance she could see the cars streaming down Gower Street and, beyond it, Tottenham Court Road. Pedestrians, mostly academics carrying briefcases, hurriedly left the university or stepped lightly from the north entrance of the British Museum. The heavy winter air, damp and spongy, smelled of taxicab and red bus, of motorcar and the accumulated dust of the ancient city, and she breathed it in gladly, this smell which was so unlike those of the cities she knew well at home, a redolence of gear and engine, of the sweat of struggle and defeat, of the strain of life, the jostle and rumble of crowds.

She considered it: this was the first time in years she had been abroad purely for pleasure, though now that she thought about it the word seemed inappropriate. There was nothing in the least pleasurable about the trip, in fact the more she thought about

it the more she realized that the essence of her journey was necessity, not enjoyment, that it was akin to a kind of penance,
that there was something pushing her away and something else
pulling her towards it, and she began to walk away from the hotel, following the sidewalks around the square, taking by impulse
a tree-lined side street and ending up in yet another square. There
were no cars, no people, and the quiet that hung over it was a
steady soothing hum. She might have walked through a tunnel
into another century. She stood and looked at the street lamps in
the mist, the elegant doorways, the living rooms that glowed as
an occasional figure stepped in and turned on a light or sat gazing
at a television. She looked at the sky, a deep soft slate, as if the silence had somehow originated there, and the thought occurred to
her that she had been on this spot once before, with Peter. After
dinner one summer evening they had walked in the neighborhood and ended up in this square, on this small street, and she
mouthed his name, Pe-ter, like that, in two syllables, because at
that moment she felt most keenly this emptiness that accompanied her now everywhere.

Now it began to rain. What had earlier been snow and cold
had become warmth and rain, and the drops fell heavily, as
though the clouds had grown heavy and fullish, and foolishly she
put her hands to her head, as if they might keep her dry. She
turned onto a street off the square and walked with increasing
speed, her shoes clacking against the gritty paving stones, and a
moment later found herself in another square, one wholly unfamiliar to her. Or yet it was familiar, for it resembled to a large degree the one she had just been standing in when the rain began to
fall. She stepped into a doorway. A car passed, a blue Ford, and
then a taxi. She lifted her hand and called out, but the driver
must not have seen or heard her, for he moved on, the light on his
roof disappearing in the distance. Now she ran across the square,
down another avenue, and found herself in another square, and
when she looked around her she began to laugh for the first time
since Peter's death, a throaty, rich laughter. Someone stepped out

of a house and hooped his umbrella and looked at this woman who stood alone and wet and terribly amused on a quiet London street. Jill said, "I'm afraid I'm lost." She told him the name of her hotel. And he lifted his hand and pointed to the big brick building just beside her. She had known it all along. She just hadn't seen it.

CHAPTER *13*

She was too tired to go to the theatre, or even take in a film. She
sat on the edge of her bed and watched the news on the television.
The IRA had announced that its annual holiday bombing cam-
paign on the mainland was about to commence, and over photographs of policemen squatting to view the undersides of cars
and vans the newsreader suggested a high degree of vigilance was
in order. The Queen Mother examined a thoroughbred in New-
market, this small woman in pastel blue and feathered hat touching the beast's neck and smiling just at the moment the animal
lifted its tail to relieve itself and the camera prudently turned
away. Jill laughed and began to towel her hair. She was not feeling too bad at all, already things were better, and the beginnings
of an appetite, a small hollow feeling, made her realize it was

time for lunch. Or, rather, dinner. It was almost half past six. A
reporter on the television interviewed a cabinet minister with astonishing hair who spoke nonsense in the sensible tones of an
Eton choirboy. An elephant had escaped from a circus in Dorset,
and in this regard an elderly woman stood at her front gate speaking of the terrors to come, of stampede in the suburbs, possible
impalement, it was shocking she said. A three-car accident had
taken place on the M-40 earlier that morning; footage showed fog
and twisted steel. A new movie was opening in London that
night, something unprovocative and thus suitable for the whole
family, for the Prince of Wales and his wife had been invited,
though only Diana was expected to attend, her husband remaining behind to brood in splendid solitude in his Gloucestershire
country home. That day the Princess had visited a hospital ward
where painfully thin men reached out to shake her hand. She held
a baby in her arms, and a voice mentioned that the infant would
not live much more than a month or two. She seemed untroubled
that she was surrounded by death, that on the margin of the glit-
tering material of her day was this terrible darkness, this place of
sores and contagion, of skeletons that hung onto life as old
clothes beyond taste and use are supported by the sturdiest of
hangers.

Jill stood and looked out the window. Save for the lamps that
must have been in place there for a hundred years or more, the
square was black with night. Cars moved slowly around it, taxis
discharged passengers; now it was time for a drink. She took the
elevator to the lobby and stepped to the entrance to the hotel
restaurant. Normally she would have been more adventurous, she
would have experimented a little, tried a new restaurant, taken
the tube to Kensington or Hampstead, eaten something unfamiliar. Once she and Peter had dined at a Chinese eatery in Soho
where the menu remained untranslated, and the corpses of water-
fowl hung dismally in the windows.

The restaurant was quite empty, and she was seated near the
kitchen door. She ordered an Absolut on the rocks, then changed

her mind and asked for a whisky, a Dewar's in fact, and sat waiting for it, gazing across at the empty tables. The restaurant walls
were heavy with wood paneling, bearing framed prints of a fox
hunt, and they reminded her of Blackjack, standing in his stall,
waiting for her, thoughtfully chewing his hay. She wondered
when she would hunt him again. It had been weeks, maybe even a
month or two, since she'd last ridden to hounds. The Secretary of
the Hunt, a lively and enterprising woman, had come to Peter's
funeral, taken her aside, urged her to return to her riding. She
thought of galloping Blackjack across the stony horizon and felt
her mind grow calm, as if astride her horse, reins in hand, solitary
atop a panting beast, she was only then truly in control.

A few couples entered the restaurant and were seated some distance from her, as though she had caught some disease and were
in danger of passing it on by proximity to others. Through the
kitchen door came the language of food preparation, the melange
of accents, the laughter and the chop of knives. The waiter
brought her the drink and set it down on a little napkin. She
wished she had asked for a double, though when she sipped it she
realized she was perfectly free to order another. She could order
three more, four if she liked. If she did so, would they talk about
her tonight in the bowels of the hotel, would this middle-aged
woman who drank in solitude become the center of interest? She
smiled to herself and the waiter came and raised his eyebrows.

"I'm not ready to order yet," she said.

"Ah."

"Wait. Tell me. The last time I was here there was a Mr. Longman working at the desk. Is he still employed by the hotel?"

"Let me check for you," he said, and disappeared through the
heavy door into the lobby. Now she saw that she would be spoken
of not only as a lush and a loose woman, but also as someone pursuing hotel employees. She laughed a little and chewed on some
bits of ice, and when the waiter came back he said, "Mr. Longman
retired last year. He lives in Devon these days."

"I see." She considered it apt that Mr. Longman had disappeared from his post. When Peter left so passed also some of the associated details of their courtship. Perhaps she would encounter more examples of this, and she considered it a kindness that she would no longer have to face the people and things they had looked at together.

He took the empty glass from her hand. "Another of the same?"

"Yes. Please."

"And something to eat?"

"All right." For the first time that evening she glanced at the menu. "I'll have the sole." The words meant nothing to her.

"The dinner."

"Yes, please."

"A glass of wine?"

"Just the scotch for right now."

He paused for no more than a second, but in that brief interval she saw what was passing through his mind. Somehow it didn't matter. Somehow he could just go fuck himself.

She ate the sole mechanically, fork to mouth, fork to mouth, tasting nothing, as though she were eating scraps of paper. She carried the glass to her lips, she drank, she returned it to the table. She reviewed the events of her life since the time she left her office at the university the previous afternoon. It was amazing how far she'd traveled, what she had done.

She looked at her watch. It was still early. There was a glass of wine on her table, though she didn't remember ordering it. When she looked up to question her waiter she could see only a full restaurant, every table occupied. From the kitchen voices rose, someone said This is the bloody wing, isn't it? and she remembered with great vividness the faces of some of those with whom she flew, faces she had studied at the waiting area by the gate, the old man in dark glasses, the French family with two boys, the young American student who actually spoke to her, telling her his name, his place of birth, the college he attended. He was from the Midwest, in fact he was a junior at the University of Wisconsin. He was traveling to London to study for a semester. "I know someone in Wisconsin," she said. "He's a teacher in the history department." Her eyes grew large with hope.

"I'm majoring in environmental studies."

"I also teach history."

"But history is my favorite subject," he lied.

"Do you know Greg Nyman?"

"No. I've never heard of him."

"He teaches in the history department." She realized that she was surrounding herself with a halo of words, as though Greg's name and department were elements in some incantation. The young man looked down in discomfort. He could not find the words for the occasion. Jill felt ridiculous. His blond hair and freckles and fresh open looks were unattractive to her. He exuded a disturbing air of innocence. He was the type who on the brink of orgasm would whisper endearments and professions of love, as though he wanted to dignify a pleasurable little fuck into a lifetime's commitment. She said, "Well. Good luck in London."

He looked up at her suddenly. "Why are you going? Sorry."

"Don't apologize. I'm going to recuperate." She smiled. "I've just had a tragic loss in my family." The phrase struck her as maudlin, something uttered in a bad television show by someone in a tight dress. She corrected herself: "My husband was murdered." She could see his eyes reading the movement of her lips. She wondered if her widowhood had bestowed upon her a sensuality altogether invisible to her, or if she exuded an odor of desire and need. She considered how she might extricate herself from the conversation, simply to spare the young man the painful silence. She said, "I wish you the best, then," and he smiled and blushed and thanked her and turned away, plunging his hands into his backpack, searching for nothing in particular.

Jill turned to the book she'd brought, one in fact she had read twice before, Daniel Defoe's *Journal of the Plague Year*. Defoe wrote as if he had lived through the Great Plague of 1665, though the novel was a work of trickery. Defoe had only been five when Death had come to London, and had written the book from the point of view of a witness and survivor. Her copy of it was heavily annotated, she had used different colored inks to signal passages that she would discuss in various sections of the article she was in the process of writing. Surrounding descriptions of fear and suspicion, of screams behind locked doors and the death of maidens and children was the tiny handwriting of the professional academic, filling the margins of each page as though trying to take possession of this tale of apparitions and visions, bodies and souls.

She had asked for, and was allotted, a window seat. She wasn't sure why. In the past Peter had always demanded they sit close to the aisle, in fact each of them in an aisle seat, preferably across from one another. He spoke of accident and escape, of statistics read in *The Wall Street Journal*, of being able to take her by the hand if, say, the plane began to lose altitude, dropping a thousand feet per second, and she laughed at him, this cautious Swiss, because to him danger lurked everywhere, at the stable, on the sea, in suburban thoroughfares, everywhere but in a rundown hotel.

Aloft she thought about Carrie, who knew nothing of her mother's whereabouts. She had visited her daughter the day before her flight and had informed Dr. Bradley of her plans. There would be no problems, she was told. Carrie's life, an unending routine of waking, sleeping, with periodic interruptions of meals and exercise, would remain the same. As would Peter's grave.

It was an absurd notion, stopping in to see your husband in a box in the ground. There was nothing to see, no one to talk to, nothing to say. Yet she felt compelled to stand there the afternoon before her flight and gaze down at the earth above him, as if the mixture of sand, loam and pebble might like an obscure poem yield up its meaning only after close scrutiny. She referred to the little map the man at the cemetery had given her. It was odd that every time you turned you always seemed to be in the same spot. Perhaps that was why a map was required, to display for you the sectors of the graveyard, the numbers and letters that designated

your loved one's final resting place, as if death and interment possessed a code all their own. She parked the car and began walking
over the freshly mown grass, past other graves with their floral
tributes, American flags, Mylar balloons. An unsealed letter had
been left on the grave of a fourteen-year-old girl named Kelly
Ann Flynn, propped up against the polished granite stone. Jill
reached down and touched it, then picked it up and opened it,
then put it back very quickly, for it was not for her to read, these
items of news from life in the high-school corridors, in fact probably the very school Kelly would have attended had she lived. It
occurred to Jill that Carrie and Kelly Ann Flynn had something
in common, that adolescence and maturity were passing them
both by, that they would never know the lush fullness of one's
first love, the terrifying rush of pleasure in someone else's bed, the
bewildering heartache of abandonment.

One day Carrie would lie here, and there would be no news for
her, for even now she lived in a world where nothing happened,
and time moved like thick syrup into something unimaginable
called the future. A fresh mound of dirt lay over Peter's coffin.
The stone had his name cut into it and the dates that defined the
limits of his life. She knelt down and touched the letters, feeling
the groove of the P, the elegant curve that created the G. She felt
as if she should do something, as though were she simply to walk
away after a few minutes' quiet meditation Peter would show his
displeasure in some esoteric and symbolic manner. She felt foolish
looking through her bag for something to leave. She had nothing
save some coins, twenty-dollar bills, passport, driver's license, her
blue tampon holder, lip gloss. She could write him a note in the
little pad she always carried around with her, Dear Peter, I was
here, where were you? I love you, I miss you, why did you go get
yourself murdered in a filthy hotel?

She knelt and touched the stone. Beneath her knee was Peter's
head, his beautiful face, his body, the birthmark on his breast.
She could not turn away from the thought of him that last morning as he tied his tie, talked about his trip, touched her hip when

he kissed her goodbye: the ceremonial recovery after sleep, dreams, the heat and steam of lovemaking. So much had happened since then. It was as if someone had taken a scissors and severed the expected course of her life. She ran her fingers along the edge of the polished monument, desperately wanting to touch Peter, to hold him in her arms, to feel his soft flesh against hers, to make him take hold of her. A sense of despair and a feverish anger rose at once within her. He had departed without explanation. He had gone from her without saying goodbye. He had left her bereft of farewell.

It was ridiculous of her to think this way. Peter would have found her laughable. He was dead, he was under the ground, and she thought of him there, in the excruciating and profound darkness, still, unthinking, without voice. That was what death was, the loss of word and expression, the sudden disappearance of gesture and intent. She remembered when Rose Keller had been taken away by the men from the ambulance, how much she had felt the absence of this silent woman who smiled and waved to her, who said little but was a weighty presence in her life, a landmark in time, someone who anchored the day for this curious little girl. What had made her lose her voice, her ability to communicate, what had cut her ties to the rest of the world?

She was disturbed by the shadow of the waiter as he stood waiting for an answer to a question she hadn't heard. She wasn't sure what to say. It seemed to her that the waiter had taken a liking to her, or else had been directed to keep close watch on this strange woman who drank too much and peered at her plate and seemed lost in thought. She remembered that the English disliked making scenes, in fact they would do anything to avoid one. She looked up at the waiter and for no obvious reason said, "Thank you very much."

"May I show you the dessert trolley?"

"No. I don't think so." She played a little with the empty wineglass.

"More wine?"

She shook her head.

"Another scotch?"

"Not tonight."

Bits of fish lay stuck to her tongue. They had the texture of parchment and torn callus. She sipped some water, and it had a sour taste. Was it her or the water? Getting to the door was going to be difficult. She looked at her watch. It was only seven. Within her it was still early afternoon, and yet she felt as though she were craving a long sleep, as after a spicy meal the mouth thirsts for unending water. If she went to bed then, if she went upstairs and washed and climbed into bed, she would wake, and she counted the hours off on her fingers, twelve one two, somewhere around three in the morning. She would open her eyes in the middle of the night as she did every morning at seven or eight, refreshed, ready to face the newly risen sun, only to find herself in a darkened and silent city. She could walk, listen to the echoes of her shoes against the paving stones. There would be a mist, or a fine rain, and beads of water would cling to her hair and clothes. And then tomorrow, what? What?

With exaggerated and imprecise indifference she made her way to the front of the restaurant, colliding twice with a chair, attracting curious pairs of eyes, pulling hard on the door when she should have been pushing. Behind her she felt the stares and smiles of the waiters and the man who tended the bar, and as she crossed the lobby she had the momentary and vivid sensation that the present had disappeared and she was on the brink of meeting Peter, as she had that time in this same place thirteen years ago. It came to her as a physical sensation, something visceral, akin to how she felt as a child on Christmas Eve: the ripe and expectant feeling that something good and inevitable was tipped just beyond the horizon of midnight. And as she rode up in the elevator it began to drain from her, floor by floor, and it was replaced with the aridity of loss, the great dry darkness that lay around her.

She sat on the edge of the bed and took off her shoes and switched on the television. Now Jill was beginning to feel it.

Two weeks after the murder of her husband. One week after his burial. Now it was coming to her, something heavy and large that took its place upon her chest, a great weight like that of a creature who had climbed from a deep pit and had come to perch soundlessly on her heart. The noise in her ears was that of the blood coursing through her, flowing down the small and large channels, fanning out to her extremities and the deltas of her body which had so opened themselves to Peter's desire. With the pain came the fear, a great comprehensive fear, a terrifying rush of dread that defined itself not in words or thoughts but also as something within her body, some hitherto unknown organ which had finally burst, spreading its vile liquid about her heart. This was the fear that comes with being alone. This was the horror of being her age. This was the blank sheet of the future that she watched being crumpled before her eyes.

CHAPTER *14*

She slept and then she woke, as she feared she would, some time in the middle of the night. The television was still on. Since she had last been in London the United Kingdom had embraced the technologies and tastes of the late twentieth century and come to recognize that people either stayed up past midnight or owned a VCR, and so a movie was being shown, *A Clockwork Orange*. Malcolm McDowell was merrily brutalizing a woman in her house while he sang "Singin' in the Rain," slapping her face, cutting her clothes, crippling her husband when he had a moment to spare. For a few minutes Jill leaned on her elbow and watched this spectacle of mayhem and melody and then she rose and switched it off and went into the bathroom. Her head ached. She looked at herself in the mirror and commented aloud on how she looked like shit. She took a washcloth and rinsed it with tepid water and held it against her face and then she hoisted her skirt and pulled down her panties and sat on the toilet. She listened as the bowl filled with everything she had drunk that day, the scotch, the wine, the pernicious water, and with dispassion the clarity of her evening returned to her, the vast wave of terror that had come upon her. It had nothing about it of grief for Peter: this feeling of loss was entirely selfish because it was her loss, it was she who had been left bereft, and because she had now become reduced to one there came a lucent and clear sense of her body, this five-foot-eight, 132-pound thing that helped define her. Before it had been something pretty, aging with grace, becoming not wrinkled and soft but rather enriched and embellished. It was what made Peter lower his gaze, it was what made his eyes sparkle, this object of his desire. Now, without him, what would happen to her? Would she begin to grow indolent and formless, relinquishing any illusions that she might ever be attractive to another? Or would she grow grey fast, every part of her, achieving a hazy colorlessness that would make her invisible to everyone else?

While earlier she felt that Peter's death had drawn a line in her life, that time would always be measured against that event, before or after, now she began to see that her thoughts were turning from Peter to herself. There was nothing she could do to bring him back. Even entertaining some vague illusion that, like Elvis Presley or Jack Kennedy, he was still alive in a universe of convenience stores and roadside gift shops, in Hyannis hideaways or exclusive Palm Springs nursing homes, seemed absurd to her. Although she felt twisted and wrenched with grief she knew that Peter Freytag hadn't disappeared, as she had at first thought, and with it the implication of return; he was dead, he was finished, there was nothing more of him save her memories. In time they would grow dim, the sound muffled, the light faded. As in old photographs what had been brilliant outline and exquisite contrast would transform into something brown and uniform. Her memory would become refreshed with new sights, intriguing sounds. Peter was dead but he would never die. Instead he would step into the background. And with that thought she realized that as long as he was there, standing and facing her, there would be also the mystery of his death, a smudge, a nebulosity, a palpable vagueness that would linger not over his memory but rather within her like an embryo forever turning in its fluid, kicking at the walls, sucking at the juices of her body.

She flushed the toilet and pulled a brush through her hair, and looking at her watch, seeing it was nearly half past three, decided to undress and return to bed. She lay there in the darkness and, because since Peter's murder she had come to disdain the quiet, listened to the radio. On one of the BBC stations a university lecturer spoke tediously of Renaissance verse. He spoke of Spenser and Sir Philip Sidney and Shakespeare and Thomas Nashe. *Brightness falls from the air,* he said, and she switched him off. She lay in the silence and looked at the window as dawn cautiously began to fill the space. She felt an odd sort of stillness and calm, as if she had come through a car accident, a bad fall from a horse, childbirth. Her mother walked towards her on the windy beach, along the margin of the tide, holding her wide straw hat against her head. Beyond her were the boats, their sails swollen and white in the sun. The sound of things flapping, wings and kites, the crests of waves, the sheets of vessels, filled her head. Her mother bent to pick up a shell from the sand and placed it against her ear, and then, because she realized she had something important to ask her mother, she woke up to the rain and grey of a London morning, and once again felt herself drowning in ignorance and mystery.

She showered and as she washed herself and shampooed her hair she began to plan the events of her day. There was no reason why her trip should be a pointless one. There were things she could see, plays to attend, paintings to gaze at, small moments and events that might add up to something substantial. If she wished she could even do a little research for her paper. Her identification card from the university allowed her to use the British

Library. The last time she had been there, when Peter was chairing a seminar one Wednesday afternoon, she had sat for hours transcribing text and taking notes from the six volumes she had chosen from the catalogue. Some of the books were very old, published in 1667, a year after the Great Fire had devastated London, and when she received them from the hands of the woman who had fetched them she bent her head to sniff their pages, imagining that the air of decades and centuries might bring her some small insight. She read over records of the Plague, and accounts by people of the time, tradesmen and clerics, who only weeks before the coming of pestilence had seen swirling suns in the heavens, weeping eyes and tokens of Armageddon. The great round reading room smelled of ancient dust and dying wood, and when someone cleared her throat or shut a book, the sound circled the room and lasted for what seemed an eternity. She remembered that on a wall in the ladies' room someone had written *Margaret Drabble is a thoroughly wretched vixen*. Afterwards she had walked down into the depths of Soho, past the discreet sex shops, their windows filled with garish red lingerie and leather garments, the peep shows where men urged you in with impossible promises, and where occasionally she would catch a glimpse of a middle-aged woman in a scanty costume, wiry wisps of hair escaping from her G-string, leaning against a wall and yawning, savoring her break with a cigarette.

But this time she would not be a scholar, she would not bury herself in old books. This time she would press forward, she would escape thought and idea and deal with sensation and people. When she came downstairs the waiter from the night before smiled a little to himself and showed her to a table. She ordered eggs and bacon and toast and coffee. At other tables American tourists looked over their guidebooks and speculated on the value of the pound sterling. She remembered that Claire and Michael Hollander lived in Hampstead. She wondered if she should call first or simply take the tube up, surprise them, impose herself upon these old friends of hers and Peter's. She had known them for, and she began to count out the years silently in her mind, eight nine ten, nearly as long as she'd been married to Peter. It was funny that she had never really taken a liking to Claire, but had preferred Michael's company, his sense of humor, his ease with her. Perhaps it was too obvious to her that Claire was attracted to Peter and had sensed in Jill a rival. In fact Michael was so comfortable with her in such an unspecific way that she assumed he would be the same way with most women. She wondered whether this was an attractive quality, if what women really wanted were men who were unafraid of them, who would allow no threat to enter the air; or if in reality, in the blacker depths of their hearts, they preferred men who treated them like garbage, who offered them correction and taming, as though marriage were an extended wrestling match, full of sweat and noise, destined to die suddenly of heart failure.

Peter had always been respectful of Jill, polite and tender, though capable of great passion, of losing himself wrapped in her limbs, or simply taking her as he had that afternoon on the Vineyard. He was a man of contrasts, or rather a man who loved contrasts. He enjoyed it when Jill wore a little something when they made love in the fading light of afternoon, even a strand of pearls, as though in this way her nudity was all the more blatant. He loved the demarcation between the hirsute chaos separating her legs and the smooth whiteness of her thighs. He was aroused when this woman of intelligence and lucidity put her hands to her body and lost herself in gratification before his eyes, as though at that moment she had stripped herself of the accretions of years of learning and prudence and were touching something primitive in both of them. Most of all she could trust Peter. The years of their marriage, their months and days spent together, had created in them a bond that would let nothing escape. Within the bounds of their relationship anything could take place without shame or embarrassment. It was as if they each owned a portion of the other: an intimate shadowy square yard marked by tussle and clench that would forever be hidden to others.

She spoke little of her marriage, even to her closest friends, and especially not to Sally, as if to utter a word about it might create a breach in its walls, allow others to invade it, or cause the escape of something of its potency. Now that Peter was gone there was nothing left to be said. Whatever had led him to the Hubbard had cast a different light on their thirteen years together. What before had been the calm complacency of wisdom had become the clamor of doubt.

She finished her breakfast and lingered over a last cup of coffee. She watched the waiter from the night before organizing menus for that day's lunch. Every now and again he would glance at her with interest, the corner of his mouth turning up wryly whenever her eyes met his. He set down the menus and came to her table, leaning slightly towards her. Very quietly he said, "Is there anything I can get for you?"

She smiled at him. "No thank you."

For a moment he said nothing. She watched his eyes as they moved away from hers. She had put on a cashmere sweater, in fact a sweater she had bought on her last trip to London, and his glance took in the shape of her breasts visible beneath it. She saw that he had meant her to follow the direction his mind was taking, as though his intention were a road on a map, clearly delineated as it cut through the landscape of her torso. He was a tall, dark-haired man with what seemed to be black eyes. Or rather he was a tall, dark-haired man who wanted to fuck her, and this was the story his eyes told. She wondered what her eyes were saying. She said, "I'm sorry about last night."

He lifted an eyebrow.

"I must have drunk too much. I was exhausted from my flight."

"You're American, then?"

She smiled.

"I was in America two years ago," he said. "I was in New York and Frisco. Are you from either of those places?"

She told him where she lived, and when he didn't recognize

the name of the town she described its location, moving her finger in the air to indicate its distance from the border of Maine and the city of Boston. He watched her hands with interest, her colorless fingernails as they sketched out the coast with its capes and bays.

"What brings you to London?" His voice snagged on a tiny laugh, as if it were absurd that anyone would want to visit this city purely for pleasure.

"I needed a rest," she said, weighing her words with some care. "I recently became a widow."

"I'm sorry."

"My husband and I met here in London, in fact in this hotel. That's why I asked you about Mr. Longman. He was working here when we met."

He continued to look at her with eyes that, because they had learned new facts, showed a new light. She placed her napkin on the table and stood, knowing that he was now seeing new areas of her, her waist and hips, her legs in the tan trousers she wore. She felt nothing for him, not that he didn't appeal to her but rather because since Peter's death to feel lust and need might somehow be construed by her as a forgetting of Peter. Yet here was a man who wanted her, who could easily have her, who might, in the twist and thrust of bed, help her take a step away from her grief. And she smiled at him and walked away.

When she returned to her room to prepare to go out she realized she had been aroused by this encounter. It had left her a little edgy, as if an itch had invaded her body and could not be located or relieved. She wondered if it would go away. She was afraid to help herself, fearful that in the midst of this private ardor the image of Peter might come into her mind and destroy her pleasure. But if it didn't, was it an indication that Peter was beginning to fade from her mind? It was a ridiculous notion, in fact it worried her more than a little: she had buried her husband only a week earlier. Why this distance that, still in its unmeasurable stage, had come between them, between the living woman and the memory of her dead husband? Clearly her reactions were abnormal. Widows wept and pined for their mates. Queen Victoria had donned black on the death of Prince Albert and remained in her weeds until the last day of her life. Death was like a magnet, pulling you towards it, holding you within its field of attraction. Eventually the force wore off; in time you could move freely, you could think what you wish, you could be drawn elsewhere.

She lay back on the bed and stared at the ceiling. She was both flattered and disgusted with the waiter's desire for her. She wondered what, apart from Peter himself, she missed most: was it the feel of a man beside her, someone she could touch and who would touch her, the heat of him, the pressure of his lips against her neck, the weight of him against her body? Could it be something as simple as that? Was it that and the notion that within a few moments she could arouse a man, make his body stretch and yearn, cause him to want her as much as she wanted him? She unbuttoned her trousers with her thumb and forefinger and slipped her hand inside them, under the thin slippery material of her underpants. She was hot there and cold elsewhere, as though the temperature in her body had drained away to that one spot, a place of focus, a knot of tension. She shut her eyes and began to breath deeply, rhythmically, feeling the muscles in her thighs tighten as she turned in circles, big ones growing small and smaller still. It would take only a few seconds, the man with the black eyes was on her and then Peter was on a table, cold and dead and colorless, and she opened her eyes and looked through her tears at nothing but the whiteness of the ceiling, a sheet of paper from which image and word had been erased.

The incident left her shaken, terrified of the power of her own memory, bewildered and apprehensive: would it happen again, would Peter always be there, a ghostly presence, a tumor on her conscience, to step between her and her pleasure, her life, her future?

But her tears hadn't been for Peter: they were for herself, for her own weakness, her inability to be alone and thrive in this solitude. She lay there for a few minutes more, and with each moment came a growing feeling of superfluousness, as though every thought and action that was hers was without purpose or meaning. She stood and rubbed her knuckles into her eyes and buttoned her trousers. Without looking into a mirror she brushed her hair, took her bag and left her room. The prospect of stepping outside into the noise and pollution of a great city, of being jostled by crowds and passing in and out of others' conversations, the weaves and knots of their lives, appealed to her.

She crossed the square and, checking her map of the Underground, cut through the gardens and walked towards Tottenham Court Road and Goodge Street tube station. She hadn't bothered to call ahead. It didn't much matter if Claire and Michael were in or not. The trip to Hampstead would not be wasted. She could always walk through the Heath, or shop on the High Street. She could have a decent lunch. She could pass the time.

She stood on the platform and looked again at the map. Two lines constituted the Northern Line, only one of which went directly to Hampstead. The signboard indicated that a train was on its way, but that its destination was High Barnet. If she took this one she would have to get off at Camden Town and wait for another train to Hampstead. Or she could wait for the correct train and not bother with changing. Suddenly the air began to change in the station, or rather it began to move, flustering her hair, rolling like a wave, as though betokening a cataclysm, and then the train was in the station, lights and noise and doors, and for some reason she got on it, for to wait for another one seemed at that moment intolerable to her.

The train was not especially crowded. There was a Sikh gentleman beturbaned and bearded, and a few young German men with backpacks who got out at Euston Station. When she alighted at Camden Town the platform was empty, or at least she thought it was. A woman sat slouched on an orange plastic seat. Between her knees was a plastic shopping bag. Jill stared at her because there was something imminent about her posture, as though she were

on the brink of action or thought and would suddenly spring to
her feet with enlightenment. In moving light the signboard indicated that her train was due in four minutes. She regretted not
having bought a newspaper or brought a book. She looked at the
advertisements for employment bureaus and department stores.
Posters announcing the latest West End hits brightened the dark
walls of the tube station. During the Blitz people took refuge
here, people drawn suddenly from their kitchen tables or bedrooms, whole families and engaged couples, illicit lovers and the
solitary, all streamed down to the depths of London to sit in silence, whisper prayers, sing quietly and listen to the bombs tumble onto their houses and flats. It was always astonishing to stand
in a place of upheaval and renewal, where plague and war had de-
scended upon the population, and where those who survived were
able to turn their faces away from the darkness and once again
take hold of time.

She watched with an unfathomable fascination at the slouching
woman. She seemed somehow suspended in time, as if ready to
topple out of life into death. She could go to her, offer a hand,
hand her a pound note, tend to her pain. She could leave her alone,
turn her head, swivel and dance within the aggrieved borders of
her own life. Now the wind came again in swirls and sucks, and
when the train pulled to a stop the woman remained where she
was, and where Jill Bowman presumed she would be long after she
had arrived in the rolling rich avenues of Hampstead.

At the tube station an elevator carried her and other passengers
to the surface of the earth. No one spoke; everyone diverted eyes
from everyone else. She watched them, though, she followed the
furtive looks as men sought out cleavage and women gazed with
pointed interest at the dirt in the cracks of the walls, she watched
as people visibly relaxed when the elevator came to a stop. She
stepped out onto High Street and tried to remember the way to
Claire and Michael Hollander's house. The man running the newspaper stand outside the tube station was talking to another man,
I said fuck off to her, I said it and she scarpered out of there but

quick. Oh yes guv I gave it to her but good, and the other man laughed and shrugged his shoulders and sucked hard on his cigarette. Now she remembered, it was the Greek restaurant across the street that brought it to mind, and she made a left turn and began to walk down the hill. They had actually eaten there that last time, she and Peter and Claire and Michael had walked up to the place and taken lunch there. Claire and Michael had just come back from a month on the island of Ídhra, they had rented a house from a writer friend, and they had miraculously returned with a comprehensive grasp of Greek cuisine, culture, history, manners, and alcoholic beverage. They had dragged Peter and Jill up the hill and had picked small fights with the waiter, for he could not for the life of him understand the way they pronounced names and words that appeared on the menu. The thought made Jill pause for a moment, for she wondered why she had bothered to travel all the way to Hampstead to see these people. She had little in common with them. In fact it was Peter who was much more their equal, for he and Michael, at least, spoke the same language, knew the same people, read the same books. Jill was more observer than participant, and yet she knew why she had to see them. They had belonged to the life of her marriage. Now she had to take her leave of them.

Now she was lost. She knew there was a left turn off High Street, and she stood in front of the pub, in fact directly in front of the entrance, and looked at her map book, seeking out the correct page, turning it so that she could match picture to reality. She became aware that a man was standing in the doorway of the pub, sipping coffee from a cup, balancing the saucer with elegant precision on his fingertips. She would remember nothing but his pose, and the poise of him. She made the turn and found herself beneath the leafy shadows of Flask Walk. The leaves held the raindrops of the previous night, and when the wind came to disturb them, points of moisture fell against her hair and face. She stopped and looked up at the trees, and then at the buildings. She was so far away from home; it was as if Peter's death and everything connected to it, Detective Sergeant Resnick, the trip to the morgue, the Hubbard Hotel, had become relegated to a period of history that somehow predated her. Yet she also knew that the Hubbard still stood, containing the room that had witnessed Peter's last moments; that Resnick would some time that day sit behind his desk and sift through the evidence relating to her husband's death; and that soon she would return to it, as a fly who has escaped the spider at dawn inevitably blunders back into the web at sunset.

CHAPTER *15*

The person who answered the door was unknown to her. In fact she took two steps back to make sure she had come to the right place. Now it came back to her: the blue enamel house numbers, the white planters beneath the windows, the stone urn on the top step, the polished brass letter-slot: all of it was hazily familiar to her. The young woman waiting in the doorway looked at her.

"I hope I haven't come at a bad time," Jill said. "I've just stopped by to visit Claire and Michael Hollander. They still live here, don't they?"

The young woman smiled a little and continued to look at her. She wore blue jeans and a sweatshirt and nothing on her feet. Her hair hung straight to her shoulders and her thick nose and lips recalled Claire to Jill's memory. "Yes, they're here," she said.

"You must be," and the young woman said, "That's right."

Jill stepped in. The odors of the house, fresh flowers and something acrid, some cleaning fluid or chemical, came upon her thick and malign. It made her regret again having come this far. Anything would have been preferable to a prolonged session of condolence and succor, even an afternoon's shopping, a horrible matinée at a bawdy boulevard comedy, a bout of intense nausea.

The young woman pointed out the living room. The sunlight jutted through the windows in sharply defined angles. Two or three vases of flowers stood on various tables. One entire wall was covered with shelves of books. Jill turned her head a little to read the titles. Stuck unobtrusively among the volumes from university presses and philosophical works by Iris Murdoch and Ludwig Wittgenstein were popular sex manuals and books on toilet-training your cat, the odd title by Robert Ludlum and Catherine Cookson. She knew that if pressed Claire would claim these had been used by her as research for an essay on the role of popular fiction in contemporary British society. It was what Claire did for a living: write pieces for weekly publications and appear on radio round-table shows where the intelligentsia of London spoke with weighty significance of a new film or art exhibition. Occasionally these pieces would be collected between hard covers, or she would come out with a short novel, usually an acerbic and witty dissection of the sort of people who lived in the neighboring houses.

Michael was a neurosurgeon who had achieved fame by writing a readable history of the treatment of mental illness. He was a calm man, or rather a steady man in both his speech and the way he fixed you with his pale blue eyes, and this gave him an air of immense confidence. For years there had been some discussion of his hosting a ten-part television series on the same subject, and this possibility hung before him, precious and tantalizing. In fact, Michael had been very useful to Jill when it came to dealing with Carrie. When on a visit to the States some years earlier he had examined her and conferred with Dr. Bradley and explained to Jill that her choice of institution and physician were good ones. Beyond that there was nothing more he could do.

Jill could hear muffled conversation coming from another room; she could make out the chick-chick of shears in the back gardens. Someone somewhere was playing a radio or a record. She thought that each sound belonged to a different member of the family, that it was an identifying characteristic, and now she recalled that Michael was a keen gardener, that he and his wife were the parents of a college-age daughter, and that Claire was forever seeking out an argument.

"Well this is a surprise," Claire said as she entered the room, surrounded by a dusky nimbus of indignation. Jill turned to her. She didn't know what to say. Claire was wearing a Laura Ashley dress that must have been at least fifteen years old. She said, "God you look wonderful, Jill," and she stepped forward and kissed her cheek. "Did you bring that husband of yours along?"

"What?"

"Peter. Where's Peter?"

Michael came up behind her and smiled. He wore a tan shirt with rolled sleeves and epaulets. The hair on his arms was thick and bleached by the sun. He stepped forward and kissed Jill on the cheek. She wondered what the hell one did in the garden on a day in December. He said, "Well this is very nice, Jill darling."

"Was that your daughter?"

"You met Jen then, did you. It's been years since you last saw her, she was just a girl then. She just finished up at Cambridge. Now she's joined the ranks of the unemployed."

"The last time we were here I remember you had just come back from Greece."

Claire looked at Michael. Her husband smiled. "Since then we've bought a cottage in the south of France. In a little village called Pierrefeu. Charming, really. It needs work, though. It's where we spend all our holiday time. Anyway, our French is a great deal better than our Greek. Come, sit and talk to us."

Michael said, "We were so worried about Peter. I mean, we were expecting him."

"Where'd you leave him?" Claire said, looking around, as if Peter were a Chihuahua, hiding and wriggling behind a chair leg. "We even went to Heathrow to meet his flight. Of course when he didn't get off we checked with one of the girls there and she said his name was on the list but he hadn't boarded the plane." Claire looked at Jill.

Jill said, "Peter died that evening."

"What?"

"Peter had an accident that night."

"My dear, you're joking." Swerving cars and distressed steel must have raced through their imaginations.

"Why didn't you call us?"

"There was too much to do."

"But we waited for him."

"I'm sorry."

"But."

"Peter was killed," Jill said. "He was found murdered in a hotel."

Claire's eyes grew wide. Her mouth twisted into a primitive grimace, a look of both disgust and alarm, a figure in a painting staring into a pit of hell. She held her fingers to her mouth as though she were about to vomit her breakfast. She said, "My lord my lord."

"I buried him a week ago." To them it was irrefutable: Peter had all along been alive; he had missed his plane, or come down with the flu, or met with some minor mishap, and had simply overlooked ringing them. His death was real to them only as a series of words and sentences spoken by this American woman who had flown all this way to impart such news. They had not seen him on the table in the morgue, they had not looked up at the window of the hotel in which his body had twisted and wrenched as the blood flowed from him, they had not been witness to his funeral, when the heavy casket sold by the man named Kelly was lowered into the earth. All they had was what these two people dealt with each and every day of their lives, the very currency of their careers, the words of one person. But had Jill the time to reflect she would have seen that for them Peter had been alive these past days, in fact in all of the minutes and seconds since she'd come into their house. That although she had seen him with her very own eyes in the chill certainty of his death, for Claire and Michael Hollander he had been a living, breathing person, a respected psychiatrist, and the notion of it would have made her head spin.

"But you didn't tell us."

"You should have called," Jill suggested.

"We were there to meet the plane," Claire said.

"We were early," added her husband.

"But when he didn't get off you should have called. I couldn't get in touch. There were just too many things I had to do. I was at the hospital the whole night long."

"But we assumed."

"But when he didn't show up," Jill said, beginning to argue.

"We just assumed."

"It doesn't matter now," Jill said. "Peter's dead and I'm here." She didn't know why she said such an inane thing, Peter's dead and I'm here, but it came out and she realized by the expressions on Claire and Michael's faces that the balance of power in the room had shifted away from them to her, that it was as if she had broken into their home with the intention of weakening their hearts through the admission of shocking news, that now she was firmly in place she had no intention of leaving.

"You're welcome to stay, of course," Michael said at once.

"No no."

"Yes, of course you must. You can have Jen's room. She can camp out down here."

"I have a room, though, I have a hotel."

"We'd be thrilled to have you."

For a moment or two she seriously considered it: long wine-soaked meals and discussion of matters literary and psychiatric. "No thank you," she said. "It's kind of you to offer, though."

"Stay for lunch, at least," Claire said.

"Yes, do," her husband added.

"All right."

They looked at her and said nothing. Words had suddenly grown cheap and useless. She could see it in their eyes as they shifted here and there, seeking out the phrase and utterance that would save the moment, spare them pain. She said: "It's good to see you," and that too seemed like a bit of weed carried by the air.

"I only wish circumstances were better," said Claire. "I can't tell you how much of a shock this is. If there's anything at all Michael and I can do, please don't hesitate to speak up."

"It's very kind of you."

Michael stood and left the room. Jill could hear him in the kitchen, she could hear knives and forks and the rattle of dishes.

"Would you like a drink?"

"Yes, please."

Claire walked to a table on which stood an array of bottles. She held up a bottle of gin.

"I'd just like a little vodka."

"With ice?"

"Please."

Claire handed the drink to her and was astonished to see that by the time she sat down Jill had finished it. "Michael's just getting lunch. It's been such a hectic year for us, you can't imagine. It looks as though the BBC may be doing that series with Michael. At least he's submitted two sample scripts to them, and they've liked what they've seen so far." She looked at Jill. "Are you still teaching at that university?"

"Yes, of course. I've taken some time off, just for a month."

"Quite right, too."

"I'm still working on the Plague."

"Are you?"

"I thought I might do a little more research while I'm over

here. It's just that," and she too ran out of words, as if the narrative of her life, the course of daily events, of hopes and dreams and frustrations, had wearied her. "I don't know," she said.

Claire joined her on the sofa and took her hands. "I still can't believe it," she said. Jill looked at her. "It's just too much to take in. Are you all right, though, are you managing somehow?"

"I'm still half in a daze over it," Jill said. "I can take it in easily enough. I just can't accept it."

"No. Of course not."

Jill didn't know what to say. The bars of sunlight had grown dimmer, greyer, as though filtered through bands of smoke. The houses across the road seemed handsome and reasonable; there was order and symmetry, and the serene white of their façades spoke of purity and sense. They had been designed and built at a time when God ruled the heavens and the monarch the territories of the earth. Everyone had her place in the world and would stay there until death. Even Freud had lived not two blocks from here. Jill didn't know why she was there. She wondered why she had flown to London. It was like a vast pretense, as if she were going through a series of motions whose object remained hidden from her. Had she come to find something, and if this was so, if she had come in search of something, was it to do with Peter or herself?

Claire continued to hold on to her hands, to gaze into her eyes and exude some sort of silent sympathy. Jill realized that it was like eating too many sweets, boxes of marzipan or rows upon rows of truffles, that she had had enough of it, enough of people's wordless looks and tears, offers of help and their soft and gentle touches. It was unnourishing food, glutinous and heavy, and it weighed on her like an indecent roll of flesh. Her world seemed to have grown soft and pale, formless and oppressive. What it lacked was angles: those provided by a window cutting through the darkness of night; the X of a glistening city intersection, the shapely V of passion.

Jill held up her glass. "May I have another, please?"

"Of course, darling."

Jill looked around again. "You really do have a lovely house."

"You're welcome to stay as long as you wish, you know."

"I'd prefer to be on my own just for now."

"Where are you staying?"

Jill told her the name of the hotel.

"That's a splendid place," Claire said.

Michael joined them and made himself a drink. "How's your little girl?"

"She's fine, Michael, she's grown so much." He looked at her. "She's fourteen now. I miss her a lot." For a few moments she said nothing. Michael seemed to wait for more. She said, "Nothing's really changed. I usually go to see her once a week. She doesn't even seem to know I'm there."

"Yes she does," Michael declared. "I've told you this before. She knows it. She just can't express it."

"She's all I've got left," she said, setting down her empty glass.

"We shall have wine with lunch, if you like," Claire said.

They went into the dining room and took seats around the table. "Jen won't be joining us, I'm sorry to say. She doesn't eat lunch these days."

Jill said nothing.

"Do you intend to stay where you are?" Claire asked.

"Do you mean in the house where Peter and I lived? Yes, of course. Where else would I go?"

"Well, I mean."

"I intend to keep teaching. I want to finish this essay. I have to go on, you know."

"Of course you do," Claire said.

Jill put food into her mouth without looking at it, without knowing what it consisted of. For all she knew she could have been eating crumpled paper or crushed cigars. The two drinks had gone to her head and now she was drinking wine. She developed an itch and without a second thought scratched at her breast through the cashmere of her sweater.

"I'm sorry you weren't here a week earlier," Claire said.

"I was at Peter's funeral."

"Let me put on some music," Michael said.

"I took part in a symposium on *Madame Bovary*," announced Claire. "It was very interesting. We did it at Logan Hall at London University. A very diverse group was involved. Fay Weldon was marvelous. The general consensus was that Flaubert had overstepped his bounds by writing a novel about a woman. He'd got everything wrong, you see. Because as a man he couldn't see things quite the way poor Emma had."

Jill smiled and nodded a little. Now she was drunk. She felt like taking her clothes off and swimming. She felt like running through wet grass. She felt like dancing, even though she hadn't danced since somewhere around 1969. The music was vaguely familiar to her. "Satie," she said, and Michael said it was by Federico Mompou. They ate in silence for a few minutes as the piano music came out of the speakers. Names of dances started racing through her mind, and she smiled a little, hully gully, frug, twist, the loco-motion, and she remembered having been quite a good dancer back in those days when she wore miniskirts and tight shirts and was willing to fling herself about with abandon. For a time she'd even taken to wearing hot pants. She liked white tights because she'd been told they showed off her legs the best. She owned two halter tops and three work shirts and no bras. She'd been to see the Grateful Dead at the Café au Go Go in the Village, before they were really famous and when Pigpen was in the band. She'd seen the Mothers and Paul Butterfield and Jimi Hendrix's first night in New York after Monterey, when nobody knew who he was. She'd been seeing in a serious way an English major, in fact the very man with whom she had painlessly given up her virginity during an uninspiring and unsuccessful evening on his mattress in an apartment in Amherst. Until then she'd been involved with various high-school and college boys, dry-humping on Friday nights to the hue and cry of Led Zeppelin. They had met at a bookstore in South Hadley and he'd invited her out for a muffin and coffee at the café next door. Dave? Don? Drew? His name escaped her. This man whose slim, shapely penis could still be summoned up from the depths of memory, whose intelligence and humor dazzled and delighted her, was like a man drowning in a distant lake, his body visible, his name unknown.

"Peter was murdered in a hotel room," Jill said, and Michael and Claire remained silent. "He was supposed to meet me for dinner before flying out to London. He went to a horrible hotel in the worst part of the city and he was killed. No one knows why. Nothing makes sense."

"Shh," said Claire, touching Jill's hand.

"I don't even know how he was killed. Isn't that strange? The detective was evasive." She stared at the soup and toyed with its contents with her spoon. "I saw his body, you know," and she looked up at them. "I saw him at the morgue. There was something strange about his neck and head."

"Don't," said Claire.

"I had a dream about him. I dreamed that he went to this room, and I was there also, and someone took out a razor and cut his throat."

"God," said Claire, her hand flying across the table.

"Leave her be," said Michael.

"Cilantro," said Jill, tasting the soup. "This is very nice."

"Good. I'm glad," said Michael.

"It's a recipe we got from a neighbor in France."

"No no, Stephen Spender gave it to me," said Michael.

"Did he?"

Jill poured herself another glass of wine. "I didn't sleep well last night," she said.

"I can give you something for later, if you like," Michael said.

"This is delicious," Jill said, putting her soup aside and pushing solid food onto her plate from the serving dish. "I woke up in the middle of the night and watched some of *A Clockwork Orange*."

"Ah Kubrick. Of course he has much to answer for. The moral

dimension was utterly missing," and Michael said that Anthony
Burgess was furious that Kubrick had not filmed it the way he
had written it, that there was a discrepancy between the American and British editions of the book. "There was a problem with
the ending. Not to mention that the absolutely gratuitous violence is not clearly shown to have a root cause."

"But it was society," said Claire. "That was the whole point.
That's what leads to the Locarno Technique business."

"Ludovico," said Michael.

"At first they thought that Peter had been killed by mistake,
you know, that he had walked into the wrong place and was murdered. But the detective," and Jill sipped wine, "the detective
said that he knew exactly what he was doing, going to the Hubbard. Then he thought it might have been a patient."

"Ah yes," said Michael.

"His name is David Resnick. I like him. He's very kind." She
even missed him a little. He had become something reliable for
her, someone whose steady temperament brought a constant heat
to her life. Yet she had tried hard not to think of him, for to think
of him meant to acknowledge him in various ways. He was someone with whom she might potentially fall in love. Was it his
looks, his manner, the way he spoke to her, the way he used
words? Or would it happen simply because he was there, he had
slipped in under her skin just when she was most vulnerable, as a
virus enters the system when a body is at its weakest? And didn't
love and companionship also imply a future absence, as Peter had
in his turn disappeared from her life?

He also represented the murder of Peter: with his own eyes he
had seen the hotel room as she imagined he must have found it,
with her husband lying in an awkward tumble on the floor in his
grey suit, the pools of blood around and beneath him, a stained
mattress on a steel bed frame, and because he had witnessed this
he possessed more of the truth than she did. Was he holding back
because the investigation required it, or were there things he was
not ready to reveal to her?

In truth she didn't want to think of him because to think of him led to thinking about him on future occasions, when he was not dressed, lying in bed beside her. And because he straddled the two worlds of death and desire he became someone dangerous to her, someone who might bring forth something dark and unseen within her. And yet she toyed with his image in her mind, especially now that she had been drinking, she played with it as a cat dallies with a mouse, with the tips of its claws.

Claire looked at her watch. Michael rose to put on another recording. Jill smiled to herself. "And then the strangest thing happened." She said nothing more. A sense of merriment and gaiety seemed to lighten her body. She thought of Resnick touching her back. She remembered him raking leaves with her, and the memory of it came to her as something intimate and rhythmic and utterly physical.

Michael wandered in musing aloud about another film he had seen about a psychiatrist who was murdering his women patients. Claire stared at him with ferocity while he smiled to himself and babbled, "I believe Michael Caine was in it. The upshot of it was that he was putting on drag and arming himself with a razor. Of course the film was horrible, absolutely terrible. I'm sorry. I shouldn't have mentioned it."

"I remember that. In fact Peter and I went to the movies to see it. There was an opening scene with Angie Dickinson in the shower, masturbating."

"I seem to recall that, too," said Michael, looking at her with surprise.

"Good God, look at the time," cried Claire. "I've got to be at the studio in an hour." She turned to Jill with a look of alarm. "I'm taping a broadcast."

Jill saw at once that it was a lie, and the moment she saw it she realized she had somehow overstepped her bounds as a guest, that she had said and perhaps even done things that would be remembered always, that would become stock tales at the Hollanders' cocktail parties. "I must go," she said. "I'd like to get to sleep a little earlier tonight."

"Come see us again," said Claire.

"I'd be glad to give you a lift to the hotel," Michael said.

"I'd appreciate a drive to the BBC," said Claire.

"I think I'll just take the tube home," Jill said, walking to the door.

"Are you sure?" said Michael, and Claire said, "She'll be fine on her own."

"I'll be fine," said Jill. She kissed Claire on the cheek, and then Michael kissed her and she felt the flat of his hands against her lower back, pressing her very slightly towards him. She said, "I'm sorry I didn't call you. You and Peter were such good friends. It was stupid of me." Claire and Michael said nothing. She shut the door behind her and wondered what they were saying about her, how much of an idiot she had been, how she would never be able to face them again.

The sun on this December afternoon was floating just above the horizon, tight and clear like something ripe. Soon it would grow dark. She walked up to High Street and began to look into shop windows. There were shoes and expensive blouses and novels and necklaces. She had brought traveler's checks and her credit cards, and now she wondered what she might be tempted to buy. There seemed no reason to buy anything at all. To admire herself in a new wardrobe while her husband was in a freshly dug grave seemed heartless to her. Yet that implied that Peter would somehow learn of her misbehavior, that from his distant dwelling place he might reach out and punish her in some way. But she knew better than that, she knew that her husband could be found in any number of places even closer to her: he was in her heart, her mind, and he was always in her conscience.

Twenty minutes later she was waiting in the Underground in a state of remorseful sobriety, holding on to a bag with the sweater she had purchased. She had made a fool of herself, she had dishonored Peter's memory by way of a capricious transaction of ninety-five pounds, and now that she was no longer drunk she began to review the events of the afternoon. She held her hand to her head and tried to recall whether she had actually begun to dance in front of Michael and Claire or had simply imagined it.

Now it was rush hour, and the platform was crowded with a melange of tourists and city dwellers, suitcases jostling with briefcases. She looked at the lighted signboard: it seemed to her a good omen that the train was going to her stop, that she wouldn't have to change at Camden Town. Now things would begin to take a turn for the better. You climbed up the mountain, you sweated and suffered pain, and then you reached the summit and came down a different path, gathering speed, moving with ease. Perhaps she should sell the house and move. She could live in the city, take an apartment near the river, buy season tickets for the symphony, go to film festivals and attend exhibitions at the museums.

All the seats in the train were taken and she had to stand in the middle of the carriage, holding on to the pole. She could move to the city. The drive from there to see Carrie took only twenty minutes, and there was no reason why she couldn't combine a visit to her daughter with her riding. She could hunt on Saturday mornings and then stop to visit Carrie on her way back. Once she had Peter take Carrie to the annual Thanksgiving Day Hunt at Groton House Farm, open to amateurs and experienced riders alike, marked by chaos and accident and frayed tempers. They arrived just after Blackjack had been trailered over by the stable manager, only moments after Jill had mounted up. Blackjack was skittish, bobbing his head, pawing the ground, wondering whom he might kick to death. Jill had spent all the previous day grooming him, combing his mane and tail, braiding him and trimming his whiskers and ears. He looked wonderful, he shone in the misty midmorning sun; in a few hours he would be muddy and soaked in sweat, and she only hoped he would not take a fall or injure himself at a fence. She watched as Carrie stared at her, she said to Peter, "Don't stand too close. There are too many horses out here. And Jack's a little nervous." Carrie's eyes were like those of a person who was about to drown in deep water.

Peter blocked the sunlight with his hand. "What?"

"Get back behind the fence. It's too much for her."

"What?"

She walked Blackjack closer to them and leaned over. Carrie lifted a tentative finger towards the horse's face before whipping her hand behind her back: "Please take her beyond the fence over there. We'll be setting off in a few minutes and it's going to get very busy." She knew that Carrie had caught sight of the doughnut-and-hot-chocolate concession just outside the gate. She herself had settled for a ceremonial swallow of port by way of the owner of her stable, the Secretary of the Hunt, who had trotted up alongside her, glass in hand. "Look at this, for God's sake," she said quietly to Jill. "I mean, really, everybody and her maiden aunt is here. I've already spotted six mounts that aren't sound and at least twenty riders who would be better off sitting at home playing gin rummy. If we survive this nonsense you can come back to my place afterwards and we'll have something a lot stronger than this port."

The hounds arrived and began running here and there between the horses' legs, sniffing the ground, being playful, and then, just before the hunt began, Jill turned to where Carrie and Peter were standing. They still hadn't moved. She waved her hand as if to say Get back, get back, and Peter waved, smiling, and then took Carrie's hand and made it wave in the air. The hunt was about to start and Jill knew what Carrie would feel, how it would affect her, nearly a hundred horses moving off across the field, the ground thundering as their hooves hit the earth. For Jill it had always been a thrilling moment. It had nothing to do with wealth or the fine jackets of the riders or your family's venerable name or how much you paid for your tack; it had everything to do with strength and composure.

She didn't see Carrie's reaction that day, for the moment they started out she was interested in nothing more than staying on her mount, ascending the hill, moving off with the field. The air grew rich with loam and leaves, and these odors mingled with the leather of her saddle, the delicious pungency of her horse. She rose and fell in her saddle as Blackjack broke into a fast and comfortable trot. It was only later, when she returned home, that she discovered Carrie had grown instantly bored with the event, turning and tugging at Peter until he bought her a jelly doughnut and some cocoa.

She would move to the city, then.

She had friends there, mostly from the university. She would meet new people, she would keep busy, she would write her essay on the Plague. In her mind she envisaged the cinemas she would go to, the bookshops she would frequent, the subway lines she would take to get to them. To stay in her house meant that her life of the last thirteen years, the life she had lived with Peter, would continue on without interruption. Everywhere she went she would be accompanied by the tangible presence of his absence. It would linger beside her like a phantom, something weighty and malign, it would lie beside her in bed, sit across from her at meals, whisper fragments of words and obscure phrases, it would quietly whistle the music Peter had always loved. A move away would be an affirmation of a new direction, it would vanquish the ghost and leave her heart refreshed.

She would take long walks in the city, spend Sunday mornings reading the papers at cafés. There were riverside festivals and open-air concerts. She would participate more in the life of the university.

She would be near Resnick; she would be near the Hubbard.

In the city lay the heart of everything.

CHAPTER *16*

She had thought about Dave Resnick so often that afternoon that
she wondered if she should call him, find out how the case was
proceeding, listen to his voice crackle into life three thousand
miles away. She thought of the color of his hair, his small slim
hands, his blue eyes, re-creating him with stunning meticulous-
ness in her mind and then suddenly losing him as she came to
doubt her memory.

She thought too of the photo of his wife on his desk, the way
she had turned to the camera, the sensuous curve of her smile. She
taught third grade at a private school, he'd told her.

She remembered the conversation they'd had when he walked
out of the woods and knocked on her door. She had asked him if
it was his day off, and he said something about if it were his day

off he'd be with his family. This was a man who divided his life in
two, and she pictured a thin steel blade, razor-sharp and reflective, cutting his family off from a life of assault and battery, of
armed robbery, of the swift end of Peter Freytag.

Her head ached with premature hangover, and the glare from
the lights in the train forced her to shade her eyes with her hand.
Her forehead felt moist, and within her was a feeling not of satia-
tion from the meal but of a hollowness that might be associated
with dread. She leaned slightly forward and rested her cheek
against the metal pole. It was warm and slightly greasy from too
many hands. When the train pulled into the next station she
craned her neck to see where she was and only too late realized she
had just then missed her stop. People had gotten off and new people had come to take their places, a great many more people. She
felt a hand or knee pressed up against her buttocks, an elbow beneath her armpit. Whenever the train negotiated a curve, the passengers moved as one, swaying this way and that, passing the
weight from one body to the next. She felt damp and filthy and
wanted nothing more than to shower away the smell of the city,
the horrible events of the day. Now nothing seemed funny, not
the hully gully or the food or the way Michael had so innocently
spoken of Michael Caine as a psychopathic version of Peter.

She twisted her neck to view the tube map over the door. The
stop coming up was Leicester Square. She could either, and she
felt the pressure on her back even more intensely now, she could
either get out and cross over to the other platform to get a north-
bound train or she could leave the station and walk back to the
hotel: the heat and airlessness of the Underground or the fresh
breezes of evening and a solitary walk on damp pavement.

The train began to slow down, and as it did so she started to
mumble excuse me and sorry as she disengaged herself from the
crowd. She realized then that someone had been touching her,
someone in the thickness of the crowd had placed his hand on her
breast, for she had felt something come away from her, something
that had formed a curve around her through her sweater. How

long had it been there? Had the person known her husband had been murdered so recently would he still have treated her like a piece of fruit you might weigh and heft and assess in a market stall? She needed to get away. She had to get away. Run run run. There was no other possible response but to flee, to race towards the escalator, to open herself to the air outside and return to the hotel as quickly as possible. Hold on, someone shouted at her, hold on, hold on, now just a minute, but she pushed and shouldered and found her way out of the crowd and onto the escalator as it moved at its extraordinary angle past the advertising placards and graffiti, Mistress Janet awaits you, Fuck the government, Kill the Queen, Ring Olivia for Colonic Irrigation, Millwall Rules OK, and then she was outside, sucking in the diesel air of central London, the stink and wet of the streets, the blessed stale freshness of the city.

In the city lay the heart of things. People were born there, they married there, they fell into betrayal and then they died, and in the end they came to understand the maze that had been their lives, the corners and dead ends, the secret passages and the disappointments. Would it end? Would it? Hadn't Peter betrayed her by going off to the Hubbard and getting himself killed? Wasn't that what Resnick had all along been saying? Please help us, he had begged her, help us find what drew him to the hotel room. Dig deep into your memory, Ms. Bowman: that's what he had meant. Tell us about the past betrayals, about the times he had walked out on you, stayed late after work, not come home one night, two nights, three.

Jesus, she said quietly as she entered the hotel.

She sat on the edge of her bed and looked in her address book and dialed the number. "It's Jill Bowman," she said when he answered. She pressed her fingers tightly against her scalp and drew them violently through her hair. She looked at her watch: it was just past noon there.

"You're back?"

"I'm still in London."

He said nothing.

"I need to speak to you," she said. "I wish you were here so I could say it to you directly."

"I'm listening to you, Ms. Bowman."

"Peter left me six years ago. Or rather he didn't leave me, he cheated on me." And when she said it she remembered Dennis and his bimbo, and the time she had come home early one wintry Thursday to find them on the bed. She remembered his thrusting body, the way her thighs seemed to take possession of him, the way her body sucked at his. She recalled the noises of their pleasure, the throaty animal moans and sudden gasps. She had stood there for what seemed many minutes, watching them, watching her husband as he slobbered at the other woman's breast.

"He had an affair," Resnick said.

"He was fucking someone else."

The words made him speechless. After a moment he said, "Do you think this has any relevance to the case?"

"I don't know."

"You're saying that if he left once he might have done it again."

"Affairs don't get you murdered, David." It was the first time she'd called him by his name. He had introduced himself to her as Dave and she had called him David, and there was something both intimate and infantile about the way she had chosen the more formal version. She felt like a mother tying her son's tie, brushing his hair, sending him out into the world and begging him to return. Yet by speaking of her husband's infidelity she had stepped over a line that divided her from the detective, she had revealed something immensely personal about herself. She had tried never to speak to anyone of either of her husbands' transgressions, as if by doing so she might somehow reduce the value of herself in others' eyes. When a man cheated on a woman he left behind him soiled goods, faulty merchandise, old trade-ins, all for a weekly visit to the city of gold.

"They do more than you think," he said. "Why are you really calling?"

"Because I feel reassured by you. I didn't realize until I got here how unsteady I am, how much Peter's death has affected me."

Again he said nothing.

"Is there anything new?" she asked.

"The fingerprints we lifted from the room either belonged to your husband or they didn't match up to any we have on the computer," and he seemed to stop short. "Do you feel I need to know about Dr. Freytag's affair?"

"I don't know."

"It snowed here yesterday, you know. Early for the season."

"It was nice here in London. I visited friends. Friends of Peter, really. I was uncomfortable. And then," and she let it drop, the story of the tube ride, the hand cupping her breast, the anonymous sweat of unknown people.

He said, "This is going to cost you a lot of money, Ms. Bowman. Hang up and let me call you back."

She gave him the number as printed on the telephone. "I'm in room 33," she added.

She hung up and sat with her hands folded, her knees slightly apart. She gave off an odor of things that had been discarded, as though she had been curled up in a lost corner of a big city. She took off her shoes and pulled off her sweater. She wanted nothing more than to have a shower, wash her hair, put on clean clothes and have a drink. She thought of the waiter from the evening before. She wondered if he would be there again tonight. She wondered what she might have done had she met him six years earlier. The ringing of the phone startled her, and she clutched the sweater to her chest. Resnick said, "There's something I think you should know. We've been in touch with your former husband in Seattle."

"This has nothing to do with him."

"We need to speak to anyone who might even remotely be

considered a suspect. You understand this, don't you? We just needed to know where he was on the evening in question." He said nothing more.

"What did Dennis say?"

"He was surprised, of course. He was sorry to hear about Dr. Freytag."

"Is he," and she tried to find the correct words, the tactful and strong way to ask.

"Is he still married? Yes, apparently so."

"And he didn't kill Peter."

"He was home on that Friday evening. So that rules out your first husband. But I'm interested in this woman Dr. Freytag knew. Did he actually move out for a period of time?"

"I only knew about it afterwards. He told me when it was over."

"This was six years ago."

"Yes."

"And the name of the woman?"

"I don't know."

"You mean he told you everything but her name?"

"He said she was a patient."

"Do you know if she did this with him willingly?"

"I assumed so. It was very painful for me."

"I can imagine it was."

"I was hurt."

"But you forgave him."

"Peter said that it lasted only a few months. That it was just one of those things."

"One of those crazy things," he said, and she laughed.

"And?" he said after a pause.

"He said they went to bed a few times. More than a few times."

"In her apartment?"

"I don't know."

"In hotels?"

"He never said. Of course I wanted to know all the details. He told me as much as he thought I should know. I didn't have any trouble imagining the rest of it."

"But you didn't know where they would meet."

"They would never have gone to the Hubbard."

"You can't be sure of that."

"They would have gone to a motel."

"There are no rules when it comes to infidelity."

"It was what he told me. He said they went to motels. They met outside the city. There are motels there which cater to adulterers. They have waterbeds and adult videos and mirrored ceilings." For one vertiginous moment she recaptured the pain of those months, the nausea of a sudden descent, the ruins that had become her life.

"Was he still treating her at the time of his death?"

She'd never thought about it. He had said it was over, that he had asked her to go to another psychiatrist. He had spared Jill nothing. The details were served willingly to her. He had spoken of his lover's youthful beauty, her perfect figure, her firm breasts, his inability to resist her. What did she have that Jill didn't possess; what could she do that Jill didn't do? Together Jill and Peter had grown adventurous in bed, they tried new things. Within the realm of the painless they went to the edge. Suddenly Jill said to Resnick: "She was an actress. Or a dancer."

"Are you sure?"

"Is it important?"

"Maybe. Maybe not. What makes you think she was a dancer or an actress?"

"Because Peter told me. He said she had been a performer. He didn't say in what. But he said something about her legs. That she was known for them."

"She could have been a model."

"I suppose so."

"She could have been a stripper."

She said nothing.

"Why did it come to an end?"

"Peter said it was because this woman wanted to marry him. And he wasn't willing to leave me."

"He just wanted a little fling, then."

"That's what he told me."

"And she became more involved with him than he'd counted on."

"I guess that's right," she said. "You can catch all sorts of things when you sleep with a stranger."

"And since then?"

"Everything's been fine. We went together for counseling. He grew more serious, but everything else was fine."

"And the sex?"

She said, "It was good."

"Nothing different about it?"

"What does this have to do with Peter's death?"

"Nothing different about it?"

"Not really, no."

"Was he more adventurous?"

"A little, maybe."

She heard a page being turned and imagined a sheet of yellow paper curling in the light of the midday sun as this lurid story from her past became a series of penciled lines on a legal pad. The words she had spoken had gone straight into Resnick's mind, they became yet another aspect of the person known to him as Jill Bowman. She wondered how he thought of her; she remembered how he looked at her. The sun shone on him while beyond her window night was falling, a vast starless shadow over an ancient city.

"Tell me something about this woman. Was she from this area?"

"I think so. I'm not sure."

"Do you know if she was married?"

"He never said so."

She could hear him taking notes, repeating words and phrases to himself. He said, "Do you know how long he treated her for?"

"I told you. He never brought his work home with him. Everything was confidential."

"Your husband was a real professional, then."

"Yes, that's right."

"Except when it came to women."

There seemed no point in defending him.

"Why didn't you tell this to me before you left?"

"I've never talked to anyone about it, David."

"It didn't come to mind when you learned your husband had been murdered?"

"I didn't see the connection."

"I'll have another look through Dr. Freytag's records. What you've told me just now may be helpful in our investigations. When do you think you'll be back?" Now she could hear it, the interest that lay over his words like a summer haze, shimmering and ghostlike, something potential, heat lightning riding up from the western horizon.

"I'm not sure. I'd been thinking about going to Paris." Again they came back to her, a street, a shadow, things elusive. "I think I'll stay here for a while." And she felt memory slide quietly away from her, like the sea withdrawing from the smoothness of sand.

"And then home?"

"Of course."

"And then?"

"I suppose I'll try to work on my essay." She was about to mention her plans to move, then thought better of it.

"I look forward to seeing you."

"I," and she smiled. "I'll call you when I get back."

Now things were different. The weight of the day seemed to lift from her back, and her headache, the piercing focused pain of the afternoon, was beginning to fade. She stretched her arms and opened her hands. She gazed out the window as she slipped out of her trousers. Her room was still dark and the light outside was a strange grey.

She stood under the shower, passing her hands through her

shampooed hair, letting the hot water strike her skin until she felt herself growing tired. She had an entire evening ahead of her and nothing planned. She was in London, there were plays to be seen, and so far she had done almost nothing for her own pleasure. She dried herself and wrapped the towel around her shoulders. She stood before the mirror, in the white glare of the bathroom lights. In the brilliance her body looked alert, more firm. She rubbed her hair with the towel and let it drop to the floor. She stepped back until she could see most of herself. It was strange thinking of all those years ago, of Drew or Dave or Don and how they had met. Little details returned to her: the table they had shared in the café next to the bookshop, the ring he wore from his private school in Connecticut.

She switched on the hair dryer and vigorously pulled the brush through her hair as she turned her head this way and that, her eyes always fixed upon herself. Now her sobriety was absolute: the giddiness and panic of hours earlier had disappeared completely. Had it been merely a by-product of passing time, or had her conversation with Resnick, her confession of a betrayed woman, caused this sense of well-being?

What had happened to him, this lovely boy she had first slept with in Amherst? Was he teaching somewhere, was he writing, had he made something of himself, and did he ever think of her? To forget someone is to let that person die. There were some people she thought of at least briefly each day, her mother, her father, Rose Keller, Greg, and even Dennis, who in the beginning, when they were first married, was the wisest and most pleasurable man she had ever known—each passed through her mind in a sudden noisy blur, a reminder of what she once had possessed and lost. Now Peter would join them. Once the pain had diminished, once she had come to understand that his return was impossible, his face, his voice and touch would become a memory printed upon her life.

And how was she in the memories of those still alive? Younger, certainly; prettier: someone who had not lived through the tragedy of her husband's murder, someone who could not foretell the future, as those who sat by phones, tarot in hand, were paid to do.

In the mirror she was a forty-two-year-old woman, attractive, nicely built, intelligent. She was certainly a better lover than she had been fifteen or twenty years earlier. And as she looked at herself she suddenly realized that the years of her life had passed as if in a dream, with excessive brevity and speed, and that one day, when she was eighty, she would stand before a similar mirror and think of all those she had lost. Would Peter's name escape her, would he become Phil or Patrick, or would he, as she stood staring at her sagging breasts and wrinkled flesh, at the useless unalluring parts of her that had so drawn him to her, return to her with a youthful vividness that would bring her up short? Would he then become an anchor to these closing years of her younger self, someone who though gone would keep her in her prime, make the best years of her life last forever?

For her Peter would always be standing in the kitchen, speaking of his trip to London, lightly touching her hip as he turned to kiss her. At seven, then, he would be saying. At seven. At seven. At seven.

Her hair was dry. Deodorant had been rolled onto her armpits. Too late she ran her fingers along her calf and thigh and was pleased to see she hadn't needed to shave her legs. Tomorrow night. Tomorrow morning. She walked naked into the bedroom and pulled the curtains shut before switching on a lamp. She dabbed a little perfume onto her neck, on the shadow between her breasts, and began to dress.

When she came down to the restaurant off the lobby about half the tables were occupied. Her waiter from the evening before showed her to a table, a considerably better one than the night before. He said, "You see? You have a view of the square." The greenery had already begun to blend in with the night. It was like staring into a wall, or the depths of the sky.

She realized that he had an accent she hadn't really noticed before. As if trying to guess his origins she looked at him, she smiled and tilted her head.

"Is everything all right?"

"You're not English?"

He laughed.

"French?"

"No no, I'm Greek actually. I've lived here for many years."

It was as if her recognition of his foreignness had liberated his tongue. Now she could hear the accent, thick and Mediterranean, as he spoke a little of his background. She thought of Michael and Claire and their adventure in the Hampstead restaurant with the uncomprehending waiter from Athens, the way he had stared at them, secretly laughing as they turned his language into nonsense.

"I trained as a gymnast. I was hoping to go into the Olympics," the waiter was saying. His eyes shifted here and there, up and down, as though out of shyness.

She didn't know what to say. She didn't know what to believe. Was it a line, a hook thrown into her heart that would lead him to her bed? His history insinuated a body in perfect physical shape. From what she could see of him, his black hair, dark eyes, olive skin and long fingers, her imagination stripped him bare, constructed his body from the evidence at hand. His eyes fixed her. His voice was like a silken sheet. Men were never what they said they were or what they seemed to be, they were experts in duplicity and artfulness. *Take me for what I am:* she had heard that one more than once. And what face did she put forward, how was she perceived? She thought herself an honest person, someone who had no reason to hide aspects of her personality. She was exactly what she seemed to be, and she smiled to herself, for she sounded no different from the men she had met. Now she had outgrown the desire only for physical beauty, for the handsome face and lean body.

She ordered a vodka on the rocks and watched him walk off.

She began to feel the urge to take a risk, to toy a little with the unknown, as if the act might erase the excruciating sadness of the past weeks. How far could you go, how many steps could you take before shadow turned into night, and night into death? She considered how the evening might unfold, the clarity of it stunning in its predictability, and yet she also felt something shift a little in her body. Sometimes sexual desire was based on a certain person and sometimes it was unspecific yet necessary, an itch that required scratching, a desire simply to be held and touched by someone. At its heart lay something dangerous and fatal, and this was another reason why she missed Peter: the familiarity and safety of him, the way she could give herself totally to him and emerge unscathed, unscarred, satisfied. She could fuck the waiter and in the morning take a taxi to the airport, return to the safety of her suburban house three thousand miles away. She could go out into the streets, to the pubs and cafés and restaurants, she could roam the cinemas of London, slither from neon flicker to alleyway, she could find men, anonymous voiceless lovers, and each encounter would leave her wanting more. Would she then have lost her identity as Jill Bowman, Professor Bowman, scholar and teacher, equestrienne, decent neighbor, loving mother, and would she then become something loose and dangerous, always one step away from the end of herself, from the fatal encounter that she knew was waiting for her, just as it had waited all those years for Peter?

Or she could refuse it, she could walk away from it. She could return to her routine of her life, the regularity of meals and coffee breaks, of papers to read and grade, of books to consult and department meetings on Thursday afternoons. She could rake leaves and weed her garden and rent interesting films on weekend evenings. She could live alone with her cat, the castrato Hector with his white face and black mask, an aging awkward beast full of thwarted desires and unrealized dreams.

The waiter brought her the drink. She found herself asking his name, and he said it was Nicholas, though he was known to his friends as Nikos. She tried it: Nico? Nikos, he said, simply that, just Nikos will do. She regretted having asked his name, it was a gesture that could be interpreted as the first step in a quick seduction, the sort of thing done in bad films in smoky bars filled with floozies and wiseguys. She wondered if she should reveal her own to him: it seemed to her an even more intimate and brazen thing to do, as if in those four letters there might be found a hidden message of invitation and promise. She could call herself Delores. Or Sally. Helena. Virginia. Hillary. Or even Sandra.

She didn't know what to say. She smiled and nodded, as if the name rang a bell in her mind, or had a special meaning for her. Without Peter her nerves were nothing. "That's nice," she said, for reasons unknown. "Nikos. Nice to meet you."

"Good to meet you, Mrs. Bowman."

Of course he had looked it up, he had made inquiries, he was interested, and now he made her aware of it. Once again she wanted to flee, to fly away from the hotel, turn away from the edge of possibility. She was in no mood for little dramas between her sheets; she would find the sounds of it unbearable, the touch painful. This was not why she had come to London, why she had left her home and flown for seven hours. This was meant to be a way to forget things, to cast memory aside, to shed the skin of her forty-two years.

"Are you all right?" he asked, bowing a little as if to have a better look. In a split second he took in the shape of her breasts.

"I'm fine," she said. "I'll have the salmon. And the rice. And I'd like a small salad."

"A bottle of wine, perhaps? A half-bottle?"

"I'll have another vodka, thanks."

No. She wasn't all right. It had been like a whisper, an undertone, something lingering and uneasy that had troubled her throughout the day, that hid in the depths of her throat and skittered about her lungs. Was she ill, had she somehow contracted food poisoning? She wondered if she should call Michael and Claire to see if they were well. She thought of Stephen Spender's soup recipe. She imagined the two of them lying on their living-room floor, their bodies contorted, their faces green, tongues swollen and extended, all their appointments and television appearances broken and meaningless, and the image, melodramatic and comical, made her smile a little.

She felt as though she was definitely coming down with something. She was tired and warm and what seemed at first to be hunger came to her in waves as malaise and decline. But this always happened to her when she visited London: between the overheated shops and the damp beyond the door, the sudden changes in weather and the uncertain quality of the food, she was bound to catch something. Her symptoms were vague; it was more a feeling, a sensation, an odd distancing effect, as though a veil, a web of cloud had come between her and the world. Possibly this was nothing more than a physical reaction to Peter's death, to the disorder and sadness of the previous days. By flying to London she had tried to forget herself, to walk stealthily away from her past, as if to shed a layer of skin. Instead she continued to run into herself, indistinct and edgeless in shop windows, clear and vivid in mirrors, her mind brimming with memory and concern, past and future.

Now things would change. She had had enough of herself. That night she would see if she could get a ticket for a play, or perhaps see a film. Tomorrow she would go to a museum, buy Carrie some toys at Hamleys on Regent Street. There were postcards to send. She would go to Liberty and Harrods and Harvey Nichols and buy herself some new clothes. There was no reason why she should have to deny herself such pleasures.

Nikos brought her a second drink. He smiled as he set it on the table and she watched his hands as he clasped them in front of him: slim hands, delicate long-fingered hands, the hands of a musician or dancer, made to sketch moods in the air, to direct and deny, to lift and set down. Quietly he said, "How long are you in London for?" His tone was intimate and the words came quickly from him, as if he were engaging in an act of espionage.

She looked up at his face. "I'm not sure."

"You find it changed since you were last here?"

"More American," and she smiled.

"Is that good, then?"

"I live in America. When I come to Britain I want British."

He smiled and walked briskly away towards the kitchen. Now the restaurant was almost full. Other couples, many Americans, sat at their tables, slightly bewildered by jet lag and uncertainty, busy converting pounds into dollars. She had always been a good traveler. Flight agreed with her, and when she landed she somehow adjusted to the pace and rhythm of a city. She knew how to comport herself in London and Paris, in Montreal and Moscow and Munich and Berlin. She had done it in Amsterdam and Copenhagen and Bruges. She knew what to look at and what to avoid, how to be gracious and when to say no. She spoke enough French and Italian and even a little German to make herself understood where those languages were spoken. But now she felt as though something in the world had changed, that at some recent point in her life things had shifted slightly away from her, to a different angle, and she had not yet been able to adapt to it.

The waiter returned with a tray. He set the salmon and salad down before her. He stood and waited for a moment. Without looking up she thanked him.

"A glass of wine?"

"No thank you."

"Another drink?"

She looked at him. "No. No thank you."

He walked across the room and, pretending to busy himself with sugar bowls and creamers, watched her.

At a nearby table a woman and a man were drinking coffee and smoking cigarettes. The woman spoke quietly, rapidly, almost under her breath, and then the man reached forward and touched the woman's hand, gently, with a clutching movement, taking the breath from her, and Jill felt more alone than she yet had since Peter's death. This small act, this intimate gesture, made her feel her loss more acutely than the big sweeping generosities of those who attended the funeral, or the easy words and inept distances of Michael and Claire.

She envied this young couple, she coveted their future together, the hours that lay before them. Undoubtedly it would not last; her sense of a future had been reduced to the word itself, to something abstract and ungraspable. Things come and then are taken away, and sometimes they step back and remain just out of reach, tantalizing, taunting you simply by existing. David Resnick was like that. He was there and not quite there, he was hers and yet he belonged to someone else, and the moment she thought of it she felt ashamed of herself: as if someone could belong to another person, as though possession were a literal affair in matters of love. When she was younger she had always been willing to meet people, to make friends, to give herself to others. Now she feared the stranger's reach, the gentleman's words, the soft smile; now all the lessons of childhood made sense: don't accept candy, don't get into an unfamiliar car, don't wander off. Because they will tie you up, hold you down, reach for the blade, hasten the night.

The smell of food nauseated her. She picked at the salmon and put some in her mouth. She could tell it was fresh and properly cooked. It stuck in her throat and she washed it down with some vodka. Had she been at home she would have offered it to Hector, and in her mind she saw him flinging the meal with a flick of his paw, leaping to it, devouring it with feline certitude before it had even finished scattering to the floor. She took a mouthful of rice and a little salad, and things were better for the moment. She seemed to have lost all interest in food; what had once been pleasurable had become a chore, a necessity, as if she were forced to swallow medicine three times a day. She set down her fork and drank a little more vodka. Now she could define it. It felt as if something in her life were impending, an exam, an appointment, something frightening and unknown which had set itself in the days of her future. This was the feeling of nerves: it lay within her stomach like a bowl of something stewing, roiling and steaming, thick and unpalatable.

It was a familiar mood, in fact a version of it came monthly, just before her period, as if in those moments of percipience she could discern within herself a murderess named Jill, coldblooded and trigger-happy in a world of eggshells and stained glass and the pearl-hued complexion of saints.

She took a few more bites of the salmon and regretted having ordered it. Now Nikos would stroll over and inquire with solicitous hand wringing if the fish had not been cooked to her taste, if he should summon the chef with his white hat and waxed mustache, or even a doctor, someone hastily dragged from his surgery to tend this nauseated American woman. She remembered only once before having had a feeling as intensely and frighteningly oppressive as this seemed to be. A year after she and Dave, Don or Drew had broken up, she had become involved with a man named Geoff who worked locally as a restorer of stringed instruments. Between them there had been a succession of lovers, boys from her historical theory class, or those who chatted her up outside lecture halls and in the student unions, over coffee and cherry pie. She hadn't looked for involvement; love went unsought.

She had met Geoff at a bar where students and townies mixed in a haze of benevolent inebriation. She and a friend would occasionally go there, drink beer, listen to the music. Even their teachers, mostly from the English and philosophy faculty, could be found at the bar, bleary-eyed and grinning as they eyed the girls and bitched about tenure, drowning their failed hopes and wasted dreams in cheap pitchers of beer.

He'd been playing eight ball at the pool table in the back of the room. There was something elegant and feline about his body as it moved swiftly around the table, as it bent and curved, as his fingers held the stick and his eyes fixed his target. He wore jeans and a black T-shirt, and when he stooped to take a shot a lock of hair would fall over one eye. She wanted to take him in hand, comb his hair, launder his clothes, as if he were an animal requiring domestication. He had seen her too, sitting on the stool, her legs crossed, she could see it in his eyes as they lifted slightly from the point on the cue ball and met hers. It had become a game, the sport of crossed looks and silent signals, of intentions real and assumed.

She had seen him before: walking down the street, at concerts or the movies, and yet she knew she probably hadn't ever laid eyes on him. He had simply stepped into an idea that had always lurked in the shadows and alleyways of her mind: a type, a face, a body she had always liked. That night a certainty had come into her life. Looking at him, watching him look at her, she knew that she would be with this man forever; that her life, which until then had proceeded in predictable ways—home, high school, college, like a mathematical progression that could be continued with regularity, obeying the laws of some high invisible power, would begin now to move to the rhythm of her heart. It would be a time of farewells and shut doors. Her future, so carefully laid out for her, graduate school, a lectureship, publications, would dissipate like the smoke of his cigarette. Her parents would rage and stamp, they would make calls and touch heads with psychologists and advisors. But she knew precisely where she would be going.

She knew it then and she felt the thrill of change. Things would be different. Yes.

When she went to the bar for another beer she felt him beside her and when she turned he smiled at her and stuck a Marlboro between his lips. Without thinking she pushed the hair away from his eyes.

He drove a battered Chevy pickup. The house he rented was in the country, where academia gave way to farmland and woods, and where the valley that held them all became a great cleft cutting through the hills. "It gets foggy here at night," he said. "Sometimes it comes in so thick you can't see the lines in the road." He spoke in the cadences of a folk song. He turned and smiled until his eyes narrowed and creased. "You're a student."

"How could you tell?"

"Everybody's a student around here."

"You're not."

And in the darkness of this clear night he touched her knee. She could feel each joint of each finger delineated and muscular as his hand moved up her thigh. The skin of her body grew tense, things tingled, dampened, swelled.

"Where are you taking me?"

"Home. Not so far from here. It's not bad. I share a place with a couple of people. But at least we all have our own room. It's cheap. It's not bad."

She tried to remember him in detail now, as she sat in the hotel restaurant, looking at the salmon at which she could only pick, the rice and salad she would force herself to eat, she tried to recapture, even for a moment, how she had felt that night when he had taken his clothes off, when she had laid her hands on him, touching him everywhere as though in disbelief, and when he had parted her legs and pressed himself to her: a long moment of suspension, when breath and beat had ceased to matter, and time had lost its meaning. It was the beginning of what was to be the end of illusion, the shattering of dreams.

The next day he had taken her to the workshop in town above the real estate office and had shown her the guitars he was about to repair with their inlaid fingerboards and varnished necks. It was an impossibly romantic profession, one linked to the ancient guilds, to the dark workshops of the Gothic, or the Renaissance studios with their clarity of light and sound. Yet he looked upon it as a job, a dead end, a way to earn a minimum wage without physical exertion or intellectual engagement. He was a man without ambition or object, who, as if myopic, was unable to see what lay in the distance.

Now she could remember very little about him. She recalled his looks, his lean thighs and hairless chest, his muscularity, his perfect shoulders, and they no longer moved her. He had been a clumsy lover, awkward and ungentle, quick to finish. Yet at the time he became everything in the world, he was like a bright exploding sun, its light and blaze blinding her to the things of earth.

Now he had nearly disappeared from her memory, he had become sucked into the event that had destroyed her love for him, as if into some tremulous galactic warp where dimensions counted for nothing, and past and future were noises without meaning. She had probably become pregnant that night, or perhaps the next time they had gone to bed. She had been off the pill for nearly a year: it had given her chronic headaches and sudden pains in her chest, and her doctor at the college clinic had told her to throw them away. On a plastic cross-sectioned vagina he showed her how to use a diaphragm, sticking his hairy fingers up the lurid canal with its painted veins and indistinct muscles. He suggested she augment the device with foam and condoms. Before then her lovers usually withdrew from her, spewing their seed onto her stomach and breasts, or into her mouth, or even on her hair, where it grew sticky and then stiff, and smelled like decaying cod.

She came up to his workshop on a Thursday afternoon. He was resetting frets into the neck of a Gibson. He said James Taylor had dropped it off hours earlier. She said, "I'm pregnant." It had no connection to the astonishing pleasure she had experienced with him.

He looked at her with bafflement.

"I just got the results of the test back."

His hair hung in his eyes as he bent over the workbench, and she didn't bother to fix it.

"What are we going to do?"

He shrugged. "That's up to you, isn't it? I mean, it's," and she said, "It's up to us."

"Us."

"You and me. It's your child, too."

"Yeah."

"What's that supposed to mean?"

He stopped his work. Quietly he said, "Let's go someplace and talk."

They went down the narrow stairway and out onto the street. They crossed and went into the luncheonette. The conversation came back to her now with amazing clarity, as those who have suffered the shock of a natural disaster or the assassination of a beloved leader will forget not a single detail surrounding it. Old men sat smoking at the counter, grumbling and scratching. The waitress came over and Jill ignored her. On the radio a war was being fought and newsmen spoke of it as if giving a lecture in statistics. Geoff ordered tuna on rye, a side of French fries, a Coke. She stared at him. Within her was something that was growing larger every day, something that contained a part of this man now so blithely eating his lunch. She thought of the fetus, coiled and wormlike, and she remembered seeing photographs of them in *Life* magazine, haunted creatures in the cathedral glow of a womb. "I don't want it," she said. "I want to get my degree and go to graduate school. I don't want to sit around changing diapers."

He looked at her. "How can you be sure it's mine?"

"Because I haven't fucked anyone else since I met you."

"That's what you say."

"Don't you believe me?"

He lit a cigarette and blew smoke from his nostrils. In bed he'd called her Cinnamon Girl. "I've heard that line before."

"What am I going to do?"

His shoulders lifted and fell. He was full of shrugs, and now that they had come to this moment, this warm afternoon in a greasy luncheonette, she realized that whatever life might have bestowed on him had toppled to the ground and shattered.

"Have an abortion."

"It's not so easy. It's not legal, you know. Are you going to help pay for it?"

He laughed and said that she knew very well he hadn't any money. She thought of how he reluctantly pulled wrinkled bills from his jeans pocket when he filled the truck at the Texaco station, or borrowed two or three dollars from her every time they went out for a beer or hamburger.

He looked away. His nerves showed in his callused hands, the way they moved and shook, the way his fingers gripped the cigarette. "What if you're just saying this? What if you're not pregnant? I told you before, I don't ever want to get married."

"You think I'm tricking you."

"I don't know what to think. All fucking women are the same."

"Look at me. Look at me, damn you."

His face showed nothing but indifference. She looked at him for a moment and her humiliation was complete. "Don't you even care?"

"I care," he said. "I care."

"Then help me."

"I don't have any money."

"Help me get some money."

He shrugged again as if he were shedding water after a quick swim. "I don't know anyone with money."

She rose and walked out of the restaurant. She wondered how he was going to pay for his lunch.

Through a friend of a friend she found a doctor from Boston who performed abortions for a flat $450, no questions asked. She couldn't call her parents. Instead she borrowed the money from ten different people and took the bus to Park Square. Without thinking she began the long walk towards the big Citgo sign, past the joke shop with its whoopee cushions and rubber vomit, the drug store, the tobacconist. She went alone, and only when the car pulled up to where she had been told to wait for it, by the record store in Kenmore Square, did she realize that her life was no longer her own, that for the next hour or so it would belong to others, to the hands of strangers, and now as she looked back on this she thought of Peter in a hotel room, being taken in by amiable people who would strip him of his life.

When she got into the car a woman wearing a soft pink woolen hat told her to lie down on the backseat. The woman got in beside her and covered her over completely with a grey blanket. "Hand me the money. We don't go until I've counted it. You understand why I'm doing this, don't you? We have to protect ourselves."

Jill took the roll of bills from her bag and held it out in the air. The woman took it from her and counted it. Quietly and gently she said, "Don't look up. Don't take the blanket off until I tell you to."

The driver turned the key and Jill felt the car move slowly forward. "Where are we going?"

"Don't be scared."

"Where are you taking me?"

"Don't be frightened."

No one knew where she was. Now her life would change forever. She would not spend her days in Geoff's rustic hideaway, listening to Neil Young records and watching him play eight ball. She would not drink beer in his funky kitchen and play native to his missionary. She would go somewhere strange and be left to die. She would bleed to death on a plastic tablecloth in a kitchen reeking of Lysol and fried chicken, and the police would find her, thighs spread, eyes open, drained white. She wanted her mommy and daddy more than anything in the world, and she said so, she cried it into the blanket, and one of the women must have misunderstood her, for she said that this had nothing to do with God, that what she was going to do was her choice. The woman repeated it so often, in so many different ways, that it seemed as if the law had endowed her words and phrases, the little formulae of critical encounters and criminal standoffs, with the magic of immunity.

They drove for what seemed to be about twenty minutes. She remembered there was a time they were on a quiet, clear road, with no traffic lights or sounds of other cars. Then they came into a town or another part of the city. "The doctor works out of a house," the woman said to her. He doesn't live there and he doesn't have an office there. Nothing's going to hurt, okay? Okay?"

"Okay," she said into the blanket.

"I'll stay with you the whole time."

"And then it'll be over?"

"It'll be over."

The woman helped her out of the car and Jill saw they were inside a garage. The driver of the car, another woman, small and chubby and masculine, opened the door that led into the house. They walked through the kitchen into the living room. Jill took in everything. The painting over the fireplace was of a child. There were framed school photos of a girl, gap-toothed and smiling before an indistinct azure background. The television was built into a console. The photo on the cover of the *TV Guide* was of Archie Bunker looking querulous. An open bag of Oreos was on the coffee table. "The doctor's waiting in the guest room," and the woman pointed towards another door.

"How long?"

"No more than fifteen minutes."

"I meant how long will it take?"

"Just as I said."

Jill looked at her. She wondered how they were going to do it in such a short period of time. The woman told her to wait and went into the other room. The shorter woman switched on the television and lit a cigarette. Sheriff Taylor was looking at Deputy Fife, whose eyes were bulging because he had locked himself in a cell. Jill watched with alarmed interest, the light in the room, the sunlight coming through the windows, blinding her. Oh Barney Barney, said Andy, shaking his head. Her mouth went dry and her memory went blank. She was going to have an abortion. She had fallen for a man in a bar and now she was going to have something cut out of her. A story had gone around college about a girl named Stephanie Gabriel who'd gone home to Baltimore one Thanksgiving, had an abortion in New Jersey, and didn't return to school. It was thought that she had not survived the ordeal, or that instead of going through with it had fled to Mexico. No one bothered to call or write her parents. Save in the imagination of her friends she had ceased to exist, and the wound of her absence quickly closed and healed over in the tight little community of Mount Holyoke College.

Somehow she had managed to finish the salmon. The rice had been overcooked and lay on her plate like the early stages of a city sidewalk. She had eaten half her salad. This was a memory she had always shunned, physically turning aside from it whenever something, a sound, a piece of music, an odor or an uttered word, summoned it from her past. She remembered how the doctor wore a white surgical mask and black-rimmed glasses so that he remained in a state of sanitary anonymity. He pulled on latex gloves while she took off her jeans and panties and lay down on the bed. It was covered only in a quilted mattress pad. For a moment he gazed down at her. For a moment she thought he might comment on her appearance, about how pretty it was, what a nice bit of snatch she had. The woman who had sat with her in the car handed him a length of rubber tubing. He squeezed a little lubricating jelly onto his fingers and smeared the end of the tube with it, then inserted his fingers into her, spreading her apart, and the noise of the action was of something being sucked. "Just relax," he said, pressing his fingers into the tender flesh of her thigh.

"What is it?"

"Just a piece of surgical tubing."

She felt it snaking up inside her, tickling and irritating, and she moved her hips this way and that. Nothing made any sense. An abortion meant that something was being taken away, and yet the doctor was pushing something inside her. The woman with the woolen hat gently touched Jill's forehead with her fingers. Quietly she said, "Everything will be all right." The doctor was pushing something inside her, not taking anything away. The doctor was sticking something inside her. The doctor was inserting some tubing. She said it over and over again in her mind, trying to understand why it was happening, why he was putting things inside her.

"It's over," he said, walking out of the room. She heard him ascending the stairs, and she heard footsteps overhead, the creaking of old wood.

The woman with the pink woolen hat stood over her. "We'll take you back to Boston now."

Yet she could still feel the thing inside her, and she wondered whether a mistake had taken place, if by accident the doctor had overlooked something. She put her hand between her legs and felt the end of the tube sticking out from her. This is what $450 got you: a piece of rubber up your twat. The woman said, "In a few days it'll come out."

"What?"

"In a few days you'll have your abortion."

"You mean it's not over?"

"It's begun but it's not over."

"It's just a rubber tube."

"It's going to irritate the lining so you'll discharge it all by yourself. There may be a little pain." The woman pressed a tube of pills into her hand. "Take these only if you need them."

"It's not over."

"Get dressed, we have to get back to town."

"But it'll fall out."

"Not if you're careful it won't."

"But I don't understand."

It wasn't the fact that she was going to end the life within her that so unnerved her. It was that something foreign had been placed within her by people she neither knew nor trusted, that someone had interfered with the chambers of her body. She lay under the blanket and listened to the intermittent small talk of the two women, and the songs that came from the car radio. She didn't know then that not one of those songs would ever sound the same again, that Janis Joplin and Eric Clapton and Fleetwood Mac would forever be linked to what had happened that day, that hearing them on someone else's radio or in a record store, even twenty years later, would bring to mind the smell of the house, Deputy Fife's bulging eyes, the face of Archie Bunker, an open bag of Oreos, the feel of surgical tubing inside her.

When she got off the bus in Amherst she waited for a shuttle to Mount Holyoke. It was February and bitterly cold, and she waited inside the bookshop. She looked at everything and nothing. She grew angry and she bit the inside of her cheek until she could taste blood. She considered calling the police, reporting these thieves who had taken her money for nothing. She realized it would be like stealing from a bank robber and complaining because there was nothing smaller than a fifty or a hundred. Geoff's shop was just two doors down, over the real estate office. She could go up there and tell him what had happened. She could take off her jeans and panties right there in the middle of the place, she could show him the inch of tubing that stuck out of her, and he would shrug and repair another guitar. She thought of names for him, cocksucker, prick, scumbag, nothing seemed strong enough for this man who had treated her like shit, or rather not like shit, because at least you dispose of shit, you send it sailing out of your sight. He treated her as though she weren't even there. A face in the crowd. Just another piece of ass. She pressed her fingernails into her palm and hoped to draw blood. She wanted to kill Geoff, she wanted to kill him slowly, she wanted to force him to lie naked on a table and invade his body with things not of this world, she wanted to shove objects down his throat, to make incisions in his stomach and fill him with garbage, and she knew that were she to do it he would say nothing, he might even doze off, because nothing ever bothered him. His life would go on as before, he would play eight ball and drink beer and pick up girls and use the same tired lines on them, talking with folksy sincerity of his simple life where dreams didn't exist and the future was just another day.

Now things were different for her, just as they had been after Rose Keller had died. It was like trying to look out of a window and suddenly finding that one curtain had suddenly been lifted and a little light could come through. Now another one had been taken off, just as after Carrie had been born and she and Dennis were divorced yet another was swept away. Peter's death had removed them all. The window was clear. Now it was night. "Thank you," she said to the waiter, and walked out of the restaurant.

CHAPTER *17*

She had told David Resnick she was too old to start again. But it wasn't true. All that had been before was now gone. Forty-two years. She would have to start again, or she would be forced to give up. Going back to zero and beginning afresh: that was how it felt. None of her experiences, her abortion, her marriage, her miscarriages, Carrie's birth, Peter's murder, seemed to have prepared her for what lay ahead. It was as if everything she had learned had been proved wrong. Things would have to be done differently now. She felt a sudden heat in her heart, in her throat and head, and she touched her forehead and felt the damp tight skin across it. She would move to the city. She would move to the city with Hector and things would be different, and the thought of it made her anxious to return, to pack her belongings in boxes and await the movers, to turn her back on the house and leave it forever. What had begun as a whim became a certainty in her mind, and in her imagination her house was as empty as it had been the day she and Peter had first looked at it thirteen years earlier.

The previous owners had moved out a month before, and the broker was apologetic as she showed them through the barren curtainless rooms, sunshine glaring off the polished wood floors. As she and Peter walked through the structure, up the stairs and into the bedrooms, footsteps echoing in the hollow corridors, she was somehow able to see them beginning life there, and that this would alter forever the course of their lives and those they touched. Because it was new she had imagined Carrie getting better and moving into the room next to theirs. After a few years she would let her pick out wallpaper, and together they would hang mobiles and a bulletin board. There would be a desk in the corner, and bookshelves, and on her bed, ranked along the pillow, would be her collection of stuffed animals, the kittens and skunk and chipmunk and dolphin and the three teddy bears. She shut the door to the room and looked at it, touched the pale painted wood. Carrie would grow there, she would achieve height and weight, and the features of her face would gain definition and beauty. She thought of herself ten or eleven years hence, knocking lightly, calling her daughter for dinner while she listened to music or talked on the phone to school friends. She imagined waking her for school, or coming upon her reading in the corner on a Sunday afternoon. For a year the room remained empty. Jill would not allow it to be used for storage. Then she decided to turn it into an office, where she could sit at her computer and work, and look out the window onto the view that rightfully belonged to Carrie.

She would have preferred never to have set foot in it again.

She was glad she hadn't pursued Nikos, hadn't encouraged him to go wandering through the corridors of the hotel, looking for her room, tapping lightly, begging for admission. Yet his in-

terest in her meant she was still attractive, as women in mourning are fabled to be. What was it about them? Were they wan
and vulnerable, easily bedded, or did they have about them an air
of having survived great cataclysms, walking from the quake, the
fire, the wreckage, and therefore wrapped in history? Was it
something sexual perhaps, did they exude an irresistible odor, the
stink of rut, a scent of the forbidden? Or did it lie somewhere in
between, were they perceived as drowning in the depthless solitude of their lives and thus eager to submit to the gentle words
and groping hands of the first available man?

There was something forbidding about Nikos, something
about him that reminded her of Geoff, and she realized it was
that which had brought back all those memories. That and the
way she had felt: a fatal combination. The waiter's charm and
confident manner, the slightly boyish way he looked at her, the
little shy uncertainties of his gestures, were the same qualities
that had attracted her to Geoff. Since then she had always found
herself drawn to men like him: attracted but now aware of the
dangers. Dennis had been just the opposite; Peter different in his
own way. None was like the other; yet she had lost them all.

She had thought about going to a play that night at the Barbi-
can and yet after dinner ended up in bed, lying very still and
watching television. A woman at a desk spoke of war. Children
had been nailed to trees. Women were being raped. She spoke of
atrocities by the case and in detail, as many as she could fit into
her report, touching upon the small facts, the age of the victim,
the number of assailants, the implements sometimes used. A
sixty-year-old grandmother had been violated and afterwards her
uterus was cut out of her by soldiers. Jill Bowman lay there and
listened to the horrors and watched the footage of toothless
speechless people who had lost their faith in this world.

She turned all her lights off and lay in the darkness watching
the television screen. She was seized by the feeling that the point
of her life was eluding her, as though she were a word without a
definition.

But now there was no feeling of oppression. It was as if a weight had been lifted from her, and because for hours her body had fought against it, had stiffened and resisted, she had been left exhausted, powerless. Now, over twenty years later, she could think of Geoff without anger; whether he was dead or alive was of no matter to her. He was not dead, not really: like all of the people in her life he remained alive, hiding behind the faces of others, or, as in a child's game in a book, outlined by the artful arrangement of branches in a tree or objects on a shelf. Often she would catch glimpses of people: her mother in the shape of another woman's hand; her father when Resnick zipped his jacket the day they raked leaves together. Old lovers would reappear in the title of a book or a few measures of music, in the acrid scent of tobacco or the taste of mint. Geoff existed in her memory as a fugitive, attempting to escape her, hiding his face, running flat out through the convolutions and curves of her mind, always fleeing. And though it no longer much mattered, though the fire of her anger had long died out, she would never reach him, never complete what should have been done all those years ago.

The day after her trip to Boston she had sat on the toilet to move her bowels and like a snake relieving itself of its scales the tube slid out of her into the water. She covered her eyes and cried for fifteen minutes, and then she took the tube out of the shit and piss and let it soak in Listerine in the sink. She would put it back in herself, she would lie down on her bed and stick it in, let it coil within the curve of her womb. She could even reproduce the abortionist's little hideaway, she could get a *TV Guide* and a television and a bag of Oreos, and she could throw money away, four hundred and fifty dollars out the window. She was glad her roommate was in a class. She was glad no one was there to see her final humiliation. She pulled up her panties and jeans and without bothering to fasten them went out to the pay phone in the hall and called Geoff. His boss said that he was on a cigarette break. You weren't allowed to smoke in the workshop, so Geoff had to go out in the street and lean against a lamppost and puff away while he eyed the girls and sniffed the air like a dog seeking bitch. She was nine weeks pregnant. Her breasts had begun to swell a little. In fact she'd noticed that her body had begun to round off a bit, as though she were filled with the events of the past months, the hours of passion and the misery of the truth. "I'll wait," she said.

"It's your dime," the man said, and she mouthed the words Fuck You Baby.

"Yeah hello," Geoff said after a few minutes.

"You're going to listen to me."

"Oh hi."

"I went to have an abortion. I got together four hundred and fifty dollars and went to this place outside of Boston and the doctor stuck a tube inside me. I hope your prick falls off."

He said nothing.

"It was supposed to irritate the fetus until it fell out. The tube fell out instead." She didn't know what she wanted from him. Was he supposed to hop on a bus and stick the tube back in her? Did she expect him to perform the abortion himself, this man who fixed guitars for folksingers and rock stars, whose undelicate thick fingers were toughened with callus?

"I'm sorry," he said.

"You're sorry."

"I am. I really am." Yet his voice spoke not of sorrow but of boredom, of an extreme lassitude. She imagined him as a baby in his layette, snoozing and crumpled in the sunlight, sucking on a rubber nipple while his aged mother knitted sleepwear for him.

"I'm going to kill you," she said. The words had come from nowhere, they were spoken by someone else, someone lurking about inside her.

"I know I know," he said.

"What am I going to do?"

"I have to go. I have to go back to work."

"What am I going to do?" and her voice was so loud it was like white light, the flash of explosives, the illumination of sudden death. But Geoff had hung up. For a moment she entertained the thought of taking a bus into Amherst and actually causing him some harm, driving a hammer into the bones of his hands, gouging out his eye with a chisel, snipping his balls off with her mother's garden shears. But he wouldn't feel a thing. There would be only slight discomfort. Dripping and bloodied, crushed and mutilated, he would go across the street and eat tuna with the unshaven old men and maybe have a beer later that evening, see a girl, get laid. She didn't want to kill him, she wanted to kill herself. Her sorrow was not translated into a despairing silence and a river of tears. It was like water boiling, she was shedding heat and fury and soon she would explode, she would scatter her ferocity over everyone near her. She hung up the phone and went back to her room and sat on her bed. She wanted to reach into her chest and tear her heart out. Her eyes ached from staring at nothing. She suddenly felt so tired she could barely sit upright. She kicked off her shoes and pulled off her jeans and underwear and got under the covers and punched herself in the stomach. She lay there and blinked until she could see again: John Lennon in the darkest glasses imaginable; Oscar Wilde leaning against a wall, casually anticipating a bit of rough trade; Virginia Woolf in her grey madness; a travel poster for Tahiti, a woman in a sarong holding a shell to her ear: these were some of the posters she and her roommate had hung up in September. The shelves in the room contained their books, and on her desk was a paper she'd been working on, something on John Donne. The silence of the room seemed to come from a suspension of time, as if everything that had happened to her had taken place in a second or two, and it was all a kind of illusion or dream. In a moment she would awaken and find that nothing had happened, that she hadn't met Geoff, that she wasn't pregnant, that time was about to resume. But she knew that wasn't the case, it wasn't ever the case, even when you slept and dreamed. You always knew precisely where you were, and only artifice and contrivance could save you from the inevitable progression of present, future, the end. She had the

sensation that she was going to die in her sleep, that Annie was
going to come back from Victorian Lit and find her dead in her
bed, and that before she was buried they would dissect her and
find the fetus that so resembled that bastard Geoff. She thought
of her mother and father at the funeral, and her sister Sally, and
she thought of them weeping over her coffin. She wondered if
when she died Geoff's life would change. Would he be contrite?
Would he leave the area, have nightmares, live in endless shame?
He would flee to Nevada and live in motels and change his identity. He would take menial jobs and find himself incapable of
having a fulfilling relationship with a woman, because he had
caused the untimely death of this promising young student
named Jill Bowman. Or would he suddenly become religious,
would he haunt the confession boxes of municipal cathedrals,
contemplate shaving his head and joining an order? Perhaps it
would be too much for him to bear, the thought that he had
killed Jill Bowman, pretty Jill with her good legs and long hair.
What is it he'd said to her? I love the skin on your thighs, and
he'd rub his stubbly face against them, and she would lie there
and writhe and grasp the hair on his head and pull him against
her until he finally got onto his knees and stuck himself inside
her. Oh yeah, he would say, oh yeah oh yeah, and then he would
come and all his words would run out. Time for a smoke. Time
for a pee. Something to eat? Yet for those moments she was the
only woman in the world, and he the only man, and it didn't
dawn on her until months later, even a year after they were finished, that these were lines he used on other women, that every
girl he ever went to bed with had great thighs, oh yeah oh yeah,
and then he'd come and fall silent and get a cigarette and talk
about having to go back to work, or do something with his truck,
something about the fuel line.

She lay there with her eyes shut and listened to the birds outside her room. She was a student at Mount Holyoke, she was priv-
ileged to be there, her teachers liked her, she would graduate
with honors, she had a brilliant future, what a good girl and so

pretty too. She thought of all the words that had been applied to her, all the phrases and praises, and she felt like shit, like garbage in the street, like the most disgusting thing in the world. She waited until she stopped crying and then she went back into the hall and called the operator. She told the operator the number she wanted and then she asked that the charges be reversed. Her mother answered and then she cried some more. She said, "Mommy, I'm in such trouble you just don't know," and her mother said, "What is it my darling, what has happened?"

"I'm pregnant," she said, and her cries became spasms, and after a moment or two her mother said, "My darling, you must be mistaken."

But a week later she was no longer pregnant.

She never saw Geoff again. In truth she passed him many times, on sidewalks and in restaurants and bars, and by not looking at him she did not see him. Her father had flown down to Washington with her. He had spoken to her advisor at the college and arranged for her to take a leave of absence for two weeks. He promised she'd keep up with her work while she was away. He waited for her outside the recovery room and bought her roses and *Newsweek* and horse magazines and a packet of Hostess cupcakes. Afterwards he sat and held her hand, and later her mother called to see how she was. Abortion had been legalized there only two weeks earlier, and she'd been checked into the eighth floor of a huge hospital overlooking the seat of power, the places where men in suits pushed pens across paper, vetoed bills, waged war.

For a few years afterwards she'd heard bits and pieces of information from old friends, edges of rumors and reports of sightings of Geoff: he had moved to California, he was living on a sloop off the coast of Maine, he had hitchhiked to Alaska to fight fires. All of these were within reason. It would have astonished her to hear otherwise, that, say, he had moved to London to become an investment banker, or had gone to Vienna to take master classes in vocal technique with Elisabeth Schwarzkopf. He was a man who lived on the outskirts of involvement, who left doors open for himself, who never carried a return ticket in his pocket. He preferred the fresh air because you could run away without having to excuse yourself, speak polite words, look someone in the face. He had eluded her, and although she bore the pain of it, to him she was nothing at all, a familiar face, a vague name, a good fuck like all the rest of them.

Now that her husband was dead, now that such a finality had come into her life, would she ever again see another man, would she ever find herself so entangled with another, save in the world of dreams and possibilities? Would she ever allow herself to toy with heartbreak, to risk it all? She had grown comfortable and complacent in her marriage, she had never once guessed there would come a time when she would be expected to date another man, to go through the motions of advance and retreat, to utter the faded phrases and excuses, the double entendres and tiny encouragements. She couldn't quite imagine having dinner with a strange man, making conversation, going back to his place so he could sit beside her and say How beautiful you are and feel her up. She couldn't bring herself to imagine an adult engaging in such behavior, yet when she thought of Resnick she thought of precisely that, of dining with him and making conversation, of unbuttoning his shirt and trousers, falling into bed with him, discovering his shape and form with her own hands.

The next morning she went shopping. At Hamleys she bought Carrie a little stuffed tiger and a smiling stuffed snowman and debated whether or not to buy her anything associated with Britain: a toy double-decker bus, Postman Pat books to read aloud to her. Would Carrie mind that she had gone away? Or had Sally been right all along, that Carrie wouldn't even notice, that the fact would remain unregistered? London was nothing at all to Carrie. She couldn't possibly even know where she herself lived, or why. Her condition was like a mask locked tight over a bright and responsive child, a girl screaming to be let free. It was why Jill always hoped that one day the child inside would break through, or that she would reach her, and the notion felt to her like the stretching of an arm and the grasping of a hand, and the ascent of her beloved daughter up from a dark soundless pit. And would she then emerge with all the knowledge of a fourteen-year-old daughter of Jill Bowman, would she yearn to ride Blackjack, would she remember Dr. Bradley, would she call Hector to her lap, and speak of her favorite foods, and those she disdained?

She flipped through one of the books. Postman Pat lived in an idyllic world with his black-and-white cat. The people to whom he delivered the mail lived in thatched cottages and village schools. No one was murdered there, no children were born wordless and numb. She decided to buy two volumes in the series. Postman Pat's cat Jess resembled Hector, and she thought it would make Carrie laugh, the cat's fat cheeks, his smile, his nose. She hoped the sales clerk wouldn't ask how old Carrie was; it had happened before, when buying a coloring book or a Madeline story, that Jill had admitted that Carrie was a young teenager, and the clerk had stared at her. She's young for her age, Jill would say. It was at such times that she felt her life was ringed with lies.

When she got back to her hotel she sat on the bed and placed her hand on the phone. She remembered that she had told Resnick about Peter's infidelity. Perhaps further questions had arisen? She tried to remember how much she had told the detective. There were things she hadn't revealed: how hindsight had given her a clarity in the way she looked back on this period of her life, how it had endowed her, even in those hours immediately after Peter's admission to her, with a perspicuity that only made her realize her ignorance. All along she had seen it, she had smelled it and sensed it, it had lain beside her palpable and alive, it had been evident in the way he had made love to her, how much more vigorous he had been, what new moves he had been trying. It had been obvious in the way he had been dressing, how he had lingered before mirrors, primping and combing. They had fought afterwards, they had fought bitterly over it, or rather she had fought and he had stood calmly by, as if he wore his hours of pleasure like plates of armor. She remembered the night he had confessed it, how they had lain awake until dawn. Her questions had been intimate ones, calmly put: what did she look like, did you go down on her, had you talked about marriage, were you intending to leave me? He told her everything, how beautiful she was, how they spent their hours, how the future had begun to take shape, as though it were a game of wits played between exhibitionist and voyeur. He told her how different she was from Jill, as if the whole matter were no reflection on his wife.

"But it's over now." He touched her arm and she sprang away from him. "It's over, Puppchen," he said. He never spoke of her again.

After lunch at a little French restaurant in Mayfair she walked down towards the river. The streets were simultaneously familiar and strange to her. The intricacies of this city were lost on Jill Bowman, and yet she found herself oddly comfortable here, as if were she to become lost she would always turn a corner and discover herself in front of something familiar or historic, a tower, a statue, a museum or hotel. She preferred the older quarters, with their gnarled streets and hidden turns, the veins and arteries of some vast aged body that bore traces of its past in every crevice and cell. The Plague had wended its way down the ancient airless lanes, a shadow blithely breaking the angles of Clerkenwell and Holborn, Spitalfields and Aldgate, picking off the healthy like some great blind ravenous beast. And then, some twelve months hence, it departed, leaving the survivors forgetful and full of hope, sensing paradise in the cool breezes and pink sunsets that augured the Great Fire, which not much later would destroy the city that had survived the Plague. Perhaps Dora Castle was right; maybe carrying a photo of her ancestor was a way to remind her that history could stretch its sinewy arm and pluck you out of the future.

She became aware of the edges of the city, of the wasted people who lived beneath bridges or in doorways. Is this what death did to you, were you suddenly endowed with the ability to spot it in your midst, in the drawn faces of those who were stepping away from life? It was as though death were a neighboring country, and the more you experienced of it, the more visits you paid to the frontier and the border posts, the better you were able to find your way there in the end.

She thought again about returning to her room and calling David. Surely there was something she had forgotten to tell him, something that might lead the detective to the answer. They had to catch these people who had done this to Peter, and the moment she thought it she saw how absurd it was. She didn't care in the least who had done it or why. Peter had taken a taxi to the Hubbard; he had gone there just before he was to dine with his wife and fly off to London: this was what had happened. She desired only the chance to speak to David again, to hear his voice, to try to gauge it by the tone and phrasing, to read in the way the syllables emerged from his mouth whether his interest in her was equal to hers in him. He was a married man, he had children. He was a married man, he had children, and when he walked out of his house and shut the door he was someone else. Everyone was someone else beyond the door, just as Peter had undergone a transformation when the door to the hotel room had shut behind him. She began to find herself caught up in a tangle of illogic, of excuses and impressions and elucidations, and none of these were based on any evidence. She was doing precisely what she counseled her students against doing. History could be interpreted only after the facts were established. She taught them to be responsible in their research, penetrating in their questions. She wanted them to go out into the world and demand that records be made public, to attend hearings and stand up and ask embarrassing questions, to read every word of original documents and letters. And here she was in London, creating in her imagination a man and a feeling, a collection of images and emotions that probably had nothing to do with him. And she was doing it not because she was dealing with history but because she was creating the future, and this seemed to make the act legitimate. To interpret the future meant that you had to create it, and the thought of it, the sheer freedom of it, made her feel the weight of risk and loss all the more acutely. She imagined him at this very moment, standing and holding his wife's face between his palms, kissing her and speaking of his love. And was he thinking of her, and had she become an element in his mind, the subject of his dreams, a name he could utter with his silent lips only in the dark hours of the night?

And did she, in the end, truly need him? Couldn't she stand on her own feet and move forward, as a child does, with tentative first steps and stumbles? With Peter gone she was beginning a new life, starting at zero, entering a world that seemed altogether different to her. Surely her desire for David Resnick was irrational, emotional, completely and utterly pointless.

Yet without him she sat alone in the wreckage and fragments of disaster, as if she had been the sole survivor of some great catastrophe, earthquake, avalanche, the falling of metal and stone from the sky. As a detective, a man who spent his days and nights observing corpses, questioning suspects, speaking to witnesses, he had grown used to violence and loss, he had become her guide to this devastation.

CHAPTER *18*

Sell. Move.

Now it was becoming something certain, it had gained texture
and solidity, it was growing within her like a tumor. Sell. Move.
It was like a child's excitement with all the frenzy and hysteria,
the sense of things anticipated, Christmas, a birthday. She began
to work out the particulars in her mind. She could feel it in
the muscles of her body, as if she were about to sprint a great
distance.

Now that she was eager to return home London seemed more
welcoming, it had opened its gates to her. Either it came from
within, or something had changed in the city, a rise in temperature, a shift in the wind: whatever it was, she no longer felt detached from things. She began to move more easily, to take long

walks, and as she progressed through the streets, she felt for a few moments that curious notion of being part of two worlds. It was what had originally drawn her to her profession, what had given her a passion for history, as if by knowing as much as possible about another age she could move between the past and the present, evading and hiding, endlessly retreating.

She was glad she hadn't gone to Paris. Things could never feel the same: though the street may not have changed, and the man on the balcony might still be there, things had taken place, the angle of light had shifted and nothing would ever again strike her in quite the same way. Now she no longer cared. She could feel it inside her: the great hollow of longing had shriveled to nothing. The past had already had its moments.

It was time to go home. It had hardly been worth the trip. She'd originally planned on staying abroad for two weeks, and now she found herself wanting to return. Sell the house, move to the city: this is what she reminded herself. She had been thinking about it constantly. Sell. Move. It was better than thinking of Peter in the morgue, or of building and furnishing in her imagination the room in which he had been murdered, the immense frenzy of blood and steel and severed arteries.

Sell. Move. Run.

She returned to her hotel at two-thirty. She had spent the morning at the British Museum and she felt as if it were eleven at night. She lay on the bed and looked at her watch and still looking at it counted back five hours. At home it was only half past nine. Carrie had finished breakfast. Her shirt would be soiled with milk and cereal. She would be in one of the big rooms downstairs, where some of the patients sat at tables and drew pictures with thick stubby crayons. Sometimes they would get into fights, and it was odd to witness boys and girls and adults alike arguing and contorting their faces and banging the air with their fists, for here they were all children, impatient and selfish and cranky. Carrie drew sudden storms, swirls and slashes in green and purple and red, and once she seemed to have created a face, a self-portrait, for when Jill saw it she said to Carrie, Is this you, my cookie, is it Carrie? and Carrie said Um and seemed to smile. Jill took it home and bought an 8-by-10 frame and hung the picture on the wall in the living room. She remembered Peter coming home and looking at it and asking what it was. "Carrie drew it. It's a picture of herself." He stared at it for a bit and shook his head a little, and Jill took it upstairs and hung it in her office. Later that evening he asked Jill why she had done such a thing. "Because you didn't want it in the living room."

"No no, it's just."

"It's just that you want all the good pictures there, don't you. The lithographs and paintings you buy. The pictures by trained artists, the gallery posters."

"It's not that, it's," and she said, "I understand how you feel. Well I like Carrie's picture. I love it. I'll keep it where I can look at it," and for some reason she grew teary and sullen and gave up on reading essays by her seminar students. She turned on the television and watched a few minutes of the late news. Her mood grew black, her breathing became deep and angry. Peter hated to go to the clinic. He called it the Hospital, even though the people who ran it referred to it as a clinic. It wasn't so much that he was against such institutions; he only disliked having to witness the terrible extremes contained there. His notion of a psychiatric patient was of a complex, civilized and excessively hygienic person given to baroque neuroses and harmless quirks and perhaps chronic masturbation, who at the worst heard voices and took too many pills, and who, during working hours, could function quite capably as a museum director or concert pianist or publisher. He found distasteful the twisted expressions and immature grunts and howls of the people at the clinic, their dead eyes and the smell of them, the shit and vomit and pee that lingered in the air like a rank fog. He complained about the lighting, the color of the rugs, the decor of the rooms. He hated having to wait while

Jill fed her daughter. He hated the staff there, the way they talked to the patients as if they were incapable of understanding a sentence of reasonable length and complexity. He hated Carrie.

That was it. It had come to her before, years earlier, but never so articulately. Peter had hated her little girl. He hated her because she needed attention. He hated her because Jill had had two miscarriages with him. He hated her because the child was not perfect, and once, she remembered it now with the pain and acuity of a bee sting, he had asked if Jill would have loved Carrie so much if she hadn't been born that way. She had wanted to slap his face in response and instead went up to the office she had made out of what would have been Carrie's room, she shut the door and sat at her desk and wept into her hands. She cried out of disappointment in her husband, in this man from whom she had expected so much that was good and reasonable. She sat there while he came to the door and knocked, begged to be admitted, asked to speak to her. After a while she said he could come in, and when he did she told him that if he found Carrie so offensive he should consider leaving.

"But I'm not married to Carrie," he said. "You're my wife."

"But she comes with the package. When you married me you knew about Carrie, you'd even seen her at the clinic."

He looked at her and at first said nothing.

"You've spent all these years blaming yourself for Carrie's condition."

"I haven't blamed anyone for it. It just happened. It's no one's fault."

"Yes, but you must understand, you may say that, but."

"Don't psychoanalyze me, Peter."

"Ah."

"You just don't like my daughter."

"I never asked to be her stepfather."

"I know that."

"I'm not really suited to the role, you see," and the words came out crisply, in his severe Zurich accent.

"I suppose you're going to blame your father for this," she said.

"My father died when I was very young."

"That's why I said it, Peter."

"Don't be so snide. I only meant that I never wanted to have children."

"Then why did we try all those times?"

"Because by then I had changed my mind."

"Sorry I couldn't accommodate you."

He waved his hands in the air. "It's just that Carrie demands so much of your attention."

"Children do that, you know."

"But you have to admit Carrie is different."

"At least she doesn't live at home."

"I suppose I was never destined to be a father."

"Then you shouldn't have married a woman with a daughter. Especially a retarded daughter. Go find yourself some cute young thing and have her sterilized, for Christ's sake."

"I don't need to listen to this."

"No you don't. And the next time I go to the clinic you can stay home. And when I take Carrie out for the day and bring her here you can drive down to your office or play squash at your club. You'll never have to see her again."

He walked out and gently shut the door on her anger. He was not given to rage or violence, and sometimes she wished he would show his temper or put up a fight. Now that he was dead she found herself remembering all the wrong things about him, as though the skin of his life had been peeled back to reveal the tumors that had lain beneath. She had to remind herself why she had fallen in love with him, and as she lay on her bed in London she did so, slowly and in stages, and the thought of it made her smile in a way that for the first time since his death meant serenity and contentment.

She shut her eyes and when she woke it was nearly four. She gazed at her watch and sat up on the side of the bed, rubbing her face. She didn't remember her dreams, or even if she had dreamed or not, but she woke with a sense of certainty. She picked up the phone and went through the lengthy process of making an international call. The man who answered said that Detective Sergeant Resnick was away from his desk but was expected back at any moment. She looked at her watch again. It was eleven in the morning there. She imagined he must have stepped away to get coffee or to use the toilet. She said that she was calling from London and that she would wait. "I'll see if I can find him," he said.

Within a minute Resnick was on the line. He said, "Jill? Ms. Bowman?" and she felt it inside her, something banging at her chest. Her mouth went dry and her scalp itched.

"How did you know?"

"I was told I had a call from London. Who else would it be?"

"I'm only calling to let you know my plans. I'm coming back the day after tomorrow."

"I thought you were staying two weeks."

"There's no point. There are things I need to do at home," she said.

"We need you here. We'd like you to have a look at something. We found a tape. A film. A videotape. I wasn't going to tell you about it until you returned. I didn't want you to worry about it."

"I don't understand what you're talking about."

"Your husband had a safe-deposit box. Actually he had two of them. The first one you know about, it contained his will and some documents pertaining to a trust he had set up. We found the other one really by accident."

She imagined the film was of Peter's murder, that whoever had been responsible for it had recorded the proceedings from the time he came through the door to the moment he crumpled to the floor and bled to death, and the thought of it erased everything bad she had been thinking about her husband. "I don't want to see it," she said.

"I think you'll have to, Jill. I'll need you to try to identify the person with your husband."

"What?"

"The film is of Dr. Freytag and another person."

"A woman."

"That's right."

"You've seen it."

"Yes." He said nothing more.

"The woman he had an affair with six years ago."

"There's no way we can come to that conclusion. But I think it's important you see it. Maybe you'll be able to identify her."

"I don't think so." Now she was sorry she had called him. She had to remind herself that she was attracted to a man who was also investigating her husband's murder, and that death would forever be imprinted upon their relationship, in the same way a tattoo becomes one with the skin.

"But you'll have to see it. I'm sorry, Jill. That's just the way it is."

"Tell me about it." It would be like having to identify Peter's body in the morgue, it was something she could gaze at only with averted eyes.

"Not now. I've got a meeting in three minutes."

"Have you been well?" She began to speak as if she were holding on to the end of a rope made of words that linked her to him, and she refused to let go.

"I'm fine. And you?"

"I miss speaking to you."

"Yes."

She was sorry she had said it, she should never have been so intimate. She wanted him to say something encouraging, something personal, I miss you too, I want to see you, I can't wait until you return. The fact that he had called her by her first name now carried no significance. She felt ashamed of herself, and the feeling was that of an adolescent in full blush.

"I," she began, and he said, "I've got to go."

"I," she said again.

"Call me when you get home, okay?"

And she hung up. Now she felt as if she had been punched senseless, or as if someone had taken her day and tipped it at an angle. Nothing was as she'd had hoped it would be. She'd been seeing things all wrong. Her expectations had been dashed to the ground. Resnick had talked only about a videotape and she wanted to hear more, she wanted to hear it in the way he spoke, the warmth and softness of the silences between them. She continued sitting on the edge of the bed. She said Oh Fuck and then she went to the bathroom and brushed her hair and washed her face and looked at herself, at her sullen face and miserable eyes. She felt like a fourteen-year-old. The weight of things unfair seemed to lie on her shoulders. She even laughed a little at her folly, at the structure she had erected in her imagination, this thing called David Resnick, this assembly based upon her own desires and hopes, which, toweringly high, had collapsed in a matter of seconds to the ground.

Her trip was supposed to have been a time when her desires would be diverted and memory would lapse. Now it was nearly five and darkness had begun to fall on London, and it came like a veil over the city, the obscurity of the hour turning a sudden blinding grey. She went out into the square and began walking west towards Charing Cross Road and Shaftesbury Avenue, where the theatres were, where people congregated. Jill noticed that men were looking at her, giving her frank appraisement and offering smiles. This was what life should be, this was what it was in dreams and twilight, a place where anything could happen, where you were on the brink of fulfillment, and it occurred to her it was like what was so powerfully gorgeous about sex, those endless minutes before it was over, when her body audaciously filled with drama and she alone could let go. She loved the look of the city this time of day, when light withdrew and neon sizzled into life. For a moment, a passing minute, she contemplated moving to London. You could get lost there, you could start over and lose your past, leave it far behind you. It was an absurd notion. She had grown accustomed to her life at home, to her Volvo and her stable, to the video shop in town and the place where she bought morning-glory muffins for Sunday breakfasts. She would miss her work. To abandon it all would be childish. But she could move to the city. She could sell. She could move.

She wasn't sure what she would do that evening. There were concerts being held that night, and every block or so she would see posters and signs for them on walls. Alfred Brendel was giving an all-Beethoven recital at the Royal Festival Hall. The ballet was doing *Romeo and Juliet*. Tosca would die at the opera house some time before midnight. There was a selection of singers and jazz groups and plays to see, and in the end she decided against all of them. To sit in the audience meant to be still and attentive, and all she could think of was to start moving, to take strong steps forward, to begin again.

Now she felt it, now it struck her with a warmth that was almost sexual: it was good being alone in the world. She who for so long had feared solitude, who had dreaded being only one, now had a glimpse of the strength of her singularity. You belonged only to yourself, you coined your own decisions and paid for your pleasures, you suffered without the words of others and your dreams were shared with no one. Yet these were mere excuses that brought a smile to her face, they were the musings of what could become a bitter and detached woman. In truth it was good being one because it was better than being zero. That was it. She felt herself filling with an elation she'd felt when she'd come to the decision to sell the house and move. Yes, she thought, yes yes, and she said it aloud, oh yes.

CHAPTER *19*

Because the floor was strewn with mail and newspapers that had been delivered in her absence, she stepped carefully around them and left her bags at the bottom of the stairway. She reminded herself that she was going to sell the house, and she had to stop herself from calling a broker there and then, before she had even caught her breath and unpacked, as if she were working against a deadline or an impending disaster, an eruption, an anticipated rending of the earth.

She turned on the kitchen tap and the pipes clanked and sucked until the water ran cold and clear into her glass. Time, which had moved with astonishing speed on the plane and the drive home, began to slow down for her. A tomato she had left out had become a mass of pulp and seed, slowly bleeding in the

middle of the counter. She turned up the thermostat and listened
as the burner switched itself on. After a minute or two warm air
was exhaled from the vents in the walls. Every step she took lifted
the dust from the floor, and it rose in a fine cloud, spreading and
scattering as the house shuddered into life. She listened to the
messages on her answering machine as she gathered the mail and
papers from the floor. My name is Howard Duke and I'm calling
about aluminum siding, how are you today, Mrs. Freytag? Her
attorney, Neil, called to see how she was, to see if she needed him
in any way. There was a message from Sally, Hi Jill, hope you had
a great trip, give us a call when you get back, and in the background she could discern the shrill horror of her children sacrific-
ing their youth at the altar of Nintendo. Another was from the
museum she belonged to, asking if she wished to give money. She
went there five or six times a year, to special exhibitions, or to see
the John Singer Sargents she liked, or simply to have lunch with
a friend and buy Christmas cards at the shop. She always felt
slightly awkward standing before a painting, turning her head
this way and that as if confronted with a great puzzle that required decipherment. It was of no matter to her what messages
these canvases bore; she was more interested in the relation between the bit of red here and the yellow triangle there, or the face
that grimaced in this corner, and the wild-eyed horse in that; she
preferred to imagine a living person standing before it in a clut-
tered studio reeking of acrylic and gesso, enmeshing himself in
this intricacy of color and line, shadow and flare. And yet there
was comfort to be had in a gallery, before these mute signs from
another's imagination. To see them made her think of Carrie, of
someone confronting chaos and trying to squeeze some meaning
out of it, or even, conversely, of someone bound to the rack of order and attempting to shatter the structure forever. Peter, of
course, looked upon art as a form of investment, something associated not with old clothes and spattered shoes but with fine suits
and reputations, as with that Hans Hofmann he'd been eyeing a
few years earlier. "I don't especially like it," he told her when

they'd gone to see it at the dealer's in Manhattan, on Eighty-second Street. "But I want it nonetheless."

Hi do you have big tits, said a breathless boy of twelve.

Julius Rosenzweig's secretary called to say that the next department meeting would be deferred until December 18.

There was also a message from Dora Castle, apologizing for not having made an appointment with her. She said, "I'm really sorry. I didn't know what to say to you. I just. It's just. I'm very very sorry about your husband. I don't know how to say it. Just sorry," and Jill smiled a little to herself. She thought fondly of Dora, whom she would often find sitting on the floor outside her office, on the slick linoleum of the corridor, smoking and reading, waiting for her advisor. She had few friends. Jill suspected she hadn't any lovers, either. Yet Dora was a pretty young woman, thin and a little mysterious looking with her huge dark eyes and black hair in a long braid down her back. She had broken all the rules that Jill had taught her about her profession and had discovered a passion for history not in the shards and pieces of things left behind but in the stories of her grandmother and aunts, in the oral tradition of family remembrance, an unreliable mixture of embellished memory and superstition and folk tale that belonged more to the realm of literature. Yet Jill encouraged Dora to pursue this course. There was something calamitous about this young woman, as if she contained the germ of her own destruction, as if she would hang on to life only as long as her elderly relatives were still able to provide her with a past.

The last message was from David Resnick. She felt her eyes bulge slightly and her tongue go dry. She felt it also in her bladder and her legs, this weakening, this fear that all potential involvement carried with it. He had called the night before. She listened carefully to his voice. Jill it's Dave Resnick, I'd like to hear from you. Play it back. Jill it's Dave Resnick, I'd like to hear from you. From you. From you. To hear from you. The heat of his words. I'd like to hear from you. There was a pause. He wondered if she needed a ride from the airport. If you need a lift. If you need a lift. He laughed a little. I suppose you're still in London. Ha ha. I suppose you're still. Give me a call when you get back. We need to talk. We need to.

We need to talk: those were his last words, and to Jill they sounded like I'll never see you again, I need to make things clear. I'm very much in love with my wife, I have two wonderful children, I don't want to see you again and this will be the subject of our conversation.

But he hadn't said those things. She had only imagined it. We need to talk: amazing how much could be packed into those four words, how much nuance and suspicion and excuse and dismissal. Yet she'd only imagined it. We need to talk. It was what detectives said to informers and suspects. It was what they did with lawyers and executioners and governors. Did he speak to his wife in this way? We need to talk, darling. She picked up the phone and dialed his number at work and he picked it up. "It's Jill," she said, and immediately he said, "You're back."

"I got your message."

"I'm glad you called," he said, and she took her cordless phone and walked into the living room with it. She sat on the sofa and put her feet up on it, the dead filth of autumn stuck to the soles of her shoes. She said, "How are things going?"

"Not too badly. I'd like you to see that tape." He laughed. "Actually it's not a question of my liking anything. You'll have to see it. There's no one else who can help us at the moment."

"Has anything else come up?"

There was a small pause. "Possibly. How does tomorrow sound for you?"

It took her by surprise. "Yes. Yes, of course." Tomorrow began to run through her mind like miles of film footage. Tomorrow she'd hoped to visit Carrie, or rather she would visit Carrie, no matter what, and then she had thought of stopping in to see Blackjack and of running one or two other errands. That was

what tomorrow meant. It meant going to the bank and paying
bills and she had considered stopping in at her office, checking
her mail, having a glance at next semester's schedule, bringing
Hector home. Her poor cat would be stunned senseless by his
boarding ordeal at the vet's, a place of howl and protest and the
mingled smells of disinfectant and shit. Her mind began to move
rapidly, dizzyingly, through the sequence of her days, through all
the days after tomorrow, and she realized that she was still five
hours ahead and utterly exhausted. Outside the sun shone weakly
on discolored mounds of plowed snow. The sky was of a sinister
colorlessness, the air was grey. Taped to the windows of the house
next door were construction-paper turkeys the neighbors' children had made in school for the holiday, now almost two weeks
past. Soon Christmas would be here; the new year would come;
soon the terrible isolating freeze of February would arrive. In a
moment her conversation with David would end, as would her
time away from the house. Before her departure it had been a
place profoundly haunted, aswirl with ghosts, the remnants of her
marriage to Peter, the shreds of his death that clung to the walls
and hung from the ceilings. She had gone to Europe to get away
from them, and now she was back. It seemed somehow unfair that
she should have to face it again. "I'm moving," she said suddenly,
and Resnick said, "I'm sorry?"

"I'm thinking about moving."

"To where?"

"The city."

"Really."

"I don't need this house anymore. It's too big for me. And I'm
just as close to Carrie if I live in the city."

"I guess that's true."

She didn't know what to say. She said, "I'll see the film tomorrow, then."

"Yes."

"Is it upsetting?"

"It might be."

"Is it," and she couldn't think of the words.

"Are you asking if it's sexual in nature? Yes, it is. It's very graphic."

"You want me to identify the woman."

"If you can."

For one absurd moment she tried to remember if she and Peter had ever filmed themselves, and she imagined Resnick sitting in his darkened office, seeing Peter rising and falling between her legs. But it had never gone that far. She had no desire to watch herself, to see herself at the mercy of another in the tarantella and distraction of passion.

"I want to see Carrie tomorrow morning. And I have to get my cat from the vet."

"How about twelve. Or one. If you like we can have lunch together."

This was sunrise. This was blaze and spark. "That would be very nice," she said. She chose a time and said goodbye. She had forgotten how determined she had been when turning her back on the waiter Nikos. But this time it was her choice. Resnick was hers. No one was forcing her. The risks were many: he was married, he had children, he had much to sacrifice. She had nothing to lose. This was her choice, and she rubbed her head as she thought it, it was her step, the bend and strain of her own leg.

She shut her eyes and fell into a lightheaded little sleep. Instead of dreams and faces she drowned in a sea of voices, and when she woke four minutes later she went back into the kitchen. Peter had not been a participant in those words and cries, in fact his role in her memory had been brought into question. Was she already forgetting him? Was there a possibility that Peter might one day simply withdraw from her mind altogether, as an uncomfortable guest slips away from a wedding, and would the mystery then be solved, would it be seen that she, Jill Bowman, was the true murderer of Peter Freytag, the one responsible for his disappearance? Wasn't that why Dora Castle carried a photo of her lost relative, to keep her alive, to deliver her from the endless tale of shower and oven?

She put on the kettle and got out the teabags. She opened the refrigerator and saw what had gone bad during her absence, the cheese, the milk, the raspberries, as crimson as menstruation when she left, now green and furred with age and neglect. The kettle whistled at her and she poured the water into her mug. She looked at the clock and then looked at her watch. In London it was nearly six; here it was barely one. She thought of her room at the hotel, she imagined it as she had left it, in the growing twilight of another evening. She considered the waiter Nikos, at that moment delivering pasta carbonara to another woman. No one she had met or talked to in England would linger in her memory for long. It was as if she had never gone abroad, never seen anything, never walked the long galleries of the museums. A piece of time had been removed from her life. Now that she was home, walking up the stairs to her bedroom and office, she saw that all the changes had taken place within her alone. The house still contained the image and scent of her husband, the residual pain of his murder. She had come back to it from the hospital, she'd returned to it from the funeral, and now that her trip was over she realized how recently she had lost him, how far she had moved since then.

She placed her suitcases down on the bed and unzipped them. A plastic bag contained her laundry, panties, bras, tights, shirts, a camisole or two, jeans, socks, and these she took into the little alcove off the hallway where the washer and dryer were installed. She unpacked the things she had bought for Carrie, the books, the stuffed snowman and tiger. She wouldn't give these to Carrie all at once; she'd put one or two aside for Christmas and her birthday. To overwhelm her with gifts now might be taken as precedent. It had happened before, she'd come bearing a few extras, and the next time, having shown up with something small, she'd been assaulted by her daughter, who raged and roared and pummeled her mother with her hands. Carrie would turn fifteen next September. She wouldn't outgrow the presents before then, she wouldn't outgrow them when she turned twenty or thirty or even fifty, if she lived that long. There was every chance she would outlive her own mother. Or she could die tomorrow.

She put the rest of her clothes away and cleared the bed and lay on it, and when she awoke it was dark and still and two in the morning. She lay there with her eyes open. Sounds were swallowed by the snow that fell in delicate flakes from the sky. Things had changed. She no longer felt the pain of her solitude. Her place in the universe had been shifted, she was no longer at the center of it, no longer the object of pity, of eyes that looked and mouths that spoke. Now she could walk about the house without fear of encountering the gossamer memories of her marriage. She took off her clothes and put on a sweatsuit and went down to the kitchen. She broke two eggs into a bowl and agitated them with a small fork. She added a little milk to it and poured the mixture into a hot frying pan. She watched as the liquid grew quickly firm, and then she turned it over. The toaster oven beeped twice at her. She buttered the bread and peppered the omelette and then folding it made herself a sandwich and looked through the newspapers and magazines that had been delivered in her absence, at the mail that had come, the free offers and renewal forms and bills. A few envelopes contained notices of donations that had been made to various foundations in Peter's name, and she set these aside. An anonymous donor had contributed a thousand dollars to an AIDS charity in memory of Peter. Another had thoughtfully given to a fund for autistic children. In a week or two she would sit down and acknowledge the kindness of her friends and those who had brought flowers to the funeral, who had remembered her husband through their gifts to heart clinics and cancer institutes and psychiatric organizations.

She was pleased to find that half an hour later she was tired again. She went back to bed and woke refreshed at six. She could hear the plows and sanders on the roads, and the sun rose into a cloudless crystalline sky on this first morning of her return, on this day when everything seemed utterly new.

CHAPTER *20*

The drive to the clinic took longer than usual. A few minutes after she got onto the highway she saw the string of brake lights, endless miles of them twisting into the distant wooded hills. She listened to the radio, pressing buttons as she searched the wavelengths for a traffic report. Twenty minutes later she reached the accident scene and stared out the window as four men tried to jack up the car to release the man trapped beneath it. He was wearing a tweed jacket and a blue shirt and tie, and although his mouth was moving, though he was talking to the people trying to rescue him, she could also see what he could never see, a valentine of red flowing from where his legs would be, spreading rapidly, a shock of color, forty years of life turning into a stain in the road, something that might fade with time, over the course of three or four winters perhaps. Doctors attached tubes to his arm, prepared to administer oxygen. Someone, possibly a priest, knelt beside him and gently touched the man's head and seemed to be talking to himself. Earlier in the day the man had kissed his wife and children goodbye, he had unlocked his car and switched on the radio and now he was dying, his ribs crushed, his heart bearing the weight of two tons of metal, and Jill Bowman put her hand to her face and wept into it.

People died every day. You opened a newspaper and read about shootings, stabbings, overdoses, diseases, bombings, long silent falls down shafts and stairwells. She prayed the traffic would move on, terrified she might be a witness to the moment when a grey blanket was hauled out of the ambulance and draped over the man's head. She turned her eyes towards the car beside her. A young man in a baseball cap sat with his girlfriend. They bobbed in their seats to the beat of unheard music. They laughed and lit cigarettes, and the young man reached over and gently squeezed the girl's breast and she laughed some more and then they looked at her with disdain, they read her expression, they found her pathetic and ludicrous, this driver who jeered their pleasure. Jill fiddled with the radio, making it louder as if to drown out the horror in the roadway. She moved from station to station, seeking word and distraction and noise. A man sold Toyotas in a flat accent. Another gave a ski report. A woman reported on human rights violations, and to Jill it was like hearing something from the ancient past, the bestiality of men in names from antiquity, Serbia, Croatia, Macedonia. She looked up at her rearview mirror and saw that all activity had ceased. Overhead a white helicopter whirled and spun and flew south. Now the emergency vehicles would pull away, one with the body of the man in the tweed jacket, another with what remained of his car. A trooper would direct the traffic to move on, people would gather speed to make up for lost time, and in twenty minutes the victim's family would hear the news. She imagined his wife taking the call at her office, being summoned from a meeting. Jill could see the expression on her face, she could understand the agony of her grimace. Perhaps the man was a father, and now the children would be taken from school to be told the news. Their mother, who had given birth to them, would have to speak of a death. The weight of the moment was hers alone. She had given birth to them and now she would have to announce a death. Would she talk in metaphors and convolutions, would she speak as in a fairy tale of Going to Sleep and Heavenly Peace and afterwards discuss the accoutrements of paradise, filmy wings and golden harps? Or would she be abrupt and businesslike: Daddy's dead. In an odd way she was glad she and Peter had never had children. To have done so would have meant that she would have had to wind words about their incomprehension, invent tales and make excuses, and like her they would have had to grieve his loss. Or was it that she feared having to share her misery? And the thought made her wince a little as she shifted into the right lane and slowed down for her exit.

She followed the curve of the ramp and drove up to the clinic, stopping briefly to exchange a greeting with the man at the gatehouse. She said that she had called earlier that morning. "Dr. Bradley's expecting me," she said, looking at her watch. He raised the barrier and she said, "Thanks, Bill." Outside the gate two patients stood in their overcoats, staring at her with lugubrious eyes, their arms hanging limply by their sides. She parked and went in through the door and waited for Jean in the lobby. Patients were only permitted there when they first arrived, or when they were leaving for a day out with their family. On other occasions they reached the world outside through a supervised area towards the rear of the building. On a polished table were copies of *Time* and *Newsweek* and *The New Yorker*. Often back copies of these magazines would be distributed among the patients, and with children's stubby scissors they would cut out pictures, an odd assortment of Hamilton cartoons, Chanel advertisements and photographs of the starving and suffering of the world, and paste them to poster board in strange and eerie combinations of the dying, the dead, the bored and the gorgeous.

Dr. Bradley stepped out of her office and shook Jill's hand. Then she reached forth and embraced Jill, holding her for a few moments to her body. "How was your trip?"

"Very nice, thanks."

"I'm afraid that Carrie had an episode while you were away." She said it as though it were in quotation marks or italics. "It had nothing to do with your being away. In any event she had no idea."

"How bad was it?"

"Let's go into my office."

Jill looked at her. She began to tremble. "Is she all right?"

"She's fine. Come in and we'll talk about it."

The office was large and furnished with a desk and a sofa and two armchairs. Dr. Bradley sat in one of the chairs. Jill sat on the sofa.

"Actually there are two things I wanted to mention to you. A detective came up here to speak to me."

"David Resnick?"

"That's right. He said he was investigating Dr. Freytag's death."

Jill couldn't understand why David would bother with Carrie. She had nothing to do with the case. She had nothing to do with Peter.

"He said it was just some routine questioning. I let him see Carrie through the window."

"He wanted to talk to her?" Nothing made sense.

"He wanted to see me. He wanted to know Carrie's history." She looked at Jill. "He wanted to know if Carrie's condition was natural, or as a result of abuse."

"Abuse."

"Physical violence. When she was an infant."

"My God."

"He said it was just a routine part of the investigation. He asked if Carrie's father ever visited her."

Jill looked at her.

"You know that he's never called my office. In any case I've always assumed you kept him current on Carrie's situation."

"He's really not interested."

"But I'm glad you are. Believe it or not we have families who never visit or call. I told Sergeant Resnick that you were an attentive mother. I also told him something of Carrie's history. That seemed to satisfy him."

"But I had already told him all of this."

Jean shrugged and smiled. "So. How are you holding up?"

"Not badly."

"You're well?"

"I'm well."

"You weren't traveling all that long."

"I decided to come back early. There seemed no point in staying on. I'm thinking about selling the house and moving to the city."

Dr. Bradley said nothing. Jill looked at her. Something was wrong. She said, "What's happened to Carrie?"

"If it had been serious I would have called and left a message on your machine. If it had been very serious I would have called your sister and asked her to get in touch with you."

"She had no idea where I was staying."

"Carrie became very angry one afternoon. It was funny because it was the day you usually come to see her."

"I don't always visit on a regular day."

"Not since Dr. Freytag's death. But before then it was almost always Sundays."

"So she'd been expecting me?"

"I don't know if we can say that. But she had a tantrum at dinnertime."

Jill looked at her.

"She refused to eat, and then she threw the tray on the floor."

Jill looked at her, as if seeking out meaning.

"We had to restrain her. It went on for a long time. She's a

strong girl, and she can be an angry one. Without words she has
few other ways to express herself."

"I hope you didn't use a jacket."

"We had to use a jacket."

"God."

"It's the only way, Jill. We didn't keep it on her for a long
time, just until we could give her an injection and the drug
calmed her down."

Jill said nothing.

"She's getting older," Dr. Bradley went on, "and stronger."

"But there are no other changes."

"No. Not really."

"Not really?"

"Not at all. Unless we interpret her anger as being directed towards your absence. In which case we'd be seeing a marked improvement, an ability to make fairly complex connections in her
mind."

"I don't like her being treated with drugs."

"We had to in this case. She was completely out of control."

"Did she hurt herself?"

"No. She began menstruating the next morning. There may
have been a physiological connection. That kind of violent reaction works like a shock to the system. It might have brought on
her period."

"And there was no problem with that?"

"No. She woke up with blood on her panties and sheets, she
showed it to Frida and we went in and cleaned her up and gave
her a pad. She didn't seem to mind one way or the other."

Jill thought of the blood coming from the man under the car.
Jean Bradley looked at her and Jill told her briefly about what she
had seen. "Things are a bit overwhelming at the moment," Jill
said.

"I think it might be nice if Carrie had a day out with you. I
know it's been cold, but if you could take her shopping or off to

see your horse or even for trip into the city, I think it would be good for her. A change of scenery, some quiet time with you. I think it would be good, Jill."

"All right."

"Why don't we go up now and see her."

"I have a few things for her," and Jill picked up the bag by its handles. They walked up the staircase to the second floor and stepped into the elevator. Hanging on three of its walls were thick mats, like those used in gymnastics classes. Jill leaned against one and momentarily closed her eyes to shut out the harmless light of the little box. When they reached the third floor the door opened with a hum and a clank. Jill counted off the doors to Carrie's room, one two three four, and when Jean unlocked it she found her daughter precisely the way she had left her, sitting on the bed, gazing out the window and holding a small blue kitten to her cheek, and her heart seemed to break as she looked at her.

Dr. Bradley said, "Let me know if you need anything," and shut the door.

Jill sat beside Carrie and put her arm around her and kissed her. "My little sweet, my baby."

Carrie said nothing. She smiled a little, not at her mother but at the toy she held against her face.

"Pretty kitty," Jill said. "Have you given her a name yet?" It seemed absurd to her, speaking to Carrie in this manner, as if Carrie were fluent with words and nimble of tongue, as if the godlike procedure of nomenclature were somehow within her grasp. Yet she had always talked to Carrie this way, slightly over her head, as though it were a kind of stretching exercise for her daughter.

"I've missed you so much, my darling," Jill said. "You know you've grown since I last saw you." She thought how much she missed her baby, how she would love to have her living at home, sleeping in the room next to hers. Gladly she would remove the desk and computer, the myriad objects of her professional life.

She would buy pretty curtains and mobiles and toys for Carrie, and it was pointless to think this way, because it would never happen, it could never come to pass. Now that she was alone she saw that all she had was Carrie. Anyone else who came into her life could never share it in quite the same way. He would always be on the outside, in the borderlands, a figure in the distant frontier.

But he would be there.

She crossed the bridge at eleven-thirty and sat in traffic on the drive by the river. A few sailboats were out on the brisk and treacherous day, their exquisite sails swollen and breastlike, impossibly white even in the grey sunlight. Carrie had seemed brighter that day, and when Jill thought it she meant it almost literally. There was a glow and a shine to Carrie's face that hadn't been there before. Perhaps her episode in the past week had caused this change, perhaps those passing moments of violence had brought something out in her, something ripe and glorious.

Now the traffic began to move again, and as she began to pick up speed she felt it once more, just as it had come to her in London, this wave, this fire and ice, and her body shivered momentarily before it passed. She told herself things: she was coming down with a cold, with the flu, with food poisoning, she thought of what she had eaten the previous night and that morning, eggs and toast, an innocuous raisin bagel, all of which had been cooked until nothing could possibly remain raw, until even the pathetic raisins burned her tongue, and she could feel herself beading with sweat. She opened her window, in fact she opened them on both sides of the car, and was glad to have the breeze off the water. Now she was feeling better, now she was herself again, and she was certain this had everything to do with having to view the video with David, a manifestation of apprehension and alarm on her brow, in her chest.

But it was more than that. The thought of watching this film didn't trouble her as much as seeing David Resnick again. Since the last time she had been with him, since just before her trip, things had changed, he had ceased being simply a detective, a nice guy with a case on his hands. Now he had achieved complexity, layers of identity, and so in her mind she couldn't quite define him, he continued to shimmer between policeman and friend and lover and policeman and lover and friend and stranger and policeman and the more she thought about it the less clearly she was able to bring him into focus. At the light she sat in her car and stared at the police station, the great tower made up of cells and interrogation rooms and offices and laboratories, a place where people were pinned to guilt with words, where flakes of blood fell from old bones, where savagery achieved silence and where trained eyes sought the outlines of those who had disappeared. On the corner a man in a hooded jacket stood with his hands in his pockets, staring with pained eyes, withstanding the wind as it gathered and tumbled down the hills and corridors between the skyscrapers of the financial district. On the radio a man with an amicable voice said that the composer Don Carlo Gesualdo, Prince of Venosa, had found his wife and her lover in a bed and had taken a knife and murdered them and then had gone out and composed exquisite music about the flight of the soul. *Shed thy tears like a torrent, day and night, and let not the apple of thine eye be dry,* the announcer translated.

She parked the car and got out, and when she stepped into the building David Resnick came up behind her and touched her shoulder and when she turned she brushed against him, so close had he come to her. She had to keep herself from embracing him. He wore a blue Oxford shirt and pale yellow crew-neck sweater. The details filled her eyes. He said, "Welcome back," and the breath flew from her mouth.

"You startled me."

"Would you like to have lunch first?"

"I," she said, and he said, "It's up to you, Jill." He spoke so quietly that he was nearly whispering.

She looked at him. "I'd like to get it over with."

In the elevator they had little to say to each other. For a woman to whom words came gracefully and with ease, Jill could only open her mouth to silence. David said, "We'll do this in my office. We won't be disturbed."

They walked down the corridor, David slightly ahead of her. She noticed that the hair on the crown of his head was beginning to thin. "Is it long?" she said.

"Exactly forty-nine minutes and twelve seconds. You don't have to watch all of it." He shut the door to his office. "All I want you to do is try to identify the woman."

"I don't know her," she said.

"You haven't seen her yet, Jill."

"I knew about my husband's affair. He never told me the woman's name."

"Did you ask?"

"No. I didn't want to know it." Without knowing her name or seeing her photograph she had been spared not the details but the reality of his love for this person. Sometimes Jill would wonder if this woman's face was prettier than hers, her breasts bigger, her legs longer, her mind more cultivated, her fingers more skillful, her lips fuller. Not knowing made it that much easier to forgive Peter. To forgive, but not to forget.

"But you may have seen her," David said. He sat behind his desk. To the side of it, on a metal stand, was a Sony television and a VCR. On both machines had been taped a bar code and printed number. She imagined Resnick having to requisition them from some central audiovisual office, much as she had to do at the university when she wanted to show a film to one of her seminars. He said, "You may have seen her walking out of your husband's office. Or at a cocktail party."

"We went to very few parties."

"But I assume Dr. Freytag must have sometimes invited his friends and colleagues to your home?"

"Sometimes."

"Younger women? Attractive women? I'm sorry. That wasn't meant to be a reflection on you."

She laughed. "I didn't take it that way."

"The woman in the film is a lot younger than your husband. That's what I meant."

"I understand." For a moment she said nothing, and the moment was held in suspension. She said, "I suspected she was younger. I asked him a lot of questions about this thing of his, this affair. But," and she laughed a little, "I forgot to ask him how old she was."

"Are you ready to watch this?"

"I'm scared to death, David."

"I understand how you feel." He stood and handed her the remote control. "One more thing: do you own a video camera?"

She shook her head.

"Did you ever have one, you and Peter?"

"No."

"I'll leave you alone in here."

"Wait. Tell me about this. How did you find it, how did you," and she didn't bother finishing her sentence. He said, "You know that your husband had a small stereo system on the shelves behind his desk, a collection of CDs and cassettes. When the office was cleaned out we found a key inside an empty CD box, Mahler's Second Symphony. It was obviously to a safe-deposit box. It was just a matter of tracing the code and number on the key to the bank." He told her which bank it was in. He looked at her.

"What else was in the box?"

"In the bank?" He considered it for a moment or two. "There were some greeting cards. A valentine, a birthday card. That sort of thing."

"How were they signed?"

"Affectionately," he said.

"Intimately," she said.

"Very much so."

"Was there a name?"

"No. Whoever wrote them was very careful not to leave anything on them which might identify her. It leads me to believe she was also married at the time. She made very sure no one would ever be able to identify her."

"Especially me."

"Especially you."

She felt a vast emptiness within her, as if everything she had depended on in her marriage, the companionship, the friendship and love of her husband, had been nothing but masks and cheap songs. She wanted to take David's hand, just to feel some warmth between her fingers, to hold it to her cheek, to assure herself that such a thing as affection was still within her grasp.

He looked at her. "When you've seen as much as you need to see, just switch it off and open the door. I'll be in the next room doing some work."

"So you're not going to watch it with me?" She regretted saying it; it sounded as though she almost wished him to view it, as if there might be the slightest chance that they might become aroused by the scenes enacted before them on the nineteen-inch screen.

He said, "I think it's best you watch it alone," and touching her hand lightly he rose and left the room.

She waited for nearly a minute. She turned on the television. Bert and Ernie were sparring over a cookie. She pressed the button and listened as the click and whirr of the mechanism began to run the tape. She could hear her heart beating, and a rush of blood to her head made her a little giddy, it turned her stomach, and then her bedroom came into view. There was the bed, covered only in a sheet. There was her bedside table, and there the book she had been reading at the time. Where was she, Jill? Teaching, researching, traveling, eating lunch in the city, at the university cafeteria? She could hear voices too low to be discerned from one another. The woman fell backwards into the screen and onto the bed, and her youth and beauty were astonishing. She wore a yellow silk dressing gown, and Jill lifted herself from the chair when she saw it, because it belonged to her, Peter had not only fucked this woman in their bed, he had also allowed her to wear Jill's clothes. The woman had short brown hair and pale skin. She smiled at the lens and slowly began to unbelt the robe. She let it slip from her shoulders as though she were teasing the camera, baring her skin, parting her knees, until it came away from her completely and she tossed it, Jill's garment, in fact a Christmas gift from Peter, onto the floor.

Now Peter came into view, and she felt her head spin, for the last she had seen of him he was a waxwork in a box and now he was alive, nude and aroused. The colors were heightened by the quality of the film, the screen filled with inflamed reds and purples. I don't know her, she said aloud, and she turned off the tape. Grover was talking to Oscar. Oscar said I hate peanut butter and jelly but I like peanut butter and ketchup, and she switched the tape back on again. The woman was fellating Peter and touching him with her hands and the expression on his face was like nothing Jill had ever seen in her life with her husband. She felt as though what had begun six years earlier, this humiliation of her, was now completed in a posthumous crushing of her pride, her spirit, her love. She turned off the tape and the television. She felt ridiculous as she wiped the tears from her eyes. It no longer mattered, certain things had been erased from the tables of blame by Peter's terrible death. And yet she was still alive, and didn't that, for God's sake, matter? Peter couldn't feel anything, he was beyond voice and touch, and yet she had to sit here on earth and endure this. Peter no longer mattered, he was a memory, something abstract, and the apparent cruelty of the thought came to her as something sensible and reasonable and clean. Now she was left, she and Carrie, and only the living possessed any value. She felt as she had when she'd returned from Boston with the tube inside her, and Geoff had become like the air itself, invisible, utterly neutral. She opened the door and David looked up. Tacked to a board beyond him were photographs of a room, things in it, a person, and they came to her in a momentary undefining glance. He walked directly to her and shut the door behind him. She put her hands on his arms and he cupped her elbows with his hands. Without looking at him she said, "I've never seen her before in my life."

"Are you all right?"

"Of course not. How would you feel if you had to watch a film of your wife and her lover?" Her tone was so familiar as to be almost sexual.

He said nothing.

"I don't know her," she said, drawing away from him. "She's nothing to me." She thought of the woman in the film as a girl, and her mind began the critical process of reduction: the girl was young and inexperienced, sexually unadventurous, obviously not attractive in person. One day her pretty little breasts would sag. One day she would grow old. Yet Jill felt like a hag, lustless and on the verge of reeking old age. Now she wanted David to touch her not as though she were a helpless invalid, someone who needed his support, but as a man who desired her, who wanted to feel her skin, to taste her body, to drown in her pleasure.

"Let me get your coat. I've got the afternoon off. Let's have a drink and something to eat."

"This hurts so much."

"I understand how you must feel."

"At least she can't see Peter anymore," she said, and they walked to the elevator.

They avoided each other's eyes and only began talking once they got into his car. David said, "You're sure you saw enough of it to know if you'd ever seen her before?"

"I've never seen her before."

"Now you understand why the funeral was filmed." He seemed to have forgotten that the radio was on. It was a phone-in show. A man said that someone ought to take a gun to the governor, and David switched it off. He turned to her when they stopped at a light. "It's a matter of routine when the deceased is a victim of an unsolved crime."

Jill looked at him.

"She wasn't there," he said.

"Do you think this woman killed him?"

"I never said that."

"But it's possible."

"That she did it alone?" He shook his head. "I doubt it very much. It looks as if more than one person was involved. And nothing indicates that she was actually a part of this. All we have is that videotape, and no evidence that it's in any way connected to Dr. Freytag's murder."

"But if there's no evidence, then everyone's a suspect."

He laughed. "Logically speaking, yes. But you're certainly not one."

"I was at first."

"Most murders are committed by people intimate with the victim. Husbands, wives, lovers, companions."

"So this woman could have done it."

"Or arranged it."

"But why?"

He had moved rapidly through the streets and now he pulled into a parking garage across from a converted marketplace. Once it housed dealers in produce and grains and slabs of meat. Now it contained endless shops and restaurants. In the warm weather people congregated in the courtyard and ate hot dogs, slices of pizza, sandwiches loaded with sprouts and feta cheese and avocado, and then went off to buy jeans and paperbacks and Mylar balloons. He switched off the ignition and seemed content to sit for a moment. "Could you possibly put a date on that tape you saw?"

"Probably from six years ago. When Peter had his affair."

"But if you know nothing about the woman involved how can you be so sure of it?"

She saw where his words and mind were taking her. "You mean he might have had more than one lover.'

"It's not unlikely. People who take lovers and get away with it often go from one person to another."

"They take risks," she said.

"And they usually get away with them. The more they get away with them the more daring they get."

"Then they get caught."

"Maybe not."

"But Peter told me about his affair."

"He told you what, that he was seeing another woman and that it was all over? You took his word for it."

"I believed him."

"He took advantage of your trust."

"Why are you doing this to me, David? I loved Peter, I was in love with him, I didn't," and she lost her way in the sentence, "I wasn't cynical about him, I trusted him. I believed him."

"Put a date on the film, Jill."

"I can't."

"Does he look younger than when you last saw him?"

"Peter always looked younger than he was."

"It was shot in your bedroom, wasn't it."

"How do you know?"

"Because it doesn't look like a motel or even hotel room. There's a book on the bedside table. It's a paperback edition of a novel by Henry James."

"*The Wings of the Dove.* I was reading it."

"When was this?"

Her eyes moved here and there, "I'm not sure. I read so much that I forget when I've read something."

"But reading is like listening to music, isn't it?" and she could hear him leading her into a kind of thinking that would arrive at the truth, he was prodding and pushing her, gently moving her this way and that.

"You mean I can associate the book with something."

"Some event. An anniversary, something to do with Carrie. Something even to do with your horse. Your teaching. Something in the news."

"I can't remember," and her hands moved rapidly through the confined space of the car.

"How old was he in the film, Jill?"

"I don't know."

"For Christ's sake, you lived with him for thirteen years, you saw what he looked like. People change the length of their hair, they get greyer or balder, how old was he, Jill?"

"I don't know."

"It wasn't six years ago, was it."

"I don't know."

"Was it earlier? Later?"

"I don't know." Her face was covered with tears of frustration and agony.

"Tell me, Jill. When were you reading *The Wings of the Dove?*"

"I read it last year."

David said nothing.

Then he said, "Was it the first time you'd ever read the book?"

She nodded. "Yes."

"This film was made last year."

"Yes."

"And you knew nothing about this woman."

She shook her head and said the word No, but no sound came from her mouth.

David opened his door and came around to her side. He unlatched the door and reached in and took not her arm but her hand. He held it lightly for a moment and he leaned down and gently touched the side of her face. He tugged lightly at her hand until she got out of the car. He shut the door and locked it. She felt ashamed and disgraced. She held so tightly on to him that she imagined she could feel his heart beating beneath his ribs. Although she knew it didn't matter, she wondered what she must seem like in front of this man she so liked. Stupid? Ignorant? If Peter had been having affairs all along what did that say about her? Had he been pretending all those times they had made love, had his moans and dramatic ejaculations, the way his hips thrust against hers, the way he used his mouth on her, were these all mere rehearsals for the real thing with his women? Hadn't she pleased him, even a little?

Before they left the garage David stopped and turned to her. He said, "You understand this may make the investigation move a lot more quickly now." It was beyond her, such a statement, not because she couldn't grasp the words but because she hadn't the ability to see it all in the way that David could. It was like viewing a painting close-up, examining the detail, the brush strokes, the fine lines in a person's face. But to step back, to see the frame as well as the scene—this was the pleasure and prerogative of the detective. Now it came to her that the room in which he'd been waiting for her while she watched the video was the situation room for Peter's murder, and the photographs she had glanced were of Peter in the Hubbard Hotel, and she wondered why so much trouble was being taken to uncover the truth about the death of her husband. It was not as if he were an innocent child, brutally murdered one December evening in the woods. In fact there was nothing innocent at all about the man. Peter had left the film in a safe-deposit box; he had left the key in a CD box, in the set of Mahler's Second she had bought him a few years earlier for his birthday, the version with Solti conducting the Chicago Symphony Orchestra. Had he meant one day to destroy the film and return the key, or had he expected to die knowing that someone somewhere would find the tape, sit Jill down in front of a television, play it for her? She thought of the girl with the short hair falling into the scene, as if until then she had been very close to Peter's body, growing aroused, anticipating the effect of a camera on her exposed body. Jill had known his body so intimately she could speak of the freckles and tiny moles and now she saw that other women were also privy to these details. The knowledge of it diluted her memories of Peter. She saw him as he was in that photograph in her office, his eyes hidden behind dark lenses, unreadable, unreachable, unloving and corrupt. Jill was sorry she was about to have a meal with this man she liked so much. Her appetite had fled her, in fact it was as if she had no need to eat ever again, as if food would go down and be instantly ejected from her, and the notion of finding pleasure in edibles and things to drink seemed to her the height of absurdity.

CHAPTER *21*

The restaurant was located on the bottom level of the building. Lunch hour was over and now only one or two couples and a few people in business suits remained. She was about to say something to David, about to ask him to take her back to her car, but a choice had to be made. She would prefer to be with him. To be alone suddenly seemed a dangerous option, a fatal one. The restaurant had a southwestern motif, the colors on the walls and ceilings and rugs were ochres and deep blues and warm yellows, and the air was peppery and faintly redolent of smoldering wood.

"Will you have a drink?" David asked. With his elbows on the table he held his hands loosely together. He smiled at her.

"Vodka."

"Tonic?"

"Just an Absolut and ice."

David ordered a light beer. Had he not been involved with this case would he have had something stronger, a double whisky, a dry martini, something that would fuddle his brain and tie his tongue? He'd said he had the afternoon off, but she knew very well he would be working, that every moment of this meal, from the first sip of alcohol to the last drop of coffee, would be part of the investigation. She had watched the video and had come to certain conclusions and now she could look back on her marriage and see it all differently. A change of perspective, the introduction of shadow and contrast, would suddenly shed new light on the case of her husband's murder. Which was worse: dying in ignorance, or living with the knowledge that all along she had been missing the point?

He looked at her. "How was your trip?"

"I'd almost forgotten about it," and she smiled.

"It's good to see you."

"Especially now that you've made me look at that tape."

Together they laughed a little, a bittersweet knowing laugh.

"No, I mean it. Beyond the fact that I'm in charge of the investigation, I've been enjoying talking with you."

"I'm sorry if I bothered you with my calls from London."

"No no."

"I was feeling low. I hadn't felt all that well. I suppose I just needed to hear a friendly voice."

"I was glad to hear from you. Was the trip worthwhile?"

"You mean did I get my?" and the waitress was there with their drinks and they waited silently for her to go. David touched his glass against hers. He smiled and looked her in the eye, and they drank.

"Did I get my mind off Peter's death?"

"I'm sure it's not as easy as that."

"It was a strange trip," she said. "It was really a waste of time, a waste of money. I didn't do anything. I saw a few of Peter's friends. I didn't go to the theatre, I only visited two museums. A Greek waiter tried to pick me up." She laughed, astonished to believe it had actually happened.

"I traveled to Europe with a girlfriend when I was in college. We flew Icelandic. Remember Icelandic with its cheap fares? We went to Amsterdam and Copenhagen and Paris, and all I remember is my girlfriend, because we spent all the time arguing over whether we should get married or not."

"Did you marry her?"

"She's the one that got away," he said. "I met Susan just after I became a cop. She was teaching at a day care center that had been broken into one night. I was sent to investigate. They'd wrecked the place, broken the toys, kicked the little wooden cubbies, torn the pages from the books. Susan was devastated and the kids were terrified and one thing led to another." He shrugged. "Now we usually travel some place the kids like. Disney World, Epcot. San Francisco. Last summer we went to Washington. It's expensive traveling overseas." He sounded disappointed.

"Especially with children. I'm so sorry Carrie wouldn't appreciate trips like that."

"How is she?"

Now she remembered. He had been there, he had asked questions, his trust in Jill was limited, it was as thin and delicate as a spider's filament. "I heard you went to the clinic while I was away," she said. "Why is it any concern of yours if my daughter is there or what kind of mother I am?"

"You know that I need to look at everything. I need to see the whole picture."

"But what were you trying to find out?"

"The conditions under which your daughter was admitted. If there'd been any signs of abuse."

"From me?"

"From your first husband. If he'd in any way abused your daughter, then he might be concerned that a psychiatrist like Dr.

Freytag had married you. I'd asked the Seattle police to interview him. It seems he travels a lot for his work."

"I thought you'd already spoken to him."

"We had. But I knew that he was involved in computer soft-ware development. There was a convention here in town the weekend Dr. Freytag died."

"What does this have to do with Carrie?"

"I was just trying to find out if he had caused your daughter any harm."

"Or if I had."

He said nothing.

"Or if I had."

"I need to look at everything," he said.

She looked away from him. "Was Dennis here that weekend?"

He shook his head and it forced her to turn and look again at him. "No," he said.

She considered ordering a second drink. She imagined David arresting her for drunk driving the moment she pulled away from the station in her Volvo. Was he always a cop, was he forever in-vestigating, even in bed with a woman? Did he seek out evidence, stray hairs, bits of flesh under the fingernails, the unfamiliar scents of suspects and thieves?

Although she only wanted a salad and a roll or two, or maybe just a bowl of soup and a glass of wine, David insisted she eat something more. The menu sickened her: tortillas and enchiladas, things smothered in peppers and cheese and onions, culinary re-minders of a trip to Taos she had made long ago with Dennis, a vacation notable for the amount of time she had spent sitting on toilets, bending over in pain, lying awake in a heavy sweat. A bowl of salsa and a basket of chips sat on the table between David and Jill. She watched as he sampled them, she watched his mouth move, and she took in his blue eyes, the same eyes that had seen Peter on the floor of the hotel room. Yet there was something charming in Detective Sergeant Resnick's choice of restaurant, as though he had seen something in her that made him think of spice and heat, of desert sun and long siestas.

"Are you working on any other cases at the moment?" she asked.

"A few. But not another homicide."

"It's a difficult one, then."

"So far, yes."

She looked at him. He folded his arms on the table and leaned forward a little.

"Why is it different?"

"Because we thought by now we'd have a motive and at least one suspect. But we don't have either. Usually when someone's killed outside his normal environment a story begins to emerge almost immediately. So far we have nothing. A hotel like the Hubbard attracts a certain class of people for very particular reasons. Drugs. Women. That's about it. Your husband wasn't an addict, he didn't have a trace of an illegal substance in his body when he died. Women? Possibly. Maybe even likely. But I don't think it was his style to go to a place like the Hubbard for a casual reason, especially when he was intending to eat dinner with you before his flight. He might have gone to a motel, or one of the better hotels in the city, some place where he could have a shower. I happen to think that the story can be found closer to home."

"His personal life."

"That's right. We've questioned all of his patients. All of them have been cleared."

She said, "That room you were waiting in. Those photos on the wall. Those were pictures of Peter, weren't they."

For a moment or two he said nothing. "It was stupid of me to wait there for you."

"I didn't get a good look at them."

"I see them every day. I look at them three times a day, four times, as often as I walk by them."

"You'd gone to the Hubbard before you came to the hospital."

"Are you asking me if I had? I went there just after we took the call here."

"So you saw Peter."

He said nothing.

"Was there a lot of blood?"

"The waitress is coming." He looked again at the menu. "What are you going to have?"

"I don't know."

"Aren't you hungry?"

"I don't know."

"You have to eat something."

She smiled. "Is that what you tell your kids?"

"Three times a day."

"A hamburger, then," she said.

"How about a steak?"

"I'm not really all that hungry."

"Have chicken."

"No thank you."

"Fish. The shrimp is good."

"Oh God."

"Look, have a hamburger, then."

"Okay. But very rare."

"I'll have the same."

The waitress watched and listened to them and wrote it down in her pad. She returned to the kitchen and Jill looked at David. "Tell me what you saw in the room. Tell me about Peter."

She could see that he was considering it, she could see it in the way his eyes moved, the way he held his head, the set of his mouth. "I really can't, Jill."

"Show me the photos, then."

"I don't think so."

"Do you think they'd be any more upsetting than the video you made me watch?"

"I always believe it's better to know and hear and see only what you need to know and see and hear."

"Ignorance is bliss, then."

"I suppose so," he said.

"How was he killed?"

Resnick said nothing.

"If this ever goes to trial I'll have to hear it anyway. I'd might as well know now."

"You want to know everything," he said.

"I'm a historian. I do research, I deal in the truth."

"Not when it's so close to you. Not like this."

The waitress returned, asking if they wanted something else to drink. Resnick ordered another beer. Jill wanted a second vodka and realized if she drank it the afternoon would go by in a blur. "A glass of red wine," she said, and the waitress walked away. Jill watched as David's eyes followed the young woman and she saw the light in them change.

Suddenly he looked up at her. "There's no reason for me to tell you any more than you know, Jill."

Until then she hadn't even noticed the music in the restaurant, some sort of country-and-western tune that normally would have grated on her nerves, all twang and complaint. The waitress brought their drinks and served some people at another table. Again David took her in, looking at her face, her breasts, her fingers as they wrote out the order.

"She's pretty, isn't she," Jill said.

"Very pretty."

Jill sipped from her wineglass. She felt the day sliding between her fingers like the fall of sand, and she realized that if she let it go, if it simply escaped her, she would never see David Resnick again except in a courtroom, or his office, or in the guise of a voice over the phone, asking questions, probing for answers, keeping his distance. She couldn't find the necessary words, I'm glad we did this, or Let's do this again sometime, or I like being with you, none of these seemed anything but trite, unreal, infantile, as though they belonged in some other world where people weren't murdered and heartbreak was just another ailment, like a bout of flu or a bad sunburn.

"Tell me about your wife," she said. "Tell me about your children."

"My wife is a teacher at a private school."

"Third grade."

"I remember telling you all this."

"Tell me more."

"Her name is Susan. We've been married," and he raised his eyes a little because the number was not quite in sight, "fifteen years. We have two kids, Jake and Molly, and you don't really want to hear this, do you?"

She smiled. "Of course I do." She said the name in her mind: Susan Resnick. She thought of the photo on David's desk, a wife taking a lock of hair away from her eye, a sexy smile. This was the woman who kissed him, who touched him and who was touched by him, who could hold him in her arms. Did she know where her husband was at this moment? She was tempted to ask him, to pry a little, to find out how he wished to conduct his life from this moment on.

"There's something I have to tell you," he said. The tone in his voice was ominous, like summer's distant thunder. He looked at her, and she felt something sink within her chest. "It's about the safe-deposit box. The one your husband had. The one I spoke to you about."

She felt a vast wash of relief come over her.

"There were more than just a few cards there. There were twenty-two of them."

She looked at him. It all seemed irrelevant how many cards were there, whether there were two or twelve or thirty-five didn't make any difference. Peter had had an affair with this woman and it had lasted longer than he had claimed. Resnick looked at her as she stared at him. "The cards were written out by three separate people, all women. There were no envelopes, no names mentioned, ever."

"Oh my God." They were the first words that came into her head, more appropriate to a natural disaster or a fatal accident, yet she felt as though someone had shot her through the brain, tearing a hole through the memories that constituted her marriage to Peter Freytag. "You mean that Peter had been seeing three different women?"

"Not necessarily at the same time. But we had the handwriting checked and it was clear there were three different writers."

"I'm not a bad person," she said, and the words simply came out of her mouth without prior thought. "I'm," and Resnick said "Shh," and his head turned a little, as if to ensure that no one was witnessing this scene. He waited for her to quiet down. She drank from her glass of water. The wide blades of a ceiling fan slowly swept through the air above them. The restaurant suddenly took on a melancholy aspect, as though it were precisely what it was pretending to be, a crumbling roadhouse in the New Mexico desert. There was no place to go, no one to run to, no shelter or sanctuary. Three women; thirteen years of marriage. It seemed there had been no room for her, that a crowd had begun to form almost from the very beginning, and her mind filled with the fiery uncertainty of speculation. Her husband's death was like the opening of something utterly forbidden, each day bringing forth a new demon, something clawed and vicious that attached itself to her and tore at her heart. Now she wished she were about to flee to London or Paris. Now she needed the time away. Now there was no place to go.

Resnick said, "This has nothing to do with you personally. Your husband undoubtedly was very much in love with you. There's no evidence that he was doing anything but playing around. I mean, were you always faithful to Dr. Freytag?"

"Of course I was."

"You were never tempted?"

"Once or twice."

"And?"

"Nothing ever happened. One of them was a colleague."

He looked at her.

"And the other was a student."

"And nothing happened there."

She finished her wine. "Nothing happened anywhere."

"But you were tempted."

She wanted more wine. "Yes." She looked for the waitress. Greg walked into her memory, bearded and smiling, as distinct and alive as if she had seen him only that morning. It was difficult thinking of him, it was like wandering into a labyrinth, a place of distraction with no apparent exit.

"Was it mutual?"

"I think so," and she handed the glass to the waitress and indicated it required refilling. "I'm certain it was."

"Don't get drunk."

"I won't."

"You won't be able to drive."

"Put me in a cell, then."

"It's better than going off and causing someone's death. Or your own."

"How's the food in your jail?"

He laughed. "I've never tried it."

"And how about you?" she said. "Have you always been faithful to Susan?"

He smiled at her. He said nothing. For one passing moment she saw that she had begun to build her future upon a mound of daydream.

The waitress brought their food, and a sense of exhaustion suddenly came over Jill, as though the knowledge she had just gained were too weighty for her body. Later it would hit her with immense clarity, later she would lie down and think about what she had learned, and the sensation would be not of fatigue but of drowning. And when night came and the air had grown silent, when her solitude was all the more acute, she would see that she had been deceived more than once or twice or four or five times, but ten times, twenty times, eighty times.

"I'm sorry I had to tell you about the cards," Resnick said. "But I thought you should know. We have three nameless women."

She remembered the postcard she'd received from Greg.

"Who may have had nothing to do with my husband's death."

She could phone him.

"But I told you, Jill, we have to examine everything."

She put her hands to her face and laughed into them. She could call Greg. He had taken a step towards her. Now it was her turn. She wondered what it would be like to fulfill a fantasy, to have exactly what she wanted. She was old enough to know. She knew it in her heart. There was no point in pursuing it to its logical, disappointing conclusion.

"It's very embarrassing," she said. "I mean it's ridiculous, Peter and his women. That tape. I never saw it coming."

He let her go on.

"I wasn't bad, I wasn't ugly, I was a good lover, I was tender, I pleased him. Why did he have to go out and do this?"

"Does it matter?"

"It does to you." Still she didn't look at him.

"Only because it might help us find his murderer. But it's done, Jill. He's gone."

"When he had that affair six years ago he told me not to take it personally."

"Then you shouldn't. You still shouldn't." He picked up his hamburger and bit into it, and the juices ran out over his fingers like blood from an open gash.

"You can't understand how this makes me feel."

"Eat your lunch before it gets cold."

"I hate this music."

"So do I." He looked at her and set his hamburger down.

"What's worse is that I can't confront him, I can't tell Peter what he's done to me."

"He probably never thought about it. Look, you're a very beautiful woman. What your husband did probably had nothing to do with you. What I mean is that maybe it wasn't a reaction to what you were. Or who you were. Am I making any sense?"

"No. But it doesn't matter."

They said nothing. They ate. Resnick said, "What are you doing for Christmas?"

Was it an invitation or mere curiosity? "Selling the house," she said, and he laughed.

"I'm serious. I told you before, I'm thinking of moving to the city. I'll get an apartment. I don't want to live there anymore. There was no happiness there."

"But there was," Resnick said. "You described your marriage as a happy one."

"Not anymore it isn't."

"But at the time it was to you."

"Peter was just pretending."

"Maybe not."

"I wish I knew what he got out of it."

"It's still a nice house. It's big. Not like mine."

She listened. For some reason every word he said about his life seemed utterly vital to her, of immense importance. He said, "We've lived there for almost as long as we've been married. Everything's changed. We have two kids, the neighborhood isn't the same. I don't know, I suppose we should move, too," and words like Lived and Married and Changed seemed highly charged, as though he were speaking in a language with which she had only a passing acquaintance and she needed to translate each word, extracting every nuance from it, weighing and savoring the tone of his voice, its volume and the way his eyes looked.

"How does your wife feel about it?"

"She's looking for another position."

"So you'll have to move." Her abruptness startled her.

"No. She'll have to commute."

She stared at him. "How did Peter die, David?"

"No."

"You have to tell me."

"No, Jill."

"We've gone this far together." The phrase seemed of tremendous consequence to her, as if not only her voice but her heart were somehow behind it. She watched him as he composed himself; she knew he was about to tell her the truth, the details of Peter's death. His face seemed to alter its shape and his eyes clouded over slightly, as if he were looking back in time through the door of the hotel room at his first glimpse of her husband in the stillness of death.

"Your husband suffocated and bled to death. His throat had been cut with a very sharp blade, a straight razor. At first we thought it was suicide, but we couldn't find the weapon. And from what we could see he had no reason whatsoever to commit suicide. He wasn't in serious debt, it doesn't look like he was being blackmailed, there were none of the usual factors staring us in the face in a suicide case. And the circumstances were unusual. The kind of hotel he chose, the fact that he was going to have dinner with you and fly to London. Suicide didn't make sense. And there was nothing in the room that could have caused the wound. A few days later we found the person who had come across Dr. Freytag's body and called us. He was the one who took the razor. He'd washed off whatever prints were on it. He was a drifter, he was a drunk, he took what he could get his hands on and didn't bother going through your husband's pockets. He said he heard nothing, that he'd been trying all the doors and this one was unlocked."

"He didn't try to take Peter's money?"

"He said he didn't want to touch him."

She looked at him.

"There was a lot of blood, Jill."

"Are you sure this man didn't kill my husband?"

"Absolutely certain. He's been questioned, cleared and released. He couldn't have done it, he was a lot older than Dr. Freytag and not very strong. Your husband was in excellent shape. It was obvious he worked hard at it. For all we know he may have committed suicide. But we still have to rule out all possibility of homicide. In any event your husband choked on his own blood."

"Jesus." Yet all along she had known it, dreamed it, thought of it. The detective touched her hand and rubbed his thumb lightly along her finger. At that moment of pain, of pointed grief and disrupted memory, she felt herself moisten and grow aroused, and she shifted herself in her chair. "He might have killed himself, then." Somehow she could accept that more than murder. It implied that Peter's death was an act of free will, and yet as she thought about it she realized that by killing himself he was also killing something in her.

"Look," he said. "I know this is hard for you, I understand how you feel about it. These things take time. Nothing we can do can bring your husband back."

"I don't want him back." And her voice rose to such a degree that others in the restaurant turned to look at this woman who had achieved sudden clarity and certainty on this blue December afternoon.

CHAPTER 22

Her last thought that evening before going to bed was that she hated her husband. Her memory began to unravel like yarn from a skein, and she followed it down the years, discovering how every inch of her past had been a confirmation of her dislike for Peter. Even when she recalled the happier moments, and there were many of them, thousands of them, she realized that even then he had been deceiving her. While he sat across from her at dinner, while he walked with her on the beach, while he caressed and loved her, his mind was elsewhere, in another woman's life. Jill had married him because Dennis had betrayed her, she had married him because he was unlike anyone else she had ever known, she had married him because he was intelligent and cultured and Swiss, she had married him for reasons she could pluck from the air at will, the way he looked at her, the shape of his fingers, the manner in which he kissed her, and yet she knew she had married him because he intrigued her and brought laughter to her lips and made her feel like the only woman in the world. She hated him because he had betrayed her and now he was gone and beyond retribution, and no one, no one at all, deserved not to be able to look a thief in the face and speak every word that burned on her tongue.

Yet David, too, had in his own way betrayed her, playing little games with her reactions, watching her eyes, saying things he never meant. Was he also betraying his wife? Did he take Jill out to lunch and tell Susan something else? She wondered what he might have said, she imagined he spoke of going out with the boys, the other cops, the fellas, dining at some local eatery, plunging their forks into four-alarm chili or boiled cabbage and pickled eggs and kielbasa, speaking of informers and street garbage, of crackheads and two-bit whores, while all along he'd been having a mildly civilized luncheon, drinks included, with Jill Bowman, whose husband had been murdered by person or persons unknown. If he lied to his wife, if, as he admitted, he had lied to Jill, did it mean he lied to everyone, was his life just like Peter's, was it a web of falsehood, a place of awkward symmetry, a room full of mirrors, and was he, in the end, to be as elusive and ungraspable as water, as sand, as the poisonous mercury?

When they rose from their meal Jill felt herself suddenly tip into a state of vague inebriation. It came upon her not as something solid and stunning, but rather as a kind of gentle wave that she could feel in her head and between her legs. Perhaps it was because she was with a man who attracted her. Perhaps it was because she had finally severed herself from her husband. Perhaps it just didn't matter. David opened the door for her and touched her arm lightly as she slid into the seat. He shut it and when she looked at the window she could see him looking at her. He got in behind the wheel and put his key in the ignition and without starting the engine sat back and said nothing. She wondered if she was meant to reach over and take his hand or touch his thigh, or even go further, unzip his fly and slide her hand inside his underwear, find the heat, and she found herself toppling into awkwardness and absurdity. She wondered if he would reach over and put his arm around her neck, if his hand would move into her blouse and under the material of her bra, or even lower, if it would engage the fine elastic of her panties and entangle itself in her lush moistness? She didn't know what to do because it had been so long since she had been with a man. Even after Dennis had moved out she'd seen no one, she'd been too busy with Carrie, and when the time came for her and Peter to make love they simply took their clothes off and climbed into bed, quietly, so as not to wake the baby. But there was nothing to fear. Instead of riding sleep with the buoyancy of a swimmer, someone floating on the easy waves of a gentle harbor, Carrie would sink into unconsciousness, rising up out of it at dawn with an accepting incomprehension, her big unquestioning eyes staring into nothing but the shallows of her reality.

For a moment Resnick said nothing, he didn't even turn to look at her. The silence disturbed her, and yet she sensed a tension between them, a kind of sexual tingle, not even that, it was like the sniff of ozone before the onset of thunder and rain, and this stillness and potential lay between them like a cloud, to the extent that she could no longer see him as Detective Sergeant David Resnick but rather as someone with whom very possibly she would make love. It was both utterly thrilling and as filled with despair as an eye swelling with tears. That sense of adolescent failure returned to her as vivid as it had been when she was fifteen and sixteen. She hadn't been unpopular in high school, merely bookish and a little distant, unsure of herself. She hadn't had a serious boyfriend, just boys who were also friends, and who, in an occasional playful mood, would feel her up or kiss her. She wondered if life henceforth would be like that, if, now that she

was no longer married, no longer complacent with Peter, unan-
chored and alone, she would be compelled to go through the ritu-
als of dating, of holding the same conversation with a series of
different men, of waiting for someone to make the first move, of
waking up beside a man who in the light of day was repellent to
her, reeking of stale cigarette smoke and alcohol. These were trivial matters in a dangerous world, and the thought of it reminded
her of the sheer casualness of some people during the Plague, people who danced by the river's edge and bragged of immunity and
God and who, in the end, collapsed into agony, into pain and
death, their twisted corpses a reminder to others of a certain fate.

"I don't like to speculate aloud," Resnick said. "I'm not really
supposed to be doing this. But I consider you more than just a
person involved in this investigation," and he looked at her.

"I don't know what you're saying."

Together they watched as a couple made their way to their car.
The woman put her hand on the man's neck and they touched
lips, and Jill felt embarrassed, as if unsure of what she was supposed to do, how to proceed without the distance of a public
place, within the intimate space of the front seat of David's car.

"There are public crimes and there are private crimes. There
are crimes people stumble into, holdups and snipers and street
mischief. Then there are crimes committed by people known to
the victim, friends and lovers. Babies are murdered by the people
who brought them into the world. Husbands shoot their wives.
Friends kill friends. Your husband had virtually no public life
apart from his professional one. He attended conferences and gave
speeches, and most of his time he was in his office treating his patients. I feel fairly sure that your husband's death had something
to do with one of the women he was seeing. It's the only area in
his life where there was a lot of uncertainty. He took chances
there, he risked exposure and possibly blackmail. We've gone
over everything a hundred times, Jill. We've examined his
records, we've looked at his appointment and address books, and
there's nothing that indicates he'd been involved in anything ille-

gal, or that would bring him into contact with anyone likely to kill him."

"He committed adultery."

"I'm speaking of murder. Your husband was killed. It outweighs everything else. We have to look at this from all different angles. The person who killed him is perfectly capable of going out and doing it again, finding himself another victim. If a crime can be prevented, then we're responsible for making sure it doesn't happen."

"It could have been one of his women." She had been tempted to use the word whores.

"Or a woman's husband or lover. Obviously we're looking into that. It's why I had you view the film. One of the women might have been as jealous of you as you would have been of her."

"But it was Peter who died."

"And then, you see, no one can have him. Everyone loses."

"So now what do I do?" It seemed an idiotic statement, the words of a weak, unthinking person. Resnick started the engine and looked at her. She felt as if she were starting from zero, as if she had divested herself of everything she had carried in her life until then. She looked at his hand on the steering wheel, and for some reason the sight of it aroused her, it became an element in her imagination, she could feel it against the skin of her body, and she wanted to see it there, on her breast, on her thigh, hand against flesh. He said nothing, yet his silence was full of intention and word, it was as if a line had been drawn between them, and each were waiting for the other to cross it. She wondered how she looked to him, if the fact that she had taken so much trouble over herself that morning had been noticed by him. She wondered what was going through his mind, if the quilt of desire had begun to piece itself into a dazzling pattern. She realized that she had taken a long time to get ready for what turned out to be a hamburger lunch. She had worn her best underwear, lace and brief satin, she had dabbed perfume on her body, she had been meticulous with her hair and face, and yet she felt not quite there,

not entirely in the present, as though through some abnormal
phenomenon she slipped into another grammatical tense. Even
David had noticed it.

"Are you all right?"

"I think the drinks hit me."

"I don't want you to drive home yet."

"What am I going to do, sit in the police station?"

The sunshine was almost too bright as they emerged from the
garage. The traffic was heavy, a knot of construction causing two
lanes to merge into one. She watched as the huge machine ham-
mered the ground with merciless force. Out of it erupted cables
attached to generators, peeling and filthy in their orange paint.
Standing calmly around the machinery were overweight men in
hard hats and work boots. A ditch had been dug and she could see
the layers beneath the road, the asphalt and gravel and the red
dirt of the city. Beneath that was the debris of the centuries, and
if they dug deep enough they would uncover house foundations,
broken pottery, discarded kid gloves and brass shoe buckles,
beads and brittle tibia. All of the details of the scene seemed to
leap out of her as if she were in the grip of fever. She wasn't
drunk, she was ill, and she was certain that whatever she had
caught in London was still with her, lingering in her system, sap-
ping her strength. Although outside it was cold, the sun coming
through the window heated the seats and the air smelled like
melting vinyl, and the contrast between the wintriness beyond
and the stale warmth within frustrated her and made her yearn
for either one or the other, bleak January or overwrought August.

"It's funny," Jill said. In her mind a door shut and the air filled
with the sounds of violins and cellos, and the smell of that time
was as rich and alive as if she were still there. Their conversation
had sent her memory back thirty years. "I saw someone murdered
when I was a girl."

He looked at her. "Are you serious?"

"I didn't see it. But I knew it was happening."

"You heard it."

"I only knew afterwards." She told him the story of Rose Keller. As she related the facts and impressions heightened by recollection the scene came back to her with especial brilliance and acuity. She remembered the bracelets Rose Keller wore on her right arm, the sound of them as silver and gold collided and jangled, and how, to Jill as a child, they seemed just right, absolutely suited to the way Rose dressed and the tone of her voice. When she thought of Rose Keller she saw ochre and deep rich browns, and the red of her hair. She saw the face powder on her cheeks and the color of her lips, and she remembered the little wristwatch she wore that was ringed with tiny diamonds. She could hear the music that came from her apartment, and she remembered also the sound of her being murdered. "I saw the man who did it," she said to Resnick. "I watched him when he left. He stood in the hallway for a little while."

"Murderers don't hang around."

"He did. But not for very long. He waited. He stood. He was picking his teeth, and I remember," and she lifted her hand to the air, as if she were sketching it on a pad of paper, "how he worked at it for a few seconds. He looked so thoughtful."

"You said they arrested someone else?"

"My mother showed me the photograph in the newspaper. I'd been sick for a few months. I hadn't been able to talk."

He looked at her.

"The doctor said it was a trauma."

"Like Carrie."

"No," and the word was like a shout, "it's not like Carrie. She was born that way. That had nothing to do with what happened to me. I knew what was going on, I was able to go to school and read and write. Carrie can't deal with reality, she can't," and Resnick said he was sorry, he didn't mean it to be taken like that, although when Carrie was diagnosed the first thing that had come to her mind was Rose Keller's body beneath a sheet.

"But I want you to understand," she said. "I mean, you went to the clinic to see if my baby had been abused. You still don't get it, do you."

"I said I was sorry."

"What happened to me was curable. It was a form of shock. Otherwise everything was normal."

"But you didn't actually see the woman being murdered."

"I saw the man come out of her apartment and then later in the afternoon the ambulance came and took her away."

They stopped at a light. He turned to her. "So you have no idea who killed her."

"I told you, I saw the man come out of her apartment."

"Someone else might have stopped in afterwards. It may even have been a friend or a lover. You'd said she was married, right?"

"No. Or at least she didn't live with anyone."

"You know that most people are murdered by people they know, people they're intimate with. Did you watch her door the whole time?"

"I don't think so. No, of course not."

It hadn't occurred to her. She tried to remember how long it had been between the time she saw the man and when Rose was taken away. "I lost my voice for four months," she said.

Resnick looked at her and said nothing. When they got to the station he asked how she was feeling, and she said she was feeling better, and she meant it. Yet she felt distracted, not quite there, and she knew it was because a piece of her mind was puzzling out the story of Rose Keller.

"We're going to need to talk again," Resnick said.

"I'd like that."

"We'll need to keep in touch about the case. I'm going to have another look at Dr. Freytag's appointment books and patients' files. If there's any discrepancy I'll let you know. I'm also going to have to question some of his friends, other psychiatrists. I need to know if they were aware of his private life."

"He belonged to an athletic club."

"We've already interviewed both men he played squash with,"
and he reached into his jacket pocket and took out a little notebook, "Harbison and a psychiatrist, a Dr. Frank Jacobson. I'll
have to talk to them again. Sometimes people tell their best
friends things they would never tell their spouses. I'm just telling
you this so you know. In case you ever hear from them or run into
them."

"I didn't know all his friends."

He said nothing.

He turned towards her, raising his knee slightly on the car
seat. "I'd like to do this again some time soon."

"I would too."

"When do you return to work?"

"In a few weeks. After the Christmas break's over. I'm going
into the office on Monday to look through my mail, speak to my
department chairman."

"Are you ready to go back?"

"I have nothing else to do. I'm going to call a broker and see
about putting the house on the market. I just want to make a
fresh start."

He seemed about to say something, words of weight and significance and risk. She watched him reach over and place his hand
over hers, and she could feel herself beginning to tremble, as if
this were the beginning of true illness, the descent into something feverish and visionary. She grabbed hold of his hand with
hers and he leaned towards her very slightly and then turned
away and opened the door and let go of her hand and got out of
the car and her lungs gave way and the breath fled from her body.

Now that they were on the street by the station voices grew
louder and more public, together they spoke briefly about her
ability to drive home, she thanked him for lunch and he said it
was his pleasure and he wished it could have been a more interesting meal, hamburgers not exactly being what he'd had in mind,
and there was a little nervous laughter, and she got into her car
and put her head back on the seat and realized she had broken

into a heavy sweat all over her body. She opened the window and turned the key and went around the corner and drove up the ramp to the highway leading home.

She went over the bridge and then drove through one town after another until she came to the interstate, where the road widened into four lanes and the view became distant and panoramic. She switched on the radio. She was surprised to hear that snow was expected that evening, a storm whose effects could not now be predicted as it raged and tore up the coast, swirling and casting its arms wider and wider, over the ocean and far inland, and the ferocity of the storm would be determined by its direction. She was amazed to hear this, and yet the sky was blue and unblemished, containing no signs or portents of such fury. When Peter was alive they would together cherish the anticipated blizzard, the notion of being trapped alone in their house. They would bring in armfuls of wood from the cord they had neatly stacked by the back door, and lay a fire that would blaze and cast heat. They'd drive out to the supermarket and fill a basket with food and forbidden things, quarts of ice cream and bags of popcorn and two pounds of roasting chestnuts and tins of anchovies and a container of feta and red and green and yellow peppers and mushrooms and grated mozzarella and a plastic bag full of raw pizza dough, or else they'd bring in Chinese food and sit by the fire and get greasy while they ate spring rolls and Szechuan dumplings, and twirled their chopsticks in containers of lo mein. And sometimes the storm wouldn't come, and the electricity wouldn't suddenly cease, and they would do it all anyway, switch off the lights and eat by the fire and listen to music and then go upstairs and make love, sometimes attempting to find new sensations that until then had not been mentioned by either of them. And now that she thought back with fondness on such matters she realized that these new sensations were new to her only, that Peter had all along been reveling in more than one life, two and three and possibly even four of them, he had given of himself so extensively that it must have taken all his energies to keep names and techniques in order. She was just one of many. This man of many layers had chosen to live with her. Would he have stayed had he survived? This was the question that couldn't be answered, this was but another mystery she would have to leave alone, as one does a dying animal found on the road, turning one's back on it, praying never to hear the screams of agony, the last breath, the horror of a creature's lonely death.

The house smelled fusty and uninhabited. This is how it would be all winter: shut up and stale. She opened the refrigerator and realized she hadn't much more than half a quart of milk, some orange juice, a grapefruit, a little leftover tuna. A half-full container of blueberry yogurt, bought weeks earlier, had turned strange and wondrous colors and stank like death. She was sorry she had drunk so much at lunch. Now she felt exhausted and ready for bed, and she made a pot of coffee and went through her mail, tossing onto the counter the horse magazine and the catalogues, and into another pile the bills: from the stable, the farrier, her dentist, Blackjack's dentist, Carrie's clinic, the gas, the cable service, the Optima card. There were a few more condolence cards, she hoped the last of them. Since Peter's death friends of hers wrote her notes and even longer letters and sometimes left messages on her machine, and because they respected her solitude, because they could see that one day they, too, might become widows in the course of an innocent Friday evening, they didn't demand that she speak or write to them at once, and she kept her distance not because she had nothing to say to them, but rather because she knew her friends wouldn't be able to find the words, they would be caught between ritual and silence, trapped in a stutter of incomprehension.

Now it came to her in a moment of brightness and lift that she had still not responded to Greg's postcard. Earlier that day she had decided not to reply, that to write back was to invite something that had passed to enter into a very different present. Her relationship with Greg belonged to another time, he was no longer her type, she was too old for him, she filled her mind with a thousand different excuses and picked up a pencil from the counter and wrote on a slip of paper normally used for shopping lists, Write Greg N., and then she crumpled it and threw it away.

She poured her coffee and sat at the table. It was still early. Again she wondered about dinner. She wasn't even hungry, but she would be at some inappropriate time, say nine or ten or eleven, and that would entail her driving out to the chicken place or the Chinese, or sending out for a pizza, none of which appealed to her. She picked up the phone and did what she had meant to do for years. Luc answered. He said that Sally would be there in a moment, she was just getting out of her car, what do you think of the weather, why don't you come and visit us, how have you been and what are your plans for the future, and Jill responded as best she could, she said the weather wasn't bad and she'd love to come and visit and she'd been fine and she was working on the future, and she continued to make up answers that would preclude any further conversation until Sally got on the line. The high and bright timbre of her voice for some reason angered Jill. "How've you been?" Sally said.

"I'm fine."

"Great. We're getting a dog, you know."

"Congratulations."

"The kids are thrilled."

Jill said, "Have you got a few minutes?"

"Of course. What's wrong?"

"I have to ask you about something that happened a long time ago."

There was a pause.

"Do you remember when I lost my voice?" Jill went on. "I was twelve."

Sally said nothing.

"You do remember, don't you. It was after Rose Keller died."

"The witch."

"She wasn't a witch. She'd been in a concentration camp. She'd lost her family."

"She never talked to me."

"She wasn't a witch, Sally."

"Everybody else thought she was."

"I didn't."

"But I did."

"I thought she was very nice."

"She scared the hell out of me."

"Do you remember what happened?" Jill said, and she carefully recounted the events of the last day of Rose Keller's life. "And then I lost my voice. I couldn't speak for four months."

"Yeah," said Sally.

"Did mother ever talk about this to you?"

"She said you were being willful."

"What?"

"She said you were doing it for the attention. That's what everybody else thought, too."

"I saw the man who killed Rose, Sally. I saw him. I saw him come out of her apartment. I even think I heard it when it happened."

"Why are you bringing this up now?"

"Because I need to know the truth."

"Why are you doing this?"

"Just because I have to."

"Why are you involving me?"

"Because there's no one else left from back then."

"Suddenly you need me."

"Yes, I need you to speak to me, that's all."

"When I invited you up after the funeral you refused to come."

"I wanted to be alone, Sally."

"When I offered to come down there to be near Carrie you refused."

"You have your own family. I didn't call to argue about any of this. I just want to know about when Rose was murdered."

"Does it really matter to you?"

"What is your problem, Sally?"

"I'm really sick of your crap. I'm really tired of the way you're always trying to steal the attention."

"What?"

"That's what it was all about, that silence of yours. It drove us all crazy. Daddy nearly had a heart attack because of you."

Now Jill didn't know what the truth was, whether she had been a witness to the murder of her neighbor or had invented it, creating this elaborate and difficult story to account for four speechless months. It was as if her entire childhood had lost its anchor, as if, like a great balloon, her life had suddenly let slip its moorings and begun to float away from the earth, only to rise into a vast unknown emptiness in the exhilaration of flight. She thought of her father taking her down to Washington for her abortion, how he waited for it to be over, and the little gifts he had bought her, magazines and cupcakes and flowers. After Geoff the kindness of men was little trusted, hard sought and much welcomed. When they arrived home all her mother could say was, "So you're back."

Jill said, "What do you mean Daddy nearly had a heart attack? I never knew about this."

"Mother was afraid to tell you. Everyone was afraid of you. Everyone was fed up with you."

"I don't understand what you're saying. I know what I saw."

"Mother and Daddy didn't believe it. But everyone had to tip-toe around you, everyone had to be sweet to sister Jill."

Her comments were laden with the unspoken: Carrie's condition; Peter's murder. In some way, the silence said, Jill had been responsible for both. She didn't know what to say. Or rather she knew precisely what to say, she'd been storing up comments for years, hoarding ammunition for this moment, and yet she found that she had nothing to say, or no will to say it, as if, were she to let loose her barrage of complaint and criticism, she would be reduced to becoming what Sally was so good at being. Now that she thought of it she remembered Dr. Angelico speaking to her of her relationship to Sally and her father and mother, and it was as if she were being stripped of all the certainties in her life, the things seen with her eyes and heard with her ears, and she was left with this: Peter had been murdered. She couldn't even say for sure what Carrie saw or how she felt or how long it would last. Doubt was like suffering from a disease that daily progressed through your system, that could be traced by a physician and yet eluded diagnosis. It was why certainty, even the certainty of failure and loss, was so perversely satisfying. It meant that decisions had been made. It meant an end and a beginning. She had buried Peter and on her own two feet had walked away from the grave. "Sally," she said, "just shut up for a minute," for Sally was expelling thirty years' worth of venom and envy. Jill felt a peculiar calm come over her. There seemed no point in further words. She took the phone away from her ear and looked at it. Sally's voice grew smaller and less distinct, and after Jill gently let it come to a rest on the hook she realized that now she had begun making her farewells.

CHAPTER *23*

When she arrived at the university on Monday morning she saw things had changed. It was like a shift in perception, an optical illusion whose trick had become known to everyone. No longer was Jill Bowman the object of curiosity. Her colleagues and students had assimilated the fact of her husband's murder, and now they were able to look her in the eye, speak of matters both mundane and academic, travel the familiar paths of their life together.

On the way there she had watched the landscape on either side of the highway unfold like a great roll of paper, white hills one after another, slopes and cliffs, the fresh snow of the weekend, spotless and smooth, billowing by her. It had been a weekend of silence: no one came knocking at her door, the phone had not rung, and occasionally she would lift the receiver, just to see if the equipment was out of order. At first the snow fell lightly, riding the soft breeze like spirals of lacework. Through the window she could make out individual flakes as they rocked gently in the air, only to settle dryly on the ground. As dusk came and night fell it began to snow more heavily, the winds raged, and what had been a lovely wintry scene had become the terror of a blizzard. When the snow finally stopped late on Saturday morning she put on her green Wellies and warm jacket and gloves and walked out into the soft spoonlike drifts, elegant sweeps of white cupping the air, embracing the trees and poles, descending like the tails of ocean waves. She walked out in the road as one or two cars, their drivers brave enough to attempt the crusty and dangerous avenues, slowly and uncertainly passed her by. Some of the houses were decorated with Christmas lights, a few displayed plastic reindeer or members of the Holy Family, Mary and Joseph and the infant Jesus out in snowy suburban New England with its Volvos and Cherokees, instead of the heat of the ancient desert.

Until she reached the shops she walked deliberately, cautiously, picking up speed where the road was clear. She looked at her watch: she had been walking for nearly forty minutes. Neighbors and people she knew by sight were fetching their mail from the post office or buying newspapers at the corner store. She pushed open the two doors of the coffee shop and stepped in and was astonished to see how crowded it was. Though normally a gathering place for the elderly and moribund, disgruntled old Republicans in caps, wheezing and wrinkled, it became, in the aftermath of a storm, the most popular place in town. She noticed how people looked up at her and how their eyes caught the light of recognition. They knew her, they knew that her husband had been murdered, word had sped around town and the newspapers had picked it up, LOCAL PSYCHIATRIST SLAIN. The article spoke of Jill as the widow, and when she read it she looked carefully at that word, for now she had a term that utterly defined her. Before she was woman and wife and now she was widow, and the crested shadow that seemed to hang over the word moved her. She wondered if henceforth she should describe herself as such, speak of herself as the widow of Peter Freytag. Would she then remain under the protection of his name, his identity? Didn't widowhood imply that through death she was to be defined always as having once been married to the deceased? Would she forever be attached to this man who lay in his grave, speechless, motionless, becoming dust, this man who had cheated and lied throughout the years of his marriage to her? She decided she would not speak of herself as a widow. As she had for all of her life she would continue to call herself Jill Bowman, and on that morning after the snowstorm, that day that rose grey and dry one week before Christmas, she removed her wedding band and placed it in the bronze box on her dresser.

All the seats at the counter were taken, as were the booths and tables on the floor of the restaurant. The air was filled with steam and the smell of pancakes and eggs and bacon. There was an unceasing roar of camaraderie in the place, and most of the diners, when not carrying on animated conversations about the weather, leafed through their newspapers. She exchanged a few words with those who waved and called to her. They invited her to join them, and she said no thanks, she was just going to get a coffee and a muffin to take out and then go home and have breakfast. It was a lie, because all of it would turn cold by the time she reached her house. She was in no mood to be sociable, to make small talk and to avoid, like a bird circling a vast lake, the subject of her recent days. She wasn't ready to renew friendships or meet new people. Her change in life was a kind of sleep and awakening to find herself in a new world to which she had to adjust her eyes. Things once familiar had become strange, slightly skewed, as if she hadn't yet found the time to rebuild all the accustomed sights, pieces of furniture, pictures on the wall, lamps and telephones and rugs, into the usual arrangement of the past.

She ordered a morning-glory muffin and was told they were all out, and the woman behind the counter was so busy feeding the

affluent faces that had filled her eatery that she turned away, as-
suming there wouldn't be a second choice. Jill said, "But," and
caught a glimpse of herself in the mirror on the wall. In her
woolen hat and scarf, her face firmed and bright from the cold air,
she looked somehow different, younger, more alive, and the description came to her without discrimination, words upon words,
because it was more a feeling than something that could be defined. She caught the eye of the woman and ordered a cranberry
and walnut muffin, heated please, and a large black coffee.

"To go?" the insanely busy woman cried, and Jill said yes,
to go.

She waited and glanced at a newspaper someone at the counter
was reading. Cigarette smoke curled up to her nose, the smell re-
pelling her. Peter had been a smoker, not a heavy one, and since
his death she had grown unused to the odor. Now it simply
stank, and she held her gloved hand to her nose and breathed instead the muskiness of leather. There was a photograph of the
President jogging in a rainy Washington street followed by a
group of frowning heavy-thighed bodyguards. A child in rags
stood forlorn in a bomb crater. "Cranberry walnut muffin, one
large black," the woman said, and Jill gave her the money and
stepped outside and began the walk home. It was odd not wearing her wedding band, and every now and again, as she had
during her marriage, she felt for it with the joints of her other fingers, and it was strange to feel it missing, its absence suggesting
the loss of some protective charm. It was as if she had left the
house without her underwear, just as she had when she walked
out of the hospital the night her husband lost his life.

Now she was glad the weekend had come to an end. It was
good driving back into the city; she had missed these familiar
things, the bridge, the traffic, the view over the harbor. She could
even see Marta's, and knew that only now could she go back there
and eat, and not feel heartsick over Peter's death.

Julius Rosenzweig came out of his office. Jill was talking to his secretary about her plans. "I'm looking for something near the river," she said. "Two bedrooms, if possible."

"I have friends in real estate," Helen said to her. "Let me see what I can do for you."

Julius listened and then came to Jill and hugged her. "What a storm," he said.

She said nothing.

"You ski, don't you, Jill?"

"I never got around to trying it. Peter did, though. I guess all Swiss take to it sooner or later," and Julius smiled with some relief, for it was obvious to him that Dr. Bowman was getting over her loss and was preparing to return to her life at the university.

"So you're back with us. I'm delighted," he said. "You're coming to the meeting today, I hope?"

"I completely forgot about it," and the moment he had said it she remembered his secretary's message on her machine the day she'd returned from London.

"It's in an hour," he said. "Stick around, I'd like you to be there."

"Everyone's supposed to bring lunch," the secretary said.

"Oh shit," said Jill, and they all laughed.

"There's a turkey club special I can send out for."

"All right."

"You're a diet soda, aren't you?"

"Yes," said Jill. She hadn't expected to be caught up in a large academic gathering such as this. She'd planned on sitting in her office and working on next semester's plans, sorting through her mail, going down to the cafeteria at three or so to get a tuna sandwich and a cup of tea. Each week brought two or three books from publishers, huge history texts that she would sell to one of the shops across the river, and sometimes she would be asked to review something for a journal. She had hoped to have another look at what she'd done on the article on the Plague. On her desk in her office were volumes of Samuel Pepys's diary, one of them opened to April 1665. *Great fears of the Sicknesse here in the City, it being said that two or three houses are already shut up,* he'd noted at the end of the month. *God preserve us all.*

Christmas was one week away. She was concerned that Carrie might have another episode. Suddenly her head filled with all the things she had managed to forget over the past weeks, and they pressed in on her as time must to someone condemned to die at a predetermined hour.

There were decisions to be made about the house as well. Jill had made an appointment for the broker to view the property on Sunday. Absurdly Jill had spent two hours cleaning, vacuuming, dusting, scrubbing sinks and toilet rims, as if, were the house to appear too filthy, too much like the house of a solitary person, it would seem unsellable to this woman who years earlier had sold it to Jill and Peter. Jill felt like selling more than her house, she wanted to sell her memories and her past and everything connected to her and Peter.

And yet there was no need to sell her past, for she felt now the absence of the past, not as an emotion tinged with regrets or even happiness but rather as a fact in itself, and this alone was curiously pleasing to her. Nothing could be changed; nothing had to be changed. She knew what she had seen all those years ago. She hadn't killed her father. She hadn't been seeking attention. And whether or not the man with the toothpick had been the murderer, Rose Keller had died, something had gone out of Jill Bowman's life, something gold and rich and earthy, something that could endure pain, that could survive the press of history, something that even now she couldn't quite define. Yet she owned her past as others own their home and their car or a plot of land, and because she owned it she could also walk away from it, or redeem it, or even set fire to it.

She and the broker drank coffee at the kitchen table. The broker now had her own company. Her children had grown and gone off to college. Jill listened to her story, and thought it odd that she hadn't been asked about her life, how the years had dealt with her. But Fran would never ask. Fran knew, just as everyone knew, and because they could not find the words to approach her, the words to express their fear or shock or sympathy, they simply said nothing.

"The house looks good, Jill," Fran said. "Let me know when you want to put it on the market and I'll take a photo and write up a listing."

Suddenly she wasn't so sure she should move. Her head filled with objection. "Should we wait till spring?"

"There's no need. It looks all right with snow on the lawn. The woods behind it are pretty. It'll sell."

Together they walked to the door. "What are your Christmas plans?" Fran asked. "You have a sister in Canada, don't you?"

"I don't think we'll be getting together this year." She regretted a little the argument they'd had. Perhaps argument was the wrong word. It was more like war, something final and catastrophic, the end of the family, turned backs and seething decades of ill feeling. Even though she had dreaded seeing them for the holiday she realized that it would have been better than sitting alone in her house. "I'm not sure what I'll do."

"How about that house of yours on the Vineyard?"

"Sally and I share it. But it's closed up now for the season."

"Of course it is."

She imagined herself and David there. She suspected he liked to sail and walk the beach and cook on a grill and look at the stars. She imagined him in white trousers and deck shoes, the reflection of the fire playing on his face on which there would be a contemplative look, the look of a man weighing the hours and acts of his life, while all along she knew what would be going through his mind: the mutilated corpses of the day's murders, the pathetic evidence found in suburban homes and housing projects, bloodied sheets, brain matter, a child's doll thrown against a wall. He lived in a world of if only. If only he had been more astute; if only he had arrived there earlier.

She was glad a department meeting had been called. It gave her a sense of a portion of her life that belonged wholly to her,

that remained unaffected by death or longing, and she partic-
ipated at first with reluctance and then eagerly, contributing to
discussions on thesis review, on doctoral candidates, on political
correctness, moving in and out of the conversation as it grew
more heated and incoherent. Afterwards she ate her club sandwich and talked to her colleagues, many of whom had come to
Peter's funeral. She spoke a little of the possibility of moving to
the city, nearer to the university. Now that she had said it so often it seemed a logical, reasonable thing to do. She wondered if it
was what everyone did, if when a mate died the survivor simply
packed up and fled, as if their abode had become a house of the
dead, a place of dolor and melancholy where shadows chased the
light.

On the way home she realized that she would have to do
Christmas shopping. She had always bought a little something
for Blackjack, a box of apple-flavored treats and a big bow for his
stall door. It seemed a ridiculous thing to do, to buy Christmas
decorations and presents for a horse, and yet everyone did it.
Some even went so far as to hang stockings for Santa Claus to fill
en route to the humans' houses. When you entrusted your life to
a creature that large and strong, you pampered and loved it, you
resorted to wholesale bribery.

In a way she was glad she didn't have to buy Peter something.
Now that she knew how he used her presents, CD cases as hiding
places for keys, the idea of shopping for him would have been repellent to her. He'd been the easiest person to shop for, nearly as
easy as Carrie. She bought him English-made shirts and silk ties
at expensive shops in the city; she bought him books and music.
She wondered what he'd done with the cashmere sweater she'd
bought him a year ago, if he used it to wipe the sperm away from
between his lovers' thighs, or laid it beneath the woman with the
perky little tits and light brown hair so her menstrual blood
wouldn't stain the sheets that belonged to Jill Bowman and Peter
Freytag. This Christmas she only had to think of Carrie. Usually
she bought her daughter clothes and a stuffed animal and a book.

She had planned on giving her the snowman toy and a Postman Pat book. She remembered that Carrie had nearly finished a coloring book from last Christmas, and this gave her an excuse to take the exit for the mall.

The parking lot was filled with cars. Space was limited because the accumulated snow had been plowed into huge frozen walls in which were embedded shopping carts and hats and woolen mittens and other forms of debris, some of it several feet off the ground. She drove down one lane after another for nearly twenty minutes until she found a space that seemed a quarter of a mile from the entrance. The wind had died down since that morning. The stillness and pain of cold air had settled over the region. The weatherman said that there was a possibility the high winds could return, for the storm that had arrived that weekend was a large and powerful one and its residual effects would be felt for days afterwards. Now it was in Canada, and Jill thought maliciously of Sally in suburban Montreal, sitting by the window and watching the ten-foot drifts engulf the house, her face contorted into a rictus of fear.

The mall was so crowded, so full of grab and spend, that the air there was not of holiday enchantment or Christmas cheer but rather of desperation and delirium. A man dressed as Santa Claus sat on a gaudy throne while women in tights took money and escorted children and snapped photographs. A child sat on the impostor's knee and wept and screamed, her little fists pumping the air, her mother's face trying not to show the anger and humiliation that could be clearly seen in the tightness of her jaw, the rage in her eyes. The scene reminded Jill somehow of the lobby of the hospital the night Peter had died, the gaze of uncertainty in the eyes of those who marked time and waited.

Jill decided merely to get Carrie's presents and leave. She went upstairs to the bookshop and examined a shelf full of coloring books. Some of these had been designed by graduates of MIT and the Rhode Island School of Design, printed on good paper and published by reputable houses. They challenged their readers to play with space, to draw pictures of their grandmothers in the fourth dimension, or to imagine what the undersides of the cellar stairs looked like during an electrical storm. Others simply contained pictures of frames, so that adventurous children could flatter themselves into designing their own brilliant universes.

She wondered what she should buy for Carrie. It was difficult having a child who could express interest in nothing. Simply because it was new she loved her latest stuffed animal, whether it was a bunny or a kitten or a bear. If you put a stick in her hand she would refuse to let go of it, as if it possessed some inherent value for her. Jill found a rain-forest coloring book that invited the young artist to use her most vivid colors, but the pages were too busy, there was too much leaf and beak and monkey tail. There was a coloring book that reduced the masterpieces of the world, from van Gogh's sunflowers to a Cézanne still life, to a kind of schema or blueprint, and allowed the child to turn the Mona Lisa into a tattooed slattern, and the Last Supper into an afternoon snack at the corner deli. She ended up buying a Beatrix Potter coloring book. Jill had always liked Potter, had always loved it when her father read the stories to her. She could even remember something of *Mrs. Tittlemouse*, with the unwanted visitation of the toad Mr. Jackson. She remembered the warty amphibian as he roamed the subterranean corridors of Mrs. Tittlemouse's abode, "No teeth, no teeth," he cried when offered a cherrystone by the ungracious rodent. Once she had tried to read it to Carrie but her daughter's attention drifted to a fly on the window, and she realized that even these little stories in their pretty little bindings were too sophisticated for her.

She went next door to the toy shop and waited in a long line to pay for a box of crayons. She remembered not to buy one with a sharpener included, for the clinic would have it removed. Dr. Bradley had once strongly hinted that a patient had sat down one Sunday and managed to peel the skin off her little finger as if it were just another Crayola. A few small boys were running insanely around the store, shooting each other with unfilled water guns, their parents standing by impassively as their children toyed with death. The holiday had begun to depress her, and the feeling was of a lowness even more profound than that she had felt after Peter's death. That had been quick and acute, a twisting blade in her heart. This was something pervasive, a fog that blurred her vision and choked her throat. She hoped Christmas would come and go quickly. She even briefly entertained the thought of calling Sally and apologizing and trying to bargain her way into an invitation to Montreal. She could make a week's trip of it, she could rent a car and go north to Quebec City, stay at the Frontenac for New Year's Eve before flying back.

But she couldn't call Sally. That had come to an end. Christmas, with all its misery, would be hers to suffer alone.

On her way out of the mall she bought sweatpants and shirts for Carrie and a hundred and sixty dollars' worth of clothes for herself. She called it a Christmas present and felt much better for it.

Now it was evening.

Now it was night.

She pulled into her garage and sat for a moment or two after she switched the car off and listened as the metal began to cool and click and settle. Her body felt leaden, and she thought of what she had eaten that day: a bowl of Cheerios and a turkey club. She had drunk coffee and diet soda. She hadn't even contemplated dinner. It had been a long day. She unlatched the door and took out her purchases and the bundle of mail from the university and went into the house. She took the vodka from the freezer and poured herself a drink, and it soothed the soreness in her throat she had earlier felt. The mail was mostly junk, announcements for forthcoming books for which she hadn't any need, flyers advertising conferences. There was a scattering of mail awaiting her at home, bills and envelopes full of coupons from local pizza shops, car washes, carpet-cleaning services, pleas for money from various charitable organizations. Already the tack shops had begun to mail out notices for their February sales. She thought of what she would want for the new season, new breeches and gloves, perhaps some shipping boots for Blackjack. She looked forward to hunting again, or even just riding. A hack through the countryside or a fast gallop up by the polo field, twenty times around the ring, at the moment anything would satisfy her, anything that would put her into motion, for winter was a time of inertia and weight, of a dense solitude that seemed to draw her earthward, and whatever pleasure she took in the chilly nights of early October or the first snowfall was quickly replaced with a sense of airlessness that could not be relieved by the mesmerizing prettiness of a hearth fire or a last whisky on Christmas Eve. And now that Peter was gone, whatever he had done to her, whatever she thought of him now, she would miss the comfort of companionship, of things going on elsewhere in her house, as if the small unexceptional noises of him, the turning of a page, his voice on the phone, the way he made coffee on Sunday afternoons, had become the music of her life.

She remembered Dora's message on her machine and made a note to get in touch with her student. It had been sweet of her to think of Jill. She thought of Greg's card and wondered what she would do about it. She had stuck it on her refrigerator beneath a magnet and passed by it fifteen or twenty times a day, a couple dancing in a Paris street, *La Dernière Valse.* Save for the dancers the street was dark and deserted. The photograph had been taken on the biggest holiday in the French calendar, July 14. The couple seemed awake and alive and full of light in the year of the photo, 1955, and yet all of Paris had gone to sleep. The photograph must have been taken very late at night, certainly past midnight. The street was empty. Not even a trace of litter was in the road. She had memorized the message on the card, she had examined the way Greg had shaped his letters and the little flourish he had added to his childlike signature. Thank you for having encouraged me to become a historian. I think of you often. Fondly, Greg. Thank you for having encouraged me. Think of you often. Think of you when? Thank you for what? She had parsed the sen-

tences so often that suddenly they seemed to carry obscure emotional messages, as though he were really trying to say I can't get
you out of my mind, I need you, call me, write me, come to me.
Yet there was no address on the card, and reading it was like driving down a cul-de-sac without the courtesy of a warning sign.
Perhaps he had married. Maybe there were children, romping
about the backyard, wailing beneath the swing set. She sensed
that in her memory Greg had become more than what he had
been, that in reality he may very well have turned into a boring
little academic, someone who fussed over trifling details, who
gloried in the minutiae of faculty meetings and union disputes,
precisely the type of person she most wanted not to emerge from
her courses. And how did she appear to him, these five years later?
He said he thought of her often. How did he think of her: was she
some sexpot in black lace and leather boots, spread across the
satin sheets, all lips and breasts and moistness, the steamy intellectual type? Was she the white-bloused professor beneath whose
propriety and multilingual abilities hid a bimbo of fierce ap-
petites and unorthodox practices, who when not speaking of the
reign of Charles II said things like Oooh, baby and I like it hot
and stiff? She felt embarrassed that she had ever felt anything for
Greg Nyman, she was mortified that she had come to their meetings wearing nothing beneath her sweater and skirt, that she had
allowed herself to be overwhelmed by desire for this man whom
she had barely known. She thought again of the card, the words
he had chosen. The word Fondly struck her as weak and unimagi-
native, a verbal pat on the shoulder, a sexless salutation of
farewell. In fact his entire message was as artificial as the photograph: a staged event, a passing fancy, the counterfeit words of
affection.

It was nearly nine. She finished her drink and turned off all
the lights downstairs save that at the bottom of the stairway. She
walked back into the kitchen and took Greg's card from the
fridge and tore it into four pieces. The sound of tearing was a

pleasant noise, the feeling within her certainty and satisfaction. Hector was sitting halfway up the stairs, gazing at her, following her when she passed him. He would leap to the bed and spend the night lying beside her, pressed up against her body, and sometimes, when she awoke in the small hours of the morning, she would find herself at the very limits of her mattress, squeezed against its edge by the heavy presence of her overweight eunuch of a cat.

She washed and undressed and read for twenty minutes and then fell into sleep as if descending into a denser medium and when the phone rang she wasn't certain what it was at first, in fact in her dream Peter was alive and the call was to tell her he had been found in Sarajevo, as if his death had only been a wandering, a man astray in an unfamiliar world. She picked up the receiver and opened her eyes to the darkness. The shirt she had put on before bed, a T-shirt with the logo of the U.S. Equestrian Team, was soaking in perspiration.

"Jill?"

"What?"

"I woke you."

"What time is it?"

"Go back to sleep."

"What time?"

"It's ten."

"My God. I feel like I've been sleeping all night."

"I'll go."

She had slept for exactly eight minutes. "No. Don't. I'm glad you called." Now she was awake, and a silence hung between them.

"I'm glad you're home."

"You tried me earlier?"

"There was no one there."

"You should have left a message."

"I didn't want to worry you," David said.

"Is something wrong?"

"It's just that we've begun to make some progress on the case. I thought you'd be up. We can talk in the morning."

"Tell me now."

"Are you in bed?" he asked, and immediately she felt aroused. She wanted to tell him that she was in bed and wearing only a T-shirt, that she could speak to him all night if he wished, and without thinking about it she touched herself, gently cupping her hand between her legs. "I'm in my office," he said. "I'm working late."

She thought she could hear the slightest echo of longing in his voice. I'm in my office, you're in bed. It was like being presented with a simple algebraic problem, whose answer somehow would bring the two values together into a common expression.

"I was exhausted," she said. "I had a busy day."

"I'll hang up."

"Don't."

"I'll call tomorrow."

"I went to school and found out we had a department meeting. So I was there all afternoon. Then I went to the mall and shopped for Carrie."

"Christmas." It was as if it had just occurred to him.

"Soon."

"Next week."

"Exactly a week."

"I've been so busy I lost track of time."

"Haven't you done your shopping for the holidays yet?" she said.

"Most of it, anyway."

"Tell me what's happening with the case."

"It's not all that important. Let's talk tomorrow."

She sat up and leaned back against the headboard. Suddenly, after years of abstinence, she wanted a cigarette. It was how she felt that first time with Geoff, or with her other boyfriends at college, you wanted to talk for hours and smoke, and she remembered how little of interest Geoff had had to say to her, and how well and patiently she had listened to him, because the sound of his voice was a kind of link between her and something potent and artless. It was when he had run out of words that she had lost her faith in him. "Tell me now," she said.

"Are you sure?"

She laughed. "Tell me, David."

She could hear pages being rustled. "Lisa Bacon," he said. He waited a moment. He repeated it. He said, "What does it mean to you?"

She considered it. "Nothing."

"Think for a minute."

"I don't know the name."

"Lisa Bacon," he said.

"I've never heard it."

"It isn't familiar?"

"Not at all."

"But you might have heard it."

"I suppose I might have."

"Let me ask you again in the morning. When you're more awake."

"I'm awake, David. I'm sitting up in bed and I'm awake, and I'll probably be awake all night." She almost invited him up for scrambled eggs and coffee, then thought better of it.

"Lisa Bacon."

"How would I know her? I mean, in what context?"

"In the context of your husband," Resnick said. "Lisa Bacon. Possibly an American citizen resident in the United Kingdom. Lisa Bacon."

"A patient."

"Think. Lisa Bacon."

"I don't know the name."

"Try to think, Jill. Lisa Bacon."

"How did you get the name?"

"Just think. Lisa Bacon."

Very easily could she talk herself into having heard it at some time in her life.

"Let's go back six years, Jill. You said that when your husband admitted to having an affair he said something about the woman's profession."

He waited for her to complete the thought.

"Something about her legs," Resnick prompted.

"She was a dancer."

"Or an actress," he said. "A model."

"But it might not have been the same woman in the video."

"It doesn't matter. We need to talk to her."

"How did you get her name?"

"Through his records. He had her penciled in for an appointment. Actually five of them. But there's no file on Lisa Bacon."

"Maybe she decided not to come back to him. It's normal for people to try out psychiatrists until they find the right one for them."

"But five appointments? One for her was in London."

"Maybe she moved on to another psychiatrist."

"But why would she travel to London to see him?"

"Possibly she was another professional, an academic. Someone at the Tavistock Clinic. Or someone connected to London University, someone traveling," and the memory of her and Peter in the restaurant in Covent Garden came back to her. Peter excused himself to go to the bathroom, returning by way of the front door. Christopher Hansel, he said he thought he had seen, an old school friend from Zurich.

"There is no registered psychiatrist or psychologist practicing in this country named Lisa Bacon."

Jill said nothing. Had she crossed paths with this Lisa Bacon in London, had she sat next to her on the tube, shopped for sweaters in her presence, dined at the next table?

Resnick went on: "Of the five appointments noted by your husband only the first two were under her full name. For the last three she was down either as Lisa or by the initial L."

She didn't know what to say.

"Did Dr. Freytag ever bring his appointment book home?"

"Never. He once told me he kept it locked in a cabinet in his office."

"That's where we found it. So you never saw it, even when you went to his office."

"I almost never went to his office."

"Did your husband ever invite guests to your house?"

"Women?"

"I mean for a dinner party. Guests. Colleagues, friends. The people he played squash with."

"We rarely entertained."

"But when you did."

"We usually had friends common to both of us. Occasionally he would invite a colleague. But then so would I."

"But not Lisa Bacon."

"No," she said.

"Do you know the exact dates he traveled on business?"

"To London?"

"To anywhere."

"You have his office records, David."

"But do you have any idea? Did you keep a diary, or an appointment book for yourself?"

"Of course I did."

"You didn't save them, did you?"

"They're somewhere in the house."

"Call me when you've found last year's book."

"What exactly are you looking for?"

"Did he ever talk about his colleagues?"

"No. Never. He considered it unprofessional."

"And he never really discussed his patients," he said.

"Only sometimes. But only their conditions, their obsessions. Never their names or professions or habits."

"And when he published his articles he always changed the names of the subjects?"

"He was obliged to do it."

"Lisa Bacon."

"I don't know it."

"Lisa Bacon," and he spelled out the names, first and last. "Remember how I asked you about Dr. Freytag, how I asked you to help me, how I asked you to remember, and when you were in London you remembered and you picked up the phone and called me?"

She said nothing.

"Jill?"

"I'm here."

"Lisa Bacon."

She said nothing.

"I'll be here all day tomorrow."

"What are you looking for?"

"When you find last year's appointment book call me at my office."

And he wished her goodnight, and hung up.

Lisa Bacon.

Now she was awake.

CHAPTER *24*

She hadn't been in the attic since Carrie's birthday, traditionally for her a time when she brought up all her daughter's clothes that no longer fit her, packed them into boxes and taped the lids tightly shut. She couldn't bear to part with anything that belonged to Carrie, to haul them off to the consignment shop in town or even to donate them to the Salvation Army. It would seem as if she were turning her back on her daughter, letting her slip away from memory, as though the clothes themselves were moments from the past.

The attic was cold and airless. When the first chill nights of autumn set in Peter had come up and removed the little expanding vent screens and securely shut the windows on either side. It felt to Jill like the morgue where she had gone with David: a place of lifelessness and preservation, where nothing grew and time had lost its meaning. When they were first married she and Peter often talked about renovating the space, having it properly insulated, installing skylights. He had considered having a room to himself there, where he could sit and work on his articles and a collection of his pieces he had begun to compile but never finished. They had even called in contractors for bids on the job, and then suddenly Peter decided that he'd prefer to work in his office. "I can stay on after my last appointment and sit at my computer. It'll be easier that way. Also we'll save the money we would have spent on the attic."

"How are you going to eat dinner?"

"I can have something delivered. Or I can go out. There's a perfectly respectable delicatessen around the corner from my building."

Now that she thought of it she saw beyond the innocence of the conversation.

She thought of the film David had made her watch. She wondered if Lisa Bacon was the woman in it, the one who was wearing Jill's yellow silk dressing gown, the girl with the short brown hair and pale skin and firm little breasts and flat belly, and she felt within her a rage that could not be defined with words, that could only be translated into physical violence. Peter was dead, his throat had been sliced across and he had choked on his own blood, and Lisa Bacon was at that moment alive and fucking someone else, some other woman's husband.

Lisa Bacon. She said it aloud, Lisa Bacon Lisa Bacon, it was precisely what David wanted her to do, say it over and over until things began to click within her memory and Lisa Bacon could step out of the past and become a face, a voice, a person she had met at a party or at Peter's office, as someone casually encountered in a restaurant. She tried to remember when she and her husband were eating in the city and he might have said, Ah, now there's someone I haven't seen in years, I must introduce you my darling, and Lisa Bacon in her little blouse and skirt would look surprised and shake Jill's hand, and the meeting would pass as a moment of complete innocence, a mere ripple in the course of time.

Lisa Bacon.

Now that she had a name the old pain returned to her, she could hear the name Lisa in Peter's voice, Lisa, she could hear him saying it under his breath, Lisa, she could even imagine how he would lie awake next to his wife and think of Lisa in bed with him, she could enter the byways of his fantasies as if they were a rain forest, lush and humid and exotically colored, and somewhere amidst the moss and leaves, the vines and fruits and plumage, they would be there, Peter and Lisa, and they would sometimes talk of her, Jill Bowman, Peter would speak of how she made love, what she looked like, what she did or didn't do with her husband. She thought of the woman in the film, sitting with her legs spread on their bed, wearing Jill's dressing gown, the room filling with her odor, the irresistible stink of her, and she tried to remember that time a year ago when she'd been reading *The Wings of the Dove*, tried to recall if anything had seemed strange to her, an unfamiliar smell to the sheets, the way Peter acted in bed with her, if the name Lisa Bacon had ever disturbed the air between them.

She stood in the attic and even with a thick sweater pulled over a T-shirt her skin prickled with cold, her nipples hardened, her teeth chattered. She hadn't slept well the night before. Whatever sleep she had enjoyed before David called had been still and profound, and perhaps it had been enough for her, for afterwards she slept only fitfully, sliding in and out of dreams as if they were rooms in a mansion. Her mother sat by a window and the sunlight threw spears of light onto her and the dust rose and as though Jill were a ghost her mother said nothing. Beyond the window a sailing ship sat in a harbor. By this moment that could either be an arrival or a departure it seemed to be understood that someone dear to her had died. Carrie lay in a bath, and Jill was sure that she shouted aloud, rousing herself suddenly and painfully as she discovered her daughter lying motionless beneath the soapy water. It was nine o'clock, two hours later than she usually got out of bed. She felt unsettled and adrift, between sleep and daylight, relief and pain, between Peter and David. One was intimately linked to the other. As long as her husband's death was unsolved Peter would remain alive, a shimmering profile in her mind, a whisper breaking the surface of silence; while David would also be a part of her days, a voice on the telephone, a man in a restaurant, someone goading her into helping him come to a conclusion, and when the case was solved he would depart from her life and she would be left with nothing to look towards but the years that lay ahead of her.

She began to search through the things stored in the attic, the cartons of Carrie's clothes, her playpen and layette and even her crib with its decals of a pink bunny and a yellow duck in a blue bonnet, none of these had been given or thrown away, and she even found the toys she had bought for Carrie just after she'd been born, the little windup carousel, the monkey that climbed a string, the Big Bird doll, and she could look no longer, for she remembered her lying under her little yellow blanket, staring and soundless, unmoved by the toys that her mother so desperately displayed to her. It had been years since she had seen them. She had left them in their box and forgotten about them, and now that so much had happened she saw that there was no point in keeping these things destined for a child who might have been, these ruins of the unconstructed life of her baby. They lay there tumbled into each other, looking at her with dead accusing eyes. Whatever innocence they once possessed had turned malign and bitter. As she thought of Carrie she thought of the child she might have had by Geoff. Whatever there was of it had been through so much. She thought of the rubber tube inside her and the house beyond the city with its television and the packet of Oreos. She remembered her stay in Washington. On the flight down her father had held her hand. In everything lay the immense potential of the future. It was why people were drawn to

even the slightest glimpse of certainty and hope, as if the future
were contained in that moment of vision, gemlike and flawless,
blindingly reflective in the light of the days to come. She thought
of what David could be for her, and how she would never have
him, and the sense of something lost, something vast and warm
and rich, lay upon her like a weight that caught at her breath and
cut short her dreams.

She closed up the box of toys. Big Bird. The monkey. The creatures of heartbreak that mocked her. When she sold the house
and moved she would give them away, and no one would ever
know the history that surrounded them, the hopes and wishes
that went for nothing.

There were four or five other boxes in the corner which belonged to Jill alone. They contained old yearbooks from high
school and college, LPs she had bought decades earlier, five years'
worth of canceled checks, copies of tax returns and the diaries and
appointment books that would tell Detective Sergeant Resnick
the story of Peter's infidelities and death. To her they were merely
the chronicle of her days, the hours and minutes slept through or
lived, appointments made and kept, meals enjoyed and concerts
witnessed, visits to dentist and hairdresser, to the chiropractor
and the vet, birthdays remembered, reminders of phone calls to
be made. Out of such mundane material arise betrayal and
tragedy, just as the simple act of crossing a street can lead to the
screech of brakes, the sound of impact, the crush of bones, the
wrench and moment of death.

She got together as many of these books as she had and
brought them down into the warmth of the house. Now it was
nearly ten and because she was so cold she stood for fifteen minutes in the hot shower before she even got around to shampooing
her hair and washing her body. When she finished dressing she
called David. "I found the diaries," she said.

"You're not by any chance coming into the city?"

"I will if you need to see me."

"I think we can do this on the phone."

She could hear him flipping through the pages of Peter's appointment book.

"Let's look at this year first, and then if we need to we'll go back twelve months. Beginning with January, tell me every date you noted that he told you he'd be traveling. And that he was actually away."

She turned to the first day of the year. They had been invited for drinks and lunch to their friends' house in the next town. Her handwriting was bold and upright: she had looked forward to it. The next day she had visited Carrie. There was a reminder to make an appointment for an oil change. A week later she'd had a mammogram. It was odd looking back over the year, the time before Peter's death, the months and days before she had come to know so much about him. She thought of how much she had assumed then, and it occurred to her that ignorance was a place of expectation and hope, a golden city of possibilities, where the truth lay beyond the margins of sight. Now that she knew so much about Peter, about the nature of their marriage, she could look elsewhere, in fact towards the future, this great white and blinding light of What Might Be, a sweet state of hope. She would sell. She would move. She would meet new people. There would be David. They were like steps along a path, sell, move, meet, and in her mind they became the blank pages of the diary she carried in her bag, empty spaces ready to be filled.

"He left for St. Louis on January twelfth and returned on the fourteenth," she said.

"Why?"

"To deliver a lecture at Washington University."

"I have that also. Is there anything else for that month?"

"New York on the twenty-eighth."

"A one-day trip?"

"There was a conference at Columbia."

"Let's move on to February," Resnick said.

"He didn't travel that month," she said.

"How about March?"

"He was in London for a week and a half."

"Dates?"

"March tenth to the twentieth."

"He said he was going to London for the entire time?"

"Why?"

"Keep going."

"There's nothing else in March. He was in Los Angeles for the first week of April."

"Give me the exact dates."

She could hear it in his voice, he had caught her husband as though Peter had been walking through an airport and David had stepped up to him and touched his arm. "April first through ninth," she said.

"He was in London, Jill."

She didn't know what to say.

"He was in London. It's in his appointment book and his passport. Where did he usually keep his passport?"

"In his office."

"Locked up with his appointment book?"

"I suppose so," she said.

"So you never saw it. He was in London in April, and during the time he said he would be there in March he was in Los Angeles. Do you remember driving him to the airport, or picking him up?"

She looked back at the pages in her book. "I didn't drive him either way that time. He went directly from his office."

"He was in L.A."

"Lisa Bacon," she said.

"Very possibly. Whatever was happening, whoever he was seeing, he was keeping it from you. Lisa Bacon is penciled in for April second. Did he ever call you when he traveled?"

"Yes, of course."

"Did he leave you a number where he could be reached?"

"Sometimes. Usually if he was abroad he'd do the calling. He'd write it off as a business expense."

"So you couldn't get hold of him in an emergency. If something happened to Carrie, for instance."

"He had nothing to do with her. I was there for her. He wasn't."

"All right. Let's keep going."

Her hands began to tremble and she felt weak and unwell. Her husband was under the ground, he was cold and senseless, and yet it seemed his life was continuing on its course, rolling out its days and weeks and months of which she had never been a part. They tracked Peter from one month to the next, May, June, July, once or twice more finding him where he wasn't meant to be. There was a sense of an impending end to things, that soon, very soon, perhaps in a matter of days or even hours, the case would come to a close. David would move on to something else, something unrelated to her, the murder of a wife, the perverse logic of a serial killer, he would fade from her life like a shadow at nightfall.

"The last time he traveled was a month before his death," David said.

"He was in Vancouver."

"He was in New York, Jill."

"And then he was supposed to go to London."

"Everything concerning that last trip is legitimate. We've checked it out. He had hotel reservations, he was scheduled to speak on Sunday afternoon, people were expecting him. But instead of flying to London he was murdered."

He said nothing more. He waited for Jill to speak, to come forth with revelations, innocent little comments that would somehow clinch the case, point the finger, seize the guilty. She didn't know what to say. There were two cases here, there was the police case and there was the personal case. She said, "Let me make a call or two. Are you going to be in your office all day?"

"I'll be here, Jill."

"I want to see you," and the words came out as that, a simple, clean, crystalline statement. "I need you to be here with me, David."

He said nothing.

"I'm afraid."

"Of what?"

"I don't know," she said. "I just feel afraid. I'm shaking, I'm," and her words ran into silence. She wanted David near her so he could take possession of her fear, so he could share it with her, make it his own.

"I can't get away, I can't leave," he said, and his voice was for the first time that day warm and moist in its overtones.

"When?"

"I don't know."

"Later."

"I don't know."

"Tomorrow."

"In a day or two."

"When?"

"We're almost at the end, Jill. All we have to do is locate Lisa Bacon."

"And then what?"

He said nothing.

"I need to call London," she said.

"Are you all right?"

"I need to know what happened. I'll call and then I'll speak to you." She hung up and went down to the kitchen and made a pot of coffee. For some reason she went through the routine as if nothing at all had happened, as if it were just another day, toasting a raisin bagel, looking over the front page of the paper, feeding Hector. She looked at the clock and counted ahead five hours. She was glad Michael answered the phone. It sounded as if he were just across the street, or in the next town. The moment he spoke she realized there was no point at all in the call, that all of a sudden she no longer much cared about the truth. She said, "I want to apologize for the way I behaved at your home. I guess I'd had too much to drink."

He laughed and said it didn't matter.

"The other thing is that the police feel they've almost solved Peter's murder."

Michael listened.

"My husband was having an affair with a woman named Lisa Bacon." She was astonished at how calmly she was presenting the facts. "The detective in charge of the case is fairly sure that she's an American based in London, or at least an American commuting between England and the West Coast. Los Angeles."

Michael said nothing.

"You know the name, don't you."

"No I don't, Jill."

"But it's familiar to you. You'd heard it somewhere, hadn't you."

"I have to admit that it sounds familiar. I just can't place it."

"When Peter was visiting London on business. He must have mentioned it to you then." She imagined her husband strutting into the Hollanders' house with his woman on his arm, she could almost see him with his hand on her knee, sitting with his friends, reveling in his infidelity.

"I can ask Claire, I suppose," he said. "She's in Cambridge for the day. I'll have her ring you when she gets back."

"But Peter wouldn't have said anything to Claire. He would have told you. He liked his men friends, he enjoyed being with them, playing squash, having a few drinks. I won't be hurt, Michael, I won't fall apart and cry."

Michael said, "I'm not sure," and every word of it was a lie, for this man who investigated the devious workings of the human psyche was unable to disguise the humble noises of his discomfort.

"Let's start all over again, Michael. How much did you know about Peter?"

"I," he said, and then he fell silent. Jill waited. "I had a feeling he was playing around," he said.

"You had a feeling."

"I sensed it."

"Is this the psychiatrist speaking or the human being?" and together they laughed.

"He never said anything about it to me. Or at least nothing precise. The last time we saw him was—" and Jill interrupted: "The first week in April. He'd told me he was going to Los Angeles. Instead he went to England. You and Claire knew, but I didn't."

"I wasn't aware of that."

"Did he say why he was there?"

"Just that he was meeting an old friend from Switzerland."

"Christopher Hansel."

"I don't remember the name. He said that his friend was flying into London for a conference and that he had decided to meet him here." He said nothing more.

"So what made you think he was playing around with other women?"

"Because we'd invited him to dinner and he begged off, he said to me privately that he had something lined up."

"And he said her name was Lisa."

"Perhaps. I simply assumed he'd called an escort agency. I thought it was rather a risky thing to do. Especially these days."

Jill didn't know what to say. There seemed no point in her having called Michael Hollander. She said, "How's Claire?" and the question seemed out of place and imbecilic.

"I'm sorry," Michael said. "I'm so terribly sorry this has happened to Peter and to you. It doesn't matter what happened here last time. You're still welcome here, you're still a dear friend."

"You've told me everything you know about Peter?"

"Everything."

"So the name Lisa means nothing."

"Your husband was very discreet."

"Not enough to save his life," she said, and she hung up and dialed Resnick's office number. He picked up the phone before the first ring had finished. He said, "Jill?" and she told him what Michael had said.

"We've contacted the police departments in New York and L.A., we've fed the information into national databases. We've also been in touch with the police in London. We've asked them to check out all the nightclubs, theatres, modeling agencies, even film production companies. It may take a long time," he said, and she was secretly glad for it.

"What if it wasn't Lisa Bacon?"

"She was the only woman he'd taken the trouble to note in his appointment book. She was important to him. She was the last one he was seeing. She'll know," he said. "She'll know something."

"And then what?"

"If we can get hold of the people who were responsible for your husband's death we'll bring a case against them. Then it'll be all over. You'll go back to your classes. You'll finish your work on the Plague. I'll go find myself some more murderers," and he laughed a little, a bitter, restrained laugh.

She wanted him to say more, that the case would be over but that he would continue to see her, be close to her, that things would be allowed to grow, that time would spread out before them like a flowering meadow, anything he might have said would have satisfied her.

"I'll miss talking to you, David." The moment she said it she regretted it, and yet it had to be said, the door had to be opened. "You've been very kind to me. You've made things a lot easier. You were always there for me." Her words sounded idiotic in her ears.

"We can still talk."

"Can we?"

"There's no law against it."

"Christmas is coming," she said.

"Don't remind me."

"When can we see each other?"

The pause frightened her, it was impossible to interpret. It seemed to go on forever. Finally he said, "My next day off is the twenty-third."

She didn't know what to say. His statement communicated absolutely nothing to her beyond the simple fact of it. She remembered that she had been thinking of visiting Carrie that day, or even taking her out for a few hours. Usually Carrie stayed at the clinic for Christmas Eve and Christmas Day. The staff would throw a party for the patients and visitors and Jill would come down and spend at least one other day of the holiday with her. Sometimes films would be shown, Disney cartoons with a Christmas theme, and the patients would laugh and clap and shout at the creatures on the screen. Carrie would sit, her mouth open, spilling saliva over her lip. Peter never joined her for the event, and now that he was gone Jill let her mind wander through the labyrinth of possibilities as to what he did while she was away.

"I'm free all day," she said.

"Are you sure?"

"I'd like to see you, David," and her voice betrayed doubt and uncertainty.

"Will Carrie be coming home for the holiday?"

"No. She always stays at the clinic. There's nothing for her to do here. Sometimes I take her out for a few hours on the day before Christmas Eve. I always spend part of Christmas Day with her at the clinic." She didn't know what to say, she had been caught in the unfamiliar repartee of invitation and decision, of enticement and acceptance, of desire and desire. "I buy her ice cream," she said. "Whatever." She never brought Carrie home because she hated seeing Carrie in the house, in the living room and climbing the stairs on all fours, poking around what would have been her bedroom, sitting on the furniture and staring for hours out at a backyard that could have been hers. With its neat lawn and flower beds, in the summer a vegetable garden, with its stacks of wood and trees beyond, the bird feeders and hammock and lawn furniture from Bloomingdale's, it was barren of a child's pleasure, sandboxes and swing sets and wading pools, and this, too, broke Jill's heart. Once she'd brought her daughter back to the house and after a moment of forgetfulness realized that Carrie had wandered into the kitchen. When Jill walked in Carrie had a knife in her hand. She could see it in her daughter's eyes, the way she was piecing ideas together, making connections, and gently she had taken the blade from her hand. That was why she would move. This house had been bought for her and a husband and child, and henceforth Peter and Carrie would never live there, their voices would never sound between its walls, their laughter was like dust on a summer's breeze.

"I'll take her out on Christmas Eve instead," Jill said. "It doesn't matter."

"Don't change your plans. I'd like to come with you. If it's all right."

His suggestion startled her.

"I was thinking about bringing Carrie to the stable, if the weather isn't bad. She likes to visit Blackjack. Every year we put a bow on his door and bring him a little present."

David laughed. He said, "We always get our cats something. Usually fresh catnip. A thriving drug trade in the Resnick household," and she laughed. "I'd like to see your horse," he said.

"Are you going away for Christmas?"

"Last year I had to work. This year I'll be with the family. We usually go to Susan's mother's house. Her sisters are there, her brother. The same old thing."

"You don't mind?"

"I don't have a choice, do I?" Together they laughed.

And if he'd had a choice? But she didn't say it.

"And we can have an early dinner, if you like."

"That would be," and the word failed to come to her. "I'll make us something," she said. "We'll take Carrie back to the clinic and eat here."

"I'd like that. I'll need to be home by eight. I'll pick you up. Is ten o'clock too early?"

"No. It's wonderful." She caught her breath. Her excitement was not in the least sexual. This was something more substantial, something that had more to do with someone walking close beside her, holding her hand, or sitting next to her, talking quietly, someone who was interested in her, and who in turn interested her.

And when she hung up she felt as much in love as she'd ever been.

Now Christmas was imminent. Because they had allowed her the distance and latitude she had so desired after the funeral, her friends had retreated into silence and waited for her to call. Now it was too late. Now people's plans were laid, the hours of their days apportioned, and there was no room for Jill Bowman in the holidays of others. She considered traveling again, flying off to some warm place the day after Christmas. The idea of putting on a thin skirt and a light blouse tempted her. She'd always loved wearing white slacks and a bikini top, and not just because they were comfortable in the tropical heat. She looked good in them, she knew she did, and she wanted others to be aware of it as well. She wanted to lie in the sun and let the freckles appear on her shoulders. Years earlier she and Peter had gone to Cuernavaca, just south of Mexico City, they had rented a house from an American journalist and had spent a week basking in the sunshine and drinking themselves silly in the shadow of the volcanoes, in this place which reeked of stagnation and death, and which swarmed with senescent Americans of a forgotten generation. She could easily do it again. She could shop for clothes and pack her bags and fly off tomorrow. But for the case. But for David.

There were things she had forgotten to do, and now that she was going to spend a day with David everything began to crowd in on her, and the years stripped away from her life as if in reality she were no older than fifteen. Although over the years she had sent out fewer and fewer cards for the holiday, many more had arrived at her house this year, as if the death of husband had compelled people to put on a show of love and compassion. Yet she knew it wasn't a show, in fact she'd been touched by the sentiments that had come through the mail slot, handwritten on thick and clever cards purchased from museum catalogues or on those made up of family photos, even on those that had been cheaply printed and decorated in the sad nostalgic pastels of an imagined Christmas. She'd been touched because in those words, in those loops and curves applied by other hands, was something genuine, something that had only been suggested in the stammering and silences that had surrounded her at Peter's funeral. They had come there to bid farewell to a friend and colleague. Now they were giving something to her, to Jill, and as she sat in the hush and space of her life her heart was moved by these words.

She looked out the window into a slate sky. More snow had been predicted for the evening. There had been little sunlight since her return from London. It seemed interminable, this winter that stretched out before her. She wanted the year to run its course, the seasons to make their appearance, the days and nights to pass, so she could know what it was to live alone, without Peter, through the brightness of spring, the fever and succulence of summer, the first evenings of autumn they together had always loved. If she could do it for a year she could do it forever.

She wondered if she should visit Peter's grave for Christmas. She was alarmed to discover that she actually felt perplexed about what to do, as if somewhere within her the soot and residue of her love for her husband were still drawing her towards him, as if, were she not to roar off down the highway and stop in at section H, plot 25, something terrible might happen to her, some shadow might fall across her life. Yet often at night, while she lay awake in the darkness, blinking and gazing into nothing, she would think of that rectangle of grass and what lay beneath it. Could she still hate this man who had become inert and speechless, could you hate the dead as you did the living? She thought of her argument with Sally, the way her sister had unpacked her burden of anger, years and years of it, three decades of resentment, and it seemed to her like a great mound of gravel and dirt that would lie upon not Jill's back, but Sally's. One day Jill would die, probably before her sister. One day the weight of those years would bend the spine of her sister, and the thought of it left Jill feeling immensely, inconsolably, sad.

To travel to the cemetery, to wipe away the snow from the granite stone, to press the slush and ice until it melted beneath the heat of her hand, to feel the grass that enclosed the unimaginable cold of his grave, would serve only her. Peter had lived his life. He had done things he shouldn't have done, and together they had paid for it, as he had in his last moments in the Hubbard, as she had in the weeks of grieving that followed. She wished sometimes that she had been unfaithful in the afternoons of her own life, that she had taken Greg by the hand and driven him off to his apartment in the city, that she had seen his eyes while she undressed, that she had heard his noises of pleasure as she made love to him. There had been other opportunities, with colleagues, students. She could have taken the initiative; she could have experienced the passing gold of the illicit moment, and now, in her solitude, she could have told herself that she, too, was as human as Peter had been, that each in turn had fled the comfort and companionship of marriage. She had no right to judge Peter. She had no right to be any more hurt than she need be. He had been good to her, he had looked lovingly upon her, he had been pleased by her and he had pleased her. Nothing that was important to one was hidden from the other. He had never rubbed his affairs in her face as if they were stains on a rag, he had never mocked her. He had been her closest friend, her confidant, the person she trusted most in the world. Now it was over. Now the pain had come to an end.

She wondered if she should drive to the cemetery now or a few days later, or on Christmas Day itself, before she went to the clinic. She wondered if it would be crowded on that day, if parking would be a problem, and if she would be distracted by the presence of other mourners, other survivors, those who had also come to speak to the dead. Now she understood why people left letters on graves, now she had things to say to Peter, not words she had failed to speak when he was alive, but those that needed to be said in his death. She would kneel on his grave and brush away the snow and touch the earth, and her senses would open and thrill to the idea that she was alive and well, that there were things she could do to fill her life. The cold and ice would feel good on her hands, the air would bite at her cheeks, and even the small pain of it would please her. She was allowed to be alive now, she didn't have to die simply because Peter was dead. She would listen to the wind in the trees, as it sped through the ranks of graves, the old leaning stones from the past and the thick granite ones so recently set in place. Time was so short. The most terrifying thing about life was not that it ends in death but that she could have made so many wrong decisions, fatal ones. There were other men she could have married, children she might have had, streets she should have crossed, beds she'd have been better off avoiding. She might never have married Dennis and had Carrie. Peter might have remained a total stranger to her, and yet as she considered it she realized that he had been a stranger, that a portion of his life had been lived in secret. Had he given her the best of himself, or simply the residue? Did it matter?

She put on her coat and gloves and got into her car. She thought of her father, who had died ten years before her mother. Sally had been in Oxford on a fellowship; her mother was living on the Vineyard with her companion. It had been up to Jill to fly to New York and make the arrangements. She had always been closest to her father; their relationship had been crystallized when she'd had her abortion in Washington. All the things she had done wrong, all the terrors she had wandered into, had been understood by him. It was almost as though he had been to these places first, and had been waiting for her on each occasion, ready to comfort her, to forgive her, to heal her. He had chosen to be cremated, and she remembered watching him disappear behind the little doors, and the intense moment of the heat on her face as the man who had been her father flared up and turned to ash and smoke. Now she would never be able to find him, nothing remained but her memories. The cupcakes, the magazines, the way he held her hand when everyone else had abandoned her. Peter would never have risen to such trivialities. He was a man of words, and now that he was gone it was the silence that pained her the most.

The traffic on the interstate was heavier than usual; people had begun to travel for the holidays. Cars passed her, station wagons and vans, their windows filled with glimpses of wrapped presents. In her rearview mirror she could see the coaches plying between Boston and Maine and New York and Montreal, filled with those returning to their families, or escaping them. She thought again of Sally, of what she had said to her, and wondered at the finality of things. Eventually her children would grow, go off to college, possibly even marry. Would Jill still be a part of their lives, or would she retreat into the realm of legend, the pathetic old woman whose daughter was locked up in an institution, whose husband had had his throat cut? Her life would be reduced to these simple dramatic facts, as if she were a character in a story, or the subject of a ballad, and the complexity of her years would disappear into the wind like the webs of the autumn spiders.

The cemetery seemed deserted. She pulled into the long avenue with its willow trees and turned left until she saw the lake come into view. She thought it ironic that Peter was so near the water's edge, this man who feared it so. A jogger moved rapidly through the lanes and disappeared into the distance. A maintenance truck pulled up nearby and a man got out and began to clear away branches that had fallen during the last storm. Before going to Peter's grave she visited Kelly Ann Flynn. Her grave was barren of letters and flowers and balloons. Undoubtedly on Christmas people would come to visit her, people who had held this child in their arms when her life lay before her like a clear open road cutting through a forest. She could see Peter's stone as she stood there, and the space around it. When she'd purchased the plot the man in the main house of the cemetery had gently urged to her to buy the adjoining one, for prices were going up in six weeks, and she had agreed, on that terrible morning she would have agreed to anything. One day she would lie beside Peter, she, not Lisa Bacon, and now she regretted having bought the space. Just as the knowledge of death had entered her mind the moment Rose Keller was taken away, now that the anticipation of it had come into her life, it was visible, it could be seen there, stretched out beside the fresh grave of her husband.

Now she knew that this would be the last time she would visit him. She looked at the stone, and then at the ground that lay just above him. She felt ridiculous standing there, trying to summon up the appropriate words. Peter was the last person on earth she could imagine living on after death. The sheer absence of him now struck her. He had walked into a hotel room and closed the door and allowed himself to be murdered. The door had remained shut, and would always be shut, and as she turned and walked away she felt something in her heart lighten and lift away from her. She was speechless, and for the first time in her life she was glad of it.

CHAPTER 25

Like something transparent and winged, or even something invisible to the eye, a virus or bacterium, Lisa Bacon had moved about the world with ease, eluding them, leaving small traces of herself: a parking ticket issued to a car rented by someone with her name in Los Angeles eight months before Peter's death; a hotel reservation in Santa Monica; an entry into the United Kingdom at Heathrow Airport on April 1. "No one knew where she lived or what she did, or even if Lisa Bacon was her real name," Resnick said. As he talked he took his right hand from the wheel, he gestured with it in the air, playing with the space between them, creating intimacies.

"The other problem was that all we had to go on was what your husband told you six years ago. That the woman he'd been meeting was a performer of some kind. Lisa Bacon may be a different woman. Or she may have left her profession. It may even turn out that he had had a justifiable reason for seeing her. By knowing more about her we'll understand something about this side of Dr. Freytag's life," and the expression struck her as profoundly dark, as if Peter had lived in some subterranean region utterly forbidden to her. It was as if he were setting up the foundations for a denouement, laying out the facts, discarding theories and suppositions, preparing her for the worst. "I feel fairly certain she had intended to meet him there on that last trip he had planned."

"But that trip was legitimate, it was business."

"People do this all the time, meet their lovers when they're supposed to be elsewhere on business. It's safer in another city, there's less chance of being seen by someone known to you. You have the best excuse in the world for being away. They'd been seeing each other often, she'd met him before in London. I'd guess she had enough money to keep her traveling in comfort. Unless your husband supported her."

"He wasn't that rich."

"But he was easily able to pay for another person's air fare and hotel room."

She watched his face as he drove down the highway, how calm he seemed, how he turned to look at her and smile, and this too was a way of altering the distance between them. When she looked at him she could barely see him. Something had replaced the Sergeant Resnick she had met that night in the hospital when Peter died, something created by her imaginings and longings that moved like fluid between one and the other. She would never be able to look at him with objectivity again, never see him as she had that first time, or even the afternoon she drove down and sat in his office and answered his questions. He had become part of her life, incorporated into the milky insubstantiality of her future. She thought of how she had endured the weeks since Peter's death, the idiocies of her phone calls to astrologers and the voices of men who spoke of how they would ravish her. She wanted to reach over and grasp his hand, to touch the side of David's cheek with her fingers, almost to assure herself that he was there. She remembered her trip to London and felt the fatigue and powerlessness of one who has traveled and seen nothing. Peter's funeral now seemed to her as something perceived through the wrong end of a telescope, terribly small, caught in the great distance of the past.

She pointed to the building on the hill, with its brown towers and turrets and the breast of snow beneath it. He got off the exit and followed the curve of the road until they reached the gatehouse. Someone had put a wreath on it, and the wide red ribbon fluttered and flapped in the breeze. Jill leaned across and touched David's arm. "It's okay, Bill. We're just going to visit Carrie."

He parked and for a moment they sat and looked out the window. The sky was cloudless and the sun warm enough to melt some of the snow. Huge icicles dripped from the building's eaves. "She can be difficult," Jill said. "She's a good girl, though."

"I saw her, you know."

"She doesn't know many men."

They walked into the lobby and unzipped their jackets. Bill had alerted the doctor and she stepped out to greet them, looking with surprise at Resnick. "I didn't think we'd see you before Christmas," she said to Jill.

"David and I thought we'd take her out for a few hours. Sorry I didn't call earlier."

David shook her hand. He said, "I'm not here in any official capacity."

Dr. Bradley looked from one to the other. She said, "Is everything all right?"

"Everything's fine," Jill said, and in the hollow of her stomach she felt the first ripple of panic, not for Carrie but for herself. Later she and David would be alone. She didn't know what to say or do. Life suddenly seemed completely unnatural, as if every word and action needed to be plotted out in advance. They would take Carrie to the stable. They would bring her back to the clinic. They would go back to Jill's house. They would eat, they would be alone, things would happen, words would be said, and so frightened was she it seemed to her that whatever happened it would fail, that the day would contain the first seed of catastrophe that would begin to spread quickly outwards in time and space, beyond anyone's control. She shut her eyes as they rode up in the elevator, she breathed deeply and steadily, and when they reached Carrie's floor she felt her fear pass. It had been ridiculous of her to feel that way, to worry over the vast abstractions and suppositions that had come to her in a moment of uncertainty. They walked to the room. "Everything's been fine since your last visit," Jean said. "We've even gotten her to try her hand at a little painting."

Jill brightened. "Really."

"You remember how before she wanted nothing to do with it. She seems to enjoy it now. I think it's a remarkable step up. It helps keep her attention focused. It gives her something to look forward to."

Jill laughed aloud. "I'm so glad."

They went inside and shut the door. Instead of sitting passively on the bed Carrie was carefully arranging her stuffed animals on a shelf that had been fixed to the wall. It was clear she had a plan in mind, that there was an intended sequence to how the creatures would be placed. Jill said, "It's Mommy, darling. I've brought a friend."

Carrie looked at her face and then at her hands and then she sat down and looked out the window, posed precisely as she always was whenever her mother came to visit.

"Christmas is only two days away. That's the time for presents," and she laughed, for something small seemed to have changed in Carrie. She wondered if the natural stages of physical growth were somehow affecting her daughter's moods, her level of activity. There was something different about Carrie, something older, something beyond definition. Perhaps it had been going on for some time, and maybe she hadn't noticed it before. But now she could see it, she could stand back from Carrie and look at her and consider her as someone independent, a young woman with a will of her own. She had developed earlier than her mother had. Jill remembered too well the humiliation of being flat-chested at fourteen, of having her first period later than any of her friends. Yet by the time she was seventeen she had grown taller, she had a good figure, and she bled, as others did, copiously for a few days each month.

"Carrie, this is my friend David." She rested her fingers on David's arm. "We're going to take you out for a few hours. We'll visit Blackjack and have lunch. Ice cream, if you like."

Carrie tightened her lips in approval.

"Hello, Carrie," David said, and Carrie said nothing.

Dr. Bradley knocked lightly and opened the door. "When do you think you'll be back?"

"Around two-thirty or three."

"Then I won't send any of her medication with you. If you're running late she'll need to be here no later than five."

"She seems to be doing very well," Jill said.

"We think so too," Jean said, leaving them.

Jill pulled Carrie's seat belt across her and locked the door before shutting it. She had put her daughter behind David's seat so she could keep an eye on her, and as they drove off she turned and smiled at Carrie. "Where to first?" David said.

"Let's go to the stable." She gave him directions. They drove under the highway and went east. The traffic was heavier than usual. People were out doing last-minute Christmas shopping. For a moment she'd forgotten that David was a detective. She wondered if he looked at things differently, if certain cars attracted his attention, or if he was drawn to think twice about the way a person drove or stared through his window at another driver. She wondered if he always had his gun with him.

"I bought Blackjack a bow and some apple treats," she told Carrie. "Maybe we'll put him on the crossties and give him a grooming." Carrie stared at her. She had brought her little blue kitten with her, and when she wasn't gazing out the window she looked with pensive eyes at the toy.

"Where does Carrie like to eat lunch?"

"There are a few places near the stable where we usually go after a hunt. Peter and Carrie used to meet me there for a late breakfast."

"Your husband didn't ride?"

"He was terrified of horses."

"Are you looking forward to riding again in the spring?"

"I'm not going to give it up. It's too important for me. I've done it all my life."

She pointed to the turn he had to make. "Take your next right. It's a dead-end street that curves around to the left. Just pull into the stable yard."

The stable manager had left the top halves of the stall doors open, and the horses were warming their faces in the sunlight. Blackjack watched them park and get out of the car, nodding his head as if pleased to see them. Jill helped Carrie on with her mittens and hat. She took the bag from the car and affixed the bow to a nail already driven into the wood. She handed the box of treats to David and put on Blackjack's halter and snapped a lead shank to the ring beneath his head. "Come on," she said quietly, clicking her tongue, and her horse took two slow loping steps out of his stall. She stood with him in the sunshine for a moment and looked him over. "He's having a good winter," she said. "He's doing nicely."

She led him into another building and fixed the straps on either side of the wall to his halter. "Now he can't get away," she said to David.

"He can barely move," and he laughed.

She took Carrie's hand and brought her gently over to him. "It's okay," she said. "You can touch him," and she placed her hand on his neck, moving it along his coat. "It's Blackjack, Cookie. He won't hurt."

Carrie put her hand up. Jill took the mitten off. "You'll feel how soft his coat is without that," she said. "In the winter it grows much thicker. It helps keep him warmer. Blackjack," she said, looking at her, "Blackjack," and Carrie said, "Ba."

Jill looked at David. He didn't know what to say.

"Bl-ack-jack," Jill said carefully, stretching out the syllables.

"Baaka," Carrie tried.

"Good," Jill said. "Wonderful." She smiled at Resnick. She felt as though she were going to cry. "She's never done that before," she said, "never like that," and David put his hand on her arm and kept it there.

"You know, I've never touched a horse before," he said to Carrie. "This is probably the closest I've ever been to one."

She looked at him.

"I'm a little afraid to do it."

She looked at Blackjack.

"If you show me how, I'll try it too."

She put her hand up and then changed her mind and scratched her head until her hat was pushed crookedly up off her ears. Jill took it off for her and tossed it on the table in the corner. "Show David how you pat Blackjack." She took her hand. "Go ahead. He won't hurt you."

Blackjack lowered his head and watched bemusedly. Jill kept him calm by running her hand softly along his neck. "You try first, David," she said.

"I don't know," he said.

"He won't bite."

"I'll do it if Carrie does it."

"Why don't you show her how?"

He reached up and touched Blackjack's jaw.

"His neck," Jill said, laughing. "Touch his neck. Run your hand along it. Pat it."

He touched the neck. "This isn't bad."

"Black-jack," said Jill.

"Baka," said Carrie.

A sense of astonishment came over Jill. Her daughter had broken into language. What would happen now: would she wake up
one morning soon and suddenly begin to converse, would she be
able to give voice to her history, to describe in eloquent detail the
silent years of her childhood, to tell her own story?

"Baak-laak," said Carrie, straining and contorting her face to
mouth the word.

Jill put her hands to her eyes and began to weep, and as her
body shook Resnick took her in his arms. Carrie stared at her
with a worried expression. David said, "Mommy's fine, Carrie.
Mommy's just happy that you could say Blackjack's name."

"Baakalak," Carrie said, her eyes wide as Jill squatted down in
front of her. "Baakalak, Baakalak."

"This is my Christmas present," she said. "This is what I've
waited for. This is," and because she didn't quite know what it
was she laughed and took Resnick's hand. They brushed Blackjack down and gave him treats. They brought him back to his
stall and drove off for lunch. Jill was tempted to try other words
with Carrie, words like Mommy and Christmas and David and
Window and Saltshaker and Tunafish and Chocolate Milk, but
she was afraid of being disappointed on this day that had brought
her so much that was new. She and David sipped their coffee
while Carrie finished her ice cream. They said little, as though
words would be superfluous, their conversation trivial and aim-
less. The restaurant was hung with framed photographs from various three-day events: horse and rider in mid-jump or someone
performing a dressage maneuver. Jill knew a few of the riders pictured there, and she pointed them out to Resnick. One of them
had been killed a week after her photo was taken. She had fallen
from her horse during a hunt and broken her neck. Jill had
known her, she'd hunted with her and spoken to her at parties.
Sometimes she speculated on the last moments of this woman's
life, on what had passed through her mind, on the sights she saw,
the tilting sky, the grasping earth, the wooden beams of the fence
barring her vision. She remembered seeing her at the tack shop a

few weeks earlier, a pretty blond woman of thirty buying stirrup leathers, and after her death she replayed the memory over and over in her mind, re-creating this lost woman in her imagination, as if to do so would somehow bring her back to life even for a few eloquent moments. She wondered if as one got older the boundary between life and death grew less distinct, if it was like the demarcation between day and night, a gradual and fathomable darkening, a fading, an abandonment to black, where the constellated stars spoke in figures and symbols of this other world. "Her name was Laura," Jill said, nodding at the photo, and Resnick looked at it.

Jill wiped the ice cream from Carrie's mouth and hands, her daughter watching with interest as each finger was pulled clean by the napkin. The waitress had recognized Jill and her daughter when they came in, and she talked to Carrie with patience and kindness about Christmas, bending over and trying to fix her with her eyes. Carrie stared at her in silence. Jill wondered if she truly remembered the young woman who was serving her, and who had served them so many times before. Jill said, "What's your name again?" and the waitress said "Diane," and after she left Jill quietly reminded Carrie of it. "Diane," she said. "Diane," though Carrie this time said nothing. It was pointless to push her. "Baakalak" was perhaps the best she could ever hope for, and the next time she took Carrie out she would bring her to the stable and see if she remembered. That would be the miracle.

Who's that?

Baakalak.

It was nearly time to leave. They would take Carrie back to the clinic and then return to her house. Now she began to wonder, now the doubts came. If she took Carrie back now, on this particular day when she perhaps should spend more time with her, would it somehow invite bad luck into her life, would she never speak again, would she withdraw and grow sullen and retreat to the darkness of things, all because of her mother's selfishness? David looked at her. Jill looked at Carrie and once more wiped her mouth with her napkin. She wanted to go out and buy everything she could find for her daughter, she wanted to shower her with presents and things she loved, she wanted to go into her attic and bring down the abandoned toys that had lain there for all those years, and instead she took her hand and kissed her daughter on the lips and held her against her as tightly as she could. "I'm so proud of you," she said quietly, and for the rest of the ride she said nothing.

When they arrived back at the clinic Resnick opened the trunk of his car and took out a wrapped package. "It's just a little something for Carrie," he said, handing it to Jill.

"You should give it to her."

"It's not Christmas yet."

"But this is special, it's from you."

Carrie stared at him as he held it out to her. The air had grown cold and their breaths swelled into clouds before their faces. She didn't seem to know what to do. Jill said, "It's a present, Cookie. David's brought you a present."

He said, "It's for Christmas, Carrie. You can open it now, if you like."

Carrie looked at her mother. "Go ahead," said Jill, and Carrie took it from him and looked at it and then looked at the door. "It's cold out here," Jill said, and they went in.

Dr. Bradley came out and smiled and asked how things had gone. Jill told her what had happened at the stable. "I'm not surprised," Jean said. "She's been much more responsive lately. And you've got a present, I see," she said to Carrie. Quietly she said to Jill, "Don't get your hopes up too much. It's nice that she was able to say that, but it's very unlikely we'll see a sudden improvement. Let's just be grateful for this day, at least."

They went up to her room and Jill helped Carrie off with her hat and mittens and coat. "Let's open it now," she said, and picked the present off the bed. Carrie grabbed it from her and growled. "Then you may open it yourself," Jill said softly.

Carrie unfolded the wrapping cautiously until she could see what it was, a little soft snowman toy, exactly like the one Jill had bought for her in London. Carrie held it to her nose and smelled it deeply, rubbing it against her face, making it part of herself. "It's perfect, David," Jill said. "It's wonderful."

Carrie looked at him and smiled a little. He said, "I was hoping we'd all get a chance to build one of those outside. I thought it might be fun for Carrie."

"She's never made one. She watched me build one once, though. It would have been fun."

"Another time, I hope," he said, and Jill smiled.

They drove home on the old north route, a road cutting through towns and villages, past the fairgrounds and gas stations and diners. David spoke of Carrie, how much he had enjoyed the morning out with them both. She said, "You haven't said much about your own kids."

"But I already told you."

"You told me their names," she said. "But that's all I know."

For a few moments he said nothing, and she realized that he had never intended to speak of his family to her, that they belonged to another world, as if between his wife and children and Jill stood a thick windowless wall that prohibited sound and trespass. "Jake's in fourth grade," he said, not looking at her. "Molly's in sixth."

"How do they like a having a detective for a father?"

He turned to her. "It's no different for them than if I were a sanitation worker or a psychiatrist."

"I'm sorry I asked."

"It's just."

She waited.

"It's just that it's not important right now."

For some time they drove without speaking. He pulled the car into a Mobil station and asked the attendant to fill it. He turned to Jill. "There's something I have to tell you. We've located Lisa

Bacon. The news came through this morning. She's dead. I wasn't going to tell you today. I didn't want to tell you today. We're certain now that your husband committed suicide."

She stared at him.

"I wasn't going to tell you because it would mean the end of my investigation. I'll be assigned to other cases."

Her thoughts broke into an abstraction of illogic. Someone had died, someone had killed himself, things were happening moment by moment, passing her by, leaving her behind.

He said. "She was discovered the day your husband died. She'd been traveling before then. France. Spain. Here in the States. For a while she was in Italy."

"She was killed?"

He said nothing.

"What's wrong, David?" She could hear it in his voice, a shadow, something moving about in the background, something dark and unhealthy.

"Lisa Bacon was in London. She was staying at the Park Lane Hilton. She'd been there for three days. Then she swallowed a bottle of forty sleeping pills and a lot of vodka and died the day before your husband was expected in England. He also had a reservation at the Hilton. The hotel records show that she'd called him at his office that morning."

Jill stared at him.

"We know now that she was a fashion model. She'd worked in Paris for a few years, then joined an agency in Boston. Lisa Bacon the model disappeared about two years ago. What I mean is that she left the agency and went off to do something else. She changed her name. The fact that she was in L.A. led us to believe she'd tried some acting. In any event she'd been around." He paid the attendant and started the car. "I've seen a photo of her. The agency faxed us one. She was the woman in the videotape. The same woman in a London morgue."

"But she had nothing to do with Peter's death."

"But she obviously knew a lot more about a different side of his life. They'd known each other a long time. For years. He'd kept both of his lives separate."

"Until now."

"He probably knew it was all going to become public. Something might have happened between them. Possibly she'd met someone else. Or she was pressuring him into leaving you. Or maybe he'd even decided to give her up and make the most of his marriage. Whatever happened drove him into a corner. It happens," he said. "More than you think."

"Why was he meeting her in London?"

He said nothing more for a moment or two. It was as if he wanted her to find the words for herself, as though she would have to work it out, discover the spelling, sound out the syllables.

"She killed herself because she loved him?" It still didn't make any sense to her. She wanted to reach out and shatter the silence that lay between them, and quickly it filled with suppositions and possibilities, he had broken off with Lisa Bacon, she was pregnant, he refused to leave his wife, all of these were likely, none of them definite.

"We'll never know that," he said. "She didn't leave a note." She could hear it in his voice, the fear, the uncertainty, the sadness. "They took a chance. They had their pleasure." He looked at her. "I guess it doesn't last forever."

She thought of her husband in the Hubbard, walking up the stairs, shutting the door, cutting his throat. It seemed so unlike him to do such a messy thing. Death for Peter was as clean and pure as his life had appeared to be: a well-considered theory, its elements and paragraphs numbered and logical. You could deal with it as you could a neurosis, an obsession, you could draw out its multiple components, place them on a chart, print them on a page. Yet he had cut his own throat in a filthy hotel on a Friday evening. She imagined him lying in his own blood on a floor stained with semen and footprints, the dregs of drug deals that had turned fatal. It would look as though he'd been murdered. The stigma of suicide would not lie across his name, it would not disturb her dreams, and yet it seemed in some strange way in keeping with his character. This man who liked to be in control of every facet of his life had also determined the circumstances of his death. It would have amused him to know how much she had agonized over the thought of his body in the coffin, in the earth. She thought of him in the hospital morgue, how calm he seemed, how drained of anger and happiness and passion as he lay on the table beneath his sheet.

She looked out the window as the road cut through the marshes. A pair of geese flew overhead with elegance and consequence, moving their graceful wings slowly in the cold air. She opened the window halfway and took in the icy air. She felt unmoved. David could have told her a thousand different things, that her husband had been tortured, mutilated, castrated, eviscerated, and he had left her long ago, he had died because of Lisa Bacon, and his death had already been mourned. She considered what had become of the people in the videotape, pretty little Lisa Bacon, the man Jill had known as her husband. One day they were there, on her bed, and now they were gone. She looked at David. She realized he was as much a stranger to her as her husband had been. "Talk to me," she said. "Please just talk to me. Talk to me about you, just say something."

"I've told you a lot," he said.

"Just tell me. Make me know you."

It was as if between them were a thin cord that had begun to fray in the middle. The investigation was over. Now time and space would inflate and grow bold, come between them, blind their eyes.

He pulled into her driveway alongside her car. He turned to her for a brief moment and then opened the door. Earlier she had put newspapers and kindling and a few logs in the fireplace and now she felt foolish for having done so, for it might seem as if she had gone to some trouble to prepare a romantic setting. She was grateful she hadn't considered the possibility of candlelight and her good china. She had been so accustomed to living with Peter, to the unconstrained routine of their marriage, that she felt as though she had wandered down a vaguely familiar path, grown utterly lost and found herself somewhere in the thicket of her early twenties, when she knew as little as she seemed to now. She turned up the thermostat and hung her jacket on the row of hooks in the hallway by the kitchen. She took Resnick's and put it alongside hers. She leaned against the wall and thought of Lisa Bacon and her husband, three thousand miles apart from one another. What words had come between them to cause such tragedy, what words, what actions?

"I'd like to see the house."

"Why?" She didn't know why she said it.

"Do I have to have a reason?"

"You mean you didn't break in while I was in London?"

"I've only seen the downstairs. And that was when you were here."

She walked him through the living room and dining room. She said little. Suddenly she knew for certain she would sell the house. It no longer suited her, it belonged to someone who no longer lived there, someone who had other expectations and hopes, and she saw that the days and weeks since Peter's death had been not just a passing of time but also of distance. It was that she had outgrown the house and the years she and her husband had lived there. Something in it had died, and its death had begun to permeate each of the rooms, as if somewhere within the walls was contained the decaying corpse of an animal that had taken a wrong turn, become trapped and slowly suffocated in the airless horror.

They ascended the stairs. She showed him her office, switching on the desk lamp and resting her hand on the back of her chair. "This was supposed to be Carrie's room."

Resnick looked at the pictures on the wall, the postcards she had bought at museum shops, those that had been sent by friends, the crayon sketch of what she believed was a self-portrait of Carrie, mounted and framed in maple. He paused before a large color photograph. He turned to her. "Is this you?"

"I did a three-day event at Ledyard a few years ago. That wasn't a particularly difficult jump."

"It looks it."

"The photographer has a real gift."

She liked the photo as well: Blackjack straining into a curve over the hedge, Jill pressing close to his neck, her thighs tense in their breeches; there was a geometry and grace to the picture that had nothing to do with how she had felt at that moment of the jump, a simple matter of getting over the obstacle, a question of survival. Only afterwards could she see it.

"Those are my publications," she said as he looked at a small shelf in the corner. "Nothing sensational. Essays in journals. I'd like to do a book someday." She shrugged. "I'm hoping to turn my piece on the Plague into something bigger. It's too early to tell."

They stepped into the hallway. Now they were in the bedroom. "Let me show you something." She opened the closet and took out her yellow silk dressing gown. "Peter had given it to me one Christmas. I absolutely adored it. Peter liked me in it."

"It's very pretty."

"He also liked Lisa Bacon in it. I'll never be able to wear it again."

The day was beginning to come to an end, the light folding in upon itself, shading to grey. Resnick looked at the framed photo of Jill on the bureau, the one taken on the Vineyard. He picked it up and went to the window. He seemed intrigued by it, by the expression on her face. She would have told him everything, how Peter had come up behind her, how he had separated her thighs and thrust himself into her. But he said nothing. Perhaps it was obvious to him from the way her eyes fixed the lens, the tired, spent look of them.

"Let's go downstairs," Jill said. "I'd like a drink."

Resnick followed her and stood in the kitchen as she got out the glasses. He looked through the kitchen window into the backyard and the woods beyond. She put ice in a glass and watched him. He seemed lost in the fading detail of early twilight, the smoke threading from a neighbor's chimney, the bare branches of the oaks against the sky, as though they formed a pattern of some significance, as if their decipherment might bring him a contentment, the answer to some pressing question. She poured two scotches and handed one to him. "It's a nice view," he said. He tipped his glass against hers and the click was barely perceptible. "Merry Christmas," he said, and she looked at him and drank. "When I look out my kitchen window I see into the life of Tony and Rosie Agnelli and their four kids," he said, and she laughed a little. They went into the living room and she lighted the fire. They sat on the sofa and watched the newspapers flame up, and then with a crackle the kindling ignited. "Have you found a place in the city yet?" he said.

"I haven't even begun to look."

"It's nice up here. There are open spaces."

"It's hard living in this house."

"The memories, you mean."

"It's more what might have been and never was."

"Your marriage."

"I was thinking of Carrie. I haven't known any other place since then."

"You had a sabbatical a few years ago."

She looked at him. "How do you know that?"

"It's my business to know everything."

"I have a few secrets left," she said, laughing.

"I'll try to dig those up, too."

"When?"

"When you're not looking."

She smiled and thought of touching his hand, of taking it in hers, almost as if to thank him for simply being there with her. "I'll start dinner soon," she said.

"I hope you didn't go to any trouble."

"Of course I didn't. I expect you to do all the cooking."

"I like to cook."

"I was only half serious. But you can help me if you like."

"It was a good day for you, wasn't it," he said.

"I still can't believe it. I just don't want to get my hopes up."

"But it's a start."

"Thank you for taking us both out. I think Carrie likes you."

"She's a cute kid. She looks a lot like you."

"A cute kid?" and she laughed and looked at him. They sat a foot apart on the sofa, and the space between them was irrelevant, for it was obvious how the day would be brought to its end. Nothing had been said and nothing would be said, for everything seemed to be taking place in the silence between the words. Sounds that would have gone unperceived seemed now to fill the room with alarm and significance, as if they were somehow linked to the urgent passing of time. A car sounded its horn somewhere outside; a child laughed; a log fell and the fire blazed up. She took his glass and went into the kitchen and made two more drinks. "I just need to go out to the car for something," he said. When he came back in he carried with him the smell of winter, a crisp, clean, smoky odor that attracted her. He had a small wrapped present in his hand. "It's for you," he said, and the weight of humiliation fell upon her.

"I don't have anything for you," she said. "I feel terrible."

"Don't feel that way," he said, and he reached out and touched her arm. "This was just something I wanted to do."

"It wasn't that I didn't think of you, I just didn't want," and he said, "You don't have to worry about it." She had wanted to explain it, to say how she didn't want to compromise him with his wife, to give him something about which he would have to weave some elaborate falsehood.

She began to open it. "It's just a little something," he said.

Jill didn't know what to say. She felt overwarm and sweaty, a little lightheaded. She had always been uncomfortable when she received presents, never knowing how to react, how to show she was genuinely pleased. She peeled the wrapping off slowly, carefully, delaying the moment when she would have to say something. She opened the little box and looked at it. She could barely bring the words to her lips. "It's a bookmark," he said, and she held it between her fingers, a black silken cord weighted on one end with a small brass heart and on the other with a bird, its tiny wings outspread. It didn't matter that he had given her a gift. It didn't matter what it was, or what she would do with it, or even if she just hung it up on the bulletin board in her office. She set it down and took Resnick's hands in hers, holding them tightly, looking into his face and his eyes. He looked at her in an odd way, a curious way, as though he knew something she didn't and was waiting to see if she might at any moment discover it. She moved towards him until his mouth found hers and in the crack and spark of firelight they kissed. She could feel his lips against hers, and the dryness and texture and reality of them aroused her. She felt his hands on her back, small strong hands moving along her spine, then he gently withdrew as she touched his neck with her fingers. He looked at her and seemed to be waiting for something. Her eyes questioned him and she took his hand. She led him up the stairs and she realized she hadn't changed her sheets in a week, she hadn't vacuumed the floor or cleaned the bathroom, yet it no longer mattered because in the heat of this moment, in the rush and current of desire, nothing mattered but the press of bodies, the acute pleasure of it, the wait, the play, the gratification.

He shut the door and the sound of it startled her. The blaze of street lamp and window light caught him as he stepped nearer to her, becoming angle and shadow. She had already taken off her sweater. She was still wearing her T-shirt and jeans. She could feel her skin tighten, her nipples lengthen. He took her face in his hands and brought his mouth to hers. He pulled away, he said, "I don't," and she put her hand to his mouth, she said, "Don't say anything." She pulled off her T-shirt and bra and leaned against the wall as he cupped her breasts in his hands and pressed them together. When he kissed and pulled at them with his lips she lifted her face and let the tears course down her cheeks. He would never see the tears, he would never know what they meant, and even if he saw them he would never understand. He kissed her again and he touched her lips with his fingertip, moving it slowly along their rise and swell, and she licked at it with her tongue, pulled it inside her mouth, pressed her teeth to it. She felt him unbuckling her belt. He tugged her jeans over her hips and edged down her panties and pressed his face to her. She could hear him inhaling her smell, and the sound of it flattered and excited her. She pushed him lightly away and kicked off her clothes and went to the bed. She lay there, her hand stretched out to him, as he undressed in that funny clumsy way men do, one leg at a time, wrestling with shoes and socks, trying to keep his balance, and though she could see nothing more than the silhouette of him she knew what he would be like, she had anticipated it for a long time, and when he came into her arms and she felt the warmth of him she lay there in a great stillness, as if to gather her strength for some tremendous storm. The smile on her face was of an immense contentment. This was the end of hunger, and when an hour later it was over, the frenzy and howl of their passion, it felt not like a beginning, but the culmination of something that had lasted a long while, and had quietly run out of time.

CHAPTER *26*

She sat on the toilet and let his sperm drip from her, thick clots of it into the bowl. He stood at the sink and washed his face. This was how adults comported themselves in affairs of the heart, they fucked and then they performed their ablutions before each other's eyes, a ritual imbued with weight and the honest pleasure of things domestic. Now she could see him clearly, his body, the shape of him, his wintry paleness, and although she hadn't truly seen him before, everything looked familiar, as though she had somehow helped create him in the bright open light of her imagination. She had formed him not from her memory of Peter or Dennis or even Geoff or Greg, but from something new and unseen, something altogether novel in her mind, from material stored somewhere in what she thought of as the future.

Once again she felt the ache of desire. Sitting there as though with someone who had lived with her for years seemed as sensual and daring as baring her breasts to a boy when she was sixteen. She said, "I just realized something. I've never bought condoms in my life. I never thought I'd need to keep them here. I forgot I was single. I'm sorry. At least I'm safe. I won't get pregnant. Not this time of the month."

"I forgot also. I've never done this with anyone else since I was married."

"Never?"

He looked at her and smiled. "You're the first."

"The first you've wanted?"

"The first I've pursued."

And she laughed, because she imagined it was just how a detective would put it, this man whose life was so caught up with notions of chase and capture. She walked to the bedroom and he watched her, his eyes taking her in, and she knew he was still watching her when she bent to pick up her clothes from the floor, the curve of her back, the smoothness of her skin imprinting themselves on his memory. When he dressed and came down she was sitting in the living room drinking scotch. She wore black leggings and a long yellow sweatshirt and nothing underneath. He reached for her and she pulled him close to her, folded into his arm against his body, let him curve his hand around the weight of her breast. She lay back against David's chest and looked up at him. She took his gift from the table. She held it between her fingers and let the heart dangle below them, twirling one way and then the other. "Thank you for giving this to me." Now it was meant to begin, now something new in their life was spread out before them like the open sea, seamless and brilliant in the sunlight. It was something that lay beyond definition, something apart from the empty phrases and words. Yet she felt a profound melancholy in her heart, as if within the great heat of love was a tiny knot of ice; as if joy bore the seed of its own sadness. Now that the case was closed there would be no more meals out, no walks together. Their life would be reduced to cryptic telephone conversations and motel-room trysts across the state line. David was there now, sitting with her before the fire. His presence meant that one day, perhaps soon, he would not be there with her. As the flight of a bird in its gorgeous roundness can also be a time of departure and escape, as day with its waning sunlight implies night and darkness, love always possessed its own end.

"How long have you known?" Resnick asked.

"I don't know. It just came on me. It was subtle. It was just a feeling. And you?"

"At first I felt sorry for you. You really touched my heart, I almost couldn't bear to see how you suffered at the hospital."

She looked at him.

"And then I missed talking to you, I missed being with you. When you were in England I went a little crazy. I'm not supposed to be doing this, you know."

"Getting involved with your cases."

He nodded. "I don't want to be away from you."

The air seemed to fill with impossibility. She got up and went to the kitchen. David followed her and leaned against the counter. She gave him a corkscrew and a bottle of wine. "I thought we'd make pasta and a salad. It won't take more than ten minutes," and she smiled, because she had known days earlier there wouldn't be much time for them.

"It sounds fine to me."

"And then what? What do you do after this?"

"I'll go home."

"To Susan and your children."

"Yes."

"I'll be alone."

"You know I can't stay here, Jill."

She turned to him. She said, "Come up with me. Come up and lie next to me, David."

When he left, the house felt as empty and barren to her as it had the day after Peter's death. She had to remind herself that he had been investigating the death of her husband, that his time apart from her was being spent in other ways. He would look at photos of other victims, of bodies lying on bloodstained floors. There was evidence to be examined. She thought of the drawer full of Peter's things, his wallet and passport, his keys, the cash he'd carried, his handkerchief, the pathetic detritus of his days. David would once again go home to his wife and children, and during that time away from him Jill would be a voice, a body, a smell, a touch in the corner of his mind, always alive, always waiting.

From the door she watched his car back out of the driveway. For a second it paused. She could see nothing within it yet she knew he was smiling at her, or waving, somehow acknowledging her. She went into the kitchen and listened to the sound of her bare feet against the floor. This was comfortable, this was somehow right, her living alone. She told herself things: she wanted David but she didn't need him. She wanted him but didn't need him, and because of that simple difference she could watch him walk out of the house and drive away, knowing that in a day or two they would be together again. In her house. In a hotel in the city. In a park, in his car, close to home, far away. She wanted him but didn't need him. She thought it over and over again, saying it quietly to herself, thinking ahead one day, two days, three days, a week, a month, years, where would they be then, would Susan be the bereft one, and would she and David be lovers as Peter and Lisa Bacon had been?

She walked up the stairs and stood in the doorway to her bedroom and looked at the bed with its crumpled evidence of their ardor, the disarray of passion. She lay down and smelled the sheets on which they had made love, she pressed her face to the pillow on which he had lain his head, and preparing for bed she played it all back, every moment, as if shoring up her memories against oblivion, stacking them one atop the other as though constructing a barricade against an advancing army. Nothing could touch her, no one could take it away from her. Even her body was different, and she touched herself with her hands, she touched her arms and breasts, her legs. Now David had seen them and kissed them, he had lain between her thighs and had lifted his head and looked at her, and at that moment he'd reached down to touch her face, just as Peter had the last night of his life, plucking the hair away from her cheek.

She stepped into the shower and washed David off her body. She dried herself and stood naked in the bathroom before the mirror. It was odd how love, making love, being made love to, changed one so. There was a kind of perfection in her body now, she felt muscular and firm, and the surface of her skin seemed to glow as she looked at herself. She was bright and awake and aroused and flawless. She felt something growing inside her, a feeling that seemed to press up against the inner walls of her body, that swelled and gave off warmth. Something of David was contained within her, something of his heart, of himself, his words, the tone of his voice, the tenderness of his hands, the courteous and gentle lust of his body. It was as if she had captured something of his essence, just as she hoped she had given him some of hers. She moved her hands over her body, over her breasts and thighs and belly, and she could even feel it radiating from her flesh, this heat and desire.

Tomorrow was Christmas Eve. She would call David, wrap Carrie's presents, and she thought of David, she thought of him in various ways, how he felt against her body, in her hands, in her mouth, the sound of his voice, his laughter. She wanted to buy something for him, something small and permanent, something he could keep hidden in his desk, that he could touch and forever be reminded of her. She wanted to buy things for herself. She needed clothes, new clothes, good clothes, pretty clothes, sexy clothes, and the clothes seemed to wrap themselves in plans, in dreams. She and David would spend days together, they would go to the Cape or up to Maine, they would take Carrie to the stable.

His days and nights off became their time together. Eventually there would be more days and more nights, and they would join up like links in a chain, becoming weeks, months, years.

She lay in bed and wondered how David would pass the night. She thought of his wife Susan and their two children, how into that house of innocence would enter the ghostly third party of his desire for Jill Bowman, and not just his desire but the feel of her, the smell of her and the taste. It was like a sickness, a germ that would make its way into the Resnick family, that would touch all the members of it in some significant way. Had Peter known this when he took those first steps toward Lisa Bacon, could he have foreseen it would come to this, to his death and Jill's solitude, the immense fractures that lay in the future? Whatever had entered his system was now in hers and in David's, it moved its way through their veins and into their hearts, and for this there would be no cure.

Would she see him again?

The new year would soon be here. Spring would come, and then the years would pass, one after another, as clouds crest over the horizon, blacken the sun, reveal the light.

Could you die of love? she wondered.

But she would not die. She would not die.